PALE AS THE DEAD

Natasha Blake is a detective with a difference. She's an *ancestor* detective, an ambitious young genealogist with a passion for history. Natasha's investigations are a matter of life and death, involving secrets, scandals and supernatural happenings; forgotten tragedies and buried crimes. The trails she must follow lead from her Cotswold home to ancient houses, deserted chapels and overgrown graveyards. Her clients could be anyone for whom the past affects the present – the haunted, the hopeful or just the plain curious.

PALE AS THE DEAD

PALE AS THE DEAD

by

Fiona Mountain

Magna Large Print Books
Long Preston, North Yorkshire,
BD23 4ND, England.

British Library Cataloguing in Publication Data.

Mountain, Fiona
    Pale as the dead.

    A catalogue record of this book is
    available from the British Library

    ISBN   0-7505-2043-4

First published in Great Britain in 2002 by Orion,
an imprint of the Orion Publishing Group Ltd.

Copyright © 2002 Fiona Mountain

Cover illustration © Anthony Monaghan

The right of Fiona Mountain to be identified as the author of this work
has been asserted in accordance with the Copyright, Designs and
Patents Act, 1988

Published in Large Print 2003 by arrangement with
Orion Publishing Group

Magna Large Print is an imprint of Library Magna Books Ltd.

Printed and bound in Great Britain by
T.J. (International) Ltd., Cornwall, PL28 8RW

For Tim, Daniel and James
And for my Mother

And mother find three berries red
And pluck them from the stalk
And burn them at the first cock-crow
That my spirit may not walk

'At Last' *Elizabeth Siddal*

O pale and heavy-lidded woman, why is your cheek
Pale as the dead, and what are your eyes afraid lest
  they speak?
And the woman answered me: I am pale as the dead
For the dead have loved me, and I dream of the
  dead.

'Pale Woman' *Arthur Symons*

Prologue

They think she's too little to understand, but they're wrong. She understands that Charlotte is never coming back and that's why Mummy and Daddy are so sad all the time, why they never kiss each other anymore, just shout, as they are doing now.

She didn't believe it when Daddy said they were going to have a lovely holiday and that everything would be all right. The sun is bright and dancing on the river. But she knows by now that the worst thing can happen on the best days.

There are more daisies than she will ever be able to pick. She plucks another. The pink tips of the petals remind her of how Charlotte used to paint her nails when Mummy wasn't looking. If Charlotte was here she'd help to make the longest chain, show her how to join the two ends to make a crown. 'Your name sounds a bit like the Queen's,' she once said.

'What's the Queen called?'

'Elizabeth.'

Mummy has put her red swimsuit on and her long blonde hair is tied in a bun. She walks as if she's still angry, towards the river. She doesn't stop to say, 'Hello.'

But when she's finished her swim she might like a posy of daisies to arrange in the little glass vase on the kitchen table. She always smiles when

11

someone gives her flowers. Even now.

There are buttercups further up the bank that would look pretty with the daisies. Yellow and white. Not blue. Like the dress Charlotte was wearing when they found her, just lying there in the grass.

Daddy is in the river with Mummy now, but he's wearing all his clothes. He's shouting, even louder than before. He grabs Mummy's hair, her hands, her neck. Pushes, pulls, drags. Her arms look very white as they come out of the water and her eyes are wide open. She looks scared but she doesn't say anything any more.

Then her head goes under and her hair comes loose, floats like golden seaweed.

He looks up. He thinks the little girl standing very still on the riverbank with her hands over her ears is too young to understand what she's seeing, but he's wrong. She knows it's happening again.

She wants to go home.

She holds onto the daisies and runs.

Grandma says Daddy has had to go away for a few days with his work, but if that's true why did a policeman take him? Why does the policeman stand next to him at Mummy's funeral?

Wherever it is that Mummy and Charlotte have gone, she wishes she could go with them.

One day she will.

One

Natasha watched as the girl walked barefoot through the damp grass towards the River Windrush. She was dressed in an antique gown of dark brocade embroidered with fine silver thread. With wild flowers tangled in her hair, a bouquet clutched in her hands and the hem of her skirt trailing across the tussocky meadow, she looked like a lost bride. Bewildered, as if she wasn't quite sure where she was.

She stepped into the water, her skirt billowing around her like a crinoline as she waded through reeds towards the overhanging branches of a willow. The water and the sky were the colour of iron, and there was no shelter from the brisk wind sweeping down from the Cotswold Hills and the huddle of silent, grey stone cottages of Little Barrington. The river was no more than four feet wide, with pools of still water. In summer it sometimes dwindled to little more than a brook, but now, in the second week of December, it was running high. Midstream, it was churning with eddies and currents.

The water was soon almost up to the girl's waist, the sodden material of her dress starting to drag at her, giving her movements a dreamlike slow motion. She took another step, deeper, as if she was walking off the edge of a cliff, into nothing. She was suddenly submerged up to her neck. When she lay back, the water making a pillow for her head, her hair swirled like a mermaid's around her pale upturned face.

'It'll be over soon, Bethany. No more pain and sorrow.' Adam Mason was standing on the riverbank a few feet from Natasha. His voice was soft and low, hypnotic.

Bethany let go of the flowers, daisies, fritillary, forget-me-nots and poppies, and they drifted on the currents, some catching in her hair and in the wet folds of her gown which floated on the river's surface on pockets of air.

'You'll never grow old now.'

Bethany arched her neck, parted her lips slightly, as if to sing a last silent song.

Adam Mason moved swiftly behind the tripod. There was the click of a camera shutter, like a spell being broken.

Natasha realised she'd been holding her breath. She slid her fingers quickly under Boris's collar to make sure the dog didn't make a bid for the water and an impromptu place in the photograph.

'There's no need to be afraid,' Adam said. 'Drowning is the most peaceful way to die.'

Easy for you to say, Natasha thought. *And how exactly do you know that? Has someone come back to tell you?*

Bethany was sculling with her hands now, just below the surface of the water, out of the lens's sight, pushing against the current to hold her position, to maintain the illusion of drifting, of drowning, while making sure she did neither.

Natasha had taken a skinny dip in the Windrush in winter on the odd occasion. Just for the hell of

14

it. The chill of the water was exhilarating, but you couldn't stay in too long. She dredged up memories of life-saving lessons in the public pool, a gold medal gathering dust in a drawer somewhere. She wondered if she should kick off her boots now, just in case.

She glanced at Adam Mason as he, rather too leisurely she thought, adjusted the focus on the camera and its angle on the tripod before reeling off another round of shots. With fair curled hair, and dressed in black jeans and jacket, he looked as if he went to bed at dawn and lived on caffeine, was almost as pale as the girl. His frame was as slight as a girl's too, but wiry and tense.

'Great,' he said, and Bethany flipped over, started making her way back towards the bank.

This was certainly one of the most unusual meetings Natasha had had with a prospective client, which was saying something. Bethany Marshall had got in touch just over a week ago, said she'd be coming to the Cotswolds for this photo shoot and suggested that might be a good time to get together to discuss researching her family history. So far, Natasha hadn't had a chance to talk to her about that. She was in no great hurry though. There was a pile of work waiting on her desk, certificates and pedigrees to be sorted, but they could all wait a little longer. Just now she'd rather be out in the fresh air, as far away from her cottage as possible.

Bethany emerged from the water, her hair and gown streaming, lips almost blue, like a ghostly survivor from a long ago shipwreck.

'We've got it,' Adam said, glancing up from the

15

camera. He gazed at Bethany for a moment. 'You looked really beautiful in there.' He said it with a depth of intimacy, as if they were alone, as if no one else was listening.

Bethany smiled back at him. She seemed shaken, as if the experience had been a little too realistic. She'd freeze to death if she wasn't careful.

Natasha grabbed the towel that lay on the ground and handed it over. 'Let me help you with your dress.'

'Thanks.' Bethany dabbed at the ends of her hair, turned round slowly. As Natasha started unfastening the dozens of tiny buttons and hooks and eyes she could feel the girl shivering.

'That was interesting! I thought photographers just told you to say cheese.'

'Adam says you can only do it properly if you really get into the part, like an actress.'

'It's a reproduction of Millais' *Ophelia*, right?'

'Yes.'

She dragged a couple of daisies from her hair. With her fingernail she made a small, careful incision in one of the stalks, like the eye of a needle.

'Are you at college?' Natasha asked.

'I'm working in a florists until I decide what I want to do.' She threaded the daisies together. 'I like the way people always smile when someone gives them flowers.'

The dress fell in a circle at Bethany's feet and she stepped out of it, wearing only white bra and knickers and a silver Celtic cross on a black rope around her neck. She was small and frail. Her ribs

16

and a delicate tracery of lilac veins were clearly visible beneath her pale skin. Facing Natasha now, she wrapped the towel around herself. 'You must think I'm as mad as Ophelia.'

Natasha smiled. 'Not really.'

'Thanks for coming. I'm sorry you've had to wait around.'

'No problem.'

Bethany bent down to a crumpled pile of clothes, dragged on a loose black velveteen skirt and black shirt, then flipped the cross so it hung outside.

Natasha was reminded of the kind of outfits she used to wear as a student. 'I've done quite a bit of research on different branches of the Marshalls,' she said. 'The Gloucestershire ones mostly.'

Bethany hugged her arms around herself, glanced over her shoulder at Adam, then stared down at her bare feet. She spoke very quietly. 'You have to know a person's full name to do their family history?'

'It's kind of crucial, yes.' Natasha hoped that hadn't come out wrong. She'd meant to break the ice, not be flippant. 'Father or mother's details would be a start though.'

'My surname's not really Marshall.'

With some effort Natasha resisted the urge to ask questions, such as what was her real name. Experience had taught her that silence was more likely to produce answers.

But not yet evidently. Bethany raised her arms to lift her wet hair away from her neck. As she did so, she turned her face towards the sky in which a faint crescent moon had already appeared, even

17

though it was only mid-afternoon. 'Did you know, lunatic literally means moon-struck because people used to believe that the moon made you mad. That's quite believable if you think about it. When the moon controls the tides, and up to eighty per cent of the human body is water.'

'I can see the sense in that.' Natasha wondered how old Bethany was, late teens or early twenties perhaps, around the same age as her sister, Abby. 'Pagans also believe that the moon has the power to heal. Perhaps that means it's healthy to be a little crazy.'

Bethany gave a faint smile. 'I'd best go and fetch a jumper.' She slipped her feet into a pair of black canvas pumps and set off across the bumpy grass to where a car, a charcoal grey Lancia Delta, was parked on the track beneath a clump of trees.

Adam Mason was folding down the tripod, packing away cameras.

Natasha carefully lifted the heavy dress, spread out the skirt a little to help it dry. The embroidery and fabric were exquisite. It looked at least 150 years old, had no doubt been worn once for balls, or for a wedding, in the days before Queen Victoria made it fashionable to marry in white. It deserved more respect than to have been dunked in the Windrush.

She stepped closer to the river, crouched down and trailed her fingers in the water. It was like an ice floe. Enticing. It would make your heart race, your skin tight and tingly. You'd feel your muscles clench and the air squeezed out of your lungs. But after a while it wouldn't feel so cold. Just a

18

scintillating feeling of release, numbing, soothing, almost as if you'd left your body behind. She was tempted to strip off right now, never mind that Adam Mason was standing a few metres away.

Instead she stood, took the stiff white envelope out of her pocket, a Christmas card to Marcus, stamped and addressed but still unposted. She tore it slowly in half, then put the two halves together and tore again, and again. She scattered the pieces onto the water where they bobbed like rose petals, became waterlogged as they hurtled down stream, and quickly disappeared. Following the ancient custom, a sacrifice to the water, an offering to the river gods. She'd been carrying the envelope around for a week. Burning a hole in her pocket, or rather her heart. It was satisfying, destroying it like that. For at least ten seconds.

'Have you been here before?' Beyond introducing himself when she first arrived half an hour or so ago, the first words Adam Mason had spoken to Natasha.

She flashed a quick look at him out of the corner of her eye. 'I'm not sure. Sometimes I think we all have.'

He stopped what he was doing and stared at her. She managed to keep a deadly straight face for a few seconds, then had to give way to a smile.

Adam barked a laugh.

Sometimes a little flippancy worked wonders. When she'd started out as a genealogist seven years ago, Natasha had felt almost sick with nervousness before a meeting with new or potential clients, or worse, an interview with one of their distant relations. She'd never found it particularly easy to make polite conversation, harder still to ask people she'd never met the most personal questions about relationships and family secrets and stories, find ways to coax their most precious and painful memories out of them. But she had been determined from the start that everyone would think it was as natural and easy to her as breathing. Which they usually did.

She looked down at the water again, the trailing branches of the willow. It reminded her of another painting. Hanging over her bed as a teenager she'd had a print of Waterhouse's *The Lady of Shalott*, drifting downstream in her death-barge. She'd seen it in a shop in Bakewell that sold hand-painted greetings cards and antiquarian maps, and something about it had instantly attracted her.

The click of the shutter made her jump.

'Stay exactly where you are,' Adam commanded. 'Don't move.' Natasha took a deliberate step back, flashed her eyes at him. 'Or what? You'll shoot?'

OK, not a particularly great joke, but it deserved a smile at least.

'Can you get the dog to stand a little closer to you?'

'His name's Boris.' Natasha grudgingly rummaged in her pocket and found a biscuit, cupped it in her palm and tempted Boris to shift closer to snuffle at it.

'Look down at the water like you were doing just now, as if it's a window to another world.'

Who did he think he was, David Lean?

Natasha dutifully inclined her head. There was

the click, click of the shutter.

Adam set the camera down on top of a silver flight case that lay on the grass.

'You're welcome,' Natasha said, sarcastically.

He dragged a cigarette packet and lighter out of his jacket pocket, offered Natasha one, then, when she shook her head, he stuck one in his mouth, flicked the lighter and cupped his hand around the flame while he inhaled. 'You don't like having your photograph taken?'

'Not particularly.'

'You should do.'

'Thanks. I think.'

He flicked ash onto the grass. 'You'd rather I'd said you were beautiful? Only if I did you'd think I was trying to chat you up.'

'Would I now?'

'If I passed you in the street and asked you to come back to my studio and pose you'd say no, wouldn't you?' *Too bloody right.* He came closer, dropped his voice. 'It's a shame, don't you think, that compliments are so often taken as a threat?'

She shrugged, tried not to sound unnerved. 'That's life.'

He held out the camera. 'Take a look.'

It was one of the latest digital models, with a small screen in the back.

She saw herself as she'd been just a few seconds ago, tall and slender, dressed in her favourite coat – long, black, Edwardian, with a high collar – Boris, a Red Setter, at her side, a splash of colour against the big, white sky and the silver of the river.

'You'd be even more beautiful if you lost that

21

chip on your shoulder.' His breath brushed her ear and she almost dropped the camera. It occurred to her that it would look rather fetching wrapped around his neck. He took it, smirking, as if her anger amused him. 'I bet you went to private school, didn't you? Rambling old house with a garden like a park to play tennis and ride your pony in. Loving, encouraging parents. What have you got to feel pissed off about?'

This was absurd. 'You don't know anything about me.'

'I'm right though, aren't I? About the posh school? I meant it as a compliment. You talk very nicely. You've got style. Attitude. What did they write on your reports?'

'I can't remember.'

'Yes, you can. You were always top of the class I bet? Wanting approval, everyone to like you?' She could feel his eyes on her, didn't like how close to the truth he was. 'Model pupil? Great future ahead? Is that what they wrote?'

She wanted to shut him up and take him down a peg or two at the same time. 'Actually.' She turned on her brilliant smile. 'You're way off the mark. They probably did say I was bright. Bright but sometimes thinks she's too smart. So you and I have a lot in common there.'

He turned his attention back to the camera. 'So, what's she told you?'

Instinctively, Natasha lied. 'Nothing yet.'

'You do surprise me.'

He reverse-spooled a frame, handed the camera back.

It was a close-up profile, the picture he'd taken

without her knowledge.

She looked OK, even if she hadn't bothered to put on any makeup, had had more than usual trouble sleeping over the past weeks since Marcus had left and had to keep reminding herself to eat. Her heavy dark-gold hair was scooped up into a loose knot at the back of her head, and around her face the damp atmosphere had crimped it into small ringlets. Wide, almond shaped eyes, strong cheekbones, small nose, a high clear brow. A face she could never quite recognize as her own.

Two

Natasha was sitting opposite Adam by a huge inglenook with a fire beneath the blackened oak beams of the Fox Inn at Little Barrington. Except for a trio of walkers in hiking boots, Cagoules and rucksacks, and a young couple sharing a bowl of chips and a bottle of red wine in an alcove, the place was empty, far enough away from any town to avoid the pre-Christmas round of office parties. On the small table in front of Adam and Natasha there was a vodka and tonic, a pint of Donnington's and a white wine spritzer for Bethany, who was in the ladies drying her hair.

'Are the photos for a magazine?'

'An exhibition. In Oxford.' Adam was chain-smoking, elbows resting on the table. The sleeve of his black jacket was slightly too long, part covering his fingers. It was made of velvet, the nap worn away at the cuffs. 'The idea is to create a series of photographs in the style of the Pre-Raphaelite paintings. A modern version of them, if you like, using a modern day medium.'

'Didn't Julia Margaret Cameron already do that?'

'Quite right.' His tone was patronising, made Natasha wonder why she was bothering. She reminded herself this was a client meeting and summoned a suitably professional smile. 'Cameron was influenced by the Pre-Raphaelites but she was also a contemporary,' Adam said, offhandedly. 'No one's done anything similar for over a hundred years and I thought it would be interesting to give it a go.'

'Which other paintings are you basing the photos on?'

'Bethany particularly wanted to do *Ophelia*, because Lizzie Siddal was in the original. She's obsessed with her.' He slouched back against the settle. 'Apart from that there won't be any direct copies. Just scenes suggested by the subjects that inspired the Pre-Raphaelites. Y'know, mythology, superstition, medieval themes. That kind of stuff.'

'I can see you as a twenty-first century Rossetti.' Actually, with his dark clothes and the way he wore his hair, long enough for the curls to touch his velvet collar, he wasn't so much twenty-first century as nineteenth. Which, to Natasha made him interesting and attractive, she was sorry to admit.

He picked up his beer, drank. 'I've always liked

the idea of the Pre-Raphaelite Brotherhood. Secret societies.'

'Me too. Ever since I read *The Secret Seven*.' She smiled but he didn't.

'I formed one while I was at college. We used to meet in the evenings and sit around in candle-light, drinking lots of coffee or wine, playing records and talking about art and literature and philosophy. It was great for pulling girls.'

'I bet.' She paused. 'The exhibition sounds great. Oxford's the ideal place, with its Pre-Raphaelite connections.'

Bethany came back from the cloakroom. There was kohl around her grey eyes, pale pink lipstick on her mouth. She slid in beside Adam on the settle, nestled up to him. He turned to her, gazed at her profile for a second, almost as if he was willing her to respond, but if she felt his eyes on her she chose not to meet them, stared resolutely ahead, sipping her wine. Adam drained his beer almost angrily. He stood, said he was going to the bar for a refill, asked Natasha if she'd like one too. She said no before she had a chance to change her mind.

Bethany watched Adam walk away. Natasha recognized that look. Love mixed with sadness. It made her feel a tender concern for the girl. 'You should have had a whisky.'

Bethany cupped her hands and blew into them. 'Or a hot cup of tea. I don't think I'll ever be warm again.'

'Shall we swap places, so you're nearer the fire?'

'Thanks.' Bethany came to sit in the wooden chair by the hearth and Natasha took the settle.

25

'What you were saying,' Natasha prompted, 'earlier, about your name not really being Marshall?'

Bethany hesitated, as if she regretted her previous confidence. 'I think I'm descended from someone called Marshall. I don't know her first name, except that it began with a J. Apparently her father was a doctor who was friends with the Pre-Raphaelites. I've got her diary. My grand-mother left it to me.'

The quiet thrill in the girl's voice made Natasha like her even more. 'That's fascinating. Adam said you were interested in Lizzie Siddal. Is it because of the diary?'

'I suppose so. I had this idea, that I'd like to write a proper biography of her sometime.' She fiddled with the stem of her glass. 'I started doing some research a while ago.'

'One of the archivists at the Public Record Office investigated Lizzie Siddal's early life just through census returns, trade directories, certificates and stuff. You should give her a call.'

Bethany glanced towards Adam who was still at the bar, paying for his drink. 'He doesn't know about... Promise you won't say anything about my name?'

'Of course.'

'It's for the best,' she said, emphatically.

People changed their name for a variety of reasons. If they were running from something or someone, had done something they were ashamed of, committed a crime, or witnessed one and were at risk if they were found. For whatever reason, they usually needed to escape the past. Sometimes of course they simply had an aversion to the name they were born with. Natasha had the feeling Bethany didn't fall into that category. She put her glass down. 'Listen, are you OK?'

She gave a weak smile. 'Fine.' Adam was walking back towards them. 'This sounds like a really strange question...' she broke off.

'I'm used to strange questions,' Natasha said. 'Believe me.'

'Do you think ... is it possible that ... well, that some families can be cursed?'

Natasha thought for a second, not because she wasn't sure how to answer, but because she was worried about the reason behind the question, didn't want to be either dismissive or gloomy. 'Sometimes,' she said carefully. 'In a way.'

She wanted to explain but Adam plonked his beer on the table and Bethany made an obvious effort to shift subject, asked how far back into the past it was possible to go.

'It depends.' Natasha said. Adam hadn't bothered to fetch another chair but had squeezed onto the small settle next to Natasha. She tried to ignore his lean thigh pressing up against hers, the fact that she was wedged in so tight she couldn't budge an inch. He was pretending not to listen to the conversation but was clearly interested. 'If a family were landowners there's records stretching back centuries,' Natasha finished.

'How long does it take?'

'You could get as far as great-great-grandparents within a month or so.'

Bethany took a moment to let that sink in.

27

'Why do people want to know do you think?'

It was an odd sort of question, from someone who'd expressed an interest. 'All sorts of reasons. I think mostly it's to learn more about who you are.'

'Is that always a good thing?'

There was a flicker of fear in the girl's eyes, something Natasha understood all too well. 'I think it can help a lot sometimes.'

'Come on,' Adam scoffed. 'It's just about providing tales you can entertain your mates with in the pub, isn't it? So you can boast about how a long deceased uncle was transported as a convict for stealing a loaf of bread. It can't really mean anything in the end, what your great-great-grandfather did for a living?'

'Oh, I don't know,' Natasha said, playfully. 'Some people say ghosts don't cast shadows, but they can cast the longest shadows of all.'

'What's that supposed to mean?'

'Ancestor Syndrome.' She glanced at Bethany. 'The idea that everything that happens to you – accidents, illnesses, fears, attitudes – are a kind of inherited fate, responses to what happened to your ancestors years ago.'

'I love it,' Adam sniggered. 'Very Gothic romance. Let me guess. The only way to break the pattern is to understand what set it in place. The perfect genealogist's sales pitch if you ask me.'

Natasha turned to him. 'Works every time.'

Bethany finished her drink and put her empty glass down. 'I'll maybe give you a call, after Christmas.'

'Whenever.' Natasha would make a bet she'd never hear from Bethany again. Which was a shame. She liked her, was intrigued. She also had a gut feeling the girl needed help in some way. One thing Natasha could never resist. Helping, or meddling, depending on which way you chose to look at it.

Adam had finished his second beer and stood.

Natasha nodded goodbye to the landlord as they walked towards the door. She dropped back, let Adam go on ahead to the car park at the rear of the pub. 'Are you off back to London now?' she said to Bethany as they followed behind.

'We're staying at Adam's friend's place in Oxford, until after the exhibition.' She spoke quickly, as if she didn't want to dwell on that. There was not an ounce of enthusiasm in her voice. She tucked her hair behind her ears, securing it against the strong breeze. 'Do you really think you can inherit fate?'

'It's just a theory. But it makes sense, certainly helps to explain why some families seem to have more than their fair share of tragedy.'

'How?'

'Well, when an ancestor is the victim of a terrible crime or tragedy, say, you half expect the same to happen to you and so, subconsciously, when you reach that age, or else a certain date, perhaps you take more risks, get depressed, self-destructive, or maybe your resistance to illness drops.' She could see she had Bethany's attention. 'So it seems like a curse when a similar thing happens again, but it's more like a self–fulfilling prophecy.' The Lancia was only a few strides away now, Adam already behind the wheel. Natasha stopped, turned towards her midnight blue Sunbeam Alpine. 'When you think about it, you don't even have to be aware of the original event. Say someone died falling from a building, a fear of heights could be passed on through the generations. Or a sense of shame, even if what caused it has been kept a secret, or forgotten.'

'I see what you mean,' Bethany said, in a way that made Natasha wish she'd kept her mouth shut.

Three

The village of Snowshill lived up to its name. As Natasha drove further into the Cotswolds, small white flakes began flashing towards her in the Alpine's headlights. Because it lay high up, the village always caught the wildest weather and was often cut off for days. Snow tended to linger, in the folds of the hills, when it had long since disappeared elsewhere. You could drive down to the valleys and sheep pastures and see primroses and daffodils, when in Snowshill it still felt like winter.

Natasha's cottage was at the end of a short row dating from the seventeenth century. What she loved about it most was that inside, there was not a straight line anywhere. Undulating, low-beamed ceilings, thick slanted and bowed walls, tiny sloping leaded windows and crooked, creaking

30

floors. It was called Orchard End, though there'd never been an orchard anywhere near. From the highest south-west facing windows though, you could see right across to Littleworth Wood and the Vale of Evesham, and Natasha liked to think the person who chose the name did so because it had been possible to see the drifts of blossom from the forest of fruit trees for which the Vale was once so renowned. The house and village suited her perfectly. She preferred small places, old places, where there was a sense of continuity, and of belonging.

But the cottage didn't seem like home in quite the way it once did, when it was Marcus's home too. He'd lived there for three years, on and off. Every time he'd gone to work up at the Department of Medical Artists at Manchester University, or abroad, Natasha had always half believed he wouldn't come back. But there had been the reassurance of his belongings in every room, daily phone calls or e-mails. Since he left two weeks ago, there was no reassurance, just silence and empty spaces where his toothbrush and razor and aftershave used to be, his boots and jacket in the hallway.

She parked outside, let Boris skitter down from the passenger seat and unlocked the front door, ducking beneath the lintel. She checked her answering machine. A message from Mary, who ran the Snowshill Arms with her husband James, checking Natasha was coming round for supper tomorrow. Another from Natasha's father, Steven, and a final message from Will, a former colleague from Generations, whom she'd dated

31

eons ago. He was calling to invite her to a New Year's party. Which wasn't until 7 January. Typical Will.

She changed quickly into a flying jacket, and stuffed the bottoms of her jeans into Wellington boots. Boris started barking eagerly, his tail beating her calves. With the snow falling thicker now, Natasha was almost as excited as he was. A fresh snowfall was magical, no matter how often you'd seen it. She followed Boris as he darted, sleek and quick as a fox, towards the church and then on down the steep lane to the track that led through the woods. The leafless trees were like images in a photographic negative, white with the snow that was settling softly along the branches.

Some of the villagers, those whose families had lived in Snowshill for centuries, wouldn't go near the lane that ran between the Manor and Orchard End once darkness had fallen.

It was the Manor that brought visitors to Snowshill from all over the UK, America, Japan. When she told people where she lived, it was amazing how many had heard of such a tiny place. 'Spooky' was a frequent comment, accompanied by a shudder, as if the atmosphere of the Manor permeated the whole of the village.

'A house for the evening hours' as one of the guide books described it. It had fascinated Natasha from the first time she'd seen it. Its former owner Charles Paget Wade's extraordinary collections filled the dim rooms. Tudor panelling and medieval fireplaces set off gruesome suits of Samurai armour, Balinese dancing masks and hanging lanterns from Persia that cast weird netted shadows.

No one lived in the Manor now, and the windows were black as Natasha made her way back.

As she came towards the triangular village green the wonderful nutty scent of wood smoke drifted towards her and the glowing lights of the Snowshill Arms seemed very inviting.

But going to the inn was only a way to avoid the empty cottage which had never troubled her until recently. She walked on determinedly. Dusk was the worst time. The brief pause between day and night, when lights had been turned on but curtains not yet drawn, making every front room a taunting tableau of family bliss.

Natasha's own cottage was freezing. The cranky central heating system had long ceased to be up to the job, but she had never got round to having it replaced.

She turned on lamps, unscrewed a bottle of vodka and poured a hefty measure, didn't bother to add any tonic. Boris was waiting optimistically on the faded Persian rug in front of the inglenook whilst she scrunched up an old copy of the *Independent* for kindling. Only three logs left in the basket. She must remember to pick up some more.

She pulled over plump velvet and tapestry cushions and Boris came to rest his head on her lap, settling down with a contented snuffle. The room immediately looked more welcoming with the light of the flames on the dark oak furniture, the pewter candlesticks and knick-knacks she kept acquiring from antique fairs, the rich browns and reds and golds of the fabrics.

Natasha flicked on the television. That was becoming a habit too. Filling the cottage with the voices and faces of strangers. She channel-hopped, finding only festive quiz shows and sitcoms, then hit a local news programme, showing an item about the Samaritans gearing up their busiest period. 'There are more suicides at Christmas than at any other time of the year...'

Very cheery.

She could feel the vodka kicking in. She shifted Boris's muzzle and wandered through to the kitchen to refill her glass. Her third today she remembered. But the first had been business. So that didn't count.

Boris had padded after her and she shook some biscuits into his bowl. She fixed herself a plate of pasta with tomato sauce and took it over to the iMac at her desk. She logged onto the internet, checked what was going on at a couple of family history chat rooms and then clicked on an MP3 site, downloaded a couple of tracks.

Do something useful.

She wandered through to the hallway to the shelves of books under the stairs.

Her books were arranged in loose alphabetical or subject order. She ran her fingers along the spines and spotted what she was looking for. A volume of monographs, The *Pre-Raphaelite Dream*, one of the books her mother, Ann, had sent down from Natasha's old bedroom when she was having a clear-out.

On the gilt-edged cover was an image that had become part of popular culture, adorning

34

compilations of Victorian poetry, greeting cards and posters. A raven-haired girl draped in forest green silk, with dancing eyes and sultry red mouth, a ripe red fruit in her hand with a bite taken out of it. Rossetti's *Proserpine*. The model was Janey Morris, neé Burden.

Natasha turned the pages to find Lizzie Siddal in Millais' *Ophelia*. A beautiful, haunting painting, the colours of the dense foliage and Lizzie's face as realistic as a photograph. No wonder Bethany and Adam had wanted to replicate it. On the reverse was Lizzie as *Beata Beatrix*, both pictures so different in style to *Proserpine*. Still sensual, but saintly too, with her face turned to heaven, or her lips parted in song, and her eyes closed as if in prayer or rapture, Lizzie was an icon.

Natasha turned to the index at the back. There was no listing for a Dr Marshall. She hadn't really expected there would be.

She postponed going up to bed until the fire had dwindled to a few embers and a chill had crept into the room. She didn't stop Boris when he sneaked up the stairs behind her, and she didn't tell him off when he pushed his luck even further and jumped up onto the bed.

The last time she looked at the clock it was two-thirty a.m. Which was better than three, as it had been for the last few nights.

Four

A couple of weeks later, Natasha was woken by the post clattering through the letterbox. A mixture of birthday and Christmas cards. She sifted through them quickly. Stamped on her disappointment when she didn't see Marcus's handwriting. She'd almost given up hope that she'd hear from him. Almost.

She opened the cards. It was anyone's guess whether you'd find pictures of champagne corks and summer flowers or robins and reindeers. That was the problem with having a birthday so close to Christmas. It tended to get lost. But she didn't mind that at all. Did her best to forget the day, except for one thing.

She knelt by the black oak coffer that stood at the foot of her bed, lifted the catch.

It had become a kind of ritual. She only allowed herself to open it on this morning each year.

She had first seen the coffer about five years ago, in the window of an antique shop in Stow-on-the-Wold. She'd fallen in love with it immediately. It was Jacobean, ornately carved with roses and acanthus leaves and a small unicorn rearing up in the centre panel. She had known it would be a perfect fit.

She opened the lid and let it drop back against the foot of the iron bed. She lifted out the bundle, removed the tissue paper wrapping. With the tips

36

of her fingers she touched the shawl. It felt cool and soft, like frosted moss or flowers of ice on window panes on winter mornings. She folded back the corner and there was the postcard, a picture of the St Catherine's window in Christ Church Cathedral, Oxford, the back blank except for a single phrase, written in blue-black ink.

'We always keep everything that's left with abandoned babies,' the woman from the Social Services had informed Natasha with exaggerated sympathy. 'We give them back when those concerned have been told about their history, when they are old enough to understand.'

When were you ever old enough to understand something like that?

Natasha had been eighteen and had known for just a few days that she was adopted, that she'd been left behind in a hospital ward. She had been nowhere near coming to terms with either fact, particularly the latter. Babies were only abandoned in Victorian novels. Foundlings. Not a term that fitted in the 1970s.

This was not true though, she'd since learned. Doorstep babies, the term they used now, were on the increase, 'a tragic symptom of society' the papers said it was. Teenage sex, the lack of family unity and support for unmarried mothers, the widening social divide. Nowadays, in the UK, records showed that one baby was abandoned every week.

We always keep everything that's left with aban-doned babies. The only history they'd ever have.

Natasha had signed the release form, taken possession of the little bundle. Then she saw what was written on the piece of card folded inside the shawl.

Her name is Natasha.

The memory came to her, swift and destructive as a floodtide. Sitting in the kitchen one Sunday morning, discussing with her adoptive parents, Ann and Steven, what the new baby should be called if it should be a girl. It was Steven who'd suggested Abigail, and Ann had placed her hand proprietarily on her rounded tummy and said that Abigail was perfect.

'Didn't you choose my name too?' Natasha had asked Steven.

He'd glanced down at her, his eyes tender, with a sadness in them that she hadn't understood. 'Your mother chose it.'

She'd wanted so much for him to say yes, but she wasn't disappointed at all, was gratified, elated. Her eyes flew to Ann, expecting a smile, something. But Ann had turned away.

That was the truth. A lone truth in all the lies. Her mother, her real mother, had chosen her name. For some reason it had been important to her, that her child should have one name in particular. Natasha.

And Steven and Ann had honoured that wish, hadn't done what most adoptive parents did and renamed their baby with their own choice of name.

She ran her fingers across the letters. How much she wanted to believe that handwriting could reveal a person's character. The N bold, an arabesque, and the cross of the T, sinuous and spiky, like a leap.

38

She tucked the piece of card back under the shawl, folded the tissue paper round it and returned it to its place at the bottom of the chest.

Natasha. Russian. Short form of Natalya. She knew the entry in the *Dictionary of Names* by heart. *Natalya. Russian. A derivative of the Latin Natalis, meaning birthday, especially Christ's. Hence the tradition of so naming those born at Christmastime.*

Perhaps that was all it was.

Later, Natasha walked over the road to the cottage adjoining the Snowshill Arms. A lamb stew was keeping warm on the range and there were candles ringed with holly on the pine table. Mary greeted her with a glass of spicy mulled wine. She was dwarfed by a navy and red polo shirt, James's presumably, which, despite its size, didn't quite conceal her protruding tummy.

'How are you feeling?' Natasha asked.

'Oh, fine. For a beached whale.'

Just over five feet tall and a tiny size eight, the only clothes Mary could usually wear were outfits intended for early teens. She looked way too young to be a mother, still a child herself.

'Four weeks to go.'

James was checking the stew was done, oven gloves tossed over his shoulder. 'I can see him arriving on Christmas Day, ruining our lunch,' he grinned. Clearly he wouldn't mind one bit.

Natasha tapped Mary's bump. 'You hang on in there as long as you can little thing, unless you want one supposedly bigger present instead of two for the rest of your life.'

Just as they sat down to eat Natasha's mobile started ringing. She fished it out of her bag. 'Hello.'

'Is that Natasha Blake?'

'Yes. Oh hi, Adam.' Natasha caught Mary's intrigued grin and pulled a face at her. *Not what you think.*

'I need to talk to you,' Adam said. 'It's about Bethany.'

Five

The next day, at Adam's insistence, Natasha found herself waiting by another river.

By her guess, he was already half an hour late. She hated rushing for appointments or trains, often cursed the modern day necessity for clock-watching and it wasn't as if she was never late herself. So she tried not to be *too* annoyed.

The infant Thames was running high and swift, swollen from the recent heavy rain which had seeped down from hills and was only now reaching Oxford.

Oxford. It had seemed like a fabled city when Natasha had first arrived, eighteen years old, off the train from Derbyshire, clutching two crammed suitcases and a bag full of books.

As a student Natasha had often stopped off at the ivy-clad Head of the River pub with friends for a drink, having punted or rowed upstream. The table where she now sat would have had a bright parasol on a pole through its centre.

She turned and saw Adam strolling down the paved steps towards her carrying his small silvery flight case. He took her outstretched hand with a quick, firm shake. 'Sorry I'm late.' He didn't sound one bit sorry.

'Don't worry. It's usually me,' Natasha admitted, slightly regretting how forgiving she sounded. 'I hate wearing a watch.'

He gave an uninterested frown and stared down at Boris.

Natasha gave the dog's silken copper ears a reassuring fondle, her impatience prickling.

Adam stuck a cigarette in his mouth without either offering her one or asking if she minded him smoking. 'Can we get started? I don't have much time.'

Well, get lost then! She cursed the fact that she was too well brought up to say it to his face.

He'd played on her curiosity and sympathy to lure her here, on Christmas Eve, saying it was urgent, and now obviously didn't feel the need for even basic civility.

As if he'd felt the little daggers in her dark eyes he glanced away, at the water rushing beneath the stone arches of the Folly Bridge. A girl was pushing through one of the swing doors to the pub and a wave of noise rolled out as she entered. Natasha knew the bar would be packed. 'Shall we go in?' she suggested reluctantly.

Adam took in the deserted picnic benches around them. 'I don't mind staying out here.'

'Let's do that then.'

She went to buy drinks at the bar. When she

41

came back outside, Adam was on to another cigarette. There was a strong breeze and he had trouble lighting it. As he cupped his hand around the flame, Natasha saw that his fingers were trembling slightly.

'You said you wanted to talk to me about Bethany.'

'She's gone.'

Remembering the friction between them, it wasn't a complete surprise. 'Where?'

'I need you to find her for me.'

'Hang on a minute.' Natasha glimpsed desperation in Adam's eyes. 'Look. I'd gladly help if I could, but you've come to the wrong person I'm afraid. I don't find people who are alive.'

'You sound like a ghost hunter.'

She couldn't help laughing. 'Sometimes it feels that way I can tell you.' She looked at him. 'How do you know she wants to be found?'

He ignored her, bent down to pick up the flight case, put it on the table, flicked back the catches and lifted the lid. He drew out an olive cloth-covered book and laid it in front of her. 'I found it on the kitchen table the morning she left. A few days after that shoot you came to. No note, just this and some flowers in a jam jar.'

Reverently, Natasha picked up the green book. She knew what it was before she opened it.

The fragile pages were pocked with dull brown spots of age. It was the diary Bethany had mentioned, written in a rough and spidery hand, with numerous crossings out and blots of ink. There was no indication of the year. But it was very old. As Natasha turned the leaves with infinite care, a faint musty smell wafted up, one that never failed to send tingles down her spine. The smell of all old books, of attics and ancient buildings, faded gowns locked up for years in wooden chests, diaries, old photographs and letters. To hold in her hands the intimate records of people and emotions and times now gone, and to imagine the hand that had touched the pages never failed to excite her.

A few of the more legible phrases in the journal caught her eye. *Papa's patients. Paintings on the academy.* She turned back to the beginning, noting the initials inside the front cover – J.M.

Bethany had left Adam but she had wanted him to have this. Something that had been handed down through the generations of her family, was probably valuable, was precious to her in any case.

Natasha closed the book. 'I still don't see how you think I could help.'

He reached inside his pocket and handed over a piece of notepaper.

She unfolded it, saw her own name, address, telephone and email written in blue biro, the writing elegant and italicised, like calligraphy. 'It was inside the front of the diary,' Adam explained. 'It's almost as if Bethany meant me to contact you, wanted me to ask you to find her. Through the diary I mean. If it belonged to one of her ancestors, it would lead to her, or her relatives? You'd be able to find their address, phone number? We could get in touch with them?'

'Hmm. Unconventional idea to say the least, but it's just possible I suppose. If she wanted you, or me, to do that, though, why leave in the first place?'

He crushed the stub of his cigarette in the ash tray. 'I don't know.'

She could understand his need to avoid difficult questions, also how what he was saying might just be true: the paradox of wanting someone's love more than anything but pushing it away, half hoping they won't let you, that they'll fight to win you back. It had crossed Natasha's mind that she was testing Marcus in the same way. 'Isn't there an easier way to find her?'

'She wouldn't tell me anything about her family or even where she was living. Short of going through every phone book in the UK and telephoning all the Marshalls I don't see how.'

She looked away quickly. Should she tell him that wouldn't work? She'd promised Bethany she wouldn't say anything about her name. And a promise was a promise. What Bethany had told her proved, surely, that, for whatever reason, she didn't want to be traced. Particularly by Adam.

'Do you have any idea why she left?' She watched his face carefully, noticed the way he hesitated, just for a fraction of a second, then didn't quite meet her eyes.

'None,' he said definitely. Too definitely.

'In that case, she's a missing person. The police would have more chance of finding her than me.'

'I can't go to the police.'

She felt her heart knocking a warning. 'Why not?'

'They wouldn't do anything.'

'Let me guess. She had every right to leave you.

You can't say you have any worries about her safety. Did you by any chance have an argument?'

'Not really.'

'That generally means yes.'

'It was a stupid argument. I asked her to move in with me and she got really angry. She said I was making her feel claustrophobic, that I shouldn't rely on her being around all the time.' He locked eyes with her. 'You're probably going to tell me that makes it even more pointless trying to find her.' He paused. 'If she hadn't left the diary, I'd probably agree. But it meant so much to her. And your details inside. It's obvious what she wanted me to do.'

Not really. She didn't have the heart to point out that the piece of paper was probably left there by mistake. 'How long had you been together?'

'Six weeks.' There was a flare of challenge in his eyes. 'I know it seems strange that I know so little about her, but she didn't volunteer much information and she didn't like questions. It was easier to stop asking. It drew me to her in a way. Can you understand that?'

'Frankly, no. I'm far too nosy I'm afraid, goes with the territory.' And if you loved someone you'd want to know everything about them, wouldn't you?

There was something else. People who were secretive were not to be trusted. Like another girl who had given a false name and then vanished. She'd walked out of the maternity ward of the Jessop Hospital in Sheffield on the day before Christmas Eve twenty-eight years ago, leaving behind the baby she'd given birth to just six

45

hours before. According to the hospital records, the girl's name was Catherine Forester. She said she lived at 9 Troy Lane, Sheffield. Which didn't exist. Catherine Forester didn't exist either.

It had turned colder. Natasha could see the mist of her own breath in front of her face and the skin beneath her nails had turned a shade of bruised violet. She pushed her hands up into the opposite sleeves of her coat, tempted to suggest that they went inside now.

'We did talk, about all kinds of things,' Adam was saying. 'It's surprisingly refreshing, skipping the preliminaries. It's not necessary to rake over a person's past to feel you know them. What happened before we met seemed irrelevant, a different life.' His voice no longer had the sullen edge it had before. 'Only the present mattered, and the future. Dreams are far more important than memories, don't you think?'

Natasha was caught up in his words, so that for a second she forgot that she should respond. 'I'd be redundant if everyone believed the past wasn't important.'

And yet recently, hadn't she come to think it too? The past could get in the way, a hindrance that stopped you living. So easy to lay the blame on the generations who'd gone before, to avoid taking responsibility for your own personality and actions. Blame it all on genes and upbringing and inherited fate.

A host of questions sprang to Natasha's mind. Did Bethany talk of her job, her family, friends, school, or college, where she grew up? She had started assessing the evidence, piecing things together, trying to fill the gaps, as if she'd already agreed to take on the job. But those questions, which disregarded completely what Adam had just said about the past not mattering, seemed somehow insensitive. 'Where did you meet her?'

He leant back. 'In a café near a studio I was using in London.'

'She told me she worked in a florists. Have you tried there?'

'I never knew where it was exactly. I've checked at all the ones nearby, with a photograph, but nobody has ever seen her.'

Natasha had a peculiarly strong image of him in a succession of rooms filled with flowers, showing the picture of a girl apparently drowning in a river to people who just shook their heads.

Adam rested his fingers on the diary as if swearing an oath. 'I'm living in Oxford at the moment, renting a flat in Jericho, and the studio, until the exhibition's over. Wanted to get the feel of the place you know. Bethany came to stay at weekends. That week though, she'd taken time off from work for the shoot at Little Barrington. Friday evening we had supper at an Italian restaurant we often went to. I told her it had been great having her around all the time. We argued, like I said. But I thought it was all OK. We came home and drank a bottle of wine, went to bed and made love.' He paused. 'When I woke up in the morning she was gone; taken everything with her, except this.' He looked down at his own hand, still resting on the olive book. 'I didn't get in touch with you right away because I hoped she'd come back. I thought we were going to

47

spend Christmas together...'

'You've tried her friends?'

'She never mentioned anyone.'

'Were there places she liked?'

He waved his hand dismissively, as if he found the questions tedious in the extreme. 'Galleries, the parks, old houses.'

'I mean where she might have gone now, other areas of the country, abroad?'

'Not particularly.'

'You're not being very helpful considering you approached me,' Natasha said. 'If I'm to be of any use at all I need to know.'

'She said she liked travelling, because it gave you a different perspective. Because it made the days seem longer she said. She'd been to France recently, Italy too. I thought we'd go together sometime, but she wouldn't talk about the future, absolutely refused. I thought we really had something,' he added quietly, as if to himself. 'I just want the chance to talk to her.'

She watched his fingers, turning the cigarette packet over and over, 'I understand.'

'You'll help me then?' There was a touch of resentment in his tone, like someone who wasn't comfortable asking for help.

Natasha looked down at Boris, sitting attentively at her feet amidst the hem of her coat. She was torn. The trouble was, knowing the little she did about Bethany, she instinctively felt that finding her wasn't the right thing to do. But to her surprise she felt sorry for Adam, and she couldn't deny that she was intrigued by it all.

She weighed things up. The piles of work on her

desk, the long winter evenings ahead. She was thankful she already had more than enough work to fill them. The new millennium seemed to have made everyone nostalgic, keen to forge links with the past, and all the genealogists she knew were inundated with work. But this project was refreshingly unusual, probably impossible. But that had never stopped her having a go before.

It would be very time consuming, that was for sure. And the only way to make a decent living from genealogy was the routine, straightforward research. No one else would be enough of a mug to agree to take it on.

But Natasha could. Thanks to the small inheritance, left to her by Ann's mother which, wisely invested by Ann, had almost quadrupled in fifteen years. Natasha had been able to buy Orchard End outright. It gave her a little freedom, meant she didn't have to worry all the time about only taking on bread and butter projects that she was certain, as certain you ever could be, were going to be uncomplicated. It made her feel better about the inheritance, which at the time she'd wanted all to go to Abby. It was her birthright, only hers. But Ann, always scrupulously fair, had insisted Natasha have half, and Steven had said there was no point cutting off her nose to spite her face.

'I'll tell you what,' she said to Adam. 'If I can borrow the diary over the holidays, I'll take a look at it, make some investigations. I can't promise anything but I'll see what I can do.'

'Thanks.' Adam asked how much it was going to cost.

'We can talk about that later.' When she had more idea if what he'd asked her to do was remotely achievable.

She opened her carpet bag, slipped the diary carefully inside one of the inner pockets. 'She told me her grandmother gave it to her.'

'The only member of her family Bethany ever mentioned. She said how, when she was a little girl, eight years old I think, her grandmother told her the story of Lizzie Siddal's body being exhumed so that Rossetti could retrieve the poems he buried with her.'

The story was familiar to Natasha. How, after Lizzie's death, Rossetti placed beside her in the coffin the only complete copies of his poems, saying he had no need for them now she was gone. Years later he changed his mind, wanted them back. When the grave was reopened it was said that Lizzie's fragile beauty had not faded, that she looked as if she had died not years but only hours ago. Natasha had always found it rather appealing in a macabre way.

'It must have had a strange effect on a child's imagination, telling them something like that, don't you think?' Adam said.

'Perhaps.' From an early age Natasha had known more about corpses than would generally be considered healthy. She smiled, remembering the stories her adoptive father, Steven, had told her. About the corpse of a thousand-year-old princess, her hair and skin frozen in the ice and permafrost of the Mongolian mountains, and the bogs of northern Europe which yielded the remains of the human sacrifices of Celtic tribes, preserved in tannic acid with their throats cut from ear to ear. Egyptian tombs where mummified emperors lay for centuries until they were disturbed by explorers and robbers who were cursed for their inquisitiveness and greed.

It hadn't done *her* any harm. Then again, perhaps it explained a great deal.

'We were talking about flowers.' Adam dropped his voice. 'I said to her that it's wrong, how some people think cut flowers are ugly because they're dead.' He looked at her. 'But there's beauty in death. What they saw when they dug up Lizzie Siddal's coffin proved that.'

Natasha suddenly wanted to escape his rather brooding but beautiful blue eyes 'Do you have a photograph of Bethany that I could borrow?'

'Sure.' Adam reached inside his jacket and drew out a small black and white print which he handed across the table. As Natasha took it, she noticed how he didn't immediately relinquish his grasp, as if he was loath to let it go.

She didn't recognize the girl as Bethany straightaway. She would have assumed instantly from the sepia tint of the shot, the crimped edges, the clothes and slightly posed and solemn expression of the sitter, that the photograph was at least a hundred years old. She was standing inside a stone doorway with ivy creeping around it. The photograph must have been taken using flash. The door was open but the light didn't reach far and it wasn't possible to see anything inside. Behind her was only darkness. She wore a pale, diaphanous gown that fell straight to the floor. Her long hair was fashioned like a figure

51

from a medieval tale, held off her face by two thin rope-like plaits drawn back from just below her temples to the nape of her neck. She had a grave kind of beauty, with her head tilted slightly to one side, her eyes cast down. The image was faintly blurred, as if there'd been a slight fault in the processing.

'It was one of the first ones we did for the exhibition,' Adam explained.

'It's lovely.' It suddenly occurred to her that there was something incongruous about someone so private, so keen to keep their identity a secret, being perfectly happy to have photographs of themselves put on display.

'Was Bethany excited about the exhibition?'

'Yes.' Without thinking she knew he was lying, remembered Bethany's lack of enthusiasm. 'It was a joint project, something we shared.' He dragged his fingers through his hair. 'She knew how important it is for me. My chance to do what I want to do. No more days photographing crisp packets and cans of hairspray. I've invested everything. I just can't believe she'd go, that she wouldn't at least stay and see it open.'

Unless she needed to disappear while she still could, before her face was plastered over the walls of an exhibition hall.

Natasha slipped the picture inside the diary. 'I'll give you a call in the new year.' She stood to leave, Boris springing to his feet beside her.

'Natasha and Boris,' Adam said lightly. 'Your family tree has Russian blood I take it?'

Of all questions she should be used to this one by now, the one question everyone expected someone in her profession to be able to answer. She should be used to it but every time it opened a cavern of emptiness inside her.

'I like to think so.'

Six

Adam's comment about Russian blood hovered in the air as Natasha sloshed vodka into a glass that evening. She should really switch to something else, whisky or gin perhaps. What had started as a rebellious, adolescent statement of independence had come to seem more like a silly, ironic joke against herself, one that begged the kind of remark Adam had made. 'With your name I suppose you'd not drink anything else.' But now wasn't the time to alter habits. No other drink seemed quite so comforting, or slipped down so easily. Too easily. But tonight it wasn't helping her to relax. Christmas Eve. Her parents and sister would be leaving Derbyshire to travel down to the Cotswolds. Still too early to go over to the pub without the risk of seeming desperate.

She went over to the iMac instead. Her notepad was open on the screen, a long list of things that needed to be done, names and dates to follow up, certificates to chase, problems that needed thinking time to solve. One swift click on the mouse and they were all magicked away. For now.

There were hundreds of websites dedicated to families and individuals with the surname of

Marshall, and Natasha browsed through the main ones. Marshalls were doctors originally, of a kind. Horse doctors, grooms and farriers. Despite humble origins the name was borne by one of the most important and influential families in the middle ages. The founder, yet another John Marshall, whose son was the 3rd Earl of Pembroke, was Regent of England for a while. Then the dynasty fell into decline, all those succeeding to the title suffering early or violent deaths.

According to one chronicler, a curse lay on the Marshall name.

Bethany's voice echoed in Natasha's head, made her shiver, despite herself. *Do you think it's possible that some families can be cursed?* But Bethany said her name wasn't Marshall; she just believed she was descended from them.

And not all members of that clan were afflicted. There were plenty that were very successful, including a few with either artistic or medical backgrounds. Charles Marshall, a scene painter and master of illusion, responsible for introducing limelight. Benjamin Marshall, the sporting artist. Two medical Marshalls were given specific mention. Henry Marshall born in Stirlingshire in 1775 who reformed the way soldiers were treated, and John, anatomist and surgeon, credited as among the first to demonstrate the connection between cholera and infected drinking water. It also said he was a friend of Ford Maddox Brown, one of the Pre-Raphaelites. He died in 1891, on New Year's Day and was buried in Ely, Cambridgeshire.

There was her man, perhaps.

John Marshall. J.M. Same initials as the diarist.

On a long shot, Natasha inserted the *Family Search* CD-Rom. She did a rough mental calculation to work out the possible birth date of an offspring John Marshall may have had. Died in 1891, friends with the Pre-Raphaelites so mid-nineteenth century. She ran a check on the most common girls' names, any Jennifer, Jane or Joanna Marshalls born between 1830 and 1870 in London with fathers named John. It threw up over 100 entries. That would have been too good to be true. She ejected the disk, took the diary out of her bag.

Even with Natasha's palaeographic training, it had taken several minutes to decipher a single page of the scribbled handwriting. She'd mentally translated a dozen or so pages on the train back to Moreton-in-Marsh from Oxford. Several of the entries had made her laugh out loud.

My appearance is moderate generally and sometimes pretty good. That is the truth with no vanity or false modesty, J.M. had written, going on to say that people called her Sunshine as a child because she smiled a lot. Natasha had formed an instant picture of her. Single-minded and slightly crafty. Someone who'd be amusing company so long as you didn't get on her wrong side.

Reading the diary didn't feel like work. *But it is so keep your mind on the job*. What she really needed was to find some clue, any clue, that would help to pinpoint J.M.'s identity. A starting point from where it would, hopefully, be possible to trace forward through the records to Bethany or her parents.

The entries were brisk and chatty, slightly acerbic sometimes, full of interesting little details of clothes, music, travel and flirtations. In the space of twenty pages, J.M. had been through two thwarted relationships, been clearly hurt at first but stoically shrugged off her disappointment. Good for her.

The first liaison had been with a guy named John Wood, who kept sending family tickets for the opera so he could enjoy the proximity of seats, from what Natasha could gather. Until J.M.'s mother was alerted and returned the next batch of tickets with the excuse of a previous engagement. *What an awful shame and a fib too!* J.M. complained.

Natasha turned to the next page. An Aunt Julia was mentioned. *The perfect chaperone. She sits by the fire and shuts her eyes!*

Natasha skipped forward. Apparently J.M. had worked her way through a couple more affairs. Helpfully, she had even summarised them.

First, John Wood. About thirty, called me 'dear' until Mama put a spoke in his wheel. He departs and is married in sixteen months. Second, Harold Archer, over thirty, short and faithful. Danced with me six times and that was that. Third, Archibald Leslie Innes, lieutenant in the Cambridgeshire Regiment, about twenty-four, appeared to like me very much. Gone to Ceylon. No money anyway. Fourth, Herbert Thomas, tall, red-headed but very clever, about forty. Afflicted with intense staring and makes embarrassing speeches, very nervous and awkward. In short, all bad symptoms. Papa did not approve or encourage. Married ten months after. There you are!

You could read an old document and it seemed just that, fusty, dead. But sometimes the words leapt off the page, as if they were written only yesterday. Natasha almost felt J.M. was speaking to her directly, could hear her voice. It was a good feeling.

Suffice to say what odd creatures men are, J.M. had concluded.

Which made Natasha think, as she often did, how little people changed over the centuries. Situations altered only on the surface. It was the same characters, the same emotions and dramas played out again and again.

Was that reassuring or depressing?

Natasha slipped the photograph of Bethany out of the front of the diary's cover and tilted it towards the desk lamp.

There were a pair of small initials in faint white print, in the right hand corner of the frame, where artists traditionally signed their work. T. R. Puzzling. Since Adam had said he'd taken it. Don't say *he* wasn't who he said he was either.

She went to put the photograph back inside the diary and noticed something else. The lining of the cover was uneven, the ridges of a square showing through, as if something had been inserted and stuck beneath it.

She peeled back the corner. It came away surprisingly easily, had clearly been done before. Underneath was a piece of lined paper which looked as if it had been torn from a spiral-bound notepad. It was perhaps ten centimetres in diameter, folded in two, similar to the paper which Adam had shown her, on which Bethany had written Natasha's address. The writing was the same as well. Elegant, looped and sloping, like a medieval manuscript, written in blue ballpoint. A light hand which had left no indentation.

One of Natasha's first clients had made her shiver when he told her, 'You've brought the dead back to life.' She'd heard it many times since then and had come to think of it as the most rewarding aspect of her job, making the past and a person's ancestors real for them, rediscovering those who'd been buried and forgotten. Now her own words came back to her as she stared at the note, her mind resisting the obvious. *I don't find people who are alive.*

An image flashed into her mind, Bethany as Ophelia, driven insane after her lover had rejected her, walking into the river to drown.

Say no goodbye,
I am gone to the unknown land,
Where at last you will be mine.

Seven

Bright sunshine woke Natasha on Christmas morning, but it was deceptive, gave off little warmth, just enough to melt the snow. When she took Boris for a walk out on the Broadway Road, it was already disappearing fast beneath the piercing blue sky. The sounds of dripping icicles, droplets tinkling from black branches forming rivulets in the steep lanes, the thump, thud of snow slipping down roofs and crumpling to the ground.

Two little girls who lived at the other end of the village came skipping up the path in spangly wellingtons, tinsel crowns and paper angel wings clipped to their shoulders. Their father ambled behind them, and wished Natasha a merry Christmas.

On the way home Natasha wandered into the church, a squat little building with a square castellated tower, braced low against the ever-present winds. She let Boris follow her inside. It didn't seem right that God's creatures weren't welcomed in His house.

Boris padded down the aisle, then stood muscles tensed, nose in the air.

Natasha spotted Mr Nicholson, the warden, busy in the vestry preparing for the Christmas service.

'Sh,' Natasha whispered as Boris snorted. 'Sit down.'

Boris chose to ignore her completely and remain standing, tongue lolling, staring up with complete disrespect at the silver crucifix.

Natasha looked up at it too.

She'd always been drawn to churches. The atmosphere of sacred otherworldliness. The drama of stained glass and candles, crucifixes, statues and tombs, soaring gothic arches. She hadn't attended church regularly since she'd left her parents' home but she liked the fact that her work often took her to deserted chapels, draughty vestries, overgrown graveyards. Small, ancient, isolated places of worship where you could still hear the whispered prayers of the past. She found in those places something calming, an assurance that you were never entirely alone, that unspoken worries and fears were universal and shared.

She closed her eyes for a moment. *Be careful what you wish for, it might come true.* Was it the same with prayers?

The whole concept of luck was superstitious, irreligious. But there was no doubt luck played a part in genealogy. Sometimes it took years to track a person down, but with others she stumbled upon the crucial leads right away.

That was what she needed to happen with Bethany. So she prayed for a little luck. Might as well cover both options.

There was something else she prayed for, something she couldn't quite put into words. That things could be put right between herself and Marcus. God literally knew how. 'If you do, let me in on it, will you?'

She almost believed she heard the answer. Church folk were quick to tell you that God always answers prayers. It's just that sometimes the answer was 'no'. Very convenient.

She looked up at the rays of light that filtered like a broken rainbow through the blue, green and red glass of the east-facing windows, dipicting Mary Magdalene, the Crucifixion and Ascension. Her glance fell on the plaque she'd read many times before, detailing the individual members of one of Snowshill's most prominent families to whom the windows were dedicated. Marshall.

John Marshall, died 1 July 1864.

Not the same John Marshall or course. Six degrees of separation. Everyone in the world is supposedly connected to everyone else through a chain of no more than six mutual acquaintances or relations. Were the Snowshill Marshalls linked to Bethany's ancestors? There were dozens of qualified genealogists listed with the Association of Genealogists and Record Agents, hundreds advertising their services in the back of family history magazines. Natasha wondered why Bethany had chosen her, if it might have something to do with the Snowshill connection. She couldn't help beginning to wish Adam had found someone else's details in the front of the diary.

Thank you, God. Thanks very much for dumping this on my plate right now. It's just what I needed.

She turned and walked outside into the bright sunshine, leant against the stone which was strangely warm to the touch.

Say no goodbye,
I am gone to the Unknown Land,
Where at last you will be mine.

It was just seeing Bethany acting the part of Ophelia that had made her think it was a suicide note, surely. Autosuggestion or whatever it was called.

The worst thing was that it did explain why Bethany had left behind her most treasured possession. Why would she do that? Unless she no longer had a need for it. Or wanted Adam think that was so.

Adam said Bethany hadn't left a note. Unless the verse was her parting message to him.

Maybe it was just a threat, a cry for help or attention, as suicide notes were often said to be. Natasha's conversation with Bethany echoed inside her head. Could it have been something she had said? Oh, why had she gone on about inherited fate and the curse of secrets?

Maybe Bethany *had* left the diary and the note because she wanted more commitment and reassurance from Adam, wanted to force him to make the effort to find her and win her back, and was waiting to see if he'd bother.

Bethany had asked Natasha: *How long would it take?* Natasha had said you could trace back as far as great-great-grandparents in a month. Her standard reply. Great-great-grandparents, four generations back, which, generally speaking, took you to the mid 1800s. So going forward from that time, the time when J.M. was probably writing her diary, would take you to now, to living descendants. If Bethany did intend for Adam to find her using the diary, is that how long she'd give him? A month? A month from now. No. She'd gone a few days after Natasha had met her. The middle of December. A month from then was mid January. And there was nothing much Natasha could do until the New Year.

Of course, the message could have a perfectly innocent explanation. A kind of private in-joke or reference. Which Adam would be able to explain *if* she could get hold of him. She'd left a message on the studio answering machine but he hadn't returned her call. Maybe he didn't bother to check for messages regularly over the holidays. Natasha had said she wouldn't be calling him until the New Year. In which case should she go to the police? That seemed extreme.

Adam had said the police wouldn't do anything anyway, because he and Bethany had had an argument; she was perfectly within her rights to walk out on him. But a suicide note, if that's what it was, would change all that. Natasha had checked on the internet, font of all knowledge, and found a paper on the Home Office website outlining police procedure for missing persons. Adults who disappeared of their own accord were described as non-vulnerable. Children and the elderly were vulnerable. But threats of suicide or risk of mental instability made adults vulnerable too, highest priority. Hospitals would be contacted, detailed investigations carried out amongst friends and family. They'd want to talk to Adam, would track him down wherever he was spending Christmas, ask questions. There was no way Natasha could initiate that without talking to him first. The note didn't say enough. What could Adam tell the police anyway? He didn't even know Bethany's real name!

The police would of course dig around, maybe find the reason she didn't use her real name. Natasha wasn't sure she had the right to stir all that up either. Not without knowing Bethany's reasons.

No. She'd just have to wait until Adam called

back. Try not to think about it until then. Easier said than done.

When she got home, she couldn't resist skimming another few pages of the diary whilst she dried her hair after her shower.

She gave a whoop when she found what she was looking for. A mention of a visit to see relatives in Ely. *Sundays are quiet here and no mistake. The people so small (not just in stature) and narrow.*

It was confirmation that J.M.'s father *was* the John Marshall she'd found on the internet, whose family came from Ely and who was buried there.

Eight

There was a knock at the door. The diary still in her hand, Natasha went to answer.

It was Mary, holding a beautifully gift wrapped bottle of Smirnoff and an engraved silver goblet to go with it. 'Just came to wish you a Merry Christmas.'

'Time for a coffee?'

'No, but I'll have one anyway.'

Mary swiped the diary from Natasha's hand as she passed her in the hall. 'What's this? Not work surely? Don't you ever stop?'

'Remember that guy, Adam, who called when I was having dinner at your place? He's asked me to use it to trace his girlfriend who's gone missing. It belonged to one of her ancestors.'

Natasha discussed most of her cases with Mary,

64

did not see giving her the bare bones as any breach of confidentiality, since Mary, who usually ended up helping with the investigation, was always a good sounding board.

Mary insisted that she was 'no good' at school, had left at sixteen with one O-Level in home economics. Her dad, a carpenter and fanatical sports fan, didn't have time for academic pursuits, always told her it was more important to be good with your hands and with a ball. Something Mary had gone along with for a few years, playing netball for Gloucestershire, training to be a hairdresser and experimenting in the kitchen in her spare time.

Then she met and married James and they took over the Snowshill Arms. Mary loved running the place, supervising the catering and the B&B business, but had become hooked on the challenges of genealogical research, due primarily to the fact that the inn stood on the site of an old monastery and was reputed to be haunted by a hooded monk who also prowled the lane outside the Manor. Since moving there, Mary had been 'privileged' to see him half a dozen times and it was this, she claimed, that had instilled in her a profound interest in history.

Natasha thought that it was more likely to make a person want to sell up and move. She herself had developed a rather pragmatic approach to ghosts over the years. She believed in them as firmly as she believed in God, which seemed a sensible comparison since she'd never seen either, despite the numbers of graveyards and vaults and supposedly haunted houses she'd visited. She wasn't sure how she'd cope with her job if she was as sensitive to these things as Mary, who could walk into a room and sense or feel if there was anyone there 'from the other side'.

Mary's interest in history had been nurtured and stimulated by her friendship with Natasha, who had found that Mary had an appetite for learning similar to a child's as well as a keen nose for the kind of detective work needed in genealogy. She often came up with a fresh slant on things, her viewpoint uncluttered by academic indoctrination.

'Modern day missing person,' Mary said now. 'Isn't that something for the police to deal with?'

'She's not really missing, just walked out on her boyfriend. I don't think the police would want to get involved every time that happened.'

'Sounds interesting, though. If there's anything I can do to help...'

'I'd counted you out for the next few months.'

'Don't you dare. There's only so many bootees and bonnets a girl can knit.'

Were there? For a second Natasha thought how she'd be quite contented to sit by the fire, with a baby growing inside her and a devoted husband making her cups of tea. The thought gave her a shock. *Get a grip.*

'Who is he then?' Mary asked. 'A broken-hearted one night stand?'

'Not quite.'

'Have a row did they?'

'Kind of.'

'Better be careful then.'

'He's nothing I can't handle, don't you worry.'

Natasha wrapped her fingers more tightly around her cup. 'What do you mean anyway? What's likely to happen?'

'You've obviously not watched enough television detective shows. With missing persons or unexplained deaths, suspicion falls heaviest on the person who raises the alarm.'

To her dismay, Natasha found she couldn't entirely laugh that off. She felt a tug of unease. She'd not tried as hard as she might to confront Adam with the note, was putting off revealing it to him. Because she didn't entirely trust him.

'So what's he like then?'

'Artistic. Interesting. Cute, if you're into still-waters-run-deep kinda guys. But not my type,' she added.

'Artistic, interesting and a complete flake no doubt. Sounds exactly your type to me.'

Nearly ten o'clock. If she didn't get a move on she'd be late for Christmas lunch with her parents and Abby.

She dressed quickly. Long, black velvet skirt, black laced boots, a boned, dark red bodice. Impatiently, she raked a brush through her unruly hair and fastened it at the nape of her neck with a silver clasp. Ringlets sprung loose around her face and impatiently she smoothed them back.

Boris streaked to the door, leaving pale strands of copper fur glimmering against the black of Natasha's skirt as he brushed by.

'Oh, I suppose you can come too.' She unlocked the Alpine and let him scramble up onto the passenger seat. He wouldn't be allowed into the hotel but he was used to waiting in the car when he went with her on research trips.

In any weather and at any time of the day or year, Chipping Campden looked welcoming, with its broad, curved high street and almost unbroken terrace of gabled shops and cottages and grand wool merchants' houses. Natasha agreed with those who said it was the most beautiful high street in Britain. Stately and imposing, but not at all aloof.

It was late morning but the town was deserted. There was no snow at all here, just ribbons of frost edging the pavements.

The hotel was a noisy contrast. Ann's choice. Natasha knew Steven would rather stay beneath the ancient beams of the Lygon Arms in Broadway, but Ann preferred the Cotswold House Hotel, with its impressive main entrance, airy Regency architecture and famous winding staircase.

She felt a rush of happiness as she saw Steven. Head and shoulders taller than everyone around him, he looked fit and tanned, dressed in slightly crumpled chinos and a dark shirt, incongruous amongst the pale English-winter faces and formal attire. He enfolded her in a bear-hug. 'Merry Christmas, honey.' People turned to look. Steven had a presence that made him dominate a room. And a voice that carried, which he never made any effort to suppress. Natasha inhaled his earthy, outdoors smell, mingled with aftershave, beer and bitter coffee. It always took her back to being a little girl, swept high into his arms as she

68

ran to meet him when he returned from one of his trips.

'Merry Christmas,' Natasha said. As a form of protest which she now saw as cruel, she'd stopped calling him Dad when she'd discovered the truth about her past. She found that she couldn't slip back into using it without it seeming awkward. She was certain he wouldn't mind if she called him by his Christian name. He used it himself now in letters and on cards. 'With all my love always, Steven.'

'Ann and Abby will be down in a while, when they've finished tarting themselves up.' He looked her up and down. 'You look ravishing as always.'

She felt a warm glow of pleasure. But it always gave her a peculiar feeling to think how he'd watched her grow, knowing all the time that she was an interloper, not a part of him at all. Now, when he complimented her or said he loved her, she didn't know quite how to take it.

He glanced towards the cocktail menu, tossed it aside. 'Whisky'll do me. You won't say no to a V and T?'

She grinned. 'I won't.'

They went up to the bar and ordered. 'Get that down you,' Steven said, clinking her glass. 'If we're quick about it we can squeeze in another one before we have to behave ourselves.'

'When have you ever?'

'All the time. It's you who leads me astray. You're a bad influence.'

'Must've learnt my wicked ways from someone.'

'Glad I taught you something useful.'

She watched his large hand on the glass. It was rough and calloused, the nails cracked. She could never quite bring herself to trust men with soft, manicured, computer tapping fingers.

Abby came bounding in, looking tanned and fit. 'Hi.' She gave Natasha a squeeze, handed over a card and present. She stripped off the wrapping paper to find a book on the aboriginal Dreamtime.

'That's great, thanks.' Natasha kissed her cheek.

'Thought it'd be your kind of thing.' Natasha opened the card and Abby added, 'It's from Australia as well.' It had a cartoon of Santa Claus and his sleigh careering along a sunny, sandy beach. How much harder it must be to convince Australian children he existed when he wore clothes and travelled in a vehicle so inappropriate to their climate.

Ann appeared by Steven's side, looking serene and lovely as always, dressed in a figure-hugging, navy blue dress with chiffon across the shoulders and a thick belt at her slender waist, her ash blonde hair tied back with a sapphire scarf. With her boots in need of a polish, Natasha felt untidy by comparison. No change there then.

When she'd once invited her parents to stay at Orchard End, Ann's evangelistic dusting and scrubbing and vacuuming had driven her mad, as it had done when she was growing up. Natasha and Abigail were never allowed to be seen with even so much as a smudge of chocolate or paint or mud on their fingers or faces. That wasn't to say Ann was overly strict. She was always ready with hugs and bedtime stories and help with homework. The perfect mum. Which is just how she wanted everything to be.

With a perfect marriage to match. Which was probably, Natasha had decided, why Ann had turned a blind eye to Steven's affairs, and never complained when he came home from a six-week trip and went straight out drinking. Maybe it was that she'd got what she wanted. Or just that she loved him. Steven attracted people to him like a magnet, by the sheer force of his personality. And once you were drawn into his sphere, it was hard to leave it.

You grow up thinking your parents are totally normal. Until you see other families and think yours is the odd one. Then you come to the conclusion that your family is normal *because* it's odd. Something of which Natasha, in her profession, had daily proof.

Ann and Steven were suited to each other as only those who appear completely ill matched could be. Steven liked clever, educated women, but there was also something old fashioned about him, a confusing double standard that made him champion Natasha's career but jokingly say he could never be married to someone like her. Ann had read history, studied to be an interior designer, then done a stint as a museum curator. She had a string of letters after her name, but her own mother, dead for fifteen years now, delighted in telling Natasha that ever since Ann could talk her only ambition had been to have a husband and a house with a big kitchen and garden. And lots of babies. Something that had jabbed in

71

Natasha's memory like a thorn. Ever since Abigail's successful conception, she sensed she was exactly that to Ann. A reminder of a time when she believed she'd failed as a woman.

'Tell me about Italy,' Natasha said to Steven, as they sat down at a small table in the corner of the drawing room. He'd been away for two months.

'You'd have been fascinated. We found evidence of a temple with a mass grave.'

Steven paused whilst the waiter distributed menus in dark green leather covers.

'Will you be going back?' she asked.

He glanced at Ann. She never appeared to mind how long he spent away. Natasha had the impression that he was grateful to her for that, but also disappointed. 'Why, thinking of coming too?'

Natasha had always been interested in Steven's work. As young as she could remember she'd begged him to take her on archaeological trips. She preferred to spend her summer holidays not digging on a beach, but with a trowel or sieve, knee deep in a muddy hole, or clambering round the crumbling walls of a castle.

'Too busy.'

'So, whose cupboards have you been finding skeletons in lately?' he asked.

She had begun to explain very briefly about Adam and Bethany, when the waiter returned with notepad and pen to take their order. Steven asked for a bottle of claret and they were ushered through into the restaurant with long French windows beside which a small choir dressed in red and white stood round a grand piano, with lanterns on sticks. They were singing

In the Bleak Midwinter.

'Didn't Christina Rossetti write the lyrics to this?' Ann said. 'Yes, I'm sure she did.' She'd been paying more attention to what they'd been saying than Natasha had given her credit for.

It had always been one of Natasha's favourite carols. 'I didn't know that.'

Steven gave her their gift then, a Victorian silver and jet necklace which Natasha knew he'd have chosen. He helped her put it on, lifting her hair to fasten the clasp around her throat. When he said how well it suited her she was aware of Ann's eyes upon her. Steven had either never noticed or had chosen to ignore what had always been blatantly obvious to Natasha: Ann resented the fact that Steven was closer to Natasha than to Abby. At the back of her mind Natasha wondered too if Ann could be jealous of their relationship, was suspicious of it even.

Hastily she handed over their presents, a silk scarf for Abby, an early edition of *The Seven Pillars of Wisdom* for Steven, which she'd found on the internet, and a Venetian glass figurine for Ann which Natasha had spotted at an antique fair in Stow.

Ann said it was lovely, then put it to one side, leaving Natasha wondering if she really liked it.

'Has Abby told you about her new job?' Ann said.

'I'm going to work for a PR company in London.'

Natasha turned to her sister. 'Really?'

'It's one of the big ones,' said Ann. 'Isn't it wonderful?' The indulgent pride in Ann's voice

73

stung but Natasha was determined, as she always was, not to let it show.

She didn't quite manage it. 'I thought you wanted Abby to settle down nearer home.'

'Derbyshire's far too cold,' Abby said. 'Me and mum went down to London last week, checking out flats to rent. We've found a great one in Wimbledon. You'll have to come and stay.'

'I'd love to. I'm glad you're not going to emigrate anyway. I half thought you might.'

'She'd never do that,' Ann said witheringly.

By the time pudding was brought to the table, topped with a blue flame of brandy, Natasha was beginning to feel hot and drowsy. She made the excuse that Boris needed a walk before coffee and Christmas cake were served. Ann said she'd go and freshen up, Abby said she could do with a quick nap. Steven offered to accompany Natasha, as she'd known and hoped he would. There were things she wanted to ask him.

Nine

Natasha let Boris out of the car, and they set off towards her favourite part of the town, past Grevel's House and up Cinder Hill Lane. The sun was a low red ball in the sky, glinting on the weather vanes high on the church tower.

'Marcus was part of our team in Italy for the last week,' Steven said, falling in step beside her.

'Oh, yes?' She tried to sound casual, kept her

eyes fixed ahead but doubted she'd fooled him. 'Was he well?'

'Seemed it. Though you can never tell with him. He's a private sort of fellow. But at least he was fairly light-humoured before … all this.' The hint of reproach in Steven's voice was unmistakable. She knew better than to think he was aggrieved on Marcus's behalf. In Steven's opinion, it didn't matter how messy your personal life got, so long as it didn't interfere with your professional one. But Natasha clung to something he'd said, the implication that Marcus was miserable too.

'I'm the last person he'd talk to, of course,' Steven said. 'Let's just hope communication doesn't break down between us altogether.' His obvious irritation irritated her back. *All right, it was difficult for him with his daughter and colleague splitting up, but what was she supposed to do about it?*

She also had a sneaking suspicion he was not so much annoyed that the relationship had finished, as that it had ever begun. There was the faintest hint of 'I told you so' in his voice.

Steven had not exactly kept Marcus and her apart, but he'd made no effort for them to meet. Inevitable they would in the end though. Steven was a lecturer at Sheffield University and Marcus was attached to the Medical Artist Department at Manchester. They'd collaborated on several museum and media projects. She'd turned up unexpectedly at a lecture they were giving together, when she was in Manchester consulting canal records for a case. The three of them had gone out for supper in one of the string of Indian restaurants in Rusholme. Then, when Natasha had been staying at her parents' house, Marcus had started inviting himself for supper. After that he'd come down to Oxford for work, and conveniently happened to be passing through Snowshill. Over three years ago now. She didn't feel like the same person.

They turned back down Church Street and outside St James they both paused, breathing in the crisp air, and admiring, or pretending to admire, the ornate gateway and pepper pot lodges of Camden House and Sir Baptist Hicks's beautiful almshouses.

'He did ask after you, in case you were wondering?'

'Did he?' She'd almost snapped.

She ached to know whether Marcus was involved with anyone else, but part of her couldn't bear to hear what she thought the answer would be. And she was damned if she was going to ask Steven.

'He's not been in touch then?'

'No.'

'He's going out to Canada first week in January, on exchange with Vancouver University for six months.'

Natasha felt a prick of tears behind her eyes.

Steven turned to her. 'Listen, Natasha. If you want to talk...'

How could she begin when there was so much she didn't understand herself.

'We were too alike, I suppose.' Even as she said it she realised how trite it sounded.

Steven found a stick, hurled it down the street for Boris to retrieve, then threw it again, running a little ahead to gain momentum.

It's a cliché, daughters wanting to marry their fathers, and Steven had always been Natasha's hero. Subconsciously she used to compare every man she met to him. Now she compared them to Marcus as well. Steven was Marcus's mentor and perhaps that explained why they were so alike, in personality and outlook. They also resembled one another physically. Both tall and rangy, with eloquent, deep set eyes, angular features and thick dark hair.

'So, it's definitely all over between you then?'

'Yes.' She couldn't help feeling Steven was in some way pleased, or relieved, despite the inconvenience it caused him. But she didn't want to argue with him.

'You were telling me,' Steven said. 'About this girl you're trying to find, the one with the diary.'

The motto of the College of Arms, the most august body of genealogists, where Natasha first worked, was 'Diligent and Secret'. It went against the grain in some way. She was never comfortable with secrets, even when they meant confidentiality and discretion. But she stuck to the promise of that motto with her own clients. Steven, though, had seemed excluded or above that. They had always confided and discussed intricate details of their work and it had always felt perfectly right to do so.

'I found a note in the diary,' she said carefully. 'In Bethany Marshall's writing. I think it might be a suicide note.'

'Good Lord. What have you done about it?'

'Nothing, yet. I wanted to talk to her boyfriend

first. The note's pretty ambiguous. I might be jumping to the wrong conclusions.'

'When have you ever done that?'

'All the time.'

'Not professionally.' This was true.

'By rights you should report it to the police, of course.'

'I will.' Soon. When she'd spoken to Adam.

'I met a girl called Bethany once. Petite little thing, very pretty. Actually, she was a friend of Marcus's.'

Natasha ignored that.

They started walking again and after a while Steven said thoughtfully, 'She poses for a photograph as Lizzie Siddal and then she kills herself. History repeating. Intentionally or not.'

Natasha stared up at the East Banqueting Hall, which offered a glimpse of what Campden House must have been like before the Civil War's fires destroyed it. 'No one knows for sure that Lizzie Siddal did kill herself. The verdict at the time was that it was an accidental overdose, wasn't it?'

'A cover-up more like.'

When suicide was referred to as 'self-murder', not so long ago still punishable by burial at a crossroads, a stake through the heart.

Nowadays taking your life wasn't regarded as such a shameful thing, such a terrible crime. Even though it was still impossible to talk about suicide without saying 'commit' before it.

Steven touched her arm, indicating they should turn and walk back in the direction of the Market Hall and the hotel. 'Of course she is buried in consecrated ground, which is supposed to be

78

sacred, a place of rest, but Rossetti didn't leave her to rest, did he?'

'Do you think what he did was wrong?'

'Yes. I do.'

Natasha was astonished. Steven regularly plundered graves and tombs. 'How can you say that? You do it all the time.'

'The bodies I disturb are thousands of years old. Well, several hundred at least.'

'I don't see that that makes any difference.' She'd always enjoyed these kinds of discussions and sparring sessions with Steven.

'It makes all the difference,' Steven said.

Natasha knew what he was driving at.

Marcus's work involved putting faces to skulls. It was disturbing, to see the transformation, a face gradually take shape beneath his hands, a reversal of the process of decay. Muscles applied to bone, then flesh. It made you look at the remains in a completely different way, when you could see the person they'd been.

Steven said, 'When they opened Lizzie Siddal's coffin she was supposed to have looked as beautiful as the day she died.'

Ten

There was one extravagance Natasha wished she were able to afford. A deep swimming pool, in the corner of a garden, shaded by trees in the summer and heated, so that steam came off it in

79

winter. Membership of the spa at the Lygon Arms Hotel was the next best thing. The pool was surrounded by soft blue lighting and mosaic floors, balconies and potted trees and a high glass roof that could be opened in warm weather. Natasha liked to go there in the evenings, late, when she often had the pool completely to herself, and could lie in the water and gaze up at the stars in the black sky.

When she arrived back home the light on the answering machine was flashing 'Adam. Returning yours.'

Shit. She couldn't believe she'd missed him. She punched 1471. He'd called at six, from the studio in Oxford. It was almost nine now. She hit three anyway.

'Hello.' A terse male voice, but it didn't sound like him.

'Could I speak to Adam?'

There was a second of silence. 'Not here I'm afraid.'

'This is the right number for him?'

'Who shall I say called?'

'Natasha Blake. He's...'

'Hi there, Natasha.'

'Hi. He's got my number.'

'Has he now? You're another one he's not told me about then.'

'I beg your pardon?'

'Granted. It's a pleasure talking to you. I hope we have the opportunity to meet sometime?'

'I don't...'

'How about you tell me what it is you want to

talk to Adam about.' The tone just a little threatening now.

'I'm afraid I can't...'

Again, he didn't wait for her to finish. 'Try his mobile.' He reeled off a number.

The line went dead.

Natasha replaced the receiver, a frown on her face. What was all that about?

She tried the mobile number, let it ring a dozen times. Then the ringing stopped. 'Yes?' There was music in the background, heavy on the bass.

'It's Natasha. Blake,' she added. Adam struck her as the type who could easily know at least two girls with the same Christian name.

'So will you help me to find her or not?' Adam's voice was faint and crackly.

She'd forgotten that she'd not officially agreed to take the project on. Well, there was no way she could refuse now. But she didn't want to tell him about the note over the phone, especially when he was obviously at a New Year's Eve party. She heard female laughter close by. 'I've started already,' she said, trying to sound optimistic. 'I'm pretty sure I've got an identity for the diarist's father.' She had the feeling Adam wouldn't be interested in practicalities, but she ran through them in any case. 'I'll go to the records centres as soon as they open in the New Year, Monday. I can find out who he married, and if they had a daughter with the initial J. Then it's a case of finding her marriage details, the birth of her children and their subsequent marriages and offspring, working forward to the present day, through several branches of the family tree if need be, until we find Bethany.'

'I understand.'

'I don't think the guy I spoke to just now at your studio did. I reckon he had the wrong end of the stick, about something.'

'What did he say?' His voice was suddenly loud in her ear. She could hear the pop of his breath, as if he was gripping the phone close to his mouth.

'Just something about you not telling him about me?'

'Why the fuck should I?'

How should I know? The line went even more crackly, as if the connection would be lost any second. 'Look. I'll need to see you,' she said. 'After I've done the groundwork at the record centres.'

'I'd like that.' Silence for a second. 'I'll be in Oxford for the next couple of weeks.'

'Great.' Natasha suggested they meet in the Opium Den.

The phone was ringing as Natasha climbed out of the shower. She grabbed a towel, ran into her bedroom, snatched the receiver.

It was Mary. 'Just making sure you're going to be here before the clocks strike midnight. Or you'll turn into a pumpkin.'

'It was the coach that did that.'

'Oh, yeah.'

'You'll have to get your fairy stories straight, you being an expectant mother and everything.'

'You're right. I'd better go. I've left James at the bar on his own. The natives'll be getting restless.

We're taking bets on who'll stick to their resolutions. Everyone has to write them down and if you've not broken them by the end of Feb, drinks are on the house for the evening.'

'Giving up alcohol's not an option then?'

'Certainly not. Bad for business.'

'That's OK then.'

Natasha had spent a pleasant few days since Christmas, going for long walks, visiting a couple of friends for lunch, drinking endless cups of tea in Mary's kitchen, catching up on reading and paperwork. A couple of afternoons she and Mary had gone swimming at the Lygon Arms, had a massage afterwards, then gone shopping in Cheltenham.

She slipped into a dress she'd bought, strappy, with a tight low waist and a bias cut skirt that reached almost to the floor, made of satin the colour of a copper beech tree. She flung a black shawl, crocheted with jet sequins and beads, over her shoulders, twisted her thick hair up onto her head, and felt much better.

It was amazing, the way you could put on a different outfit and feel like a different person. Natasha often wondered if she preferred vintage clothes, and antiques, because they were already imprinted with other people's personalities which she could borrow for a while.

Eleven

The Snowshill Arms was busier and noisier than usual. In contrast to the cold outside, it was warm and fuggy, and the glow from the hanging brass lanterns and coloured lights entwined with garlands of holly, gave the pub the atmosphere of a grotto.

Through the crowd Natasha spotted Mary's father-in-law, Arnold Hyatt, a permanent fixture on the three-legged shepherd's stool beside the open fire. As Natasha entered and Boris slunk through the forest of legs, making a beeline for the hearth, Arnold raised his tankard in silent greeting. Arnold was Snowshill's wise old sage, who'd seldom travelled even as far as Cheltenham yet had seen the world.

'Hullo, stranger,' he said to Natasha. It was a long-standing joke between them. Arnold, whose family had farmed the land around Snowshill for at least four generations, held firm to the definition that a stranger was anyone whose parents and grandparents weren't buried in the graveyard of St Barnabus.

'Just the person. I was having a disagreement with my young grandson. Can you tell me? What are diamonds made from? I reckoned with what you do for a living you'd be able to help out.'

Natasha stifled a giggle. Geology. Genealogy. Easy enough mistake. 'From what I remember,

84

diamonds are a crystalline form of carbon.'

'Just the ticket.'

Natasha elbowed her way through to the bar, where James and Mary were manning their posts.

James looked up from pulling a pint, raised his voice above the din. 'Your drink's going warm. Poured it out hours ago. Actually,' he scanned the bar top. 'Some bugger must've swiped it. Your usual, is it?'

Natasha shook her head, fancying something with a bit more bite. 'I think I'll have a whisky, thanks.'

James had only a fleeting likeness to Arnold. He'd caused a terrible rift in his family when he announced he preferred the snug conviviality and late nights of running a country pub to the isolation and frosty dawns of agricultural work. But if Arnold had not entirely forgiven James, blood was thicker than water he said, and he'd come to the decision that there was no point in losing a son as well as the land. Besides, he had more sense than to bar himself from the place that offered the most pleasure in life.

Mary came over with fingers expertly inserted to carry eight empty tumblers and highballs, which she clinked into the shelf at the back of the bar.

As the measure of Glenfiddich was being poured, Natasha dug down into her pocket for change but Mary shooed it away. 'Have one for me,' she said, patting her bump.

James squeezed past to replenish Arnold's tankard, and Natasha noticed how he allowed his hand to rest fleetingly on top of Mary's tummy, a gesture both protective and proud. Natasha felt a pang. She'd sworn that once she was here she wouldn't let herself think about how Marcus was spending the evening. If he was out on the town in Manchester, or spending the evening in a quiet village pub like this one – with someone else.

'Did your visitor find you?' James asked.

She quelled a momentary flicker of hope. 'No. Who do you mean?'

'A young girl. Never seen her before. A bit skinny and pale, striking though. With long hair. She was in here earlier, asking after you. She certainly wasn't dressed for the weather. Just wearing a grey dress.'

Natasha instantly thought of Bethany and felt a twinge of apprehension. 'You didn't by any chance manage to get her name, did you?'

''Fraid not,' he said. 'Didn't want to frighten her. She looked like she'd just seen a ghost as it was. Wandered in, asked where Orchard End was, said she was looking for Natasha Blake, and then disappeared.'

'You make it all sound very mysterious, darling.' Mary gave the bar top a wipe down with a damp cloth, replaced beer mats.

'She never came,' Natasha said. 'Or I don't think she did. I've been at home most of the day.'

'Can't have been very important then.'

Mary handed Natasha a piece of paper and a biro. 'Write your resolution down there.'

Mary peered over Natasha's shoulder, reciting as she wrote: 'I resolve not to make any more resolutions that I can't keep.'

'Cheat.' Mary tutted.

At midnight Mary and James handed round champagne and plates of vol-au-vents and mini pizzas. Following which, James grabbed Natasha's hand and they led everyone outside to hold hands in a circle and sing 'Auld Langs Ayne'.

The brittle, cold air was infused with the scent of wood smoke from a bonfire in the garden of one of Natasha's neighbours. Fireworks were set off. There was a screech like a banshee, followed by a crack like a gunshot and a fizz of stars.

At one in the morning, everyone headed home. Natasha walked back to the cottage, feeling a little drunk and sleepy.

As she opened the door Boris set up a frantic barking and snarling. 'Mad dog.' She patted his head. 'What are you making such a fuss about?' He quietened a little and skulked behind her legs, tail drooping, almost tripping her up.

She went through to the living room.

Before she turned on the light she could see the red winking of the answering machine. Marcus? She sprang forward to switch it on. The beep was followed by a few seconds of hissing silence. Then the tape clicked off again. She dialled 1471 and listened to the automated voice saying that she was called at ten-fifteen but that the number was withheld.

The girl in the grey dress? She went back into the hallway to check in case a note might have been slipped through the letter box and had drifted under the rug or been blown into a corner by the draft when she opened the door. But there was nothing.

Twelve

The seven-fifteen from Moreton to Paddington had been emptier than usual in these limbo days of early January. Natasha felt optimistic, glad to be working again, and to be going to London. It was a great place to visit when you lived somewhere else.

The Society of Genealogists was the last building in a narrow, terrace off Charterhouse Buildings. It was identified by a gleaming brass plaque on the wall that gave a false impression of grandeur. Inside it was Dickensian. Dingy, cramped and slightly shabby, but Natasha felt at home there. She could rely on meeting the same faces in the record depositories and libraries she had to visit on a regular basis.

Frank Sills was one of her favourites. He was serving behind the counter in the small bookshop that sold all the tools of the trade: library guides, computer software, record cards and pedigree charts. He gave Natasha a cheery nod as she went through to the cloakroom and lockers. He looked like a retired naval captain, though he had an eccentric taste in clothes.

'Think it's a bit over the top?' He grinned, pointing to his tie: vermilion red, with a golden and black coat of arms complete with chevrons and lions.

'It's splendid, Frank.' Natasha teased. 'Anyone

coming here should have an appreciation for family ties.'

Frank's rippling laughter followed her as she walked past the lower library, crammed with microfiche cabinets and binders along the windowsill.

The upper library was lined with bookshelves. Boyd's Marriage Index, overseas papers, peerages, the trade directories.

Natasha went straight to the rows of blue medical registers, 1858–1920, arranged in chronological order half-way down the main isle. She eased sideways, past a long, narrow table at which a long-haired young man in a moss-green great coat was flicking through a pamphlet with yellowed pages and black and white pictures of steam trains.

She selected the directory for 1861 and leafed through to the M's. She ran a finger down the page.

There were only three London doctors with the names Marshall, John. The first lived at 27a Aldeman Street, St Pancras and the second, a John Brake Marshall, resided at 21 Princes Street, Hanover Square. The third was a Fellow of the Royal College of Surgeons. Marshall, John, 10 Savile Row.

She jotted down the details, closed the directory and slotted it back in place, then skipped forward a decade to 1871. A thicker volume. More doctors, more Dr Marshalls. But yes. He was still there. Ten years older. Still living at 10 Savile Row.

It was satisfying, plotting a summary of a life to

be coloured in afterwards. John Marshall's had, on the surface at least, followed a straight and steady path. Not moving house for at least twenty years. He was still in the same house in 1881. A larger practice maybe, or a dwindling one as he grew older, more respected and selective. But still there.

It was a problem Natasha often had, getting carried away, diverted by the characters she encountered on route. She had to remind herself that it wasn't really John Marshall she should be interested in. It was his daughter. J.M.

The Member's Room reminded Natasha of her old sixth-form common room, with low, upholstered lounge chairs, photocopied posters tacked onto a cork notice board, scatterings of well-thumbed magazines.

Toby Curtis, a researcher, popped his head round one of the Formica cupboards in the kitchen area. He came over and kissed her on both cheeks.

'You look terrific,' he said, peering at her from beneath a long fringe of light brown hair.

Toby had a small boy's passion for outer space and computer games, any kind of gadget for that matter. He was the first person Natasha knew to have a Psion personal organiser, yet he dressed in Arran sweaters and faded corduroys and when he cooked her supper nowadays, in his mews cottage in Hampstead – a property investment of his father's – they would have a glass or two of port afterwards. Like children playing at being adults.

Toby was Natasha's junior by two years,

handsome, in a bumbling, boyish sort of way, and she teased that he was the little brother she'd never had. It was partly true, but was also a gentle warning off to avoid hurting him. He'd never disguised that he'd had a crush on her, ever since his brother, who was at Oxford with Natasha, had introduced them.

Toby often helped Natasha with London-based aspects of her research.

'So what brings you here?' Toby said, pouring steaming water.

'The smell of caffeine.' Natasha flopped down into one of the chairs. 'I'm trying to put an identity to a mysterious nineteenth-century diarist in the hopes that she'll lead me to an even more mysterious twenty-first-century missing girl.' She shifted piles of leaflets promoting family history societies, lectures and museums, to make room on the coffee table as Toby carried two mugs over.

'So why aren't the police trying to find her?'

'I wish everyone would stop asking me that. Long story.'

'There's plenty of coffee in the jar.'

'Another time maybe. So how's it going with you?'

'Oh you know, I've been waving my wand around in the hopes a beautiful girl will appear.'

He asked her about Christmas and then regaled her with anecdotes from his skiing holiday with a bunch of friends. Months ago he'd asked her to go too and, listening to him, she wished she had.

'So you'll have to follow a line of ascent rather

than descent to find this girl?' Toby said thoughtfully. 'They say you can never go back, but in this game that's far easier than going forward.'

'It's just the same process you'd use in probate cases, if you were trying to locate the beneficiaries of an estate.'

'I guess so. If a little less run of the mill.' Toby tore open a packet of mints, offered Natasha one. 'Well, if anyone can find her, it's you.'

Natasha popped a sweetie in her mouth. 'Wish I shared your confidence.'

Thirteen

It was just under a quarter of an hour's walk from the Society of Genealogists to the Family Records Centre in Clerkenwell.

Despite the hours she must've spent there, something within Nathasha still resisted the new building, a concertina edifice in red brick, with wide plate glass windows in an innocuous suburban street. Clerkenwell was a red light district in Shakespeare's day, traditionally associated with Huguenot watchmakers and Italian immigrants, but Natasha had tried, in vain, to find much evidence or atmosphere of its more exotic past.

The censuses were located in the Public Records Office search area on the first floor, an enormous room which also housed the wills and death duty registers. The walls of the room were lined with cabinets holding the microfilms and the centre filled with carousels for the fiches. The censuses covering 1841–91 had a designated area, with supporting surname indices, reference books and place name index.

Systematically, Natasha collected a numbered black box from the shelves in the general reference area, then found her allotted microfilm reader. She went to the area of blue files first, for the 1861 census. Not holding out much hope, she checked the lists of London streets for which no census returns from that decade survived. The complete London returns had been lost for years, turning up not that long ago, at the back of a cupboard in the House of Lords of all places. Substantial sections of it were missing though.

Yup. Savile Row was one of these. Naturally.

No matter. The Marshalls hadn't moved house over the next decade. Natasha went over to the brown files, for 1871, checked the Place Name Index to find what registration district Savile Row fell into, Westminster, St James. She made a note of the class code and folio number, took the microfilm from the cabinet, slipping in the numbered black box to mark the place.

She went back to her reader, flicked the machine on, slipped and threaded on the spool, wound it round and cranked the switch, watching the names and pages swim past. She turned the dial to slow down as she neared the correct page, refined the focus.

And there he was.

John Marshall. Status: widower. Age: 52. Birthplace: Ely, Cambridge, England. Head of the household. Occupation: Surgeon.

The details were handwritten but Natasha's trained eye could read them easily enough. Inside 10, Savile Row on the evening of 2 April 1871 were three servants: Sarah Morris, cook; Emily Cooper, housemaid, and Alfred Dunkley, footman. Also present were four of Dr Marshall's children. Three daughters, Ellen, aged twenty-nine, Ada aged twenty-one and Eleanor, aged ten. The only J, was Dr Marshall's son, unsurprisingly another John, then aged twenty-five.

Natasha's heart sank. Damn. No daughters whose Christian names began with J. She stared fiercely at the screen for a moment as if the sheer force of her will could conjure one up.

At least she succeeded in summoning an alternative.

It was regular practice in Victorian times, and before, for the first born of each sex to be named after their respective parent but thereafter known by a middle name to avoid confusion. It would be possible then to assume that Dr Marshall's deceased wife was called Ellen. Also possible, just maybe, that her eldest daughter had been given a second name which began with a J. Or perhaps Mrs Marshall's name hadn't been Ellen at all, and there was another, older girl, a Jane or Jenny or Joanna, who'd already married and left home when the 1871 census was taken.

Natasha wound the film back, walked over to the photocopying machines and took a print of the relevant page.

She went downstairs, doing quick mental calculations inside her head as she pushed through the heavy glass doors to the Office of National Statistics reading rooms. It was always exaggeratedly hushed in there, as if out of respect for the dead. You couldn't forget that you were surrounded by them, thousands of names; thousands of lives and stories.

As usual there were researchers poring studiously over the bulky indexes or conferring in whispers. There was just the occasional muted background clatter of the heavy bound registers with their brass corners being carefully hefted down or returned to the endless rows of pale grey metal cabinets.

The entry for Ellen junior's birth should be relatively easy to find. She was twenty-nine in 1871, and so born in 1842 or 1843.

Ever since Natasha had studied heraldry – a basic requirement for someone in her profession – she couldn't see any form of colour coding without automatically reflecting on what was symbolised, intentionally or not. The birth records were red, the heraldic colour of fortitude. The colour of magic. Also, the colour of blood. Green for the marriage indexes; appropriate, considering that on a coat of arms, green or *vert*, signified love. The death registers along the back of the room were, unsurprisingly, black, the shade of mourning, also the armorial colour of wisdom. Tucked in a corner next to the death indexes, not to the birth registers which was surely a more appropriate location, was another small section of books. The adoption registers, bound in red and buff with a yellow spine.

Natasha had looked in those once, found

nothing she didn't already know, and had avoided them ever since.

She went to the red birth registers at the far right of the room, beginning with the March quarter of 1842. She grabbed the fabric handle, the cloth covering slightly faded and frayed, and dragged it down, turned and rested it on the wooden angled reading shelf which ran the length of the aisle. She lifted over a wadge of waxy pages with neat, scripted entries in black ink. No Ellen Marshalls born in the registration district of Westminster St James at all. She reached for the June quarter. None registered then either. Nor during the September or December quarters. Or in any of the indexes covering 1843.

She carried on resolutely into the next year. There was no law then, stipulating how soon after their birth babies had to be registered. It was often long after the event.

And so it must have been with J.M. There she was, in the March quarter of 1844.

Marshall Ellen, J.

It was always a thrill to find, staring up at her from the indexes, or some obscure manuscript or old book, a name, a person she'd been searching for. People easily became addicted to genealogy, and that was the reason why. That sizzle of satisfaction. And she didn't want to stop there. She wanted to go on breathing the life back into them through documents which illuminated, even if only glimmeringly their character, their joys and sorrows. Natasha knew that it was the same for Steven, when he dug down and found a piece of pottery, a coin, foundations or bones, a fragment of history itself, that had lain hidden for centuries. Small, personal details from the past, the ephemera of the day-to-day lives of a man or woman or child who lived a quiet, unextraordinary life, parallel to your own.

J.M. was, in all probability, Ellen J. Marshall. Known by whatever the J. stood for. But Natasha restrained her excitement. She desperately didn't want to make a mistake. As she knew from the bitter experience of her early career, it was easy to see what you wanted to see, to waste hours, months, pursuing the wrong branch or the wrong tree altogether. She didn't have months this time. Probably no more than two weeks if her theory about how long Bethany might wait for Adam to find her was close to the truth. If she wasn't too late already. She crushed that thought, quickly filled in a priority order form for a copy of the birth certificate and handed it over with cash at the kiosk.

Now she just had to prove that Ellen J. was the diarist.

She went out into the foyer and rummaged around in her bag for her mobile. She found the number of the Royal College of Surgeons, asked to be put through to the library.

The archivist, a softly spoken, elderly gentleman with a lilting Welsh accent, politely reiterated what, from previous experience, she'd expected to be told. They would gladly undertake a search for a biography of a Fellow. If he was eminent there was a chance there'd be an obituary as well. But they were inundated with requests for such information. She'd need to write in with the details and they'd call as soon as possible to let her know what was available. Then, as soon as they received a cheque for the photocopies, she'd have her information.

'Oh. I see.' She made sure she sounded suitably crestfallen but accepting. 'I'll have to do that then. It's just that I was hoping to find something before my uncle flies back to America. You're my last hope.'

A moment's hesitation. 'Well, if it's urgent, maybe we could hurry things along a bit. Why don't you give me a call in the morning.'

The phone beeped as she terminated the call.

'My favourite girl.' She pictured Steven at his desk at the university, surrounded by stacks of books and archaeological magazines, leaning back in his chair, shoving aside piles of papers to put his dusty boots up on the desk. 'Just wondering. Have you found *your* girl?'

'Don't.'

'I suppose you've completely ignored my advice as usual?'

She didn't answer.

'I've met some headstrong, eccentric mavericks in my time but you beat 'em all hands down.' *You can talk.* 'Sometimes I wonder what you were doing when I took you on all those digs. I thought it would have taught you teamwork if nothing else.'

He sounded cross and she hated that. Hated being told off by him, however mildly, hated being told off by anyone, especially if she had a sneaking suspicion it might be justified. 'You know the only sport I ever liked was swimming.

98

I'm not a team player. That's why I left the College of Arms, remember, and Generations. I knew I'd be better on my own.'

He understood her well enough to realize it was counterproductive to get her back up. 'I realize you always think you can do the job better than anyone else. Usually you can... So long as you've thought about what happens if you're right about that note and you don't get to her in time. What if this girl does turn up; dead? If you've kept it to yourself then there's only you to blame. Still. No point in arguing with you if you've made up your mind. I just hope she's worth all your effort, that's all.'

She steered the conversation round to Italy.

'I'll be staying in London next week, funding meetings,' Steven said. 'Be great to see you before we go back out.'

'I'll see what I can do.'

As she grabbed a roll from the basement canteen Natasha was still smarting from her conversation with Steven and all the latent emotions it had aroused. Memories of turbulent teenage years, when she argued with him and Ann constantly, refused to accept their advice or rules, threw back at them words that she knew were as unjustified as they were unkind. 'How dare you tell me what to do. You aren't my real parents.'

She knew that when she got home there was sure to be an e-mail from Steven, apologizing for lecturing. He was only cross because he cared, was worried about her. Why did she find that so difficult to accept?

You always think you can do the job better than

anyone else. And that was the trouble. She might give the appearance but it often wasn't how she felt inside. 'It's wonderful to be so confident, but don't let it come out as arrogance.' That's what he used to tell her. And she wondered who he was talking about.

Still, giving the impression of confidence was probably half the battle.

She flipped through her notebook, turned back to the page where she'd made the notes on the Marshalls. Two daughters. Ellen and Eleanor. There was surely some significance in the similarity of the names. She'd make a bet that she'd be proved right about Mrs Marshall. Both daughters named after her. In which case it must have been triply confusing. Four females in one household. And three of them with the names Ellen, Ellen and Eleanor. John and John as well for that matter. No wonder Ellen number two was known by a middle name. And Eleanor so much younger than her sisters and brother. A late, unplanned pregnancy? Had Ellen senior died in childbirth? Had little Eleanor also been named in remembrance of her mother for that reason?

Fourteen

'Your hunch was right,' the archivist at the Royal College of Surgeons said when Natasha called next morning as arranged. 'The doctor's wife was indeed called Ellen.'

100

She wanted to kiss him. 'Fantastic. I can't tell you how helpful that is.'

'Glad to be of assistance.' He sounded surprised and pleased, as if he wasn't used to such unreserved appreciation. 'There's a two-page entry in Plarr's *Lives of the Fellows of the Royal College of Surgeons of England*. Would you like me to drop a quick copy in the post to you? You might as well have it now it's here in front of me.'

'Yes, please.'

'You never know. It might be useful.'

It might. But she had the information she needed. Dr Marshall's wife being called Ellen made it highly likely that Ellen J. was the eldest daughter, that there were no other Marshall girls with the initials J.M. Which meant it was a pretty sure-fire bet she was the diarist.

The 1881 census was a mine of easily accessible information. So far it was the only census that had been computerised, painstakingly, by the Church of the Latter Day Saints. The entries were all stored on CD-ROM, fully indexed by both surname and district. Natasha quickly inserted disk five, covering London, and typed in the search criteria. Marshall: head of household. There were 200. She flicked the cursor down the page and found him again. On 3 April 1881 the housemaid, Emily, was still in service. Eleanor was still living at Savile Row. John, Ada, and Ellen, had all gone.

Perfect. It was a great help in genealogy that in the past people moved around less and it was customary for daughters to remain at home until they married, then, in the absence of birth control, to have a child soon after, or sometimes just before.

One of Toby's flatmates answered the phone. Natasha caught the sound of radio pop music and the clatter of breakfast, then Toby's voice. 'You want me to help you find your missing girl I take it? So bang goes my morning raiding tombs with Lara Croft. She reminds me of you you know.'

'From you, Toby, I take that as a real compliment.' She filled him in on the background to the case. 'It's a girl called Ellen J. Marshall I'm interested in. She was still living at her father's house in Savile Row in 1871. She's gone by 1881.'

'So I've got to trawl through ten years of marriage registers to find out where she went and with whom. Original job. Not. I suppose you want it done yesterday.'

'Course not. This morning would be just fine. Her birth certificate should be waiting at the collection point as well.'

Professions, like given names, had a way of running in families. Lawyers' sons became lawyers, carpenters' sons became carpenters, military men had children and grandchildren who also joined the armed forces. Often the tradition was carried on over several generations. Natasha wondered, had either of the Marshall girls, or John junior, become nurses or doctors?

Another thought occurred. When Bethany told her she was working in the florists while she decided what to do, was she considering a career in the medical profession? Bethany said she believed the moon controlled the mind because

102

the human body was up to eighty per cent water. Natasha couldn't remember if that figure was accurate. She had an almost photographic memory, only sometimes she left the lens cap on, and sciences hadn't been her strongest subjects. Did what Bethany had said indicate a particular interest in anatomy, that she had studied biology? Was her father a doctor perhaps, putting pressure on her to follow in his footsteps, pushing her along a path she wasn't sure she wanted to take? And, if so, would knowing about Dr Marshall help her make her decision?

Natasha saw it all the time, people presented with the tiniest reference to one of their ancestors, clasping or staring at a piece of paper as if it were the most revelatory discovery, something that might totally change their lives.

She could imagine how it felt, what it meant to learn of a great-grandfather who died at sea, or a distant cousin even, who married at seventeen and gave birth to twelve children. Knowing such things helped people to make sense of their own lives. It's a universal need, isn't it, to want to know about your roots, where you came from?

Natasha was sure Bethany would be thrilled by the smallest scraps of information she discovered about John Marshall and his family. Suddenly, she wanted very much to be able to tell her about them.

Toby called back at two. 'Bad news I'm afraid.'

'You couldn't find her?'

'Oh, I found her all right. Just not in the place you told me to look.'

'She didn't leave her father's house to marry?'

'Nope.'

There was one other likely reason Ellen J. Marshall might have departed 10 Savile Row. Natasha felt her stomach knot. 'You checked the death registers.'

'I did. She's in the first quarter of 1873.'

'Shit.'

'I've ordered a copy of the certificate. Though I guess we already know what it'll say. She died a spinster of this parish. No doubt she'd have been a virgin as well. What a waste, eh?'

'Returned unopened as they say.'

Toby laughed.

'So what are you going to do now?'

'Check out the brother and sisters, I suppose. John, Ada, and little Eleanor.' Three of them. It would take time to trace present day descendants for each one. For some reason it didn't feel right in any case, as if she was missing something, had drifted off track.

'I picked up the birth certificate as well by the way. The J stands for Jeanette.'

So J.M. was named after both her parents. Jeanette the female version of Jean, the French for John.

After she'd hung up, Natasha opened the diary. She looked at Bethany's photograph and felt swamped by failure. It would have helped if Adam had given her a normal photograph instead of that small, tragic, ghostly face.

Who are you? Where are you? Are you all right? Then she said aloud, 'I won't give up yet, I promise.'

She slipped the photograph back between the

104

delicate pages, and thought of the exuberant personality that radiated from them. J.M., Jeanette, was in her early twenties then, spirited, embracing life and love. Yet in a few years she'd die.

Just thirty years old. Unmarried. Childless.

A dead end, literally.

Fifteen

Natasha had made an impulsive decision to leave the Alpine at Snowshill. The Opium Den was a five-minute walk from Oxford station and as she walked up Station Road, her legs seemed to grow heavier the closer she got to the restaurant, as if she'd been running for hours.

The restaurant was half full, students and young professional couples mostly. Adam was sitting smoking at a 'no smoking' table by the window, unopened magazines and an open bottle of Shiraz and two glasses in front of him. One was half empty.

Disconcertingly he didn't smile or say hello, just watched her as she came towards him.

'Hi there.'

He carried on staring, then caught her eye. 'You walk like a dancer.' He poured wine into the empty glass.

She took off her coat, slung it over the back of the chair and sat down. 'I studied ballet until I was fifteen.'

'That explains it then. I had this idea of doing a series of photographs of ballet scenes. How about it?'

'I told you before, I don't like having my picture taken.'

'Pity. The one I did the other day turned out well. You look very dramatic.'

'I've not been accused of that since I was seventeen.'

'You surprise me. I bet being in love with you is a real challenge. Like anything rewarding.'

She knew better than to respond. Nibbled a prawn cracker instead. 'Did the ones of Bethany turn out OK?'

'Could be better.' He crushed the butt of his cigarette into the tray. 'Dunno what went wrong. Problem with the exposure maybe. Shadows. None of the black and whites are any good.'

'What a pity. So how's the exhibition coming along otherwise?'

'Too fast.'

'Is there an opening date?'

'It's 16 January.'

Two weeks away. The deadline Natasha had given herself by which to find Bethany.

'The last shoot's this Friday,' Adam said. 'It should have been done weeks ago.' He sounded fed up. He was wearing a crumpled white T-shirt beneath his black velvet jacket. His fair hair looked as if he'd just climbed out of bed, and he needed a shave.

'Where's the location this time?'

'It's just a studio session.' He picked up a chopstick and flipped it between his fingers like a cowboy in a western twirling a pistol. He jabbed it into the table and put it down. 'So. How did you get on?'

No choice but to heap more angst on Adam's plate. 'The diarist was called Ellen Jeanette Marshall. Her father, John, had a practice in Savile Row.'

'Well done.' He must have seen her face. 'There's something else?'

'Jeanette died when she was thirty. Unmarried.'

He sucked viciously at his cigarette, exhaled, glared out of the window. 'She must have had a bastard then.'

Natasha was aware of the couple at the next table, glancing in their direction. 'It's possible.'

But not a great deal of help.

It was true that dying a spinster didn't definitely mean Jeanette had no direct descendants to whom she could have passed her diary. It was a mistake inexperienced genealogists made, finding a marriage and then searching forward for the birth of the first child, when they should also have gone back. In Victorian times, ten per cent of marriages took place after the first baby had been born, and many couples didn't wed at all. 'The trouble is, illegitimate children usually weren't registered. Adoptions certainly weren't. They're practically impossible to trace now.'

Adam snatched up the menu, terminating the conversation, erecting a barrier between himself and what he didn't want to hear.

Why am I putting myself through this?

Natasha glanced sideways. The eavesdroppers had resumed their chat, no doubt when they

107

found out the discussion was about dead people. Nowhere near as interesting as a modern day scandal.

Steven was right. It wasn't her place to shoulder all the responsibility. But looking at Adam's face, anger hiding pain, she couldn't see a way to mention the note. What if he couldn't explain it? Formed the same conclusion she had? It would be too cruel, unbearable for him, to be presented with that when he'd just learned that there seemed no quick or obvious way to find Bethany.

Still, at the back of her mind, was a niggling suspicion that she wasn't being completely honest with herself. There were other reasons she didn't take the plunge. She couldn't get over the feeling that he was keeping something from her, that things were not all they seemed.

She watched him smoking, tried to pin Mary's comment to him. *It's often them that did the driving away, or just did them away.*

Horrifyingly, Natasha found it not totally implausible that Adam was capable of either.

Adam dropped the menu onto the table. 'That's it then,' he said. 'You'd better tell me how much I owe you.'

'Nothing. I haven't done what you asked me to do. Look, there's other things we can try.' *Like what exactly?* She took a deep breath, cast about for some positive suggestions, 'As a woman, it's unlikely Jeanette left a will. But her possessions would have gone to someone. Her brother maybe, or either of her sisters. I'll trace forward from the three of them.'

He didn't seem particularly cheered by that.

Natasha wasn't either, knew she'd be wasting her time. If there was no direct bloodline then Bethany had been simply wrong when she'd said she was descended from the diarist.

The only thing left was to take the note to the police. For a split-second she wondered if she could do that without involving Adam. Of course not.

'Look, just because there's no direct blood link to the writer the diary might not be entirely useless. I'm going to go back over it, see if I can find anything else. Perhaps there's some other clue, I don't know, a reference to a place maybe, one of the doctor's patients?'

The waitress came over with her notebook. Natasha asked for king prawns in coconut sauce and steamed rice, something she'd eaten here before. Adam said he'd have the same, then slouched back in his chair. 'What if I was completely wrong?' he said in a way that made Natasha know she wasn't going to like what was coming. 'Rossetti put his poems into Lizzie Siddal's coffin as a kind of grand farewell gesture, a sacrifice. Right? Well, I've been thinking. What if the diary was Bethany's way of copying Lizzie and Rossetti's story? It would be just like her to do something like that. What if she wanted me to have it as a token, a keepsake?'

Natasha refilled both their glasses, trying not to dwell on the implication of what Adam had said.

'Look,' he said. 'I appreciate you going to so much trouble. But perhaps we should call it a day. Admit defeat.'

She held Adam's glass out to him. 'Not

something I've ever learnt how to do I'm afraid.'

She was rewarded with a thin smile, his first that evening. 'I can see that.'

How would he take it if anything did happen to Bethany? How would you ever recover from something like that? 'Tell me more about her?'

'What do you want to know?' His tone was sullen again.

'I'm not exactly sure. Anything. Everything. What music did she like?' Always a key to a person's soul.

'The Doors. Jim Morrison.'

Great. Jim Morrison committed suicide. But Natasha had all the albums too. Vinyl and CD.

'Did she like her job?'

'Very much I think. She knew a lot of interesting stuff about floristry.'

Natasha leant forward, elbows resting on the table. 'Like what?'

He gave a shrug. 'She told me about gypsy funerals. Apparently they have flowers arranged as 'broken hearts', with a zigzag of red roses to symbolize the break. During the Second World War there was a ban on transporting flowers by rail, she said, and they found this way to smuggle anemones to Covent Garden hidden in broccoli. I never knew flowers had such poetic names. Star of Bethlehem, Angel Wings, Love-in-a-mist. Love-lies-bleeding.' He lit another cigarette, taking his time. 'She had this tin box with a Victorian advertisement on it, you know for Pears soap or something. I found it in a drawer she kept her clothes in when she was staying over. She'd saved everything. There were ticket stubs from when we'd gone to galleries, the Polaroids from the photo shoots, the first scrap of paper I gave her with my phone number on it. She even saved the receipt for a cappuccino she'd bought on the day I met her.'

She must have loved him a lot. So why did she leave?

Natasha thought of the little musical box with the secret drawer where she stashed sweets as a child, and the burst remains of a glittery star-shaped balloon Marcus had bought at Stow Fair on the first weekend he'd come to stay with her. She'd felt daft, keeping it, but couldn't bring herself to throw it away.

'She gave me a photograph she said she took when she was twelve,' Adam said. He dug his wallet out of his pocket and took out a colour snapshot of a canal, with boats.

Natasha turned it over. *X Bethany* was written neatly in black ink.

Was the picture taken somewhere near where she lived, where she'd gone on holiday? Where she'd gone now? Oxford? Cambridgeshire, where the Marshalls came from? How many canals were there in Britain? Too many.

'I asked her who showed her how to take pictures,' Adam said. 'If it was her dad. She said her father never taught her anything she wanted to learn. We were in a café and she refused to finish her dinner, insisted we leave, right away, but she wouldn't say why she was so upset. I learned my lesson. Didn't try to bring her family into the conversation again.'

She said her father never taught her anything she

wanted to learn. What would make a person refuse to talk about their family, disown them to such an extent they changed their name?

'How did you two actually get together? I know you met in a café, but what...'

'I bought her another cappuccino. Then I asked her to come back to my flat. She said yes.'

'Just like that?'

'Just like that?' Adam echoed, faintly mocking. 'She trusted me.' He paused for a moment. 'She was an odd mixture. Came up with some madcap ideas sometimes. But she was old-fashioned in lots of ways. She was really into routines. She liked to go to the same restaurant on a Friday, always have breakfast together before I went into the studio. She said she liked being able to look forward to stuff that wasn't too far away. She hated it if I changed plans at the last minute. Which I have to do a lot. She never let us part without making up... And she got angry, really angry, if I was late. Which I am all the time. She'd be completely over the top, in tears, almost hysterical.'

Natasha didn't like the sound of that, even though she could relate to it. Separation anxiety. One of the problems adopted children were supposed to suffer. She swallowed some wine.

'One time she tried to hit me, another she actually passed out,' Adam continued. 'She was always terribly apologetic afterwards, promising never to be cross again. I told her not to make promises she wouldn't be able to keep. That it didn't matter anyway. But it seemed to really worry her.'

'The day she left, did she seem different in any

112

way, do anything different?'

'No. Except...'

'Except what?'

'The afternoon before, she was on the phone for ages. There's one in the bedroom at the flat and she shut herself in there instead of using the hall phone. I asked who she'd been gossiping to and she said nobody. First sign of madness I said, talking to yourself, but she didn't get the joke.'

The food arrived, interrupting the conversation. Natasha moved aside the magazines to make room on the table. She glanced at Adam's choice of reading matter as she shifted them to the window ledge. The *Independent*, and three glossy women's monthlies.

She arched an eyebrow.

'Only buy them to look at the photographs.'

A shadow fell over the table, Natasha looked up. For a moment she couldn't place where she'd seen the man before. Then it came to her. The Society of Genealogists. He was wearing the same moss green greatcoat over combat trousers and black T-shirt. His long dark hair was tied in a ponytail this time.

He gave no indication he recognised her. 'Well, Adam, aren't you going to introduce us?'

'Jake Romilly,' Adam muttered. 'Natasha Blake.'

'Ah, Adam's little secret.' He stuck out his hand. 'Pleased to make your acquaintance at last.' His voice seemed familiar. Was he the man who had answered the studio phone? He glanced round the restaurant. He was tall, strongly built, green feral eyes. 'Great place.' He turned to Adam who'd picked up one of the magazines and was morosely flicking through it. 'I'm meeting a friend but it looks like she's late.'

'Or stood you up,' Adam grunted.

'Perhaps I'll join you then.'

'Catch you later, Jake,' Adam said with finality.

'Friend of yours?' Natasha asked lightly, after he'd left.

'Partner, sort of.'

'You don't seem to like him much.'

'We've had our differences. He's a talented guy though, if he wasn't so lazy. Thrown out of Eton for drugs. Thinks the world owes him a living. He has a huge chip on his shoulder about anyone being more successful than him, at work, girls, you name it.'

'I could swear I saw him at the Society of Genealogists the other day.'

Adam spluttered an incredulous laugh. 'Jake? I doubt it.'

She wasn't convinced.

Natasha pushed a bowl of rice towards him. Adam switched his cigarette to his left hand to serve himself, sat back, studied her. 'Anyway, where were we? Your turn now I think,' he said quietly. 'Tell me about you.'

'What for?'

'Because I want to know? You went to university here?'

'Magdalen College. I read Ancient and Modern History.' She looked at him. 'I thought the past wasn't important.'

'It is to you.' He looked at her. His eyes were the most incredible blue. 'Where did you grow up? Somewhere wild and windy I'd bet.'

'Not sure I have grown up yet.' The oldest trick in the book. Compliments, personal observations and questions designed to make you feel interesting, special. Adam obviously had it down to a fine art. Natasha was annoyed to discover that guessing the game he was playing didn't entirely deaden its effect. She guided things back on course. 'You said memories aren't as important as dreams. Did Bethany tell you about her dreams?'

'She said she didn't have time for them. Have you any brothers or sisters?'

'This is weird. It's usually me asking clients those kinds of questions.'

'Do you ever give a straight answer?'

'Not if I can help it.' She didn't feel particularly hungry now, but she went through the motions, helped herself to some of the prawns. The sauce was creamy and sweet-smelling. 'I've got a younger sister. My parents live in Derbyshire, which is fairly wild and windy. That satisfy you?'

'Is their marriage a happy one, would you say?'

'That's an odd thing to want to know. It works for them I think. My dad's away a lot. Why are you so interested?'

'Where did you spend your holidays when you were a little girl?'

'Last question, OK?' She had the feeling she shouldn't be telling him all this but wasn't sure why not. What harm could it possibly do? 'We went camping in the south of France, sometimes stayed in a cottage on the coast at Whitby.'

'Idyllic childhood.'

'In some ways. How about you?'

'Not idyllic at all,' Adam lit another cigarette. 'I guess your usual work isn't this complicated?'

You could say that again. 'No.'

'Bethany said she read somewhere that family history's the most popular hobby in the UK.'

'Over half a million people are actively involved in it.'

'Do you professionals scorn dabbling amateurs then?'

'Professionals built the Titanic but amateurs built the Ark. They're my best source of income actually. When they get stuck or want advice. People tend not to dabble in genealogy though. Once you start you're hooked.'

'I best steer clear in that case.' He studied the amber glow at the end of his cigarette. 'I've an addictive personality.'

'Have you ever tried to give up?'

He shook his head. 'I've never liked the idea of old age. Enjoy yourself while you can and to hell with the consequences.'

'Sounds a bit selfish.'

'Not if what you do doesn't affect anyone else.'

'It always does.'

'I can't work you out,' he said.

That makes two of us. 'In what way exactly?'

'You don't strike me as a historian-type. It was a real surprise, when you turned up at Little Barrington in your sporty convertible. I'd imagine you working in something like television or advertising.'

'Bundle of contradictions me. I used to want to be an archaeologist. But my life's in ruins anyway.'

'I'm sorry to hear that.' He gave a slow smile. 'I

116

bet you enjoy telling boyfriends they're history?'

'Mm. Sadly too often.'

'Why's that?'

'I wish I knew.'

'Maybe you spend too much time hunting around in mouldy old documents.'

'I don't actually. Genealogy's quite high tech and sexy now. There's more web sites than for anything else, apart from pornography.'

'Must be something in it then. Maybe I should give it a go.'

'Pornography or genealogy?' She couldn't believe she'd said that.

'Whichever you think would be the most fun.'

Natasha stared down at her plate. Then she found herself wondering. What other pictures had Adam taken of Bethany?

Sixteen

Natasha had a habit of going over conversations in her head, worrying about how she could have handled things better. It troubled her, how much she'd enjoyed the evening with Adam. She shouldn't have flirted with him.

It was past eleven when she arrived back home but she didn't feel in the least bit tired. She drew the curtains, lit the fire, settled down on the sofa and picked up the diary. It made a difference knowing the writer's name. Names defined who you were, given names just as much as surnames.

It must be strange for women when they married, if they took their husband's family name, like becoming a different person. She sneaked the photograph of Bethany into the back of the diary, couldn't face her just now.

Two pages in, Jeanette's sister, Ada, fell ill. Dr Marshall diagnosed typhoid. Jeanette had taken her turn to sit at her sister's bedside through the night.

Papa came down to say Ada was asking for me. I went to her room and put my face well into the light as Papa told me. I said, 'Here I am, darling.' Ada opened her eyes very wide as if she was trying to see but there was no expression in them. When I kissed her, her skin was cold and clammy. We were all crying. At seven-thirty in the evening Mama came down and screamed, quite distraught, 'She's gone.' I comforted her as well as I could and made her take some wine.

This morning Mr Watkins came to take photographs of Ada in her coffin. She looked very beautiful.

Another branch of the tree chopped off.

A phrase stole into Natasha's mind. In the midst of life we are in death. It didn't really apply these days, at least, not in First World countries. Unless you were a nurse or an undertaker, you were shielded from death until you were nearing it yourself. Natasha knew plenty of people her own age who'd never suffered the death of someone close, never even been to a funeral. Until the last five years, when her grandparents, one either side, had died, Natasha's only real experience of death had been that of an aged aunt.

Jeanette's mother though would have half expected to lose at least one of her children. Jeanette had come face to face with mortality long before she met her own early end.

Natasha picked up the diary again.

The lid was closed with wax. I always thought there were nails or screws or something of that sort. The simple observation was strangely powerful. A doctor's daughter, with a doctor's unsqueamish, straightforward approach.

All very interesting but... As Natasha studied Jeanette's handwriting she remembered what she'd said to Adam. Perhaps the diary held some other clue.

I wish.

Ada was buried at the churchyard in Ely. It was uncommon then for women to attend funeral ceremonies and Jeanette and her sister and mother remained at home.

Natasha found herself rooting for Jeanette. She hoped she found some love and happiness before she died. At least she was soon back to her flirtations. Over the page she'd written. *Dreamt I was dancing very wickedly with Mr Brown; highly improper but one can't help one's dreams!*

Natasha rested the diary on her lap, tilted her head and flexed her shoulders. Adam's face stole into her mind and she thrust it away.

About two years ago, after the messy and painful end of another relationship, she'd gone back to see the psychologist her parents had sent her to when she'd found out she was adopted.

119

She knew it was a bad idea and she'd been right. She'd hated every minute as she had the first time, resented the prying questions. What about the physical side of your relationships? Fine, thanks. Why do you think you behave as you do? If I knew that I wouldn't be here, would I? More than that she hated the inference that she was a text book case. Adopted child who has unrealistic expectations, who constantly needs to test anyone who comes close because they crave the unconditional love only one person in your life can ever really give. Adopted child who is possessive and who fears love, because even that one person abandoned them. Adopted child who therefore underneath believes they don't deserve love anyway. And so is attracted to unattainable, unsuitable men.

It sounded very neat and easy to overcome when you put it like that.

Easier still to fall back into the same old patterns. Unsuitable, unattainable. Adam Mason certainly fit that bill. You'd never be able to trust him.

Natasha picked up the diary again. The next entry was an amusing account of an admirer, a Mr Sandwell, whose advances Jeanette didn't welcome, evidently. Jeanette had paraphrased an 'enormous' letter her fan had sent to her.

Mama read it out loud to the horror-stricken exclamations of the victim, moi, and the roars of the whole family.

He begins Dear Miss Marshall, excuses himself for not having written before and tells me I am far above him in position etc (which I am fully aware of). Then he goes on to say that he has been staring at me for several months. He compares me to a star in heaven and feels he is not good enough for me (quite right), but offers to put on livery and be my footman, or propose a compromise (oh, horror of horrors!) to be my lackey and my husband too. He goes on with a lot more twaddle and ends, Your obedient servant which is the only sensible part of the letter!

Natasha stopped reading. She imagined Bethany, as a little girl, being shown the diary by her grandmother. Being told to hold it very carefully, sitting statue still as children do when they're afraid of spilling their drink or breaking something, balancing the book on her lap, almost not daring to turn the pages. The writing unreadable as hieroglyphics to a little girl's eyes.

Had she struggled to read it herself, or had her grandmother helped her, telling her about their past, perhaps, other stories of the Marshalls and Pre-Raphaelites? Doubtless Jeanette's exploits had seemed all the more significant when Bethany herself started dating. She'd have compared the differences in her own and Jeanette's lives, and the similarities, seen Jeanette as a friend.

Why had she left it behind?

Why did she have it in the first place? If the diary wasn't linked to Bethany and her family in a directly genealogical way, there had to be some reason why her ancestors had acquired it and handed it down the generations. Why it was important to them.

About fifty pages on, she found what she thought that reason just might be. A reference that made her hold her breath as she read.

Went to the Academy to look at the Rossettis. In front of the lady in a green dress, The Blue Bower, was that nasty, common-looking creature Fanny, who lived with Rossetti and because of whom his poor wife committed suicide.

Papa has become Mr Rossetti's habitual doctor. Just the other night Mr Maddox Brown summoned P. at two in the morning because Mr Rossetti had collapsed. He has had a wretched life since his wife's death from poison she took herself. They had only been married two years and she found herself surplanted in his affections. No doubt his grief is remorse and for two years he's seen her ghost every night. Serve him right too.

It was Lizzie Siddal whom Adam had said Bethany was obsessed with, whom her grandmother had definitely talked to her about.

Lizzie. Whose example Adam had said he could imagine Bethany trying to emulate. And Lizzie had killed herself, allegedly.

Because of whom his poor wife committed suicide.

For some reason, Jeanette differed from her contemporaries, did not go along with the commonly held idea that Lizzie's death was an accident.

No doubt his grief is remorse.

In some ways suicide was a perfect act of revenge.

122

The image pierced Natasha's brain: Bethany in her long gown, walking into the water, posing as Lizzie Siddal who was posing as *Ophelia*. Who both took their own lives.

If Bethany was found dead, or killed herself at the same time as an exhibition opened in which the centrepiece was a photograph of her doing just that, it would make quite a point.

She stood up, went to the bookcase and pulled out *The Pre-Raphaelite Dream*. As she did so she noticed, a few books along, a slim volume bound in white which she'd forgotten she had. A collection of sketches, an exhibition catalogue from the Ruskin gallery in Sheffield, entitled *Rossetti's Portraits of Elizabeth Siddal*.

She took both books back to her desk, turned to the index in the larger book and found two mentions of Lizzie, in a chapter entitled 'Flower of Death'.

Elizabeth Siddal was the archetypal Pre-Raphaelite beauty immortalised in some of the movement's most revered works. She retains the reputation as an enigmatic, tragic figure. Silent, ailing and wan, with a mass of coppery-red hair and a melancholy disposition, she died two years after marrying Rossetti, from an overdose of the laudanum she took to ease her afflictions.

On the facing page were the pictures of *Ophelia* and *Beata Beatrix*.

Natasha looked from one picture to the other, saw an obvious similarity between the two.

In *Beata Beatrix*, Rossetti's post mortem tribute

to Lizzie, a wild bird lets fall an opium poppy into her open hands, symbol of the drug that killed her. But it is not only in the memorial to her that the flower of death is represented. In her most famous incarnation as the drowning Ophelia, painted years before, it trails from her fingers like an omen.

The text below that illustration read:

'Her expression varied in shades of sadness, as if a premonition of early death overshadowed her life,' wrote Sharp, whilst Ricketts called her 'A delicate wraith, a ghost in the house of the living'. According to Evelyn Waugh 'Her fading beauty bore taint of underlying decay. She brought Rossetti the icy breath of corruption and mortality.'

The image gave credence to the legend of the exhumation of Lizzie's coffin, how little changed she'd been. Even in life, hers had always been a cadaverous beauty.

Natasha closed the book, picked up the collection of portraits and glanced through the delicate pencil drawings. There must have been a hundred different versions of the same face. Some of the portraits were straight head and shoulders, some full length. She was reclining in an armchair, her hands folded in her lap; reading, head bowed; sitting on the floor, her legs tucked under her; or in a basket chair, profiled against a window. Always in the same high-necked blouse and plain long grey skirt.

The pictures seemed to reveal much more

about the artist than the model, were somehow almost harrowing. Perhaps because, like Jeanette's diary, you knew how the story ended.

But it wasn't Lizzie Siddal who was haunting Natasha. It was Bethany Marshall. Or whoever she was.

Seventeen

As a child, Natasha used to sleepwalk. Steven would find her wandering in her nightgown along the dark corridors of their house and carry her back to bed. Sometimes she'd wake to find her feet dirty and scratched, and she'd know she'd been out in the garden, barefoot.

She was pretty sure she hadn't been sleep-walking for years. But when she awoke and went downstairs to make a cup of tea just before seven, she wondered if she'd been at it again.

As soon as she reached the hallway the cold hit her. It was freezing, the quality of the air markedly different to that in her bedroom, and there was noise coming from the living room, a faint rattling. She pushed the door open. It was still totally dark outside.

The window was flung wide, the heavy drapes flapping slightly. The sound she'd heard was the iron curtain hoops jangling on the pole.

The book of sketches of Lizzie Siddal was open on the desk, the pages rippling to and fro. Standing there in only a T-shirt, Natasha shivered. The catch had somehow worked loose and the window must have blown open. That was it. But the wind, if there had been any, had died down to little more than the gusty breeze, ever present so high in the hills.

She banged the casement shut firmly. The catch was old, rusted stiff. How in heavens could it have drifted open of its own accord? A voice inside her head answered: *It couldn't.* So what then? If she had been sleepwalking it was the first time she'd headed for a window rather than a door.

She dragged the curtains across, glanced down at Lizzie's portrait. Snapped the book shut too.

Feeling a little melodramatic, she took a large pewter candlestick from the windowsill. She inched through to the kitchen, peering behind doors. Then upstairs. The house was empty.

She was wide awake now, still a little spooked. She went back into the kitchen, made tea and took it to her desk and switched the iMac on. The bright screen was reassuring. As she waited for it to run through the set-up she doodled in her notepad, flowers and spirals.

She scribbled the name Margaret Wood, circled it. Margaret was an archivist at the Public Record Office at Kew who, as Natasha had told Bethany, had done in-depth research on Lizzie Siddal's life and family, using the census returns and PRO certificates. Perhaps it would be worth giving Margaret a call. Way too early yet for sane people to be at work though.

She logged on to check for e-mails, watched messages start to pop up in the inbox, highlighted in red.

She used to love receiving letters and postcards from Steven when he was travelling, still did, and e-mails seemed to carry that same sense of expectation. She and Marcus used to send them to each other all the time. Little jokes and anecdotes about what they were up to, just to say hello. Now there was just the tiny stab of disappointment each time it didn't happen.

The iMac pinged to say all messages had been received, six in total. The e-mails comprised a new business enquiry, to which Natasha quickly replied with proposals, hourly and project fee rates. There was also a brief note from Steven letting her know he'd said it was OK for Sheffield University to get in touch directly regarding a talk they wanted her to give on internet sources for local historians. A chatty message from a friend with a joke. A quote from the Tideswell Parish News. *We apologies for the typographical error in the last edition, in which we described Mr Tom Rogers as a defective in the police force. He is, of course, a detective in the police farce.* Also a note from Will, reminding her about the party on Saturday. 'Just in case it had slipped her mind.' Which it had.

She printed the joke and clipped it to her notice board, filed the enquiries and put the University material in the in-tray. Told Will she'd see him at the weekend.

At the start of her investigation, Natasha had checked the Genealogical Research Directory as a matter of course, fired off e-mails to half a dozen researchers who'd registered that they were interested in the Marshall name. The final couple of e-mails were responses from two of them, a chap in Canterbury who said he had done some work on the Gloucestershire Marshalls and there was no recorded link between them and the Marshalls of Savile Row. He had not come across any current descendants of the Savile Row branch. The second was from a woman, Sue Mellanby, who lived in Cambridge.

Hi Natasha, I was delighted to receive your message. My mother is now in her nineties and her mind is sadly not as clear as it was but she spent many of her younger days working on our family tree and I have a distinct childhood memory of being shown Dr John Marshall's grave in Ely and being told that he was 'one of the family'. Unfortunately my mother does not share this memory, and having only recently picked up where she left off, I can't tell you any more than that at this stage. My mother has, however, told me that she made contact with several branches of our family in the Midlands and she says, though I must stress again her age and state of health, that she remembers hearing of a little girl named Bethany.

Just reading her name sent a zing of elation along Natasha's spine.

I have put out some feelers to some of the contacts from Mum's notes though I expect many are long out of date. I will, of course, let you know if anything comes of it.

Natasha replied with a note of thanks.

Boris was whining at the door to be taken out for a walk. Natasha quickly dressed and grabbed an apple to eat on the way.

It had grown lighter and there was the palest glimmer of sunshine, a tiny patch of pale blue sky on the horizon beyond the woods. The low lying mist in the valley made Snowshill seem like a kingdom in the clouds.

When Natasha was able to get to sleep at a reasonable time she enjoyed being up early in the morning, when the day was clean and new. But this time, as so often lately, seeing the dawn meant she'd hardly slept and had a headache that made the freshness seem raw, bringing a sensation of being wrenched from warmth and security.

Lizzie Siddal had had trouble sleeping too, and then she went to sleep for ever.

Sleep and death had long been linked. You saw that euphemism on gravestone epitaphs all the same, and in poems and prayers. The idea that sleep was a short death, and death a long sleep from which it is possible to one day awake. It was once believed that during sleep the soul left the body to go walking with spirits.

She helped Boris over the stile, a slightly comical procedure, then vaulted over it herself, got into a stride. Walking was like swimming: if you hit a rhythm, you felt like you could go on for ever.

She didn't have time to sit back and wait for whatever information might feed through from the Genealogical Research Directory. There had

129

to be something else she could try.

Boris chased after a Frisbee thrown by a little boy, dressed in his school blazer, with a German Shepherd. Both dogs tussled with it for a minute until Natasha called Boris off. The little boy shouted thanks as Boris bounded towards a large puddle and pawed his reflection with a splash.

Natasha decided what she'd do. If you don't find what you're looking for in the likely places, look in the less likely ones. She'd telephone Margaret Wood to arrange a meeting. Then she'd ask Mary if she was up to a trip to the records centre at Gloucester, to see what she could find out about Jeanette's brother John and little sister Eleanor, beneficiaries through which the diary just might have passed. And she'd e-mail Toby to ask if he'd do some digging around in the Pre-Raphaelite archives at his favourite haunt, the British Library, to firm up details of any links between the Marshalls and Lizzie Siddal. When all that was sorted out, she'd drive to Broadway for a swim. She'd perhaps invite Mary and James round for supper. See if Mary fancied coming swimming as well.

Everything decided, she felt better.

As soon as she returned home she opened the contacts database on the iMac, found Margaret's number and made an appointment to see her tomorrow at ten.

She put the receiver down and noticed that the answering machine was flashing. Another early bird who'd called while she was out. She pressed play.

Froze.

A male voice, young, gruff, slightly muffled as if to disguise it. 'She doesn't want to be with him any more. Just back off all right? Leave her alone.'

Eighteen

Natasha swam beneath the water, holding her breath.

She surfaced into air and light and noise.

She had never felt out of her depth before.

She should get out right now. Tell Adam she couldn't help him.

What had she got herself involved in? A simple lovers' argument, turned into a potential suicide, turned into what? There was one obvious conclusion. Bethany had left Adam to be with someone else and was afraid of telling him. The explanation fitted, yet somehow didn't fit at all.

Try this then. Someone didn't want anyone poking their nose in, didn't want Bethany found. The phone call was a warning off. Natasha could hear Mary now. Another TV detective show plot. The 'suicide note' was a plant, a cover-up. Because Bethany was already dead and someone wanted to make it look as though she'd done it herself.

It all sounded ridiculous. Then why did she feel just a little scared?

Mary was at edge of the pool, cutting through ripples, her pregnancy concealed. She reached the deep end, turned round and kicked back. Her face pale against the blueness, eyes open, her hair a cloud beneath the water.

Adam had told Bethany drowning was a peaceful way to die.

The dazed look in Bethany's eyes when she'd emerged from the Windrush. Had the experience made her wonder what it would really be like?

Surely, at some point in their lives, everyone had.

Natasha went through a phase of holding her breath under water, practising, counting, seeing how long she could last, a few seconds more once the air had all been expelled, until the pressure in her chest increased and she felt light-headed. She stopped just before it really hurt.

She was suddenly curious to see the photograph Adam had taken at Little Barrington.

If she gave up now it would be because she was afraid – no other reason. She wasn't sure how she could live with herself, what would happen if she once let fear get the better of her.

She'd rather be angry, a much more useful emotion. She tried to work herself up to it. How dare someone threaten her? How dare they think they could intimidate her?

She rang the studio from the hotel foyer. A confident female voice answered. The girl introduced herself as Adam's assistant, Angie. 'I'm afraid he's not here,' she said.

'Do you know if he's free tomorrow?'

'He's busy for the next couple of days.'

'How about Friday?'

'We're doing a shoot which isn't due to finish until five.'

The last session of the exhibition. 'Could you tell him I'd like to see him then?'

'I say due to finish, but with Adam that doesn't mean it will.' Her tone was almost obstructive.

'Don't worry. I'll drop by anyway.'

'Who shall I tell him to expect?'

'Natasha Blake.'

There was a moment's silence in which Natasha guessed the girl was waiting for her to elaborate, but all she got was a thank you and goodbye.

Natasha wondered if Angie and Bethany had ever met at the studio. For some reason she thought Adam might have done his best to make sure they didn't.

Nineteen

Normally Natasha went up to London perhaps twice a month, once a week at most, storing things up so she made the best use of her time. Now she was beginning to feel like a regular commuter. She'd arrived early enough to grab a parking space near the ticket office and had joined the other regulars at the buffet car. It made her think of something Arnold once said. 'You move to the city to get a job well paid enough to buy a house in the country. The world's gone mad.'

She drank her scalding coffee and watched the fields turn into suburbs, the water towers at Didcot looming like a Sci-Fi space station. Her

133

mobile rang, not a number the phone recognised. She hit the answer button, said hello but there was no reply. She listened to crackling silence. She waited a few seconds, then hung up. 1471. Number withheld again. She wondered if it was the same person who'd left that message on her machine. Another attempt to scare her off.

'I don't recognize her I'm afraid,' Margaret Wood said, scrutinising the photograph Natasha had given her.

They were sitting on a bench outside the Public Record Office, with egg rolls and plastic cups of chocolate that were almost too hot to hold, watching the swans, geese, ducks and the odd moorhen pecking about in the reeds. The Thames lay just the other side of the railway line, beyond the hedge, close but invisible. Instead there was a man-made river, or lake, with an artificial island in the middle, and a concrete waterfall, rimmed by a paved forecourt and lawns around which were ranged the pale brick buildings housing the Record Office's documents. Ninety-three miles of them, Margaret had just reminded her.

It would have been almost peaceful but for the constant roar of jumbos flying to and from Heathrow. They flew so low Natasha had an urge to wave to the passengers.

She took the picture back from Margaret. 'Her name's Bethany Marshall. I was wondering if she wrote or telephoned recently?'

'Well, now that does ring bells. I didn't actually speak to her but a colleague handed her details over. Before Christmas it was. She wanted me to send her...'

'Information on Lizzie Siddal.'

Margaret looked a little nonplussed. 'Yes.'

Natasha could barely contain her excitement. 'So she gave you an address.'

'Just e-mail.'

Naturally. In cyberspace you could be anyone you liked. 'Could you let me have it?'

'I don't see why not.' Margaret's eyes crinkled. 'I've known you long enough to trust you. I told her to call to arrange to come and see me if she wanted any more information but she never did. Do you mind me asking...?'

'Actually, it was Lizzie Siddal I wanted to ask you about.'

'She's definitely not telephoned.'

Natasha smiled. 'What prompted you to start researching her life?'

Margaret took a sip from the steaming cup. 'A friend took me to see a Pre-Raphaelite exhibition at the Tate. Years ago now. There was one of Lizzie Siddal's pictures there, *Clerk Saunders* it was called. A scene from Walter Scott's *Minstrelsy of the Scottish Borders*, where a woman is confronted by the ghost of her murdered lover. It was very striking, the figures rather stiff and spiky but beautiful in their own way, rather intense. It struck me that she was the only woman represented in the entire show. I read about her in the catalogue and looked her up in a couple of books, and it intrigued me because she was drawn as such an enigma. No one seemed to agree about even the basics. If she was to be recognised as an important female Victorian artist, a recognition her pictures obviously merited, it's only right that someone should attempt to shade in the landscape of her life. Don't you think?'

'Yes.'

'I started with the birth, marriage and death records, all the usual. Her father's in the trade directories, a Sheffield cutler who moved to London. And she's in the census returns too, living at home in the Old Kent Road, then listed as married, her occupation an artist/painter at 14 Chatham Place. I remember her friend, Emma Maddox Brown, was staying on the night of that census.' Margaret paused while there was yet another interruption, a tube train trundling on its way to Richmond. 'Of course, before family history started to become so popular, people didn't think of parish records and censuses as a source of historical research did they, amazing as it may seem? I wrote it all up in an article for *Family History* magazine. That's what I sent on to Bethany.'

Natasha noticed that along with pretty sapphire and diamond engagement and wedding rings, Margaret wore a third, rimmed with the tiniest emeralds that flashed like cat's eyes: an eternity ring, symbol of everlasting love, which nobody seemed to wear any more. It was an interesting contrast to Margaret's businesslike demeanour.

'I could hunt out the notes I made for the article if you think they might be useful,' Margaret said. 'You'd have to give me a day or two. I know where they are, or at least which box, but it's just a matter of getting a moment to myself. I've got my daughter and her little ones staying until the weekend so the evenings are pretty hectic, as you can imagine.'

She broke off another chunk of sandwich and threw it into the water. A duck gobbled it up greedily, a sure signal to others to come paddling over from the far side of the pond. She tore off more crust which she hurled as far as she could towards the new arrivals, feeling Margaret's eyes on her. She'd no doubt scold her grandchildren for doing the same thing, kind but firm, telling them not to waste their lunch.

'Lizzie was fairly easy to trace,' Margaret said. 'I was surprised nobody had made the effort before. It took a while, but I got there in the end, though it's only a rough sketch I admit.' She smiled at the unintentional pun. 'And you, Natasha, what makes you so interested in her? This girl, Bethany, is she a client?'

'Kind of. Bethany is obsessed with Lizzie.' *What if the diary was Bethany's way of copying Lizzie and Rossetti's story? It would be just like her to do something like that.*

'I wondered if knowing more about Lizzie might help me to understand Bethany a little more.' Bethany might even see Lizzie as a role model.

The thought had come to her unbidden and she realized that's what she'd been hoping. What she'd been dreading.

Twenty

'The Victorians celebrated death. Their funerals were elaborate affairs, even for commoners. The mourners wore black robes, veils and crepe ribbons and the hearse was drawn by black horses whose heads were decorated with tall black ostrich plumes.'

The guide paused. Natasha was standing beside him and the single other member of the tour party in the wide paved courtyard of Highgate Cemetery's oldest, western side. They had reached the imposing entrance from Swain's Lane, the neo-Gothic mortuary chapels, with battlemented parapets, lancet windows, turrets and stained glass. Beneath an octagonal bell tower was a central archway, with ornate double iron gates, through which the funeral cavalcades would once have swept.

In the early January dusk they were all too easy to conjure.

As Natasha had left the Record Office, she'd checked the tube map in her diary, counted the stops to Paddington. With a bit of luck she would make the two-fifteen train. But her eyes had been drawn to the black northern line, winding on upwards, to this other destination, further north. Highgate.

The guide was a sandy haired man in his mid-forties, named Michael, and the other member of

138

the party was a young man in a long tweed coat, who had introduced himself as Nigel Moore, explaining that he was a newly qualified doctor at the Middlesex Hospital. He wore round spectacles and had the sort of kindly, confident face that you'd be relieved to see if you were ill.

They were led towards the broad flight of stone steps that climbed to the forested burial ground.

'Cemeteries didn't exist until the 1820s,' Michael explained as they walked. 'But the churchyards were becoming overcrowded. With the population rising, graves were literally overflowing, and there was a real fear that exposed, decaying corpses would spread disease. The cholera epidemic of 1865 was blamed entirely on the rotting bodies infecting the water supply. A case of the dead killing the living. Highgate was not the first cemetery, but it was to be different from the rest, designed by architects and landscape gardeners.'

Natasha was used to wandering around graveyards, stopping to read the inscriptions. It was often necessary in her work, but she did it out of choice too. She liked the stories the stones told, and the thought-provoking beauty unique to burial grounds. She never minded being alone in them, even as darkness fell.

But this place was something else. Grand, mysterious, in an almost horrifying way.

The evergreens had grown enormous, forming a dense woodland whose branches were like the arms of candelabrum, shielding rather than shedding light. Everything was partially obscured by the omnipresent ivy, dark creepers and tangled undergrowth. Statues of guardian angels with outstretched wings, crooked Celtic crosses and gothic spires stood at odd angles, twisted and toppling, unearthed by expanding trunks and roots which made it look as if the occupants of the graves had risen from the dead and were trying to escape.

Michael was saying how the growing preference for cremation brought financial difficulties to the cemetery, and the burial ground was left to neglect and decay. It was broken into by vandals and high-spirited revellers seeking moonlit fun on Halloween. But there were serious incidents too, vaults were broken into, coffins prized open. Highgate became a centre for occultism, voodoo, witchcraft and vampire hunters.

Easy to see why.

'The decision was taken to close the place down, move the bodies and rebuild on the land,' Michael added. 'But then a band of volunteers came forward to save it and thanks to their work Highgate is now a nature reserve, home to hundreds of insects, rare butterflies and woodland flowers and ferns. That's why it's closed to the public except for these tours.'

As they walked, the doctor, Nigel Moore, had been studiously consulting the guide book, holding it up close to peer at it in the waning light, and he showed interest in the numerous illustrious medical men buried all around.

'Yup, it's a good place to be ill if you're dead,' Michael smiled. 'Plenty of spiritual doctors to tend to you. Robert Liston, the first to operate on a patient under ether, Henry James who advocated fresh air and Robert Hill who campaigned for the insane not to be treated as freaks.'

'Don't suppose there's a Dr John Marshall,' Natasha asked, suddenly wondering. The young doctor checked the list. But Marshall wasn't there.

'Is he a relative?'

Natasha explained that she was a genealogist, researching his family history for a client.

'The Egyptian Avenue,' Michael announced.

It resembled an exotic temple, something from the land of pyramids and pharaohs, yet overgrown with ivy and creepers. The entrance to the avenue formed an arch flanked with giant fluted obelisks. It had the desolate splendour of a lost palace.

Natasha's heart began to beat a little faster as they passed under it into the long narrow Street of the Dead. Like a tunnel, excavated into the steepest part of the hillside, it was overhung with dark foliage and lined with heavy metal doors, the entrances to a towering terrace of vaults.

She glanced at the names of those whose remains were interred. A genealogist's dream. It was like a ghostly gathering of the clans, up to a dozen members of a single family, generations spanning over a hundred years, who would never have met in life.

'It's a great feature of Highgate,' Michael said, seeing the direction of her gaze. 'You get a real sense of family continuity here, all the members and all generations finally united.'

Wasn't that supposed to happen in heaven?

As they doubled back down another converging

141

path, Natasha asked Michael how long he'd worked there. 'Ten years. I'm one of the few permanent staff, site manager now. I worked in the City before.'

'It's an unusual change of career.'

'I fancied something a bit different.' And this is about as different as you could get, Natasha thought. 'It's so much better than being cooped up in an office all day. I get to wander round in the fresh air, checking things are in order, making arrangements for funerals.'

'People are still buried here?' Nigel Moore asked.

'Now and then.'

They had come to an oval avenue, enclosing a wildflower meadow. Then they turned off the path away from the clearing, and in single-file, clambered through thick undergrowth.

Michael halted and turned. 'There she is.'

Natasha came to stand beside him, her initial reaction one of vague disappointment. She had expected something more ornate. But the grave was small, unobtrusive and unadorned with monuments or statues. She could barely make out Lizzie's name, weather worn and cracked, engraved on the flat stone atop.

When you'd been reading or researching a life it was always moving to see the place where the person's body lay. Natasha thought of Lizzie for a moment, tried to separate the woman from the legend.

'One of the most famous and romantic events in art history happened here,' Michael said. The three of them stood around the small grave in the gathering darkness, just as people had stood once before.

She'd read an account of Lizzie Siddal's exhumation in the guidebook while waiting for the tour to start. There were five of them on that October night in 1869. They too would have been still and silent for a while. No doubt reluctant to begin the task they had come to perform. The weather might have been similar, dreary, with a fine autumn rain, and it would have been darker then, the only light coming from lanterns and a small bonfire they had lit by the graveside for warmth.

Dante Gabriel Rossetti, who had ordered the act, was not present.

Understandably he could not bear to be there. He must have relived and regretted a thousand times his rash impulse of love and grief. Again and again the image must have returned to him, his dead wife, before she came to Highgate, lying in her open coffin at his studio. He had reached out to her, in his hand the small greybound book, the only complete copies of his poems. He had laid it between her cheek and her famous golden-red hair, saying he did not need it anymore.

Six years had elapsed, during which time ambition had created a new need.

But six years was a long time, and those sent to undertake the task must have wondered what kind of state they would find both the book and her body. It was difficult to imagine their thoughts as the men employed by the funeral company removed the heavy grave slab. It would have taken them some time to dig down to

Lizzie's coffin. Once it had been identified by the brass name plate, the ropes would have been dropped, secured and the coffin raised joltingly. Then would have come the most gruesome task, levering off the lid.

Someone would have had to reach their hand inside the coffin to take back the book. Their fingers would have brushed against her hair. In the glow of the fire, it was said to have retained its wonderful colour and sheen, to have continued to grow in death. A flaming strand is said to have come away with the book.

Rossetti had excused his actions by saying that if Lizzie had been able, she herself would have lifted her own coffin lid to return the manuscripts.

How easy it was in a place such as this to imagine a pale hand rising from the grave, a disturbed spirit flitting between the dark trees. To sense a presence, not malevolent but not peaceful either.

What must Rossetti have felt when he first laid eyes again on that little grey book, soaked through, worm-eaten and putrid with decay?

At least he had not seen her face in the flickering firelight. It must have been more unsettling, in some ways, to see her beauty untouched, than to have been confronted with bare bones or decomposing flesh.

Her corpse's perfection was a myth surely?

The date of Lizzie's death, 11 February 1862. Involuntarily, Natasha curled her fingers around the yellow post-it note inside her pocket on which Margaret had written Bethany's hotmail address. It might prove useless, but it felt like something. Something tangible that made Bethany seem a fraction closer at last.

Natasha had been staring at the gravestone and the inscriptions penetrated her thoughts. Some of the dates were very recent. The faded ones were harder to decipher but it was almost not necessary. It was the repetition of a single name that was so striking. Gabriele Rossetti, his father. Frances Lavinia Rossetti, his mother. Christina Rossetti, his sister, William Michael Rossetti, his brother. A twentieth-century Gabrielle, a little girl named after her esteemed ancestor. Another Gabriel Rossetti, who died less than thirty years ago, in 1974. They were all here. All his blood family. And to them he had sent his wife, related to them only through a short-lived marriage, who'd never been close to them in life. But if the recurrence of that single name was so noticeable something else was more so. The absence of the most important member of the cast.

'It's such a shame Rossetti's not here, himself,' Michael said. 'He should be of course. Everyone who comes here is so surprised to see that he's missing.'

'Where is he?'

'Birchington, in Kent. Apparently he gave strict instructions that he was not to be buried here on any account. It's understandable I suppose.'

Understandable because Rossetti was afraid of Lizzie's spirit? Because he felt guilty for her death, or because he had violated her grave? Because he had been haunted by her during the remainder of his life and feared his soul would have no rest if it lay in proximity to hers? Or

145

because, after what he had done, Highgate had become for him a place of nightmares?

She noticed something else about the gravestone. Lizzie's name itself was partially obscured by a little jar of fresh poppies. She gave an intake of breath.

'Are you all right?' Nigel Moore's tone was concerned.

For a moment she couldn't tear her eyes away to answer him, until she felt his hand touch her arm.

'I'm fine,' she managed with a smile. 'Thanks.'

Michael was looking at her with concern as well.

She suddenly remembered one of her reasons for coming. She took the picture out of her pocket, handed it to him. 'Do you remember bringing this girl here?'

He frowned. 'You're the second one that's asked me about her this week.'

'What do you mean?'

'A chap came round the other day, showed me a picture like you've just done.'

Adam? 'What did he look like?'

Michael shrugged. 'Youngish. Dark. Bit scruffy. Wearing a baseball cap, jeans.' *Not Adam.* He looked back at the picture. 'What's so special about her?'

'I wish I knew.'

'Well, like I told the other fellow, I don't particularly remember her. But that's not to say she's never been. Everyone who comes here asks to see Lizzie, but if it's a large group we can't let them. Lots of them bring bouquets, as you can see. But most times it's not necessary. You should

146

see it here in springtime. The whole area's a carpet of cowslips and primroses.'

But there were no growing flowers here now, only severed ones.

Twenty-One

Natasha had been sitting in front of a blank computer screen for the best part of an hour. She'd tried out a couple of messages and swiftly deleted them. *Hi, Bethany. Wondered if you'd had any thoughts following our meeting.* Too bland and crawly. *Hi, Bethany. I've made some investigations, found an identity for your diarist.* In the end she just typed: *Are you OK?* Before she had time to think twice she hit 'send'.

No messages came in whilst the modem was hooked up. Still nothing from Sue Mellanby in Cambridge whose mother thought she remembered a little girl called Bethany.

It was already dark when Natasha drove down to Oxford. It was Friday and the streets were busy with students out on the town, laughing and talking, heading for restaurants, wine bars and cinemas. Sometimes, especially in the evening, Natasha missed living in town. As she stood on the pavement of Beaumont Street she wished for a moment that she was part of the gilded student crowd again, with the evening and her life before her, exciting, filled with infinite possibilities. But when she had been in that position part of her had longed to be older and wiser, and more settled. Well, she was older.

The building was a few yards up from the Playhouse, in the middle of a Regency terrace, flanked by a dentist's practice on one side and a firm of accountants on the other, both announced by gleaming brass plaques. The canary yellow door she was facing said Bennett and Gibson Architects. She wondered if she'd come to the wrong place.

The door opened and a girl with streaked blonde hair wearing a navy trouser suit came out, balancing an enormous bundle of envelopes in the crook of her arm. As she turned to close the door behind her she dropped the whole lot, spilling them down the steps and across the pavement. The girl swore. Natasha rushed to help and received a grateful smile as they scrabbled about on the ground together.

'Thanks. I missed the post collection and they've all got to go today,' the girl explained. 'I've still a load more to do. I'm going to be here hours yet.'

Natasha helped her carry them to the post box over the road and stuff them all in. As they were walking back she asked if there was a photographer's studio in the building.

The girl eyed her sceptically. 'You're looking for Jake or Alex?'

'Adam actually.'

'Are you a model?'

'Sadly not.'

'In the basement.'

148

Narrow stone steps led down and through a grille on the ground, and a faint light glimmered from a subterranean window. Natasha spotted the inconspicuous typed nameplate, a strip of white paper behind Perspex marked 'Studio' and next to it, 'PRB'. Please ring bell, or buzzer?

She pressed the chrome button and the intercom crackled into life. It was quickly cut off, and a metallic, female voice gave a clipped 'Hello?'

'Natasha Blake. To see Adam Mason.'

There was a few seconds of static, then, 'Come in.'

The lock clicked and she pushed against the heavy door.

She was momentarily disorientated by blackness and the contrasting dazzle of a single point of light in the centre of the cavernous room. There were giant umbrellas lined with silver, a figure silhouetted, pale face accentuated, red lips. She was dressed in a black hooded velvet cloak, her long blonde hair tumbling around her face.

Adam was standing in the shadows. He didn't seem to have noticed Natasha come in.

'It's night,' he said softly, the size and emptiness of the place giving his voice a theatrical resonance. 'I've come back from the dead to see you again.' The click of the shutter. 'You don't know whether to be glad or afraid, to run to me or to run away.' A rapid bombardment, like pistol fire. 'Then I'm gone. You know you'll not see me again until you are dead too.'

There was a petite girl with cropped, spiky, white blonde hair and orange paisley, lycra-clad

149

legs leaning with one Doc Marten pushed up against the wall. Angie presumably. Without so much as a cue from Adam, she stepped into the light, put the hood of the cloak down, adjusted the folds, applied spray to the model's hair, a dusting of powder to her porcelain cheek, stood back to check her efforts, dabbed on a little more blusher and then walked away.

'This is wicked.' The model spoke with a strong Essex accent and the sudden transformation of her crimson lips, from melancholy seduction to slightly brazen smile was a real let down.

'I told you you'd be a natural,' Adam said. 'Glad I propositioned you now?'

Natasha caught a flutter of very long eyelashes. 'Any time,' the model simpered.

'Now, turn away but keep your eyes on me. Look over your shoulder. Stop. Right here, remember?' Adam poked two fingers towards his own eyes. 'A little further. That's it. Lean forward as if you're about to run, or you're backing away from something.'

The girl adjusted herself, her pose looking a little awkward from where Natasha was standing. Adam obviously thought so too. He walked over to her, stood behind her and put his arms around her shoulders, then leant his body against hers, pushing her over slightly. Surely he didn't have to stand quite so close! He lifted the girl's arm, bent it, put his hand over hers and laid it against the opening of the cloak. 'It's cold. Wrap it round you.' Then he moved to face her, placed his palms on either side of her face and gently angled it towards him. He said something else which

150

Natasha didn't catch, but it brought a smile to the girl's face.

What a creep. It troubled Natasha, the way he'd openly flirted with her at the Opium Den when he was supposed to be worried about Bethany, in love with her still. But this was taking it way too far. Why was she bothering?

Adam walked back to the camera. Angie went over to him, brushed her hand across his arm to attract his attention. Or to stake a claim.

He turned to her and she whispered something to him. He nodded and she went over to the other side of the room, came back with a white lily, which she gave the model to hold.

'It's night,' Adam began, his tone colder now. 'You've been running through the woods. You're sure you're being chased. You kissed me once but you know you shouldn't have. Look back over your shoulder. That's good. You can see my face in the darkness now. I'm catching up.'

Another staccato volley. The blanched face, partially concealed by the sumptuous folds of velvet, frozen by the flare.

'Wistful and provocative now.'

'Make love to the camera you mean?'

'Be my guest.'

Oh, please.

The final flash died, leaving a bright floating image on Natasha's retina, like the afterglow of the sun.

'OK, Diana,' Adam said. 'We're finished.'

'Oh, don't say that, honeybun. I couldn't bear it.' She glided towards him, the hemline and small train of the cloak swishing over the floor, then turned, allowing him to ease her out of it. Angie hovered close by, relieved Adam of the garment and went to hang it on a rail.

Natasha coughed.

'Sorry,' Angie muttered to Adam, flicking her eyes in Natasha's direction. 'I forgot to tell you.'

The reaction on Adam's face told her the question at the forefront of his mind was, how long she'd been standing there. He looked guilty which instantly made her suspicious.

She wasn't going to let him off the hook easily. 'I wanted to talk to you. If I'm not interrupting anything.'

'I'll be just a minute.' He glanced over to the back wall. Natasha's eyes had adjusted and she could make out an easy chair pushed up against it. Have a seat. Can Angie fetch you a coffee?'

'Lovely.' She stayed on her feet.

As Adam retreated back into the darkness, Angie cast a chilly smile in Natasha's direction and disappeared into an anteroom off the main studio. She came back seconds later with two steaming mugs in her hands, one of which she handed over. She'd made it strong enough to stand a spoon in. If she'd been given a choice, Natasha would have asked for it milky, with one sugar. 'Thanks.' But the girl's eyes were already trained back towards the spotlight.

Adam was standing on its periphery and Angie went to give him his coffee, made to his exact taste no doubt.

Natasha wondered if Bethany had ever been present when Adam photographed other girls. If she was jealous of Angie, who seemed to know

152

Adam so well she did everything before he had to ask, and who clearly shared closely with him an important part of his life? But then that was the case with most people. You spent most days of the year with work colleagues. It was they who got to share your frustrations and successes.

Natasha took a sip from the mug. Her tongue furled at the bitter taste.

As Diana headed for the bathroom, Adam made some adjustments on the camera, closing down, shutting off. Natasha couldn't help watching Angie, who looked as if she was loitering, finding things to do. She was sorting through reels of film, putting them down, picking them up again, scribbling notes on stickers, sifting through a pile of Polaroids. Natasha almost wanted to reassure her: *Don't worry, I'm not interested in him.*

Interested? You couldn't help but be 'interested' in Adam, in both senses of the word. But his life was obviously complicated. It took all sorts though. Perhaps Bethany was a free spirit, not prone to possessiveness. Could you love someone and never be jealous?

By the look of things, Bethany had more cause than most. Did she find she was copying Lizzie Siddal's life in ways she might not have wanted? Being involved with someone like Rossetti, artistic, mercurial, a womaniser, someone who gave her no peace?

Maybe she'd already had her heart broken beyond repair.

At last you will be mine.

Adam wandered over to where Natasha stood. Angie, with obvious reluctance, slung a denim

153

jacket over her shoulder. She came and offered Adam her cheek onto which he delivered a swift kiss. Then she lifted her arms up around his shoulders for the briefest of moments and as she pulled away said, 'Have a good evening.' She threw a glance at Natasha that spoke the exact opposite.

'That was brilliant,' Diana said as she re-appeared, swinging across the studio as if it were a catwalk. She scrunched up her blonde hair, securing it with a silver band. Tall and thin, she had changed into tight denims and a white T-shirt with Babe written across the breast in pink sparkles.

Adam clasped her hand. 'You were great.'

'So were you. You'll give me a call the minute I can see them?'

'Of course.'

'It's such a brilliant idea. I'm surprised no one thought of it before.'

'Thank you.' His voice sounded suddenly flat.

'And I'm so glad you've decided to carry on with it after...' she flicked her eyes at Natasha, lowered her voice. 'Well, Jake's told me what's going on. I said nothing's changed as far as I'm concerned. It's a shame about Bethany. I liked her. But the exhibition's going to be an incredible success. I'm sure of it.' She squeezed his arm, batted her eyelashes again, made her voice throaty. 'Come and see me again soon, OK?'

She walked towards the door through which Angie had just gone, leaving Natasha alone with Adam.

Twenty-Two

Adam waited until the door closed.

'It's good to see you.' The blacked out room and spotlight created an atmosphere that was unnervingly intimate, like a moonlit walk. 'You look tired. It suits you.'

Don't give me any of that crap.

He reached out as if towards her, then extended his hand over her shoulder half trapping her against the wall. He flicked a switch and the spotlight blinked off, casting the room into utter darkness. Natasha stiffened, felt a flicker of fear. You could scream at the top of your lungs down here and no one would ever know. *Too bad.*

Another light came on, weaker but positioned directly above.

'There's nothing going on. I wanted to get the best out of her, that's all.'

I bet you did. 'It's absolutely none of my business. Could I see the pictures you took of Bethany the other day?'

Adam hesitated, then led the way to the back of the studio. The door he opened had Dark Room written on it, but it looked more like an office. Small and heated, with a single stripped pine bench, an angle-poise lamp, and filing cabinets. On top of them were containers of chemicals, trays. Natasha had watched old photographs being restored, reprinted, and had always thought

155

there was something almost mystical about the way an image gradually materialised on the blank paper, floated up out of the solution. Digital couldn't compete. She was glad to see Adam hadn't entirely abandoned traditional methods.

She also noted that there was a computer on the desk.

Directly behind where she was standing was another door, with a bolt across it.

'Does Jake use this studio as well?'

'Not for much longer.'

Adam had gone to one of the three filing cabinets, carefully withdrawn a manila folder from the top drawer. He fanned out a handful of large matt black and white pictures onto the desk. 'Have a look at these first.'

The short reach of the light forced them to stand close together. Natasha felt his hair brush her face, just below her temples, caught the scent of it, clean and lemony. She wondered what it would be like to touch it. Where had her indignation gone when she needed it? Not to mention her wariness. She drew away and Adam, as if taking a hint, retreated to just beyond the fringe of light.

She picked up one of the pictures. It was a larger version of the one Adam had given to her. Not black and white exactly but various tones of grey, delicate and dreamy.

She put it aside. Beneath it was a shot of Bethany's face, emerging from darkness, the image infused with a dusky light. The simplicity of the composition made it ageless. The one beneath was almost identical, except that her face

156

was even more vague, as if she was fading away. Her eyes were trance like.

Natasha remembered the way Adam had used words to entice the emotions he wanted out of the girl he'd been photographing earlier, and she wondered what he'd said to Bethany to make her look like that.

'They're beautiful,' she said.

In the right hand corner of the picture were initials she'd seen on the picture Adam had given to her earlier, the same letters that were on all the photographs. 'What does TR stand for?'

He took the print off her. 'It's just a code.'

'Will there be any men in your exhibition?' She thought of the Cameron photographs in the National Portrait Gallery. It was the men that came to mind. Lord Tennyson bearded and wild-haired, Rossetti's brother, William, with the bright stare of a wizard. 'That's what Julia Margaret Cameron was best known for, wasn't it?'

'True. But it's much more interesting taking pictures of girls.' He still stood outside the reach of the light, like a grand inquisitor with his face obscured, making it impossible to tell if he was being glib or not.

'And the Pre-Raphaelites are remembered for their pictures of women of course. They chose models who shared traits and experiences with those they were meant to portray.'

Lizzie as Ophelia, a girl driven insane by unrequited love; Beatrice, Dante's lover in heaven. And Bethany?

'Did Bethany like what you saw in her?'

'I don't know.'

157

'Adam, are you worried about her?'

'What do you mean?'

'Do you think there's any chance she might do anything drastic?'

He turned to her. 'Absolutely not!' He seemed furious that she'd even suggested it.

Natasha tried to look as if she was reassured. But Adam's answer was too emphatic, as if he was determined to convince her, or himself. 'I'm sorry. I had to ask.'

She slowly sifted through the shots again. The pictures were all characterised by that soft focus. Was that the quality Adam recognised in Bethany? The same quality the Victorian artists had noted in Lizzie Siddal, something phantom-like, foreshadowing of an early death? Or was that just the result of the techniques he'd used?

'You know that picture you gave me, I presumed the blurriness wasn't intentional but due to a fault in the processing or something.'

'Actually, you're not far off the mark. In Cameron's case it was achieved by accident, at first.' He leant over to drag a heavy book down from the shelf above the desk and opened it at a monograph of a girl in a garden. 'See, she started off with a lens with a short focal length which only allowed one shallow plane to be completely in focus.' He indicated a circuitous area with his finger, over the filmy cascade of the model's hair, then touched her sharply defined profile. 'And the collodin emulsion they used in those days also tended to make the finished print look a bit hazy. A lot of the effect though, was down to the incredibly long exposure which meant that breathing or slight movements, almost invisible to the naked eye, were recorded on the film...' He was suddenly a different person, animated, enthusiastic. It reminded Natasha of the way Steven talked about archaeology. There was something very attractive about people who had a passion for a subject, a knowledge or expertise they were eager to share. 'I generally use one of the Victorians' less scientific methods,' he added. 'A trick of the light. If you drape fabric over windows or lamps, the diffusion gives sitters a sort of supernatural glow.' He shut the book, put it back in the bookcase. 'I'm boring you.'

'Not at all,' she said truthfully. 'It's fascinating.'

They shared a smile.

'So what eternal quality do you see in the girl you were photographing earlier?'

'Diana? Oh, she was definitely a snow queen, icy and predatory.'

'Is she a friend?' *How clumsy was that?*

'Not in that way,' Adam smirked. 'She wants to be an actress. Thinks the exposure will be good for her. We ... I met her at a party about a year ago. And the first thing I noticed were those bright red lips. They seem to shout at you even when she's not saying anything. The Victorians believed that character shaped a person's features. I think there's something in that.'

The vision was strong. Marcus, his fingers working a skull, eyes and lips and cheekbones taking shape beneath his hands. His voice, mingling with her own as they speculated together about what the person might have been like, when all they had to go on was a slowly

159

developing face. She pushed the vision away.

Adam was looking at her again.

'You're not going to ask me then?' he said. 'What characteristics I see in you.'

'I'm not sure I want to know.'

'It's a difficult one. It's my guess you're a bit of a chameleon, changing who you are depending on the circumstances.'

'That's probably very astute.' She handed the photographs back. 'I've always thought black and white is so much more beautiful than colour. Why old photographs are so much more striking than modern snap shots, I suppose.'

'Colour is too realistic. Black and white leaves more to the imagination. You wanted to see the pictures from Little Barrington, didn't you?' He turned, opened the filing cabinet and took out another folder. 'Like I said, the black and whites didn't turn out, so it'll be the colour I use for the exhibition. Think it'll work though.'

The picture was much larger than the rest, the print glossy, the colours almost Technicolor. Bethany's face was bleached out. Natasha wasn't sure now why she'd wanted to see it, what she'd hoped to gain.

She laid the photograph on the desk. 'I keep thinking. That long call you said she made before she left. I'd really like to know who it was to. I don't suppose you've had an itemised phone bill...'

As if on cue the phone rang, making them both jump. Adam snatched up the receiver. 'Yes. Can I courier them over tomorrow?' He put the manila folder down on the desk, dragged over a

160

notepad and pen.

The corner of another photograph was protruding from the folder, a single shot that Adam had left inside the file. On an impulse, Natasha flipped open the folder.

It took a while for the significance of the image to register in her mind.

Adam hung up.

'I took it the evening before she left,' he said. 'She had a thing about Sleeping Beauty.'

Natasha glanced at him, then stared down at the picture.

Bethany was lying on her back on a narrow, flat surface which looked more like a bier than a bed. Her eyelids were closed, her head fallen slightly to one side, her hair fanned out around her. Her hands were crossed loosely on her breast. The table was overhung with silk and she was wearing an organza gown, diaphanous and floaty. The drape of the fabrics and the bloodless tone of her skin gave the picture a sculptural grace. She was like a marble statue on a sarcophagus.

'Where was it taken?'

'At the flat. It was important to her that I waited until she was really asleep. She said it's one thing you can never see, what you look like when you're sleeping, unless someone takes your picture.'

There was something incredibly intimate about it. It was a lover's role, a parent's role, to watch over the sleeping. Yet it was not a lover's eyes that had watched over Bethany, but the cold, intrusive eye of the camera lens.

Adam eased the photo out of Natasha's hand. It was impossible to read his eyes. The light in

161

them was hard and yet his voice sounded sad, regretful. 'She said it would be interesting to see her expressions when she was dreaming.' He was staring at the picture now, whispering as if they were in the presence of someone whom he didn't want to wake.

Natasha forced the words out. 'She looks like she's...'

'I know,' he cut in. 'That was part of the idea. You know how commercial photography began?'

She did, but shook her head. She wanted to hear it from him.

'The first photographers who were paid for their work took pictures of the dead. Long before there were wedding photographers and studio portraits, when people died, especially children and the young, their pictures were taken as a memento for their family. Mortuary photographs they were called. It sounds gruesome, but I've seen some of them. They're incredibly beautiful.' He slid the picture back into the folder now and looked at her. 'It's not quite true, that the dead look as if they're sleeping. It's the sleep of children. Innocent, at peace. The Victorians were preoccupied with death of course. Almost as much as we are obsessed with sex. Only sex has lost some of its mystique, don't you agree? Death is the only taboo left.'

Natasha remembered Adam's directions in both the photo shoots. He was fascinated with death. She could understand that, in a way. So why did the realization make her feel a grip of panic?

'I think that's one of the reasons the Pre-Raphaelites are so popular still,' Adam said.

'They've got it all. Sex and death and drugs as well.' He broke off, tapped the file which held the photograph. 'You see, it's accepted that Rossetti painted *Beata Beatrix* after Lizzie died, but Bethany's grandmother told her he used Lizzie's corpse as a model, which makes it a kind of mortuary painting.' He looked at her. 'It's ironic really.'

'What?' That was a touch high-pitched. She tried again so he wouldn't notice. 'What is?'

'If I *had* been able to tell the difference between real and pretend sleep, Bethany might be here now.'

'What do you mean?'

'She must have been pretending on the night she left, so she could slip out without me knowing. If only I hadn't had the wine, I wouldn't have slept so soundly.'

She could see he was punishing himself. 'I'm sure it's quite easy to make someone believe you're asleep when you're not. I used to do it all the time.'

'Why?'

'I've always suffered from insomnia. My mother could never understand. It used to make her really cross. When she came up to my bedroom I used to pretend so I wouldn't get told off.'

'I bet it's the loneliest thing in the world. Not being able to sleep.'

'There've been times when I'd agree with you.'

He opened the cabinet to put the file back inside. She craned to look what else was in there. It was full almost to bursting. She caught a glimpse of titles of the other files. Anne.

163

Christine. Emma. Frances. More girls' names, a dozen of them at least.

Adam was saying something about sleep deprivation as a form of torture, but she wasn't listening. She needed to see those other pictures, and to know what was in the other two cabinets.

Before she knew quite what she was doing she'd inched back against the far door, leant against it with her hands behind her back, feeling around. Something cold, metal. She cupped her hand around the bolt, eased it silently back into her palm.

Then she said she had to be going, and felt Adam's fingers in the curve of her spine propelling her towards the exit.

Coming up from the underground room was like waking up.

It had been raining and the street was busy and bright. The glow of headlights and streetlamps and the light from windows reflected on the wet tarmac. A continuous flurry of people passed with umbrellas, dressed for the evening.

'I wish you'd let me photograph you properly,' Adam said, making even that sound suggestive.

Natasha eased away from him, thinking of Bethany. 'No way.'

'Like the joke?' He directed her eyes to the intercom. 'Borrowed from Rossetti himself. PRB. Please ring bell.'

PRB. She twigged. 'Or Pre-Raphaelite Brotherhood.'

For the first time, Natasha wondered if she was afraid of ghosts.

Twenty-Three

She drove as far as the Pear Tree roundabout, then doubled back. Until she was heading into town again she hadn't been entirely sure she was going to do it. Just what *was* she doing?

Punters were milling outside the Playhouse, waiting for the doors to open. Lights were still on in the architects' office, the girl in the blue trouser suit just visible through the slatted blinds, slaving over her computer screen which cast a blue glow over her face. The basement was in total darkness. Natasha gave the buzzer a press just to be sure. No reply.

Back on the pavement, she rang the brass bell by the yellow door. The girl opened up, papers in one hand and stapler in the other, a distracted smile on her face.

'Hi again.' Natasha slipped into her best scatterbrain voice. 'Look, I'm sorry to bother you, but I've left my phone down in the studio. Adam seems to have locked up and gone. I don't suppose there's any way in from your floor.'

'Not unless they've left the door to the backstairs unbolted.'

'Do you mind if I have a try?' The girl hesitated. 'It's just that, well, you know how it is, my life's stored on the mobile. I feel completely lost without it.'

The girl gave a weary shrug, in too much of a

hurry to argue, then led the way through a smart office towards a wooden door marked Fire Exit leading down a short flight of concrete steps with heating ducts overhead. 'It's just down there on the right, if it's open.'

'Thanks.'

The girl had left the upper door ajar so there was just enough light for Natasha to get her bearings. She stuck her hands out, tripped over a chair leg, cursed under her breath, felt the cold metal of the filing cabinets, and came up against the desk. She felt for the lamp, switched it on. She planted her phone on one of the shelves. Just in case. Her heart was hammering.

What am I doing here?

There was an A4 size address book on the desk, with black and white computer generated spirals on the front. She flipped through the pages. Prop suppliers, galleries, marketing and sales departments for cosmetics companies, fashion houses. She closed it and opened one of the desk drawers. Paperclips, Sellotape, rubber bands. Second drawer. Another address book, smaller, bound in black leather, the pages silver edged. A little black book in other words. How imaginative! Girls names were listed under the initial letter of their christian rather than surnames. Just like the arrangement in the filing cabinet. But the index had no 'B'... She ran her finger down the inside of the spine, felt a jagged edge. The page which would have had Bethany's details had been ripped out.

She grabbed a pencil, ran it carefully over the

blank sheet which would have been beneath it. She hadn't done that since she was a child playing Private Eye. She angled the book towards the light. She was mildly surprised to see the trick had worked. The word 'Blackfriars' was startlingly clear. But any words before or after, any telephone numbers, were obliterated.

Blackfriars. Was that where Bethany was living? But Adam had said he didn't know where she lived.

She set to work on the computer, found the inbox, clicked on the menu bar to arrange the contents by recipient. No messages to Bethany. It was not here that she had retrieved the information Margaret Wood had sent to her.

Natasha turned her attention to the filing cabinets, opened one at random. A girl standing in a long gown on castle ramparts. In another, she just about recognized the girl from upstairs. Christine. She was wearing a velvet dress, playing a lute. Beneath was a stunning one of the same girl standing in a circle of fire, her hair wild as a sorceress. The initials TR were in the corner of every frame.

There was nothing sinister about any of it, though. The pictures were tasteful, beautiful in fact.

She checked the other drawers. Paperwork in one, negatives in another. She held them up to the light. Pictures of gardens, an owl caught in mid-flight.

In the next cabinet the bottom drawer was filled with negatives and prints of sports cars, parked on a beach, on top of a mountain, arty shots of bottles of wine, fizzy drinks. One of them had a printed sticker on the back, the name Jake Romilly. Another folder had prints of a stud in jeans on horseback. Same details on the sticker. She quickly tried the middle drawer. An assortment of black and white shots. A motorbike cutting up a beach with jets of sand, the spray of water over a statue in a fountain, bare footprints in snow.

In the top drawer were more girls' names. Same ones as before. Christine in a barge like the Lady Of Shalott, Diana standing beside a lake, appearing to float up out of the mist, draped in a tunic like a Greek goddess. Another of her standing hand on hip cradling an urn, then with her arms arched above her head, her hair drawn severely back from her face, a crown of roses with thorns.

Natasha picked up the address book, found a biro and scribbled both Diana and Christine's phone numbers on the back of her hand, since she'd met them both, briefly. She would think of some pretence to call them... She remembered Diana's comment at the studio. 'Jake's told me what's going on. I said nothing's changed as far as I'm concerned.' It would be interesting to know what she meant by that.

Natasha looked back at the pictures. They were subtly different in style to the ones in the other cabinet, more direct and defined, less of the misted effect, but the subject matter and the overall feel of them was similar. Another photographer, same project. Plagiarism? If so you'd hardly store the copies alongside the

168

original work, pleading to be found. What then? Adam hadn't said he was exhibiting alone. Jake Romilly's exhibition pieces?

No stickers on any of them. TR in the corner again though. Adam had said it was just a code. For the show then?

She pushed back the files to see the ones at the front. Beth. Bethany. The file was bulging, the cardboard cover ripped where the weight of the contents had pulled it away from the metal hanger which ran along the top.

The abundance of them was what first struck her, and the replication. The setting and costume identical in a succession of frames which differed only by an alteration, sometimes very slight, in Bethany's pose and expression. It was unsettling seeing the same face in dozens of varied attitudes and guises. Her face reflected in an oval mirror, the impression of somewhere cloistered, a room in a tower. Another sequence: Backlit. The fragile lines of her body silhouetted. The last set: At the Bridge of Sighs in Oxford.

Was Jake Romilly obsessed with Bethany? Was it him who'd called to say Bethany didn't want to be with Adam? And if so, was that a dangerous delusion or the truth?

Male voices outside the studio, footsteps. She quickly stuffed the pictures back inside the folder, pushed it in the drawer and gave a shove. She grabbed her phone just as the door opened.

Jake Romilly was with another young man in biker gear with short cropped dirty blond hair. Jake was holding a bottle of uncorked Jack Daniels. Even from this distance she could smell it on his breath.

He looked Natasha up and down, then gave her a wide smile, folded his arms across his chest, crossed one foot in front of the other, waiting to hear what she had to say.

'I forgot my phone.' She brandished it at them, the excuse sounding lame even to her.

'Did you now? Been here with Adam I suppose? You seem to be seeing rather a lot of each other.'

'I'm a friend of Bethany's.' She knew she was pushing her luck.

'Yeah?' He took a swig of Jack Daniels. 'Only met her a couple of times.'

A direct lie, if the photographs were anything to go by. 'Oh, when was that?'

A beat of silence. 'Last time was just before Christmas.'

She had the feeling she'd unnerved him a fraction, got him wondering what Bethany might have been saying about him.

'I'll be off then.'

'You're more than welcome to join the party.' He waved the bottle. 'Stay and have some.'

'I'll pass this time, thanks.'

She'd reached the exit to the studio when he said, without looking at her. 'Nosy little cat, aren't you? Remember what curiosity did?'

Back at the cottage, Natasha took a novel up to bed, Umberto Eco's *The Name of the Rose*. She tried to read for a while but couldn't concentrate. She switched the light off, lay back and stared at the ceiling. She turned on her side to try to sleep.

She thought of the picture of Bethany, lying flat

on her back. Who actually slept in that position, with their arms crossed on their chests? Had Adam moved her, adjusted her limbs for effect, or was she really only pretending to sleep? Wanting him to photograph her that way for some reason, before she left.

Sleeping Beauty. Another Pre-Raphaelite motif.

Lizzie Siddal again, her grave, hidden behind a tangle of ivy. A tragic, twisted fairytale. For she was not roused with a lover's kiss but by a lover's greed.

She pulled a jumper on, tramped downstairs, turned all the lights on and put a pan of milk on the range. She found she was shivering. That was the trouble with old houses, drafts crept in all over the place, and you could never tell quite where they came from. For good measure, she added whisky, watching the golden drop seep into the white, like caramelised sugar.

She cradled the warm mug, wandering through to the living room, saw the *Pre-Raphaelite Dream* lying on the floor where she'd left it. She looked at the pictures of Lizzie Siddal painted by Deverell, Millais, Rossetti.

Perhaps there was nothing unusual about Adam's group of friends sharing the same models.

She closed the book. On the cover was Janey Morris, Rossetti's second muse, who inspired him after Lizzie's death, and married one of Rossetti's best friends, in order, according to accepted legend, to 'keep her in the family'.

Suddenly the whisky and milk made Natasha feel a little sick. Rossetti and Morris hadn't just

171

shared Jane as a model. Did Adam and his friends share Diana and Christine and Bethany in other ways?

Did that have something to do with her disappearance? Was Bethany not the only model Adam had been sleeping with? What a strange phrase that was. Sleep not just a euphemism for death, but for sex as well.

She wished there was someone she could talk to, someone who wouldn't mind her ringing at two in the morning. Would Marcus be in Vancouver yet? It might be a perfectly civilised time over there. Once that wouldn't have mattered. Marcus had never minded her calling him in the middle of the night.

She heard the soft tap of Boris's claws descending the wooden stairs, coming to find her. 'Hello, boy,' she said as he plonked down close beside her.

She put her arm around him and he glanced up, checking she was all right. Sometimes, Natasha thought he was the only one who came close to understanding her, the only one who would love her no matter what. She'd found him at the rescue centre, a little puppy sitting forlornly in the corner of his pen. 'Abandoned on the roadside,' the woman who ran the kennel told Natasha, and she'd bent down to stroke him, and whispered into his ear, 'We're both in the same boat then.'

She buried her cheek in the velvety fur on top of his head.

Twenty-Four

Natasha had been at her desk most of the morning catching up on phone calls, e-mails, typing up reports and notes, liaising with a contact in the States. She rang another client, a middle-aged man expecting his first grandchild. As so often happened, the birth of a new generation had triggered his interest in the ones who'd gone before. Natasha told him she'd tracked down distant cousins in Alice Springs.

'You've really made my day,' he told her. 'I can start planning my holidays now. Always fancied a trip Down Under but it seemed such a long way away. If you've got family it makes the world of difference, doesn't it?'

The call brightened her morning. She took a leisurely break to have lunch in Broadway with an old flatmate from London who was passing through on her way to visit her parents in Worcester. They went to a café, giggled a lot and pigged out on omelette and chips followed by sponge pudding and custard. It was one of the few occasions she'd taken time out from work since the business with Bethany started. It made her realise how much it was preoccupying her. She wondered if she'd lost her perspective. Finding Bethany had become a kind of personal quest. As if a successful resolution could in some way restore a balance, make up for events of the

173

past, prove that people couldn't just vanish into thin air.

Natasha had tried the model Diana's number in the morning. She dialled it now for the third time and got an answer.

'Hi. It's Natasha Blake. We met, almost, at Adam Mason's studio.'

'Oh, yeah.'

'Adam's asked me to pose for some pictures too. It sounds fun but I've never done it before. I wondered if you'd give me some tips.'

'Nothing to it.'

'Do all the girls find it so easy?'

'You'd have to ask them.'

'Adam showed me the photos of Bethany. They're so lovely.'

'Mmm.'

'You said you know her. What's she like?'

'Dunno really. She kept herself to herself.'

'Have you modelled for Jake as well?'

Diana hesitated. 'Lots of times,' she said, guarded. 'The more practice I get the better.'

'You think I should say yes, then?'

'Depends on the question.'

Which left Natasha none the wiser.

The party was to be at Will's flat, opposite Montpellier Gardens in Cheltenham. Natasha wondered who else would be there. Emily for sure, other ex-colleagues from Generations. It would be good to see them.

It was nearly seven by the time she'd showered and decided what to wear. In the end she went for the copper-beech dress and the shawl, both still hanging on the wardrobe door from New Year's Eve. She was going to be late, at least forty minutes. No point altering the habits of a lifetime.

She drove out towards Toddington, put her foot down once she was through Winchcombe.

There'd been warnings of black ice on the roads and patches of mist. Perhaps this was why the red Celica had been hugging her rear all the way, basking in her tail lights. It was beginning to bug her. If she had to brake hard he'd bang into her.

Natasha didn't mind driving in bad conditions. It made her feel alive, in touch with the elements. She pressed down on the pedal, felt the plucky engine, nearly a decade older than herself, gearing itself for the challenge, proximity to the ground increasing the pure adrenaline rush of speed. She felt the tyres slip and right themselves. There was a bend up ahead and she eased back, took a firm grip of the narrow wooden steering wheel.

The bloody Celica was still on her tail.

She hit the outskirts of town, indicated right to turn off onto Prestbury Road. The Celica did the same. She accelerated ahead again, put another car between them for a while, then it was back in her rear view mirror, the driver behind the windscreen inscrutable in the glare of the lights. She spotted an off licence next to a chip shop. She left it deliberately late to pull into the kerb, and watched the Celica shoot past.

On your own now, mate. Sorry!

She bought a good bottle of red Australian Cabernet. The bottle safely tucked under the passenger seat, she eased out into the traffic again, checked her mirror at the lights. She did a double take, gripped the steering wheel. The lights were changing back to amber. She shot across the junction. The Celica was right there behind her.

She'd only been to Will's new flat once before, for the house warming, but from what she could remember she was nearly there. Past the Holst Birthplace Museum, onto North Street, the shopping arcades on her right, then Imperial Gardens. Still shadowed by the Celica.

Up Montpellier Promenade now, past the smart wine bars and boutiques and restaurants, right again into Will's road. She parked as close as she could to the flat, watched the other car continue on. She sat rigid, daring it to park further up the street or turn back. It didn't do either. She took a second to compose herself, locked up and sprinted across the road, couldn't help glancing behind her as she waited at the door, willing someone to open up quickly.

Emily, who Natasha used to share an office with, answered with a champagne flute in her hand, looking very glamorous in white silk, her short auburn hair pulled back. 'Hi, great to see you.' She gave Natasha a hug, relieved her of the wine bottle and her coat. When Natasha had met up with Emily last, she was talking about moving in with Will. Seemed very at home already.

Natasha went through to the spacious living room. In the warmth and light, surrounded by familiar faces and normality, the incident with the Celica seemed ridiculous. *Forget it.* Just a coincidence the car had been heading in exactly the same direction she was.

Will was standing by the fireplace and came across to give her a hug. He was three years older than Natasha, worked in the department of Generations that specialized in genealogical investigations allied to genetics, for the purposes of tracking hereditary medical conditions, Alzheimer's, Cystic Fibrosis and blood disorders, for medical advancement and for people who wanted to know what genes they might be passing onto their children, or to look into the past to see their own future. It was an area Natasha had always avoided.

She was used to listening to Will though, enthusing about how genetics was going to open up a whole new chapter for genealogy, give it a new relevance, was its scientific sister. And how it worked the other way around. Using genetics to fill in genealogical gaps, to enable everyone to trace common ancestors back over not hundreds of years but thousands, to the Vikings and the Celts.

Emily joined them, topped up Natasha's glass.

'Happy New Year,' Natasha toasted. It didn't feel particularly new any more.

'Happy New Year,' Emily smiled.

The gossiped about bosses and mutual acquaintances, Emily bringing Natasha up to date with some of the contacts the company used around the world.

'It's not the same without you, you know,' Will said. 'We miss your spats with the big chiefs, waiting to see what wonderful outfits you'll turn up in. I don't drink half so many cups of tea and

177

coffee now you're gone, mind.'

'That's no excuse. You can come over for a cup whenever you fancy. Kettle's always on.'

'So how's it going, out in the big wide world?'

'Great.' *That didn't sound very convincing.* 'You should try it.'

'I don't have your dedication. And I'm rather attached to my regular pay check.'

'There is that.'

'Would you ever come back?' Emily said.

Will answered for her. 'No chance.' There was the slightest edge to his voice. Natasha knew very well what he was getting at. The end of their relationship. Her move as usual. Absorption in their work had pulled them apart, but she'd given the final shove. He'd suggested a re-match once or twice, before Marcus, and she'd told him it wouldn't work.

It was nicer having him as a friend. Not just a consolation prize, but special.

It was odd, seeing everyone. It made Natasha feel a bit remote as well as nostalgic. You forgot all the hassles of working for a big company, the politics and routine and bureaucracy, once you'd left, remembered only the gossips over coffee and the photocopier, the banter and moral support.

If Adam had approached her while she was working at Generations or at the College of Arms, she could have legitimately shared her concerns about Bethany's note with half a dozen people. But then she'd most likely not have been able to take on the case in the first instance. Not enough profit. No profit more like.

She'd had half a mind to talk about it all to Will

178

or Emily anyway. But the moment never seemed quite right.

By nine the heavy drinking had started. Natasha had to drive home so she made her excuses.

As she crossed to her car she glanced across the road to the shadowy park, almost expecting someone to leap over the railings. She checked her side mirror as she set off and again as she reached the outskirts of town. But she was alone on the road. Relief flooded through her. She opened the window, let the cold air blast in and keep her awake. The shrill beep of the mobile made her realise it hadn't worked all that well and she'd been almost dozing at the wheel.

The phone was sitting on the passenger seat. She glanced across at it warily. She let it carry on, reluctant to pick up. Why was it so damned impossible to ignore a ringing phone?

'You changed your mind then?' It was Adam.

'What about?'

'Posing.' She knew immediately what he was going to say, her mind already running ahead, working out how she was going to talk herself out of this one. She slowed down so she could pay more attention. 'Diana said you called her for some tips.'

'That's right.' *Nothing like setting a trap for yourself.*

'Where are you?'

'Midway between Cheltenham and Broadway.'

'Come over now.'

Twenty-Five

As she drove, switching direction, heading south towards Burford and the A40, Natasha examined her motives, as well as the sense, or lack of it, in agreeing to go to Adam's studio alone, late at night. Trouble was, she wasn't sure whether it was Adam she didn't trust or herself.

She tried exploring her conscience instead. Bethany had walked out on Adam, freeing him from any obligation. It was never as simple as that, though. There was no point pretending, acting the martyr. She wasn't doing this because, after her conversation with Diana, it was less complicated to go along with Adam's request.

No, she *wanted* to do it.

She wondered if she was in danger of copying Steven's cavalier attitude to the opposite sex.

Adam let her into the studio. Over his shoulder she could see he'd already rigged the lights. Beneath the spot was a plain wooden bench.

She tried to think of Jake and his friend, the threatening voice on the answering machine, the Celica, but she was having problems connecting any of it to Adam, to the here and now.

He handed her a glass of red wine.

'I've had plenty already.'

'Then one more won't do any harm. It'll help you loosen up.'

She needed that, but on the other hand she

180

wanted to keep her wits about her. *What the hell am I doing here?* A question she seemed to be asking herself a lot lately. The wine, or the feel-good factor it would induce, was too tempting. She took it.

'There's an outfit in the dark room. You can change in there.' He seemed distant, cool. Natasha couldn't help wondering if he'd spoken to Jake Romilly as well as to Diana, knew she'd been snooping around behind his back. She could leave now, walk away this minute – if he'd let her.

She walked over to the small door. 'A word of warning,' Adam said. 'The material's a little damp. I'll explain later.'

Damp was an understatement if ever there was one. Unsubtle was another. The costume was hanging on the back of the door. It was of flimsy cotton, a long white Grecian robe. Droplets of water were snaking from the hemline, making a pool on the varnished floorboards.

She might as well be stark naked. It would cling to every line and curve.

She took it out to the studio, holding it at arm's length towards Adam. 'You've got to be joking.'

'I used warm water and the lights will keep it that way. It shouldn't be too uncomfortable.'

'Yeah, right.' She hung the robe back on the door. 'Perhaps this wasn't such a good idea.'

'Aren't you even curious to hear what I want you to do?'

She snorted. 'I think I've a pretty good idea.'

'Your father's an archaeologist. He took you to the British Museum when you were a little girl?'

'Yes.'

'He showed you the Elgin Marbles?'

'He did, yes.'

'He told you their story? How Lord Elgin brought them back from the Greek Parthenon in the nineteenth century, how Greece has been fighting to have them repatriated ever since?'

'Yes.'

'Know how classical figurative sculpture was done?' He started walking slowly towards her. 'They drape the model in wet cloth.' When their faces were a few inches apart he stopped. 'I want to shoot you as one of the Elgin Marbles.'

'Explain.'

'Only if you promise not to run away.'

She crossed her fingers behind her back. 'Promise.'

She followed him back into the dark room. He took the Cameron book down from the shelf and showed her a picture of one of the Marbles, a fragment of sculpture, two female figures in robes reclining against one another on a pedestal. Headless. Alongside it was one of Cameron's photographs, the sitters on a bench, mirroring the attitude of the statues.

Adam handed the book over to Natasha.

'The particular statue was from the Parthenon's east pediment,' he told her. 'Cameron chose them for the very fact that their heads are missing. They're figures from myth and legend.' He looked at her. 'But because they're broken, their exact identities can never be known. So it's perfect, you see. You can make them what you want them to be.'

He wasn't talking about Bethany. He was

182

talking about her.

'That comment you made the second time we met. When I asked you if you had Russian blood. "I'd like to think so," you said. I knew you had no way of finding out. I can see you very clearly, with your mane of hair and your black eyes, standing in Red Square, dressed in fur with snow swirling about you. That'd be too obvious, though.' He handed her the robe. 'Which brings us back to the Marbles.'

Removed from the natural environment. Rescued by an archaeologist. Identities unknown. Very neat. 'I'm impressed.'

'I'm glad.'

She took the outfit and Adam turned to go. 'When you're ready.' She closed the dark room door, took off her dress and shoes. She decided her underwear would have to come off too. It would show through. Naked, she stood for a moment and listened, couldn't hear any sounds coming from the studio, wondered what Adam was doing. She stepped into the wet robe. The coolness of the cotton wasn't unpleasant at all, made her skin tingle the way it did when she stepped into cool water.

She wasn't sure what to do with her hair. She looked around for a mirror, seemed to remember there was one at the far side of the studio. She glanced down at herself, the wet fabric hugging her narrow waist, her hipbones jutting out, not to mention her nipples. She found she didn't care.

She adjusted the fabric slightly and opened the door. Adam was sitting on the bench as if it was in a park, elbows resting on his knees, a

183

broadsheet newspaper open in front of him.

When he saw her he folded the paper slowly, looked her up and down. He stood, came towards her, touched her hair. 'May I?'

She nodded.

He moved behind her. She felt him take the weight of her hair in his hand, twist it, then lift it and knot it loosely and expertly on top of her head. Then he adjusted the drape of the robe, pulling it lower across her arms, carefully arranging the folds, his fingers brushing her shoulders, warm against her chilled skin.

He took a stick of kohl from his jacket pocket. 'Close your eyes.'

She felt the pencil pressing down sharp on her eyelids.

'OK.' He nodded towards the spotlight. 'In your own time.'

She walked into the glare, the floor cold on her bare feet, aware of his eyes following her. She sat down on the bench.

Adam had moved behind the camera so she could no longer see him. She waited for what seemed like ages. Much longer and she'd be as stiff as a real statue. The heat of the spotlight on her naked shoulders was nice though, like a sun lamp. She could feel it drying the robe.

Then she glimpsed him, a shadow standing in shadows. He adjusted the camera, aimed it at her like a weapon, making her suddenly feel exposed and vulnerable. *He's a photographer not James Bond for God's sake.* Guns don't come disguised as cameras in the real world.

'Lean back a little. Lift one foot up onto the

seat, like in the book, remember? That's right.'

He disappeared again. Then the flash came, blinding. She was sure she'd blinked.

'Tip your head back a little. OK. Now bring your arm down across your breast. Relax.'

The flash again.

'Look to one side now.'

Flash.

'Puts a whole new twist on playing statues. Don't I get any emotional direction? I thought that was your style.'

'You don't need it. The marbles had no identity. The idea is you interpret them however you want.' She could see him vaguely through the dazzle of the afterglow, detaching the camera from the tripod. He stepped into the light, came towards her, crouched so he was at her level and put his fingers under her chin to tilt her head back slightly. 'All I want to take from the originals is the idea of classical beauty, nobility, a reflection of more heroic times. You've got plenty of that.' He draped her arm further across her body.

He kept his eyes fixed on her as slowly he lifted the camera to them, brought his hand up to adjust the lens, carefully and quietly, as if she were a rare bird he was trying to photograph without startling. The camera was a few inches away from her face.

'Tell me about your mother.' She looked down, then back into the lens, was half tempted to push it away.

'I don't know anything about her.' Click. 'Except that on one night, in 1973, she was at the Jessop Hospital in Sheffield.' She couldn't believe

185

how easy the words had come.

The camera came in even closer.

'What is it you want from her most? Love?'

'To understand.'

The camera twisted round. Another click.

'When did they tell you?'

'I'd rather not talk about it.'

'They didn't tell you? You found out for yourself?'

'Yes.'

'How old were you?'

'Eighteen.' She'd never talked about this before. Not to anyone. Hearing her own voice in the empty room was strangely cathartic. It should have felt invasive, with the camera pointing at her, but it was the opposite, gave a distance, a reassuring anonymity, like confiding in a diary, only more compulsive. She'd never understood before, why people went on television to disclose their most private problems.

'I needed my birth certificate to get a passport to go on a school skiing trip to France. All my friends had full certificates. I didn't know the terminology for them then. They were long and thin, folded into three, with details of both mother and father, their occupations and address.'

'But you didn't have one.'

'No. It had to be ordered specially. My friend Rachel said it must mean I was adopted. She meant it as a joke. We'd often talked about it. It was the perfect explanation for why our parents never understood us, teenage alienation and all that. We used to giggle about how we were different from them, compare the shapes of our noses, peculiar habits. We invented fascinating ancestors for ourselves. Decided our real mothers had given us up to pursue glamorous careers.' She paused. 'When my certificate arrived it was half the size of everyone else's, unfolded, with just my name and date of birth.'

Use your initiative. Work things out for yourself. That was what Steven had taught her. So she'd gone to the local library. They directed her to the small genealogy section in the shelves where the history books were kept. There was an entire book about adopted children, with a pink and blue cover and bold black title lettering, including a brief section on birth certificates. It explained everything quite plainly. It said that short certificates were introduced to conceal adoptions, a job they didn't fulfil all that well. Documents were normally signed by the assistant registrar, but those issued for adopted children had to be authorised by a higher authority, the registrar general. And instead of the customary national health number, they had an adopted child register number. The book gave examples of both. She photocopied the pages and then compared them when she got home.

The odd thing was that she didn't feel anything. It was as if she'd just confirmed something she'd always known.

As Marcus said: 'You've always known your real mother left you. Deep down you remember it all. You must. You were there.'

The click of the shutter made her jump.

Adam's voice. 'You confronted them.'

She sat up straight, the eye of the lens following

187

her. 'Yes.'

Everyone was downstairs in the kitchen. Ann was at the oven, stirring sauce in a steaming pan. Abigail sitting at the dining table doing her homework, physics it was, Steven beside her, helping her. A tumbler filled with whisky and soda sat at his elbow.

They'd been just a few paces away, near enough to touch, but it was as if she was watching them through a telescope, from miles away, from another planet. It took a while to register that they could see her too, that they were looking at her. She stared down at the piece of paper in her hand and crushed it.

'My dad smiled at me, and what surprised me was that he didn't seem to see anything different. He didn't notice that I'd stopped being his little girl.'

In the silence, familiar objects became peculiarly vivid, the big kitchen clock on which she'd learnt to tell the time, the flowered curtains, the rope swing in the garden through the window.

Her mother, who was not her mother at all, looked at her through a thin veil of steam and said nothing. Steven came over to her and put his arms around her. She wanted to shrug him off but she couldn't seem to summon the energy.

'We were going to tell you. When you were twenty-one,' Steven said, as if the secrecy of the thing was the only issue.

Over his shoulder Natasha saw Abigail. Her sister smiled, not understanding. A stranger. Who had always been her parents' favourite. Now it made sense.

Then it sprang into her mind, a lifeline to cling to, the pink and blue book in the library. There had been pages, several chapters even, devoted to tracing missing parents.

'I loved my mother. My adoptive mother. I still love her. But she never tired of telling me, how when I was a baby I cried at night for hours on end. But I kicked and screamed louder when she picked me up, would never let her hold me, had rejected her affection ever since. I'd always thought it was the other way around.'

But her real mother would be different.

Then Steven had ripped that away too. He'd taken her out of the warmth of the kitchen into Ann's cool pale blue drawing room. They sat opposite one another on chintz chairs.

'When she walked out of the hospital, searches and appeals for information had been made, the police and authorities had been involved. But she had never come forward. Ann and Steven applied to adopt me in January and I was handed over, the papers signed two months later, on 12 March. My parents never made a big fuss of my birthday, in December. Too near to Christmas they said. I checked back over my diaries. We always did something special on 12 March, went out for a meal, to the movies. They never said what we were celebrating.'

'The day we brought you home...' Steven had said. 'We both said it was the happiest day of our lives.'

Later, Natasha found out that they adopted her because they thought they couldn't have children of their own.

'What's your worst fear?' Adam's voice was almost too quiet to hear.

She stared into the lens. 'What I might be capable of. What I carry in my blood, that I can never know about.'

He lowered the camera, just a fraction, so she knew he wasn't looking at her through it any more, was keeping it there to let her talk. 'That's what makes you keep such a tight rein on yourself.'

'I suppose.'

'Do you ever let your guard down?'

'I honestly don't know. When I've had a few drinks maybe.'

'There's better ways than that you know.'

Now, face to face with him, she couldn't believe what she'd told him. She stood up, felt strangely light and floaty. The robe felt peculiar on her. It was completely dry now, brushed against her skin.

She took the camera from Adam's hand, lifted it to her eyes, focused on him and clicked.

Then his hand came forward against the lens and there was blackness. He took it off her, set it down, his eyes never leaving hers.

It was as if she was so used to having the camera in front of him he forgot that it was disconcerting to be gazed at so directly for minutes on end. It was as though he was challenging her. Who would be the first to look away?

She lost, intentionally. But it felt like she'd won something.

She went back into the dark room to change. She

stripped off the robe and fastened her bra. As she bent down to pull on her tights her eye caught something in the bin. Photographic prints and negatives. The black and whites of Bethany as Ophelia. The ones Adam had said were no good. Slowly, she lifted them out.

That eerie soft focus again. But this time something even more eerie, something that sent through Natasha's body a shock of coldness.

The shadow Adam had spoken of. It took the form of a luminous outline of a figure, what looked very much like a girl with long hair, lying alongside Bethany in the water, partially concealed by her, indistinct but identifiable. Like an after image, an aura. Like a ghost, invisible to the naked eye, but captured somehow by the photographic process. Was that really what she was seeing? Bethany's ghost? Or the ghost of someone else?

Twenty-Six

There was an e-mail from Toby saying he'd had a 'ferret' around in the British Library's Pre-Raphaelite papers. He suggested they meet for coffee on Wednesday.

Steven was going to be in London for his sponsorship meetings on Wednesday. She could see him afterwards.

Just after nine-thirty, Abby called from her new office to give Natasha her direct line.

'How's it going?'

'Great fun. I'm organizing a celebrity tennis tournament.'

'How come?'

'To promote cement.'

Natasha didn't even try to get her head around that one.

The tournament was on Wednesday so Abby wasn't free. They made hazy arrangements to meet up soon.

Then Mary called, on her way back from Gloucester.

'John Junior died in his forties. Left a will bequeathing all his worldly goods to his wife Helen. They had one daughter, also Helen, who married a chap called Davies, sadly. There's millions of them. I'll see if I can hit the jackpot, but I'm not promising.'

'Thanks Mary. That's brilliant.'

'If I have no luck I'll try Jeanette's little sister, Eleanor. Had a quick scout for a birth certificate but no go I'm afraid.'

'No need to be so thorough,' Natasha said. 'Just go straight for a marriage.' Before her pregnancy Mary would have worked that out for herself, and come up with some useful suggestions of her own. Natasha despised herself for feeling annoyed and disappointed that Mary's mind wasn't totally on the job.

'I popped round the night before last,' Mary said. 'You were out.'

'I was.'

'And?'

'And ... nothing. Much. I agreed to pose, for

192

Adam Mason.'

Mary gave a squeal. 'You agreed to what? No ... hang on a minute. More important question, when you say pose...?'

'As a Greek goddess. I lost my head. Not literally, as it turned out.'

'About time too. And?'

'Like I said. Nothing.'

Mary gave an exaggerated sigh.

Now, talking about it, Natasha was totally disapproving of herself. 'He's a client.'

'So?'

'He's employed me to find his girlfriend, remember?'

'The ball's in your court, then. You could be a little less conscientious than usual, couldn't you? Tell him you've done your best.'

'I might have no choice.'

'Look, Nat, I know you always get wrapped up in your work but it's more than that this time, isn't it? Why are you letting it get to you so much?'

'Am I?'

'You know you are.'

Natasha pushed her fingers against her closed eyes. The true answer to Mary's question? Because Bethany was a girl who had disappeared and this time Natasha was old enough to do something about it.

'I suppose I'm used to dealing with people who died a long time ago. It's much easier. You can't have any influence on the past.'

'Oh, I don't know. I thought that's what you historians did all the time.'

Natasha did some tidying round the house,

then picked up Jeanette's diary. Just in case there was anything else. She could use some of Jeanette's straight talking anyway.

I shall describe a charming gentleman we met in Hyde Park today. He's a barrister. Over six foot and walks well, brown hair a little wavy and lighter moustache. Very nice blue-grey eyes. His nose is not exactly perfect but the *tout ensemble* is really very pleasing, even if he does have the unromantic surname of Brown.

There were more details of how Mr Brown's path crossed those of the Marshalls on their Sunday walks, until Mrs Marshall took the step of telling him how to obtain a ticket for her husband's Academy lectures and demonstrations. Brown was invited back to Savile Row for tea afterwards.

Mama asked me today what I think of his attentions. I dare not yet commit myself to an opinion though he seemed very delighted to see me last night. But what is to be will be and it is no use worrying oneself about it.
  Little Eleanor in bed with a fever which passed by morning, thank the Lord.

Natasha realised it was one of the few references Jeanette had made to her sister.

All invited to an At Home at the Ford Maddox Browns. The flood of artistics in everything hideous in the way of costume was startling. The ladies sad and the gentlemen mad looking. Janey

Morris and her daughters were there, the former looked very well I thought in cream crepe trimmed with old gold satin and made high to the throat, a white Indian shawl over her shoulders. When her face is quiet it is fine and fascinating, but when she speaks she is spoilt.

Pre-Raphaelite chroniclers would love to get their hands on this stuff. Bethany had some great material if she did write a biography of Lizzie.

Papa, Mama and I were bid to visit Mr Rossetti's studio. The paintings were different to any others I have seen and altogether I admired them very much. Though I cannot understand this fascination for murderous queens and witches and such like. The best was Proserpina. She is dark and Papa said a glorified portrait of Mrs Morris. The face is wonderfully painted but her figure is not nice; so long waisted. Mr Rossetti was very agreeable and talked very cheerfully and was very nice altogether, but he looks more baggy and untidy than ever, and a great deal older. If it were not for his eyes, which are very observant, one would never take him for a genius.

   After we left, Papa told me the astonishing news that Mr Rossetti wants to take my face for the head of Joan of Arc if Papa and I both consent. He is very much struck with my appearance, and evidently from the way Papa and Mama grin, said something very flattering which I have not been told. I should not have thought my style sufficiently melancholy.

It was not to be, Jeanette wrote a few pages later.

Mr R fell ill I am sorry to say. Papa accompanied Mr R's brother, William, to Birchington and returned the next day. He told us Mr Rossetti was absolutely blue when he got there, dying from blood poisoning arising from congested kidneys. Papa packed him in wet sheets and in five hours brought him round, though doubts he will ever be fit for anything again. He is more plague than profit, poor creature.

A telegram arrived informing Papa that Mr Rossetti is dead. Such a waste. It is very sad to think of. If he had led a good and proper life he might have flourished. Let us hope he is happy now.

I was sufficiently idiotic to shed a few bitter tears of woe at being made to stay away from this evening's lecture. The impropriety of hearing Papa describe the muscles of the trunk in Mr Brown's presence is considered too awfully shocking.

Natasha closed the book. No wonder Jeanette found the Pre-Raphaelite models so scandalous and exotic. Over a hundred years ago, they spent hours unchaperoned in artists' studios, when regular courting couples had to be practically engaged before they were allowed to hold hands.

She stared ahead. Her appointment programme was still open on the screen. Coffee with Toby highlighted for 10 January. Steven had said

Marcus was flying out to Canada the first week in January. He wasn't going to call her before he went.

The phone rang. She let the answering machine take the call. She heard Adam's voice.

'There's something I want you to see. Are you free this evening?'

She snatched up the receiver. 'I'm busy I'm afraid.' A lie.

'Too bad.'

'What is it you want to show me?'

'A surprise.'

'I hate surprises.'

'So don't come.'

Twenty-Seven

Adam had told her to meet him outside Exeter College at seven o'clock. She parked round the corner on Broad Street and walked up Turl Street to the main entrance, the towering, studded gateway in the stone wall. A cut-out door within the door was open onto the Front Quad.

She'd only been there a second when Adam came through it, as if he'd been watching for her. In the dim light his ruffled hair seemed fairer than ever against his black clothes.

'This had better be worth it.'

'I hope you think it is.'

They walked along the gravel path round the perfectly manicured lawn, the grass like velvet in

197

the darkness, past the ivy clad, seventeenth-century terrace towards the French Gothic chapel then on to the castellated Hall. A small door led to a short flight of stone steps and onto a carpeted corridor. There was a pegboard with the heading 'Meeting and Conference Rooms', to the right of it a signpost pointing to 'Morris Room'.

'Close your eyes,' Adam said, just as he'd asked her at the studio. She let him guide her forward, then to the left, his hand on her arm. She took another step and felt him restrain her. She heard the creak of a door hinge. Light turned the insides of her eyelids rosy.

'Open.'

They were at the threshold of a long room at the end of which were tall narrow arched windows draped in dark red velvet. The walls were off white, and chairs stood in the corners, beautiful wrought-iron thrones with gothic arched backs, fleur de lis motifs and plush red velvet seats to match the drapes. Instead of the spotlights you'd expect in such a place, the gallery was lit only by candlelight. Wrought-iron candelabras were suspended from each end of the ceiling, tall ones stood haphazardly on the floor, arms twisting upwards. The whole effect was witchy, bordering on the macabre.

The photographs were displayed in rows, the light flickering over them, emphasizing their mysterious, eerie quality.

The pictures of Bethany took up half of one wall, photographs from both the files from the dark room, framed in simple silver frames. At the opposite side were the ones of Diana. Natasha recognized other pictures, the girl with a harp, the Lady of Shalott, Christine standing in the ring of fire.

'What do you think?'

She could feel his eyes on her. 'It's stunning.' She turned to him. 'I mean it. I've never seen anything like it.'

He took her by the shoulders, swivelled her slightly.

She met her own eyes, midnight black, staring out from the photograph. The expression in them rapt, pensive, alarmingly seductive. Focused on Adam. The wet robe like a second skin.

'It's not finished yet. There are more pictures still to go up. Captions. But I wanted you to see it all first.'

She looked at him. Found she was flattered and also unsettled.

She walked away from him down the room, her footsteps loud and hollow, the candle flames dancing in her wake. There must be nearly a hundred of them. How long had it taken to light them all?

Just a week now until the exhibition opened. Until it was a month since Bethany had disappeared.

She turned round. 'Where's…?'

Adam took a step back towards the door, closed it and leant back against it, as if barring her way.

Natasha looked sideways, saw what she'd been searching for. Bethany as *Ophelia*. She was hidden behind the door. The print was enlarged to twice the size of the other pictures, the vibrant colours a contrast to the monochrome.

'The idea is you see her only as you leave the room,' Adam said.

She still couldn't work it out. Why *would* someone hide behind a false identity and at the same time allow themselves to be put on such public display? As she gazed at the photograph she remembered the way Bethany had mentioned the exhibition as if she'd rather not talk about it.

Had she agreed just to please Adam, because she wanted to help his career? Because she loved him? She'd waited, hadn't she? Not left until he'd completed his collection.

Natasha looked around again. 'Are the pictures all yours?'

'No. Shall we go now?'

She helped him extinguish the candles one by one, cupping her palm over them, the smoke wafting up, a potent smell that reminded her of bonfire night. Then they were standing in semi-darkness, just a taper of light from the corridor.

On the way back down the stairs, Adam knocked at a door in the foyer that said 'Administration'. She heard him tell someone he was leaving. 'Goodnight, Adam. See you tomorrow.' The voice well spoken, young, female.

As they walked out through the gateway Jake Romilly was coming in the opposite direction, his long coat open and flapping around him. He stalked past, ignoring them both.

'Come for a drink with me,' Adam said.

They cut up Castle Street, into the broad boulevard of St Giles. Adam lit a cigarette, but it was so cold it looked as if they were both smoking, their breath transforming into white mist.

Young groups loitered in doorways, sharing burgers and cans of coke, older couples sauntered hand in hand, peering into darkened estate agents' windows.

'Eagle and Child all right?'

'Perfect.'

'Oh, I nearly forgot. I brought something for you.' Adam fished a piece of paper from his pocket. 'You seemed strangely interested in my phone bill.'

Natasha glanced at him, then took the bill as they walked. No more than three dozen numbers were listed.

'I generally use the one at the office,' Adam explained.

'The long call Bethany made?'

'Only one on 14 December. Half an hour.'

Natasha recognized the number. The British Library.

That piece of information was added to the other pieces which together were starting to make up a picture of Bethany over the days before she disappeared. Nearly drowning in a river in an antique gown. Calling the Public Record Office for information on Lizzie Siddal. Closeted in a bedroom on the phone to the British Library. To do with Lizzie again? What did it all add up to? What was the connection to the Marshalls?

At least Natasha would find out soon enough what information the British Library held on Lizzie. She'd been one step ahead there, which was a good feeling. Maybe she was on the right track after all.

The pub was heaving with students and arty types blocking the narrow flagged hallways, pints of lager and gins in their hands. Natasha shouldered her way past the oak and glass partitions which divided the inn into its distinctive, Victorian parlour-like alcoves. She paid for a lager and vodka at the bar.

Despite the crowds, Adam had found a seat in one of the alcoves by a cast iron fireplace. She squeezed in beside him.

He nodded hello to a couple of girls who came to sit opposite by the curtained windows. They were dressed to look older then they were, painted children, with what looked like native American charms, feathers and bones and teeth, around their throats.

'You come here often?' Natasha gave Adam a wry smile.

'My temporary local. I like it.'

'So do I.'

'I thought it was the kind of place you'd feel at home,' Adam said.

A lanky student came and sat down on a stool at the other side of Natasha, opened a tabloid newspaper, then, eyeing Adam's lighter on the table, asked if he could borrow it. 'Sure.' Adam reached across Natasha to hold the flame to the man's cigarette. She could feel his thigh pressing into hers, his arm against her breasts. He was doing it on purpose. There was a little round scar on his temple which looked like it might have been left over from a childhood bout of chicken pox.

202

He flicked off the lighter and drew back, not quite the distance he'd been before. She could feel the warmth of his skin through her jeans and shirt.

'Tolkien and C. S. Lewis used to hang out here,' she said. 'Rossetti and Morris would no doubt have popped in a few times.'

'Don't you wish you lived a hundred years ago?'

'Sometimes.'

'I do.' She half expected him to give the reasons everyone did, talk about technology and how busy people were and the break down of families. But instead he added, 'It must change your whole outlook. Growing up with the words of Shakespeare and Lord Byron in your head rather than the lyrics of pop songs.'

'Oh, I don't know. "I Should Be So Lucky". I can relate to that. Why did you want to become a photographer?'

'Some grandiose idea of preserving beauty that otherwise would be lost forever.' He turned to her. 'My grandmother had this big round hat box full of crystals, all different shapes and sizes, that came from chandeliers. At Christmas she hung them from the tree instead of baubles. They looked amazing against the dark green branches, like huge snowflakes or raindrops that never fell. My grandfather was a painter and decorator, so it's a mystery how she came by them. She told me she was a Fairy Grandmother, and she visited all the children, taking away their tears.'

'That's a lovely story.'

He looked at her. 'Except I never believed it.'

A thought flickered through her mind, barely articulated but there none the less, and dangerous. Bethany must have been crazy to leave him. She didn't deserve him, the efforts he had been prepared to go to to win her back. Natasha knew that the sudden upswelling of anger she felt for Bethany was irrational, fired by her own prejudices and experiences. She quashed it firmly. She needed to go on liking Bethany, otherwise she'd never summon the energy and resolve to keep on trying to find her.

'When I was about seven,' Adam went on, 'I borrowed my father's camera, tried, over and over again, to take a photograph of that tree, but I couldn't quite get it right. My grandmother said that it just went to show how clever God was. That all the brilliant scientists in the world couldn't create a camera as good as the human eye. I was sure I could make the world look more beautiful than the way we see it. Or different at least.'

He reached out and with his finger brushed a tendril of her hair that lay against her shoulder. 'Rossetti was obsessed with hair,' he said. 'To him it was the most sensual, erotic thing. But it's faces that fascinate me. Eyes and lips, skin. Why did you come tonight?'

'I didn't want to go home.'

'There's no one waiting for you there?'

'Only Boris.' She felt suddenly vulnerable, picked up the vodka for something to do.

Adam ran a finger down his beer bottle, tracing a drop of moisture. 'My flat's just round the corner.'

She drained her drink. 'I should get going.'

'I wasn't inviting you. Just passing a comment.'

She felt a flush of anger that she very much hoped wouldn't look like a blush. 'I don't think so.' She picked up her bag.

'What's the hurry anyway? No one's going to miss you.'

No one's going to miss you. Something about his choice of words, just the truth of them, perhaps, angered her even more. Also frightened her. The implication: who'd come looking for you?

'I've an early start tomorrow. Train to catch.'

'Where to?'

'London.'

'To visit the Queen?'

She looked at him. 'A contact. I asked him to research the Marshalls.'

'And has he found anything?'

'I'll be able to answer that tomorrow.'

'I'll walk you to your car.'

'Don't worry. I can take care of myself.'

They were outside the pub. 'Thanks for showing me the pictures. Goodnight.' She set off to walk.

He fell in step beside her.

She resisted the urge to shout, 'Leave me alone', remembered the voice on the answering machine. *Why can't you leave her alone?*

They were walking along a dark passageway by Merton College. Adam pulled her against him.

'What are you—?'

His hand was over her mouth. Then his lips. She felt his arm go round her, his hand cradling the back of her head. Her muscles seemed to soften, turn to water. He kissed her, pressed his leg hard up between hers, rubbed himself against her, took each of her hands in his, trapped them down at her sides, interlaced his fingers with hers. Then he slipped one hand underneath her coat, untucked her shirt and slid his palm across her back and under her bra, the caress soft and dry. She put her arms up around him, the unfamiliar leanness of his body.

The alley was deserted.

She pulled back, turned and walked away, forced herself not to look over her shoulder.

She couldn't have said if she was leaving on the grounds of common sense or out of some instinct for self preservation, or because she knew how wretched she would feel tomorrow if she let things go any further. She ignored the other voice inside her head, the one saying tomorrow may never come. And if it did, to let it take care of itself.

She'd set the alarm for seven-thirty and had just dropped off to sleep when the telephone rang. She rubbed at her eyes. The clock on the chest of drawers said it was just after five.

'Did I wake you?' It was Adam.

'Course not,' she said sarcastically. 'I've been up ages.'

'So have I.'

'This is getting to be a habit.'

'I warned you I had an addictive personality. What train did you say you were catching?'

'I didn't.'

'There's something I haven't told you.' She

waited. 'I need to see you again.'

'I'm leaving for the station at seven,' she lied.

'Call me when you're on your way.' He gave her the number of the flat in Oxford.

She watched the fingers on the clock, turned on the radio and heard the early morning shipping forecast. Gale warnings.

Twenty-Eight

The ringing at the other end of the phone was competing with the rattle of the train, the tinny hiss and thump of a personal stereo and the conversation that was going on at the table across the carriage between a young bespectacled man in a sharp pinstriped suit and a middle-aged woman with lots of blue eye-shadow and a briefcase.

Five, six, eight, ten times the phone had rung. Why was she holding on so long? Adam obviously wasn't at home.

The train had passed Reading, so she guessed it was around half past nine. Maybe he'd left for the studio already. She had her finger on the off button when the ringing stopped. 'Hello.' He sounded annoyed. She heard a female voice in the background. It sounded like Angie.

'It's Natasha. I'm sorry if I disturbed you. But you said...'

'You're on the train?' His tone had changed, was warm now. 'I was planning on coming up to town too, need to pick up some clean clothes.'

Of course you do!
'When are you free?'
'I'm meeting someone at eleven. I should be done by one.' Silence for a moment. 'Meet me outside the Tate at two.'

She knew that Toby would be waiting for her in the restaurant of the British Library, having ordered a pot of tea and warm scones with melted butter.

In many ways the Library was the perfect environment for him, like an extension of his personality, a juxtaposition of the new and the old.

Strangely tranquil, a modern cathedral to knowledge, you could sense the weight of the important material held within it. The great rooms, all white pillars, pale burnished wood and muted carpets, with rows of flickering computer screens sitting on desks inlaid with green leather. The foyers and corridors were open plan, structured like enormous balconies, so you could stand on the top floor and look down on the wide hall with its sweeping staircase. And through the centre of the building, dominating all floors, a column of smoky glass, holding old books, incongruously antiquated symbols of the library's purpose.

Not everything was sleek and computerised though. Sometimes it was necessary to cross reference in the original catalogues, a painstaking task, and you also needed special permission to see some of the more valuable documents. Which was why Toby, who knew his way around

208

blindfold and had been granted access to almost everything, often did the legwork for Natasha.

He was sitting in the café area on the second floor, amid chrome furniture and subdued lighting, the tables decorated with vases of single, long-stemmed red roses.

He beamed when he saw her, kissed her on both cheeks and pulled out a chair.

'You look wonderful,' he said, and she felt guilty because she'd chosen her outfit with someone else in mind. Beneath a leather jacket she was wearing a fishtail skirt in deep purple and an embroidered black muslin shirt. She had a black feather boa flung around her neck.

She was keen for him to tell her what he'd found but he had a way of dispelling impatience. He ordered tea, placed a pat of butter and small plate of toasted teacakes in front of her. 'Eat up,' he said, sounding like someone's dad.

'Well,' she said through a mouthful of teacake, 'what's up?'

'Your Jeanette and John Marshall were interesting characters,' he began, heaving his bulging briefcase onto the table. It was made of battered tan leather with straps and buckles, like an old-fashioned school satchel. He pulled out a wad of papers, a laptop and a large red and black notebook, the sort with small feint squares covering the pages. Natasha watched with fondness as he hit a few buttons on the keyboard, fumbled through his papers. He always seemed disorganized but had never once failed to come up with the goods.

'There's a collection, called the Ashley Library,

which contains letters to and from Rossetti and his circle,' he said. 'They were gathered by a fellow called Thomas Wise who was interested in the Pre-Raphaelites but also had a reputation as a bit of a forger. He supposedly managed to get hold of an actual leaf from the notebook that was exhumed from Lizzie Siddal's grave, but that's by the by. Dr Marshall features rather prominently in the papers. He was Rossetti's medical adviser for many years, was also friendly with Ford Maddox Brown and Rossetti's brother, William. Rossetti seems to have been a difficult and demanding patient, and never settled his bills on time. Same old story. Struggling artist who only found real fame and fortune after his death.'

'Must be a real pain that,' Natasha commented.

'Knowing you'll be worth more dead than alive? Enough to make you top yourself.'

She swallowed hard. 'But the thing is, you never know if it's glory or obscurity that awaits you.'

'Whereas the rest of us mere mortals know it's just obscurity. Maybe poor old Dr Marshall would have been quite happy to be forgotten.' Toby grinned. 'Anyway. There seems to have been a mutual respect between him and his esteemed patient. There's a letter from Rossetti to Marshall, consoling him after the death of his daughter, Ada, and there's another in which Rossetti offers his support to Marshall's application for the chair of anatomy at the Royal Academy. The application must have been successful as there's another letter congratulating him.' Toby leant forward a little. 'Marshall was the doctor summoned by Ford Maddox Brown on the night of Lizzie Siddal's death.' He looked up. 'Know that?' Natasha shook her head, wanting him to go on. 'Marshall was called back two days after Lizzie died to examine her body, because Rossetti had got it into his head that she wasn't dead at all, only in an unconscious stupor due to the drugs ... poor guy. I've always thought it really gruesome, how they used to leave corpses lying about the house for days.'

Natasha agreed. 'Did Dr Marshall give any verdict on the cause of death.'

'Can't find it, unfortunately. His opinions on Lizzie's state of health beforehand are well recorded though. He wrote to Rossetti telling him that there appeared to be nothing physically wrong with her, said her weakness was due to what we'd now call stress, I suppose. He packed her off to the Riviera and to the spa in Matlock for recuperation. There's a letter from Georgina Burne-Jones saying that she wondered how it was possible for Lizzie to suffer so much without developing a specific disease. She was diagnosed by another doctor as having curvature of the spine and I came across a suggestion that she had a Victorian form of anorexia. Seems to me that Marshall was probably right about a mental or psychosomatic illness though. It would make sense that her stress or depression or whatever was made worse when her baby was stillborn, wouldn't it?' Natasha nodded. 'Enter Dr Marshall again. He attended the birth and then was called out by Rossetti when Lizzie was distressed afterwards. There's a letter from Georgina Burne-Jones saying how Lizzie would sit rocking an empty cradle by the fire, saying "Hush, you'll wake it". All in all, it seems pretty conclusive that she did commit suicide. Evelyn Waugh, Violet Hunt, Hall Caine, they all agreed, though they're all novelists with an eye to a story, aren't they? The consensus is that Lizzie had become so paranoid that every time Rossetti left her she imagined him with another woman, and if she was in a depression after the baby... There are also claims she left a note, either pinned to her nightgown or beside her bed.'

Here Toby paused to take a bite of teacake, chewed it slowly. Natasha's mind went into overdrive. Is this what Bethany had found out during that call to the British Library? Had someone told her what was in the Ashley Papers? Natasha didn't want Lizzie to have killed herself, let alone left a *note*. Moreover she didn't want to think Bethany knew that Lizzie might have left a note. A note was the one way you'd know an overdose wasn't accidental.

A note was also one parallel too many.

'What did it say?'

'No one seems sure, which I suppose you could say is proof nobody ever saw anything. She either condemned Rossetti, or asked him to care for her brother. Hall Caine described a train journey when Rossetti said the note had left a scar on his heart that would never be healed.'

Natasha realised Toby was watching her, waiting for a reaction. She reached across the table and squeezed his hand. 'You're a star. I can't believe you managed to find so much in such a short time.'

212

She was touched by the way his face lit up at her praise, then turned to a worried frown. 'I can't see how it brings you any nearer to this girl you're trying to find.'

She sighed. 'Not immediately, no. But I'll tell you something interesting. If I believed for a second that Bethany was a direct descendant of Marshall, I'd almost believe something else.'

Because she was enlisting his professional help she'd felt obliged to brief him on the details of the investigation. Now she repeated the story Bethany had told Adam, recited to her by her grandmother, about the picture of *Beata Beatrix* being drawn from Lizzie's corpse.

Toby pulled a face. 'I've never heard that one. How grisly.'

'It would explain things though, wouldn't it? Marshall was there on the night Lizzie died. You said yourself that two days later Rossetti didn't believe she was really dead at all. And more to the point, that Marshall was called back then. He could have seen something. Rossetti in the process of painting her, deludedly thinking her still alive. If Bethany was related to Jeanette Marshall, it would be easy to assume that the tale had been handed down through the generations, from someone who was actually there. Maybe Rossetti had Lizzie embalmed or something. That would explain how she came to be beautiful six years later, when her coffin was opened.'

She'd been talking quickly, her imagination running away with itself, and Toby was looking at her dubiously. He made a bridge with his fingers. 'I do wonder if insanity is infectious.' He grinned.

'Seriously. I mean, Rossetti himself suffered a kind of derangement after Lizzie died. Dr Marshall prescribed him the same drugs Lizzie took, and died from, chloral and laudanum.' He started rummaging in his papers again. 'See what I mean?' Toby said. 'There's a letter from Rossetti to Marshall forgiving him for bringing him back to life after *he'd* tried to kill himself.' Toby paused, glanced at Natasha. 'Perhaps suicide is contagious too.'

Twenty-Nine

Natasha caught the tube to Embankment. She walked along Millbank, saw Adam long before he saw her. It seemed only minutes ago that he'd kissed her, and at the same time it could have been weeks.

He was leaning on the railings, staring down at the Thames. Just as she had been the second time they'd met, in Oxford. It was hard to believe it was the same river. The water was the colour of steel, and the weak sunlight was making no impression on it. On the opposite bank, random electric lights emanated from a jungle of tower-block windows.

It was surprisingly warm for January though, as London sometimes was. People were strolling along the pavements as if it were spring.

Steven had told her, when she was little, how large cities created their own microclimates, so that if you travelled a few miles, just into the suburbs even, the weather would be quite different. It was one thing, accepting manmade streets and buildings, but the knowledge that once created they had the power to subvert nature made them seem sinister.

She'd better watch it. She'd brought *The Pre-Raphaelite Dream* to read on the train, intending to go through it more thoroughly and had obviously been getting too involved with Rossetti and Morris and their band, picking up their mistrust of the modern world, the way they saw cities, factories and machines as corrupting, evil entities and wanting to retreat into a world of Medieval chivalry and arcane mystical religions. But then she'd always been like that to some degree. You couldn't study history, live your life with one foot always in the past, if a part of you didn't yearn to go back.

So long as she could take her sports car, iMac, MP3 player and mobile phone with her of course.

She went to stand next to Adam, not quite touching. The water was a long way down, shifting and treacherous. There was one small boat, making slow progress up towards London Bridge. The putt-putt of its engine kept cutting out.

Adam turned to face her. He slipped his arm around her waist, kissed her. The shock she felt was like an electrical charge that left her a little dizzy and disoriented.

'Am I late?'

He shook his head. 'I was early. Didn't want to keep you waiting.'

He looked at her with his direct gaze. It would be so easy to believe that she was the exclusive recipient, if she'd not seen evidence to the contrary, seen him behave exactly the same way at the studio, with Angie and Diana. He was one of those men who'd perfected the knack of making every woman feel the only one in the world. A useful skill for a photographer, perhaps. But exactly the type she could do without. *Keep telling yourself that.*

They walked back the way she'd come, towards the Tate.

'You never explained,' he said. 'Why you don't wear a watch.'

She was surprised he'd remembered that. 'Something to do with too much static charge in my body.'

'I can believe it. What happens?'

'The time goes haywire.'

'Really?'

'It's kind of freaky. Least, I thought it was when I was a kid.'

'That's when you don't want to be different. When you're older, different's good.'

'Sometimes. Sometimes not.'

Groups of young people were sitting on the steps of the gallery, knocking back cans of Coke, eating hot dogs they'd bought from a stand opposite.

Adam put his arm around Natasha's shoulder, directed her down one of the long white corridors that spidered off to the galleries.

She'd a pretty good idea where they were heading. No doubt he'd thought she'd be

216

interested, wanted her to see the paintings that had influenced his photographs. She was, but just now she wished they were somewhere else, anywhere.

She saw *Ophelia* immediately they entered the long, narrow gallery, hung at eye level on the right side of the room, halfway along the pale blue painted wall.

Beata Beatrix was hanging at the far end. Natasha walked across and stood before it.

There was a radiance about the picture, akin to the soft focus in Adam's photographs, as if light was shining through it like a stained glass window. It made the edges of Lizzie's red hair glow. Lizzie, or Beatrice, had her eyes closed, her face tilted upwards in an attitude of surrender, with her hands open in her lap to receive the white poppies. Natasha stared at the heavy lidded eyes, the pallor of her skin, and almost supine repose of her body, despite its erect position. You could imagine, all too easily, how he might have taken her dead body, sat her up and tilted her face, allowed her limp hands to rest just so.

'They should be asphodels, not poppies,' Adam whispered in her ear, making her jump.

'Why's that?'

'"My regret follows you to the grave."' Natasha looked at him. 'The Language of Flowers. Bethany was into all that.'

She turned back to the picture, seeing only the bouquet in Highgate. Fresh poppies.

Then, suddenly, she remembered the bouquet Adam said was in the jam jar beside the diary the morning Bethany went away. 'Which flowers did she leave you?' She tried to sound casual.

'They were purple, surrounded by lots of grasses and leaves, pretty. Then that was her job.'

'But what were the flowers, do you know?'

'I'm not very good at that kind of thing. African Violets maybe.' He looked at her.

'Just asking.'

He nodded towards the painting. 'There's something really disturbing about it, have you noticed? She's supposed to be praying, or contemplating heaven, and there's that phallic symbol pointing at her face.

Natasha hadn't spotted it before, but she did now. The sundial in the background was incredibly suggestive.

She moved down the room to stand beside a little family who were admiring *Ophelia.*

'She had to lie in a bath of water whilst the artist painted her,' the mother was saying quietly, as if she was telling a bedtime story. 'There were candles underneath to keep the water warm, but the picture took so long to paint that they all went out, and the water grew so cold poor Lizzie caught pneumonia. Her father was terribly upset and sued the artist.'

'How much did he get?' The little boy asked, with a glee that made Natasha smile.

'I'm not sure. It wouldn't have been as much as your pocket money. It was a long time ago.'

'Why didn't she say she was freezing?' the girl asked.

'She didn't want to ruin the picture.'

It had never struck Natasha before that paintings could be much more lifelike than photographs.

218

She glanced at Adam, watching her from a bench in the middle of the room and she realised then how brilliantly he had replicated it all in his photograph. Bethany's dress could easily have been the one Lizzie had worn, and Adam had managed to recreate the setting perfectly, down to the reeds protruding from the water and the branch of the tree that overhung it. You could almost imagine he'd come to sit on the same bank just a few minutes after John Everett Millais had left.

And Bethany must have stood exactly where they did now, studying the picture, staring into Lizzie's eyes. She must be a talented actress. For in Adam's photographs she had caught the expression exactly, the wildness and despairing sorrow.

Unless of course, there had been no need for her to pretend.

The caption beside the painting listed the abundance of plants and flowers, explaining how Millais had taken pains to be accurate and true to nature, explaining also the symbolism of them.

The willow, forsaken love; the nettle growing amongst its branches, pain; the daisies near Ophelia's right hand, innocence; the pansies floating on the dress, love in vain.

The chain of violets around her neck, death of the young.

Violets, not African Violets. But maybe in December the African ones were all that were available.

Bethany and Adam had come here together. Natasha almost sensed her now, sitting in the space between them. If she turned she almost believed she'd see her.

Lizzie. Elizabeth. Beth. Bethany.

Why hadn't she spotted that before? Bethany probably wasn't her real name either.

'You can see why they've put those two pictures together.' Adam gave a short nod towards the picture that hung above *Ophelia*.

It was of a fragile boy stretched out on a narrow rumpled couch in a garret, his head and arm lolling off the edge. He was dressed in a white frilled shirt and beautiful blue silk breeches that lent a sickly, lurid blue-grey hue to the painting. His red hair curled around his wan face.

Natasha recognised it from the book she had at home, but went to read the description anyway.

Chatterton, by Henry Wallis.
Thomas Chatterton was a poet whose spurious medieval histories copied out in a fake hand on old parchment, his melancholy life and youthful suicide, fascinated artists and writers of the nineteenth century. Wordsworth called him the 'sleepless soul that perished in his pride'.

If Bethany had stood here then she too had read it, been bombarded with those two haunting, beautiful images of suicide...

'You can see the fascination with dying young,' Adam said quietly. 'Rossetti was obsessed with the idea of earthly love cut short by early death, having a lover to worship in heaven. Like Dante and Beatrice.' What was he saying? That the idea appealed to him too? 'The fantasy came true for

Rossetti. I've often wondered if it lived up to expectations.'

She stood up.

He grabbed her hand then, aggressive, his fingers tightening on her wrist. 'There's something I wanted to tell you.'

'Let go of me. You're hurting.'

He released her. She went to sit down on a bench, shaken, keeping a distance, her eyes fixed ahead.

It was then that she noticed the small water-colour that hung to the left of *Ophelia*.

It was Turner's painting of the Bridge of Sighs in Venice.

Jake Romilly had taken a picture of Bethany beneath the bridge with the same name in Oxford. This must have been where he had the idea. They'd probably all come here then. Bethany, Adam, Jake Romilly.

Adam must have followed the direction of her gaze. 'They called Waterloo Bridge the Bridge of Sighs for a while, because there were so many suicides there.'

She stared at him. Then she remembered the conversation they'd just been having. Adam was only explaining a probable reason for the picture's presence beside the other two, why a pretty watercolour of a bridge should hang beside two paintings of people who'd killed themselves.

But she couldn't rid herself of the thought: He knows about the note. He's known all along.

This was all a trap, some kind of trick. He was toying with her, in some horrible, cruel way she couldn't begin to understand.

221

Adam's voice reached her. 'When I came here with Bethany she said something to me. We were talking about how the Pre-Raphaelites believed that evil was female in origin, that beautiful women corrupted and destroyed the men who loved them. And Bethany said to me, "That's what I'll do to you. I can't help it. I have a bad heart."'

Thirty

'Let's get out of here.' Natasha led the way back through the gallery, following the signs to the café and restaurant, under the rotunda, down the stairs to the basement. She chose the café, judging the service would be more prompt. She and Adam ordered two bottles of beer that were plonked on the counter immediately.

Adam lit up. 'What do you think she meant?'

She looked at him. 'I've no idea.' But she was thinking: Bethany's secrecy, her sudden departure. What did she have to hide?... All along it was Adam she'd been suspicious of, when perhaps, if there *was* some crime or mystery behind Bethany's disappearance, he was not the one responsible? Unless of course, he was being very clever, this was just one more lie, another dimension to whatever game he was playing. 'Are you quite sure she didn't mean it as a joke?'

He was easing the corner of the damp label off the beer bottle, the way you took a price tag off a present, so it left no trace. 'Let's talk about something else,' he said. 'I just thought you should know, that's all.'

'I wish you'd told me before.'

'Well, I didn't.'

'Is there anything else while you're at it?'

'No.'

Despite her better judgement, she'd cut back her distrust and suspicions of him to a seed of doubt. But it was like a weed, with roots too tenacious to be completely eradicated.

Her bag was on the table, the spine of the book poking out. Adam read out the title '*The Pre-Raphaelite Dream*. Do you always immerse yourself so deeply in your research?'

'I was interested in the Pre-Raphaelites when I was a teenager.'

'This job is close to your heart then.'

He was still looking into her eyes. Marcus's had been so dark, like Steven's. Natasha wasn't normally attracted to blue eyes, the colour of cold and of ice. But there was nothing cold about Adam's eyes now. They were as changeable as water that took its colour from the sky; blue, grey, green, or black as night.

She'd drunk the beer too quickly, could feel it working round her system, going to her head. She looked away from Adam. The fatal attraction of danger. She'd thought she was too sensible to fall for that.

'There's something else,' he said. He reached inside his jacket, produced a folded brown envelope. 'This arrived for her at the flat this morning.'

The frank bore the Family Records Centre logo.

Inside was a death certificate. For a man named Harold Leyburn, from Dorchester in Dorset, who died in January 1921 aged thirty-five.

After everything else Natasha couldn't take this in, make any sense of it at all.

The obvious conclusion: Bethany had started to research her family history herself and this Harold Leyburn was one of her ancestors. He could be a great-grandparent. Just three generations back.

'I'll have a contact try to track down any living descendants,' Natasha said, mechanically. It would all take time. Why the hell hadn't this come earlier?

She realised Adam hadn't passed any comment. She forced her eyes away from the certificate to look at him. 'I've been thinking,' he said. 'Maybe I should just let her go.'

'No. We can't give up looking now.'

Adam was toying with a paper flower that was stuck in a stainless steel vase in front of them. A red rose. 'The only symbol in the language of flowers that everyone understands,' he said. 'But does it mean love or the Labour party to most people now?'

'What a depressing thought.'

There were no roses in the bouquet Bethany left Adam, and she'd have access to anything she wanted surely, working in a florists?

A lot of people bring flowers, the Highgate guide had said. *Where did they get them?*

Thirty-One

Natasha met Steven in a dark, spit and sawdust tavern off Chancery Lane. He was with a trio of the team he was taking back to Italy and they'd been downing pints for the best part of the afternoon judging by the collection of empty glasses ranged around them, and the general decibel level.

Steven rose, looking steady as a rock, to kiss her. He introduced her to his colleagues, most of whom Natasha had met briefly before, in similar locations.

'V and T?' Steven said, grabbing an extra stool. 'My round.'

He came back with a double. 'You've some catching up to do.'

There was no point trying to pace yourself with this lot. 'You got your funding, I take it?' Natasha shouted above the din.

Steven raised his glass, sank half of it. 'Just a few quid short of what we wanted. It'll do for now though.'

'When do you go back?'

'Soon as possible, hey, mate?' Freddie, one of the gang, winked.

'Something you're not telling me?' Natasha said.

'Someone more like.'

'Thank you, Freddie,' said Steven.

225

'Say no more.' Natasha winked back at Freddie, to make sure he didn't for one second think he'd got one over on her. Children weren't supposed to like hearing of their parents' sexual exploits but Natasha was well used to it, unable to summon any indignation. Which worried her sometimes. Where were her scruples? But she knew none of Steven's dalliances were serious. He was like a sailor, a girl in every ruin.

'What are you doing later tonight?' Natasha asked him.

'Open to offers. Depends who's asking.'

'Me. I need a bed for the night if there's one spare.'

'We're staying at a cheap hotel in Piccadilly. I'm sure there'll be a chair,' Steven said.

'How gallant,' Freddie commented.

'For me, you idiot,' Steven said.

The hotel room was small and dingy, neon lights outside that made certain you knew you were on the outskirts of Soho. The single bed was fairly comfortable, with crisply laundered white sheets that were tucked in so tight you felt as if you were in a straightjacket.

'Are you all right?' Steven asked her.

'Fine thanks.' Which wasn't quite true.

It was still dark and the meter was already up to seventeen pounds. A scented pine tree dangled from the roof of the taxi and the smell, combined with her raging hangover, was beginning to make Natasha feel sick. She'd bought a Danish pastry but couldn't face it. The journey to Highgate seemed to be taking ages. They'd started at a crawl through Piccadilly, been swept along with the morning influx of traffic and picked up just a little speed round Regent's Park and on into Camden. Hampstead, with the Heath flanking either side of the road, had been quieter, almost desolate in comparison.

Eighteen pounds now. But at least they were moving. When Natasha had first come down to London, she'd been amazed that you were charged by time as much as distance, and could be stationary in traffic, watching the pounds clocking up.

She'd had an issue with that in her own work, since she'd set up as an independent researcher. At the College of Arms, projects had been sub-contracted out to her, with the Heralds taking a commission, handling all the client liaison, dealing with the invoicing. A similar system had operated at Generations. Natasha had worked out her own free structure, and she hated charging people if she didn't feel she'd done a good job.

Adam had one requirement only, to find Bethany, and so far she had failed. And here she was running up eighteen, no, nearly twenty pounds on expenses, clutching at straws, possibly atoning for the attraction she felt for him by working doubly hard to find his girlfriend?

She hoped she had enough change, wondered if the driver would accept a cheque, if she had her cheque book with her that was. She opened her shoulder bag, rummaged around inside, couldn't see much in the poor light. Swain's Lane was like a road in a country village, spooky, dark and winding, with just a couple of street lamps, no houses, shops or cars. Just the burial ground flanking it.

'Long way to go for a bunch of flowers,' the driver had joked in broad cockney.

Now, he reached his arm back, slid the glass partition open, allowing faint strains of country music to waft through.

'You'll not be able to get in there yet. Too early.' He threw the words over his shoulder, keeping his eyes on the road.

She realised he was talking about the cemetery, presuming she planned to take flowers to a grave. 'Do you know what time it is?'

He glanced at his watch. 'Nearly eight.' It was said with a warning note, in case she was putting on the pressure to get her there quickly. 'This the place?' he said a few moments later, flashing a look at her in the rear view mirror.

There was a painted sign. Highgate Florists. 'Great, thanks.'

It had a bowed bay window, like an old fashioned sweet shop, filled with baskets and vases of flowers. The lights were on but the sign hanging on the inside of the door was flipped over to 'closed'.

She couldn't find a knocker or bell by the shop door, so rapped her knuckles gently on the bull's eye glass. She studied the display in the bay window. It was not your typical florists, full of gaudy yellows and reds and bright blues. The muted, tasteful garlands and bouquets on show hinted at the shop's proximity to the cemetery, flowers for graves and funerals instead of for lovers and wedding bouquets.

The door was opened by a striking woman who looked to be in her early forties, but could have been older. Tall and broad shouldered with long hair a rich henna auburn, she was dressed in a flowing skirt the colours of the rainbow, and jangly silver earrings and necklaces.

'I'm sorry to trouble you, but I wondered if I might take a moment of your time,' Natasha said. 'I'm looking for someone.'

The woman smiled. 'Aren't we all?' She stood back to let Natasha in and as she closed the door behind her a tiny wind chime tinkled. The shop was filled with the heady fragrances of a summer garden.

On the wooden counter, was a little glass jug containing bunches of violets.

Natasha introduced herself and the woman held out her hand. 'Rosie,' she said. 'Appropriately, but it's my real name.' Natasha wondered how many times she'd said that. 'What can I do for you?'

Natasha handed over the photograph of Bethany. 'I wondered if this girl ever worked here?'

Rosie glanced at the picture briefly, then back at Natasha, her expression suddenly guarded. 'You're from the police?'

It was said as a statement rather than a question. It hadn't occurred to Natasha that her inquiries might be construed that way. 'No, no. I'm a genealogist.'

'I see, sorry.' Rosie looked back at the picture. 'Bethany,' she said. 'She left a month or so ago.'

Natasha felt her mouth forming a broad smile. Rosie was smiling back, and Natasha realised her own reaction must have given Rosie the impression Bethany was a long lost relative. Which was probably why Rosie's smile turned to a cautious frown when Natasha asked her next question: 'Could you tell me her full name?'

'Marshall. Bethany Marshall.'

So Bethany had lied to her employer too.

'Do you know where she lived?'

The woman was definitely eyeing her warily now. 'I'm not sure...'

'It doesn't seem right to go around giving out a person's address to anyone who asks. I know.'

Rosie smiled, disarmed. 'Well, no.'

Natasha couldn't quite understand why simply voicing someone's inner concerns helped to allay them. But Rosie bent down to a shelf underneath the till and pulled out a thick black book that looked like a ledger. 'I'll tell you what I'll do. Her details will be in the wages book. We pay staff at the end of the week, by cheque, or cash in Bethany's case as I seem to recall; she said she didn't have a bank account. There should be a phone number. I'll give it a ring, see if she minds me letting you have it. Here it is.' Rosie jotted something down on a note pad. 'Of course, it's over a month now since she left. She might have moved on. Phone's in the back. I'll just be a tick.'

She closed the book, slipped it back under the counter.

Amazed that Rosie hadn't taken it with her, Natasha leant right over and dragged it back onto the counter. She flicked back four weeks, five.

Bethany Marshall, 14 Chatham Place, London E17.

Quickly she returned the ledger to its place.

She felt an absurd urge to laugh.

She heard Rosie's footsteps.

'Sorry. Unobtainable.'

Surprise, surprise. 'Thank for trying anyway.'

Bethany had given a false name, it should have come as no shock that she'd given a false address too. It was as obvious as her choice of surname. She'd part adopted the diary writer's identity, and for her address – she'd given the flat where Rossetti and Lizzie had lived during their short, ill-fated marriage, the place Lizzie died, the place where Rossetti placed the book of poems in her coffin. Chatham Place, Blackfriars.

'I'm not sure why she left the shop,' Rosie was saying. 'She only worked here for about two months, part-time. Just came in and asked for a job one afternoon. I happened to need an extra pair of hands so I took her on to start right away. Then one evening she said she wouldn't be coming any more. That was that. Still, she did have a long way to come every morning.'

'You knew her well?'

'Not really. I'm not in here that often. She seemed a nice enough girl. A bit strange and dreamy. But she was ever so clever with the flowers, no formal training as far as I could tell, but she had a real artistic flair, an instinctive eye for colour. Katherine, my assistant, would have known her better. She's the one who generally runs the shop from day to day.'

'Could I speak to her?'

'She'll be in again on Monday.'

'Is there any way you could put me in touch with her before that?'

'She took a few days' holiday. That's why I'm in here covering today,' Rosie sounded impatient now, feeling she'd done her bit. 'I think she said she was going away for the weekend, but I suppose I could give her a ring at home, see if she's still there?' Without waiting for a reply she disappeared again.

Natasha took a deep breath.

A minute later Rosie returned, shaking her head.

'Not having much luck I'm afraid. Just an answering machine. I've left a message. The best I can do is if you leave me your number. I'll get her to call you.'

'Thank you, that would be really kind.' Natasha handed Rosie a business card, thanked her again and turned to leave. Then, on an impulse, she asked for a bunch of violets.

'I take it you know her boyfriend,' Rosie said, as if the thought had just come to her. 'Didn't care for him much myself, shifty sort of character, and too arrogant by half. Used to come and pick her up from work. He's been back here a couple of times since she left, asking if I've heard anything.'

Thirty-Two

Natasha clutched the flowers as she caught the Northern line down to Embankment. She felt adrift, thinking she understood nothing of this world or the people in it, if she could judge characters so badly. Adam and Bethany. She'd been wrong about them both.

The gusts of stale underground air that blasted through the rattling train were tempered, now and then, by a cleaner fragrance from the flowers. But it only seemed to make her feel worse.

At least the combined effects of the hangover and rage helped to stop her feeling scared. The lying bastard. Adam had told her that he didn't know where Bethany worked.

She changed onto the Circle line. Westbound would have taken her up to Paddington. There'd be a train leaving for Moreton-in-Marsh in half an hour. But she turned in the opposite direction and headed east.

She came out of the tube station at Blackfriars into a disorientating labyrinth of poorly lit underpasses, concrete paving slabs and tunnels, graffiti sprawled across the walls. The ground was littered with discarded crisp packets and sweet wrappers, apple cores and crushed soft drink cans.

She was going against the flow, weaving through waves of City workers with briefcases.

She came out high above the river and inched forward, looking down, feeling the strange sensation you experienced at the top of high buildings, as if you weren't quite in control of your own actions.

Natasha knew this part of London well, yet she couldn't quite get her bearings now. She checked the A-Z.

Chatham Place was an incongruous residential oasis hidden in a crowd of commercial properties

233

off New Bridge Road. It was part of a short terrace of four tall, narrow Victorian brick houses. They looked forgotten, left behind by mistake. There was nothing to mark out Number 14, no distinguishing feature, no blue English Heritage plaque.

Natasha stood back and looked up at its windows. One, at the very top, was illuminated with a faint amber glow and slits of light through drawn curtains. She rang the brass doorbell, heard its muffled chimes, and waited.

There was a spy glass in the door, an empty milk bottle beside the step.

She heard the sound a chain being slipped into place and the door opened a few centimetres.

'I'm so sorry to disturb you,' Natasha said. 'But I wonder if I could talk to you for a moment?'

'Of course.' The door closed for a second to release the chain, then opened wide. 'Come on then, dear, out of the cold.'

The owner was an old lady. Even so early in the morning, she had a small, beautifully made-up face, pearls in her ears, inquisitive china blue eyes, and a neat, pale blonde bun.

Natasha was ushered into a narrow tiled hallway filled with pot plants, then up a steep flight of steps. She caught a strong smell, musky and sweet. Furniture polish and pot-pourri.

'I rent out the ground floor,' the old lady explained as they came into a small, warm, living room on the first floor, decorated with cream satin wallpaper threaded with gold stripes, walnut cabinets displaying sparkling china, glass and silverware. 'This is the room where she died, you know.'

Natasha started, turned to the old lady, followed her gaze, and her heart missed a beat.

Hanging on the wall in the far corner by the large window was one of Rossetti's portraits of Lizzie Siddal. Its delicate gilt frame blended perfectly with the wallpaper, so for a split second it looked as if Lizzie was standing there, watching.

'Please, do sit down. It's Marion by the way.' She indicated a winged chair by an elaborate marble fireplace inlaid with yellow and cobalt blue ceramic tiles. There was no fire, but a large basket of dried flowers in the grate. 'There's no need to look so concerned, dear,' she added, when Natasha didn't move. 'I know what you're thinking. I must be crazy, letting strangers into my home. Well, I probably am. But if you can't be crazy at my age, when can you be?' She stood, small and thin, back ramrod straight, her slender stockinged ankles showing beneath a blue silk skirt that matched the scarf around her neck. Her voice trembled a little, as did her hands. 'It's far better to be reckless when you're old I think. Whatever happens, you've had your life. I've a little rule: after dark I don't let any boys in.' She gave an impish grin.

Natasha found herself smiling too.

'Besides, I'm well armed,' she brandished a lethal looking hat pin that made Natasha flinch, then laugh as the old lady threaded her weapon back into her scarf, out of sight. 'My young visitors are the only company I get these days,' she added, again as if Natasha would know exactly what she was talking about. 'I wouldn't miss them for anything.'

Natasha reminded herself that she'd come to find out if Bethany had ever been here. 'You said the rooms downstairs are rented?'

'Mr Braithwaite. He's a banker. With a house and a family in Herefordshire. He arrives on a Monday night and leaves on Friday morning, quiet as a mouse.'

'Has he lived there long?'

'Over two years now.'

Natasha wasn't in the least surprised that this had never been Bethany's home. 'And apart from him, you're alone?'

'Ever since my husband passed away. Except for the ghosts that is.'

Natasha wondered if the 'visitors' and the 'ghosts' were one and the same. She decided Marion was gloriously batty.

The old lady was arranging a cushion in the small of her back, plumping it up. She rested against it. 'I don't just say that to please you lot, you know.' She fixed Natasha with her merry blue eyes. 'You get a definite sense of them sometimes. You can probably feel it too, if you let yourself. It's never bothered me. In fact it's the main reason I bought the place. I was fascinated with her myself, you see.'

'Lizzie Siddal?'

Marion inclined her head.

'And your visitors...?'

'I get all sorts. Painters and art students mainly. Also actresses, musicians. People who are interested in her too. I give them a cup of tea and have a nice chat about poetry and pictures and whatnot. I wanted to be a painter when I was young. But it was frowned on in those days. As it was in hers, of course. But she had the courage to not let that stand in her way. I was too concerned with being respectable. A crippling ambition, which I'm glad to say I've now abandoned entirely. Though it's a case of the heart being willing and the flesh weak I'm afraid.'

Natasha revised her opinion. Marion was maybe one of the sanest people she'd met in a long time.

The old lady put her finger to her lips, looked Natasha up and down. 'Let me guess now. You're an art student too?'

Natasha shook her head.

'A dancer then?'

'I'm a genealogist.'

'How terribly interesting.' Marion cocked her head to one side. 'You look rather like an artist.'

Natasha opened her bag, took out the photograph. 'Have you ever seen this girl?'

Marion took the picture, reached over to the bureau behind her chair for a pair of little round glasses, then studied it carefully. 'It was only taken a couple of months ago,' Natasha explained, in case the old lady made the same mistake she had and assumed it was much older.

'And is this girl interested in Lizzie?'

'Yes.'

'Do you know, I'm not sure if I have seen her. She seems familiar. But then, as I say, I get so many. Maybe she's been here. Perhaps she's just one of those who come to look from the outside. I see them on the pavement, standing there.

Some take photographs but others simply stay a while and then walk back the way they came.' She gave the picture a little tap. 'Yes, perhaps that's why I feel I know her from somewhere. She's a pretty child.'

'Yes.'

'Friend of yours, is she?'

Natasha looked at Marion's kind, expectant face. 'I don't know who she is.' The truth of the words sunk in as she spoke them and she felt utterly despondent. She took the photograph back.

This was a girl who'd in all likelihood given a false name to her lover and a false address to her employers, who'd gone to such lengths to keep her identity a secret. And she'd succeeded.

The florist had immediately assumed that Natasha was from the police. Was that the conclusion anyone would make, if faced by someone asking if they knew a person in a picture? On reflection, Rosie had seemed oddly unsurprised, as if she'd been expecting it. As if there'd been something about Bethany that had made her suspicious, made it seem natural that the police would come looking for her.

I have a bad heart.

The Pre-Raphaelites were drawn to the idea of evil women, femme fatales, artists tormented and destroyed by female beauty. Maybe Adam had seen something in Bethany, something dangerous, that had attracted him.

She glanced up at the old lady who was watching her with interest. Natasha realised how odd her own behaviour must seem, showing a picture of someone she said she didn't even know. But that was the great thing about people who were a bit loopy, they didn't notice it in others. Marion seemed accepting and entirely at ease with her.

'Will you have a cup of tea?' she asked.

'I'd love one.'

She disappeared, leaving Natasha alone.

She walked over to the picture that hung on the wall, Lizzie's face gazing out of the golden frame as if out of a window.

The open coffin had rested in the window here, her body laid out in it, wraithlike and at peace at last, her pale, beautiful face so little altered from the way it had looked in life. She'd breathed her last breath in this very room, which had seen so much of her sorrows and fleeting joys. It was here that her little dead daughter was born, to this room that Rossetti called Dr Marshall back days after Lizzie herself had died, because he believed she could be revived.

Natasha moved across to the window, stared out at the vast blackness of the river. A gauzy mist was descending, making nimbuses round the street lamps which had not yet been turned off.

The view was eerily familiar, as if she herself had stood here before. She realized she was recognizing it from another of the pictures in the book. Lizzie, in the balcony room, standing with her arms resting on the back of a chair, tilting it onto two legs towards her, leaning over to look at a painting propped up on an easel. And behind her, through the window, the Thames and Blackfriars Bridge.

The view wasn't obscured with high rises and

239

office blocks then, but murky and cluttered with smoking chimneys. Blackfriars was the heart of Dickensian London, full of narrow alleys and cobbled streets, dark inns and chop-houses, the river in its Victorian heyday busy with barges, mud larks and warehouses.

It seemed so much quieter now. In the courtyard below a man was walking a dog. Natasha watched him cross the road, pass beneath the solitary street lamp and disappear round a corner, leaving the road empty. But not quite. Natasha gave a sharp intake of breath. There was someone down there. A girl with long hair in a grey dress. She was standing just away from the light, wreathed in mist and shadow. Natasha tried to make out her face, but she was too far away. Natasha looked for a catch in the window, tugged at it, but the window was stuck fast. Perhaps she'd see more with the light off. She glanced around for a switch. The room was cast into semi-darkness which brought the courtyard below into better focus. But the girl had gone.

She must have been one of the girls Marion had described, someone who'd come to take a picture, see the place for themselves, on some kind of pilgrimage or homage. Or just a regular passer-by.

She turned round to the dim room. The only light was beneath Lizzie's picture, like a shrine.

'Lord, I'm sorry,' Marion turned the light back on, balancing a tea tray. Must've been habit, so used to living alone. Didn't mean to leave you in the dark.'

That's exactly where I am, Natasha thought. In the dark.

Half an hour later Natasha got up to leave. She picked up her bag and the little bouquet of violets. As she reached the door she turned and held it out to the old lady.

'Thank you, dear.' Marion took the flowers. She closed her eyes and inhaled. 'What gave you the idea I might know this girl, by the way?'

'She told her boss that she lived here.'

Marion gave a wily smile. 'Maybe she does. In a way.'

Thirty-Three

Natasha guessed it must be about ten-thirty as she walked down Queen Victoria Road. It was a safe bet that Edward Deerhurst, Richmond Herald at the College of Arms and Natasha's former boss, would have been at his desk for roughly three hours.

She climbed the stone steps, signed in at the little reception desk, and walked up the wide oak staircase to the Earl Marshal's Court.

The College had been an inspiring and, at first, daunting place to work, steeped in history and ceremony and tradition, the official repository of the coats of arms and pedigrees of English, Welsh, Northern Irish and Commonwealth families and their descendants. Natasha still found it stimulating and humbling to think of the genealogists who'd pioneered and honed their skills on that site since the fourteenth century.

The door to Edward's office was ajar. Natasha tapped.

'Come in.'

He stood when he saw her, came around his carved oak desk with his arms wide. 'My dear Natasha, what a wonderful surprise.'

The Heralds were responsible for furnishing their own offices and Edward's was filled with antiques that would have looked fine in a museum or a cordoned-off room in a stately home, but were used here as originally intended. You sat on Jacobean chairs, had meetings at a cherrywood table with ornately carved legs, read by the light of lamps with gilded stands.

Natasha couldn't imagine Edward Deerhurst in any other kind of surroundings. He carried his role well; the legacy of the first Heralds who'd mixed with medieval knights and been part of the royal household. There was an aura about him that befitted the duties of the current Officers of the College, organizers of official ceremonies, coronations, state funerals and the opening of Parliament. At those occasions the Heralds dressed in their distinctive medieval uniform, a tabard, embroidered on its front and back and sleeves with the royal arms.

Edward's everyday wear was less ornate but still formal, a black waistcoat and crisp white shirt. He was tall and distinguished, with thick black hair greying around the temples, a slightly gaunt face with a large Roman nose, iron-grey eyes and

242

a deep, refined voice. He had terrified Natasha when first she'd met him.

Now he made them coffee, freshly percolated, with cream, and when they were seated in the corner of the room, said, 'I had a telephone call yesterday afternoon, a gentleman, wanting to check your credentials. Is it a coincidence you're brightening my day a few hours later?'

Natasha felt goose bumps break out over her skin. 'What did he want to know?'

'Just how long you'd worked here, when you left, what cases you'd been involved with, then information about the processes we employ, how adept and experienced you were at some of them, specially how you'd use a person's ancestors to find someone alive today. He started to ask about your background, family, but I put him straight on that, told him it wasn't at all relevant. I gave you an impeccable reference of course, told him you were a brilliant researcher, very conscientious.' Deerhurst levelled his eyes at Natasha. 'If you've decided you've had enough of the freelance life, I'd rather hoped you'd come back here.'

'You'd be the first to know, Edward. I'm not looking for a job.'

'Then what...?'

'Your guess is as good as mine.' She sipped the strong coffee, rested the cup back on the saucer. 'What would you do,' she said, 'if you were working on a case, and you started to wonder if your client, or someone you were researching, might have done something wrong, committed a crime even?'

243

His slanted eyebrows, at times, gave him the distinct look of an owl. 'We're the guardians of secrets. We're trusted with intimate family details, permitted access to the most sensitive papers, on the understanding that anything we find will be treated with the utmost confidence.'

She caught sight of the documents neatly laid on Edward's desk, embossed with the crest of the motto of the College. 'Diligent and secret,' she said.

He gave a nod. 'Diligent and secret. But, and there is a rather large But.' He levelled his eyes at her. 'We're not priests taking confessions. It's just a job. Though I know you find that hard to accept.'

She smiled. 'You couldn't just run a quick check to see if you have anything on file about a Harold Leyburn of Dorchester.' As she said the name she had a peculiar feeling of déjà vu, as if she'd come across it somewhere, before Adam gave her the certificate. She found it in her bag, handed it to Edward.

'Ah, so you didn't just come here to say hello.' He rose and left the room. 'Give me a moment.'

He reappeared after a while. 'Drawn a blank I'm afraid. There are at least a dozen Harold Leyburns in the 1891 census, none who live in Dorset, let alone Dorchester. In a few months they'll release the 1901 census of course, which might be more revealing. That's not much help to you now though is it? The College has nothing else listed under that name. But, you know, I'm sure I know it from somewhere.'

'Me too. Can I borrow your computer?'

'Be my guest.'

It sat in pristine isolation in an alcove of the room, hardly used. Natasha logged onto an internet search engine, keyed in Harold Leyburn, watched the electronic egg-timer turn and turn. Five entries. News items from six weeks ago.

Promising young Olympic sprinter Harry Leyburn, 24, died suddenly in training yesterday. The coroner has been called to investigate but so far the police do not suspect foul play. It is thought that Leyburn's death was the result of a heart attack.

No further news. Details of the autopsy had clearly not yet been released.

'Are you working for a relative of his?' Edward asked, picking up the sheets from the printer and reading what Natasha had just read.

'I don't know.' Was Harold Leyburn this Harry's ancestor then, and if so, where did Bethany fit in? 'I just don't know, Edward.' She took the copies from him. 'Thanks for this.'

'Always a pleasure.'

She set off down the corridor.

'Natasha?'

She stopped.

'Are you putting yourself in danger?'

The threatening phone call, the Celica that had followed her, whoever was poking around asking questions, one step ahead of her, at Highgate, talking to Edward. Not to mention Adam and her renewed doubts about him, and Jake Romilly's intimidating asides. She felt that the answer to

Edward's question was probably yes. She *was* in some kind of danger. But to what degree, or more to the point from whom, or why exactly, she couldn't say. Someone who wanted something she had, to find out what she knew or what she was doing?

'Don't worry, I'll be fine.' She tried to sound confident.

'Be careful, will you?'

She waved her hand over her shoulder.

When she eventually arrived home having picked up Boris from the Snowshill Arms, the post, yesterday's and today's, was lying on the mat. A couple of January bills, a large white envelope stamped with the FRC's logo. She knew what that would be; birth and marriage certificates she'd ordered on normal delivery when she was at the Records Centre, some for new leads, others just background for clients' presentation files and pedigrees. There was also a brown A4 envelope that she gave no more than a glance to as she picked it up.

They could all wait until tomorrow. She couldn't settle to any of it. Her mind kept wandering to Mary and James. When she'd collected Boris, James had said Mary was resting in bed. She'd had some contractions and they'd contacted the midwife only to be told it was probably a false alarm. They'd reassured Mary that if the baby was born imminently, two weeks early, it would be absolutely fine. Natasha imagined herself in Mary's shoes, then stopped herself. Biological clock wound up and ticking at the threat of being thirty? Surely not. Right now she seemed as far away from Mary's life as it was possible to be.

She'd skipped lunch again, but had gone beyond feeling hungry. She ate a bowl of cornflakes with milk and a sprinkle of sugar. Breakfast was the best meal, all the better for not being eaten when it was supposed to be.

She put some milk in a pan for hot chocolate. While she waited for it to boil she glanced at the envelope that was sticking out beneath the smaller ones on the kitchen table. It was franked second class, with an insignia: 'The Royal College of Surgeons'.

The biography of John Marshall. Part of her didn't want to open it. She'd had more than enough of them for now. John and Jeanette and Lizzie and Bethany, or whoever she was. Eventually, curiosity got the better of her. Jake Romilly's parting shot: *Curiosity killed the cat.* She could never resist finding out more about people she had started researching.

She tore the envelope open and drew out two sheets of photocopied paper, stapled together. The typeface was tiny, but Dr Marshall's biography spanned both pages.

Marshall, John (1818–91) M.R.C.S, F.R.C.S. Born in Ely, Cambridgeshire on 11 September 1818, the second son of William Marshall, solicitor and an excellent naturalist. John Marshall entered University College Hospital, London in 1838 and moved to Savile Row, where he remained until his retirement. In 1887 he replaced Sir Henry Acland as President of the General Medical Council. Marshall perfected the operation for the excision of varicose veins. At first violently criticised, it is now accepted. He was one of the first to show that cholera might be spread by means of drinking water and also advocated the system of circular wards for hospitals. He gave his first course of lectures on anatomy to the art students at Marlborough House in 1853, a course which he repeated when the art schools were moved to South Kensington.

A bust of him by Thomas Brock, R.A., dated 1887, was presented to University College on behalf of the subscribers to the Marshall Memorial Fund. A replica is in the college Hall. He appears in Jamyn Brookes' portrait of the group of the Council.

Marshall's wife, Ellen died in 1859, and on New Year's Day 1891 her husband followed her to the grave.

Natasha, deflected by something else, didn't spot it at first. Marshall had taught anatomical drawing to art students, so he was one of the pioneers of Marcus's profession. Out of habit, she thought how interested Marcus would be; perhaps he already knew of Marshall? Then she remembered she'd relinquished the right to share the details of her life with him.

There was a hissing behind her and she turned to see the milk seething over the edge of the pan. She snatched the pan handle, holding it at arm's length and cursing as the boiling froth subsided.

She poured what remained into a mug and

spooned in some powdered chocolate. She wandered through to the living room. As she went over to the iMac something about the last line of the biography came back to her. It had been one of the first things she'd needed to know. Mrs Marshall's name. Ellen.

She put her mug on the windowsill, went back into the kitchen and grabbed the sheets of paper.

The date of Mrs Marshall's death. It was wrong. It had to be.

She found her bag where she'd dumped it in the hallway, pulled out her file and flicked through to the photocopied census return. Little Eleanor Marshall was recorded as being ten years old when the 1871 census was taken. Which meant she was born in 1861. Two years after the doctor's wife died. Eleanor *was* named after her mother, but not after Ellen Senior. Ellen Jeanette may have died unmarried, but she had not died a virgin, or childless. She wanted to kick herself. Should have considered it before. It was not uncommon in the days when illegitimacy was considered such a terrible stigma, to bring up a child as if it was the sibling of its parent.

She went back to the living room to try Adam's number. The answering machine was winking at her. With some trepidation, she hit the play button.

It was a female voice, young, friendly. 'It's Katherine. Rosie at Highgate Florists said you wanted to talk to me. I'd really like to come and see you. It's my day off tomorrow so I can be with you by two. I hope that's all right. Call me if it's not convenient. Otherwise I'll see you then.' She left her number and the machine clicked off.

Natasha replayed the message. Just in case she'd missed something.

It's Katherine. No surname. As if they already knew one another.

She couldn't understand it. Why this girl would be so insistent on coming immediately, all the way from London to Gloucestershire?

Thirty-Four

Had Jeanette taken her secret with her to the grave?

That wouldn't necessarily mean little Eleanor didn't realise the truth. There were some things you didn't need to have spelt out for you. Things between families that, although never mentioned, come to be understood and acknowledged.

Natasha was never completely convinced or satisfied until she had proof – dates, something on a certificate. It was against her nature to leave loose ends. This was what she had been waiting for, a key that made everything lock into place.

But meeting this girl, Katherine, could prove far more important than anything that might be waiting to be unearthed in the birth, marriage and death registers. She might have information that would end the search for Bethany there and then, and make the Victorian story superfluous. Natasha couldn't help regretting that.

But she was definitely getting somewhere now,

that was all that mattered. About time, too. It was 12 January already.

One thing Katherine wasn't going to be able to tell her though: Who was Eleanor's father? Was it the elusive Mr Brown?

And how did this link to Harold Leyburn?

She lay down on her stomach on the rug in the living room, shoved Boris off, propped her head in her hands, and opened the diary in front of her.

Papa thinks there must be some explanation for Mr Brown's silence. He was so 'honest-looking', so 'polite' to Mama, so 'deferential' to Papa, was without doubt 'so much taken with me' that Papa cannot make it out. No more can anyone else, but so it is. I begin to quite forget all about him. Papa asked if I should like an Academy ticket to be sent to him and I answered promptly in the negative. I would not go a single step out of my way after him. I shall never get married to anyone else though.

Three pages on, Jeanette was talking about dressmaking, the shade known as Etna, a beautiful coppery-russet that was a fashionable colour for women's clothing then. *Everyone I see is dressed in <u>brown</u> (still my fate!). I am gradually eliminating everything <u>brown</u> from my possession. I have always <u>hated</u> the colour.*

That was the last page. Not a satisfactory ending at all. A life interrupted.

Natasha ate a slice of toast and Marmite, then took Boris for a long tramp in the drizzling rain.

251

Wet grasses tangled round her ankles as she walked, the coldness eventually seeping through her jeans. A seasoned walker had once told her that jeans were the last thing you should wear, that if you got caught in bad weather, the waterlogged denim could actually cut off your circulation. Natasha couldn't quite believe this. When she reached the Manor Farm though, she decided to double back.

She turned the bend in the lane by St Barnabus, with Orchard End up on the right. The front door was flung wide open. Knowing she'd only be out for a few minutes she hadn't bothered to lock up, but she was absolutely certain she'd shut it properly. She ran the rest of the way, paused outside, glad of Boris, though she didn't much trust his abilities as a guard dog.

She went into the hallway. Silence. She thrust out her arms and gave the living room door a push. It swung open. Her purse and cheque book were still sitting on the table by the fire place, the TV and iMac still in situ. But her desk had been ransacked. Papers were strewn everywhere, the pile of birth and death certificates rifled through, spilling onto the floor. Her notebook opened at the page where she'd written the Marshall details.

She grabbed the heavy pewter candlestick from the window ledge and made her way upstairs, treading carefully, striding to avoid the steps that creaked. She could see into her bedroom. The duvet rumpled, clothes littered everywhere, towels draped over the floor. Just as she'd left it! The necklace Steven had given her for

Christmas was still on her dressing table, next to a silver hair clip.

Not a regular burglar then, not a petty, opportunistic thief. But someone who was after something in particular.

Whoever it had been was gone now, she was sure of it. She sat down on the bed and lifted the phone onto her lap, dialled the police. They said they'd send someone round from Broadway station within the hour. As she stood in the kitchen, pouring a glass of whisky, she saw that her hands were shaking.

She went through to the living room to wait. Couldn't bring herself to sit at her desk. It gave her the creeps, thinking how someone had been here uninvited, touching her things. A violation. She started putting the papers back into some sort of order. It would take a couple of hours at least. In a flash of temper, she scooped them all up and dumped them into a pile. She was itching to fetch the polish, but with the police coming that wasn't perhaps such a bright idea. Evidence, fingerprints. Where would you be without TV cop shows? She probably shouldn't have moved the papers either. Tough.

Then she thought of something else. She nudged the mouse to reactivate the computer screen, looked at the record of the most recent files that had been opened. Bethany. The Marshalls. She'd been using them yesterday and the last changes were dated then. But someone could still have been looking.

Like all the other incidents, the break-in was to do with Bethany, of that Natasha was certain. It followed that the closer she got to finding Bethany, the more desperate whoever it was became. A positive thing then? The break-in proved she was getting warmer.

Then why was she standing in her own living room shivering, feeling lost and frightened and alone, feelings she despised more than any others?

She had been able to rationalise away the Celica, and the rest. But there was no escaping the fact that someone had definitely been here, in her home.

It was PC Walker who came with a young woman police constable. Walker was a middle-aged chap; with a paunch, thick spectacles, a double chin and rapidly receding hair line. Natasha knew him quite well. He visited the village to advise the old ladies on their neighbourhood watch schemes and to teach the school children about road safety and not talking to strangers. He had occasionally been seen having a drink in the Snowshill Arms, never after hours of course.

Natasha made cups of tea and handed round digestive biscuits.

'I'll just have a scout around if I may.' Walker munched on the biscuit, scattering crumbs as he went, trailed by Boris vacuuming them all up. 'You're sure nothing's been taken?'

'Pretty much, yes.'

'Just your papers you say. Was there anything you think anyone might especially want to get their hands on. Sure you'd not left any wills lying about?' Walker grinned 'Some great-granny coming back from the dead to see you're not tampering with her last wishes?'

Natasha managed a smile.

They sat in the living room while he took a statement. 'Perhaps you disturbed whoever it was, or they spotted you on your way back and escaped before they'd had a chance to grab anything.'

The phone rang.

'Want to get that?' Walker asked.

'It can wait.' The answering machine picked up.

'Well, I think we're about finished.' Walker stuffed his notebook back into his pocket. 'Just kids most likely. Ran amok and scarpered.'

She told him about finding the window open when she came downstairs a few nights ago.

He took a look. 'You'd have to be pretty skinny to squeeze through these mullions.' He glanced down at his own stomach with a grin. 'No harm in taking fingerprints, checking out the usual suspects, but since nothing's been taken and your door was unlocked...'

'My own fault. You've got better things to do with your time I'm sure.'

'Best lock up in future though. You can't be too careful. Rural crime's on the increase. City ruffians know the countryside's full of trusting folk who save them the bother of breaking in. Rich pickings. Worth the extra journey.'

'Thanks for the warning.'

'Thanks for the tea.'

She hit play on the answering machine, keeping one eye on the window through which she could see PC Walker, climbing leisurely into his car, checking his radio.

'You probably won't remember me, it's Dr Moore. Nigel Moore. We met at Highgate.' He'd left a number and asked if she could give him a call. 'Whenever it's convenient.'

She wondered for a moment how he'd known how to reach her. She'd mentioned she was a genealogist. He must have taken the trouble to find her details on the internet. Was it a professional call? She hoped so. Life was complicated enough as it was.

Thirty-Five

It was almost two. Katherine should be here soon.

Natasha changed out of her jeans into chocolate velvet leggings, black jersey vest top and a baggy black lace shirt, picked up the book of Lizzie Siddal's portraits. It was like those little books children used to have, of a man running or a bird flapping its wings in flight. Each picture slightly different, producing, as you quickly flipped through the pages, the effect of animation. It seemed as if Lizzie was looking down, then for a moment raised her eyes to meet Natasha's.

'What is it you want to tell us?' Natasha whispered.

She heard a car engine, then heard it stop. A girl walked past the window on the other side of the lane. There was a knock at the door.

She was slight and pretty, mid-twenties perhaps, olive skin, violet eyes and dark hair that was braided and pinned around her head with little iridescent clips in the shape of butterflies. She set bells ringing in Natasha's head for some reason she couldn't quite put her finger on. One of the girls in the photographs?

'Katherine?'

For a second Natasha had the impression the girl was weighing her up against expectations. Then she smiled. 'That's right.'

Living alone, it seemed to Natasha as if every time she invited someone else to her home she was somehow baring her soul. The decoration, ornaments, furniture, books all said something about her. As did the dust on the picture frames, the grate in the fireplace that needed a good sweep. The mess around her desk didn't, but she couldn't get into that now.

She went through to the kitchen to make two fresh cups of coffee.

When she returned, the girl was standing in the window, studying the spines of the books on the shelves, her head bent a little to one side. She caught Natasha's eye and straightened. 'Sorry. I can't resist looking at other people's collections.'

'That's OK. Neither can I.'

'Natasha handed over a mug and they sat down, Natasha in the wooden rocker by the inglenook and Katherine on the sofa. She sipped her coffee, held Natasha's eyes for a moment, then glanced away. 'Look. I might as well come straight out with it. I'm sure you're wondering what on earth I'm doing here.' She looked up. 'It was me who gave Bethany your name and address. I got it from Marcus.'

The shock of hearing his name in so unexpected a context made Natasha freeze. She wanted this girl out of her house. It felt more of an intrusion than the burglar. Why had she come?

'I'm his sister,' Katherine said, quietly.

Natasha cursed herself for jumping to conclusions. Steven was right. She'd never do that professionally. Of course the girl was Marcus's sister. He didn't often speak of his family but Natasha knew he had a sister called Katie. That was why Natasha felt she recognised her. Though on the surface she didn't resemble him that much. His eyes were intense and deep set, dark, hers almost violet, open and bright. But their lips were the same, full and wide. And something about her expressions and mannerisms, a smile that made her look somehow sadder.

Natasha sat down again.

'I'm sorry. I must have shocked you,' Katherine said. 'But you see now, why I wanted to meet you.' She tucked a stray strand of hair behind her left ear. The lobe was pierced twice, a little diamond star and a small hoop. 'It's terrible that we've never met before,' Katherine smiled. 'Marcus told us all about you though.'

'Did he?' He'd hardly ever mentioned his family, had never invited Natasha to meet them. With perseverance, she'd wrinkled out of him the basic details. They lived on the Cornish coast, his father an electronic engineer, his mother a housewife. Three brothers and a sister. He'd talked of school holidays shrimping and surfing.

258

'Mum was always telling him to bring you down to see us, Katherine was saying. 'So was I.'

He'd always given the impression he wasn't close to his family, and had hardly any contact with them except the usual, birthdays and Christmas. He'd always led her to believe he felt more akin to Steven. When he'd been staying at the cottage or she'd been at his place, she'd never once heard him talking on the phone to his mother or his sister.

Why was she feeling cheated?

'He used to come home all the time, and I used to go up and stay with him in Manchester,' Katherine said. 'Then he started seeing you and he went all strange.' She said it with no animosity. 'I could never reach him at his house and he wouldn't give me your number for ages. And he never seemed to have time to come home any more, was always busy when I wanted to come up and see him. I thought you must be some possessive and manipulative witch who didn't want him to have a family. But after you split up, and Marcus seemed so upset, I spoke to Freddie and Jack and some of the other guys who work with him and your dad and they all say how great you are, how you made Marcus laugh. So I didn't know what to think.'

'Me neither,' Natasha said, to herself. Was there just a tiny grain of truth in Katherine's first assumption? Was she manipulative, possessive?

She knew the answer was yes, sometimes.

But still. Why had he done it? Cut her out. Kept her and his family apart. Because he was ashamed of her? Because she'd never meant that

259

much to him?

'We're a bit daunting I suppose, en masse,' Katherine said. 'But you look like you'd cope.'

Natasha lifted her cup, swallowed a mouthful of coffee. There was a pain across her forehead. Understanding pierced her. He'd worried she *wouldn't* cope.

He'd thought it would be difficult for her. To see him as part of such a tightly knit family, surrounded by his relations who all looked like him, a gaggle of brothers and sisters. He thought she'd feel left out, different. Did he really think she was so fragile?

Boris thrust his muzzle into Katherine's hand, gave an inquisitive sniff. She stroked him. 'It's a shame you and Marcus aren't together any more.'

Natasha was remembering. Marcus talking quietly on the telephone, joking and laughing, when he thought she was upstairs in the bath. The phone bill she'd checked the minute it arrived. A twenty-minute call to a London number she didn't recognise. Too late anyway. But she'd still not be able to resist calling it. Had hung up when a young woman answered. Had it been Katherine?

'I'm going to move back to Cornwall in the summer,' Katherine said. 'I've been living with my aunt and uncle in London and it's been fun but I've had enough of it now. I want to get my own place back home. Perhaps you could come and stay sometime.' She was deliberately sowing a seed. Trying to play Cupid. Natasha was touched, let herself believe that what she'd suggested might just be possible. She felt the other girl's eyes resting on her. 'He didn't tell me what happened between you.'

'I don't suppose he had a clue.' She felt as if something inside her was broken, confronted with Katherine's pretty, open face, which suddenly did look so like Marcus's that she could barely stand to meet her eyes.

'I've meant to come and see you before,' Katherine said. 'It seemed like an omen. When I found a message from Rosie with your name and contact details on it.'

Natasha had almost forgotten the reason she'd initially wanted to get in touch with Katherine.

Bethany.

'It's one of those situations that seems like an amazing coincidence, isn't it?' Katherine said. 'There you are, looking for someone, who, it turns out, worked with the sister of your boyfriend.' Natasha smiled at the term. Teenagers had boyfriends. 'But you only got involved in looking for Bethany because I'd given her your name.'

'Why did you?'

She gave a little shrug. 'We have lots of people coming into the shop who are researching their family history, visiting the grave of an ancestor. We got to talking about it and I mentioned that Marcus had told me you were a professional genealogist. It stuck in my mind because I thought what an unusual, interesting job. Anyway, Bethany asked if I knew how to contact you. I told her you lived near Oxford and she was really keen that I get your address and phone number. I explained it all to Marcus when I asked him for your details, but I guess he never got a chance to tell you. Bethany got in touch though?'

'Yes. Although it's ... her boyfriend ... I'm working for now. You don't by any chance know where Bethany is?'

'We didn't keep in touch after she left the shop.'

'This may sound like an odd question. But did she ever mention Lizzie Siddal?'

'Not to me. But there was a young guy came into the shop a few months ago, and they got talking about art. Bethany was always sketching. They were quite disturbing some of her pictures. Fairies, not like the Flower Fairies, but with serpents in their hair, fallen angels and ghosts in forests. Anyway, I heard her telling this guy about Lizzie Siddal, how people should respect her as an artist. He asked Bethany if she'd like to come with him to the grave but she said no. He was quite sexy, long black ponytail and dark skin like a Cherokee. Well, you'd know, you've met him.'

Natasha frowned. 'Have I?'

'You said her boyfriend...'

'Adam. He's fair, pale skin.'

Katherine gave a little shake of her head. 'Oh well, that's not who she was seeing when I knew her. Unless of course she was going for a mixed dish.'

'Can you remember his name?'

Katherine thought for a moment. 'I'm not sure she ever told me.'

Someone with a long dark ponytail, like a Cherokee. Jake Romilly. 'I'm sorry, you were saying. When this guy came into the shop...'

'Oh, yeah. Well, they seemed to be getting along

so well, I told her I was sure Rosie wouldn't mind if she took an early lunch and went off with him, but she was quite adamant that she didn't want to go, left the poor guy standing there and disappeared into the back room to leave me to take his money. He didn't buy anything in the end. He came back the next day and she went for a drink with him, started seeing him on and off. I think they argued quite a lot, though. She seemed edgy sometimes. One time he came in and she told him to go away, she didn't want to see him any more.'

'When was that?'

'Um. Few weeks before Christmas I think.'

Natasha felt drained, as if she'd given blood. 'Did you get on with her?'

'Yeah. I felt a bit sorry for her, though. I sometimes thought our place was the worst kind of florist for her to be in. She was too sensitive. When people came in for wreaths for the graves she'd be almost in tears sometimes. But she had a nice manner with them. Sometimes they are quite upset, widows and grandchildren, young wives and husbands and mothers occasionally. Even people who were coming to see ancestors who died long before they were born. Bethany was really understanding and kind.' Katherine smiled. 'She always looked like she was dressed for a funeral. I never saw her in anything but black, long flowing skirts and baggy jumpers.' She put her cup down. 'I should be going.'

'Stay for something to eat.'

They chatted whilst Natasha made supper. Pasta with mushrooms, salad and French bread

263

rolls. As luck would have it, the cupboards were fairly well stocked after a trip to Tesco. Katherine asked if she could help, stood beside Natasha chopping the mushrooms, tomatoes for the salad. 'Open some wine if you like,' Natasha said. 'Corkscrew's in the dresser, top drawer on the left.'

Katherine sat at the table with the wine.

'Did you always want to be a florist?'

'I think so. I've always liked gardening as well as art so it seemed like a perfect way to combine the two things. My grandmother was an artist. She made silhouettes. I'm named after her. Dad remembers her as being very elegant and beautiful. A lot to live up to.'

'You seem to be doing fine.' Natasha laid the plates on the table, served up. She was glad to have company now that darkness was falling.

They talked about London and shopping, castles and old houses in Cornwall. Katherine said she'd love to know more about her own family history and Natasha said she'd gladly help her if ever she wanted to have a go. Then she remembered that it would be Marcus's family history too, the history of the children they might have had. Ghosts from a future that would never be.

'I just thought of something,' Katherine said when she put on her coat to go. 'The day before she left, Bethany asked if I knew of a local doctor and I gave her the number for mine. Dr Wilkinson. He's known my uncle for years, a friend of the family. He told me Bethany made an appointment and then never showed up. Do you think that's anything important?'

'I don't know.' Natasha opened the door, thought of something herself. On Christmas Day, Steven had said he'd met a girl called Bethany with Marcus. *Petite little thing, very pretty.*

'Have you ever met my father?'

'Once. With Marcus and a group of the other guys they work with. I ran into them all in a pub near Oxford Circus and we went out for a meal in Chinatown. Actually...'

'Bethany was there too. I know.'

'It was lovely to meet you.'

'You too.'

'You should call him you know. Marcus.'

Thirty-Six

Natasha started cleaning the desk and her iMac. Then she did the washing up, polished the dresser and rubbed beeswax into the table, donned rubber gloves and bleached the sink. She fetched a bin liner and stuffed it full of old newspaper and magazines she'd never get round to reading, junk mail. She did a sweep of the kitchen cupboards and threw in old bottles of dried herbs, a sticky jar of honey. After that she set about with the vacuum cleaner, prodded the nozzle into all the corners and crevices by the stairs and behind the doors. She didn't go round the furniture as she usually did, but pulled out the desk and the filing cabinet and TV. After a while she felt sorry for Mr and Mrs Wilson trying to sleep next door and turned it off. She took the bleach upstairs and scoured the bath and washbasin. It was therapeutic. Straightening, cleaning, putting things in order. When she stopped she'd have to think. She went through all the drawers in the bedroom and folded clothes, sorted her jewellery.

Then, carefully tucked away in the bottom of a little silver tea caddy she used for bangles, she found a diagram Marcus had done for her, the face of a Stone Age boy, with strange lines like meridians criss-crossing his features.

She remembered the exact occasion he'd drawn it.

September, three years ago. Marcus was driving back up to Manchester in the morning. It was the second weekend they'd spent together. They were sitting on the floor by the fire, eating baguettes and cheese washed down with red wine. He'd slipped her glass from her hand, set it on the floor, taken her face between his hands.

'You know. No one will ever be able to recreate your face after you've gone.'

'Why's that?'

'What I do is all based on averages. Standard faces for different ages, different sexes and races,' he spoke with a soft cadence, as if he was reciting a poem rather than explaining a scientific technique. 'You take the typical width of a mouth, or nose, the distance between the chin, the cheek bones and between the eyes. Then you make variations dictated by the measurements and irregularities of a particular skull, and so you

266

create an image that's individual. But your face. It wouldn't fit any predetermined model.' Like a sculptor he smoothed along the line of her cheekbone with his thumb. 'These bones are as fragile as a bird's. Yet it's a strong face. And your eyes.' He touched the lids. 'Statistically they'd be too large, in proportion to the rest of your features. The angle of them, a little foreign. You could never recreate that. And no one would know you had these little pale freckles across your nose, how thick and shiny your hair is, the way it curls like this around your ears.'

She thought it was the most lovely, unusual thing anyone had ever said to her. She leant forward and kissed him. His hair had smelt of woodsmoke.

She'd asked him to tell her more about his work and he'd fetched a pencil and paper and drawn the Stone Age boy for her.

She lay awake with the curtains open. The moon was full and round, so bright you could see the craters on its surface. A silver face with black pits for eyes. She tried not to listen out for strange sounds, but the slightest thing made her tense up. The slightest bump and creak from the ancient timbers, the gurgle of the hot water tank filling up, the wind rattling the casements. Tonight they all sounded like footsteps, doors being opened, someone crawling in through the window, picking the lock, creeping up the stairs.

She thought of Katherine. How strange Marcus's sister should have that name. The same name Natasha's real mother had given to the hospital. Catherine. The woman who psychologists would no doubt blame for the fact that Marcus wasn't here right now.

Impossible to think the person who'd carried you inside them for nine months left because she didn't love you. So you tell yourself that she left because she wanted something *better* for you. She left you *because* she loved you. *Ergo*, love equals abandonment.

A vicious circle. So you make sure no one ever gets the chance to abandon you again.

Marcus's voice drifting up through the floorboards, low and familiar, talking to someone in the way she thought he talked only to her, teasing, gentle. She'd crept out to the top of the stairs to listen, heard him say, 'I'll see you soon, I promise.'

She'd taken one giant leap then to what seemed the only conclusion. He'd always vowed there was one aspect of Steven's life he'd never emulate but she hadn't believed him. Instead she'd listened to the voice inside her head that said no one was to be trusted, everyone left in the end. So she'd sent him away before he had a chance to tell her *he* was leaving.

He'd come up to bed, tried to touch her but she'd shied away, lay beside him staring at the wall until his breathing became deep and regular. Then she had packed up all his things, systematically working through the house.

In the morning he'd not been able to find his toothbrush.

'Why don't you look in the boot of your car?'

He'd stared at her dumbfounded.

'I thought you were different but you're just the same.' She'd not given him the chance to lie. Not given him the chance to explain.

And now it was too late. Because of a stupid, stupid, misunderstanding.

You slept to escape. But she couldn't sleep.

She went downstairs and turned on the iMac. She opened a new e-mail message box, typed in his address. At first she wrote, 'Katherine came to see me today.' Then she deleted that, not wanting to risk causing friction. Instead she said, 'I was wrong. I should have trusted you. I'm sorry.'

There seemed nothing more to say.

She pulled her notebook towards her, opened it at a fresh white page, attempting to make her mind as fresh and blank as the paper. A new leaf. She tried out different scenarios. Adam cheating on Bethany, with Angie, or Diana. Bethany cheating on him with his partner, Jake Romilly. Bethany made an appointment to see her doctor just before she disappeared. Was she pregnant and knew Adam wouldn't want the baby, wouldn't make any commitment to her? Perhaps she wasn't even sure it was his baby. The irony made it seem almost inevitable, nearly convinced Natasha it had to be true. Bethany and Jeanette, separated by one and a half centuries, but united by a common dilemma.

Illegitimacy no longer carried the shame of Jeanette's day, but it still wasn't easy, single mothers were often frowned upon. And it was still the mother that bore the burden in the end, had to make the decision, to risk having to rear a child on her own if the father wanted out or she didn't want him on a long-term basis. Or have the pregnancy terminated. A hard, cruel word. It should be easy to see why some chose to go ahead and have their babies, then gave them away. Walked out of the hospital and left them behind, or put them on a doorstep a week later.

Thirty-Seven

Natasha woke up, remembered it was Friday the thirteenth and seriously considered staying in bed. Boris was having none of it, whining at the door to be taken out. As Natasha dressed, she balanced the phone receiver under her chin, dialled Mary's number.

No more contractions.

'Let's hope they hold off for another day at least,' Mary said.

'No sex, hot curries or trampolines for you.'

'Spoilsport. Can't hear you too well. You're cracking up.'

'I don't see how. I'm not on a mobile. Must be your... Ha ha. Very funny. Talk to you later.'

Before she left the cottage, Natasha couldn't stop herself going round the place twice, checking and then double-checking that all the windows were closed and locked.

It felt good to be out. Black clouds massed overhead but the sun was shining right through them, beautiful and ominous.

She decided to take Boris with her to the County Records Office in Gloucester. It would mean him sitting in the car for a couple of hours, but she couldn't bear to leave him behind in case whoever had been in the cottage decided to make a return visit.

The temperature had dropped in the night and frost was thick on the Alpine's windscreen. She was out of de-icer and it took a couple of minutes scraping a small round window with a CD holder, then giving up and going back inside for hot water from the kettle, before she could set off. She drove carefully, waiting for the rest of the frost to melt away.

At Winchcombe, Natasha checked her side mirror to overtake a coach.

There was a red Celica a couple of vehicles back.

There must be hundreds of Celicas on the roads. She tried to read the registration plate but it was too far away. Next time she checked, not a Celica in sight.

On the outskirts of Gloucester, she stopped at the roundabout, indicating left for Over Causeway. She changed down into first, stole a look in the rear view. The Celica was two cars behind again, impossible to see the plates or the driver. She waited for a lorry to pass, then accelerated into a gap. The Celica followed suit. She was on the dual carriageway, checked all was clear, then overtook a Mondeo and slammed her foot down to the floor. The Alpine's heart revved up to seventy. With the roads still slippery no one would be foolhardy enough to follow. Except the

271

Celica. It had no effort keeping up, and in a second it was sandwiched between her and the Mondeo. The Alpine's back window was fogged with condensation, so she still couldn't see his face. She was sure it was a he.

The Celica turned off when she did at St Oswald's Priory. She did an abrupt right without indicating, into the municipal car park opposite the County Record Office. The Celica carried on.

She switched off the engine. Stretched her arms out in front of her, gripping the wheel until her breathing had steadied.

Who the hell was it? The worst thing was, her brain kept throwing up an answer to that question, along with a whole host of other questions. She'd spotted the car behind her twice, but that didn't mean those were the only times she'd been followed. Maybe her stalker wasn't an expert, slipped up occasionally. Someone had known exactly when to break into the cottage, after all. The thought she had probably been watched unknowingly made her shudder.

She let Boris out to stretch his legs, locked up and went into the Record Office. It was in a converted Victorian School which bore evidence of its previous existence on the walls, black and white pictures of girls in pinafores and boys in peaked caps. If you looked carefully, you could see names etched into the wooden door frames of the old classrooms that now served as libraries. There were microfiche copies of most of the ONS indexes there.

Will was waiting in the foyer. Natasha had

managed to cajole him into taking an early lunch break to help since Mary was indisposed. He put his arms around her, then held her away from him. 'You OK? You look a bit shaken up.'

'Too many nutters on the road. Nothing that a sugar fix won't sort.'

Natasha treated them to mugs of hot chocolate laden with swirly cream at a greasy spoon café over the road. They carved up the work between the two of them.

It was a case of working forward through the marriage indexes to find out if and when little Eleanor married. Who she married was another matter. They might not even get that far. Until the twentieth century the indexes didn't record bride and groom together in the same entry, so they'd have to wait for the certificate to find the name of Eleanor's husband, then to find her children. There was a chance Natasha could fiddle a shortcut though.

She was taking the first possible eight years of Eleanor's marriage; Will was starting seven years later. If they had time they'd check out the Leyburns too. Logically, they should be doing that bit first, but sometimes you had to trust your gut instinct. And Natasha's gut was screaming that Eleanor held the key.

As Natasha sat at the microfiche reader, working systematically down her list, 1882–86, names swimming past, that conviction grew. She started to feel Bethany, drawing her on. The diary, the trail she had left behind, was leading to her finally, whether or not she had intended it. Natasha couldn't work out how she felt about that, or about Adam, or about anything any more.

'I've got it,' Will announced. Natasha went over to his desk, peered over his shoulder. Will pointed out the entry.

Eleanor Marshall was married in the London district of Westminster St James in the June quarter of 1882. Despite everything, Natasha felt the heady exhilaration she hoped to find in every case and found only in a few, the thrill of the chase. Here was the first step in the continuation of Jeanette Marshall's bloodline she was once convinced couldn't exist.

'Well done,' she said.

'That's it for now then.'

There was no way Natasha could stand to wait for the certificate. 'Not necessarily.'

It was almost one o'clock, the Centre filling up with researchers who came to work on their own family trees in their lunch breaks. Will said he had to be getting back to his proper job. Natasha thanked him, followed him out to the foyer, punched in the number for the London Metropolitan Archives, and asked to speak to Stuart Russell, a former colleague from the College of Arms. She gave him the volume and page numbers so he'd be able to look up the certificate. It should take fifteen minutes or so. She went over the road for a bowl of soup and a coffee, then came back to the Records Centre.

Stuart called back two minutes later. 'The groom was Samuel George Miller.'

Natasha thanked him, promised to return the favour if ever she could.

She rang Toby. His phone was turned off, a good sign since mobiles weren't allowed in the reading rooms of the Family Records Centre and there was no way Toby would have it turned off unless he absolutely had to. He was most likely still at work.

Natasha took Boris for a turn around the block, past launderettes and dry cleaners, grocers and betting shops, almost dialled up to remote access her e-mails but stopped just in time and made a bargain with herself. She'd only allow herself to look at them when she got home.

It didn't really matter if Marcus didn't reply immediately. She'd keep trying until he did.

Toby responded to her message half an hour later. Natasha asked him to look up Samuel Miller's will, and drank another bitter coffee from the machine at the Records Centre while she waited. At this rate she'd be flying home. Toby called back and said the chief beneficiaries were Miller's son, and grandsons John and Charles, with a few personal trinkets left to his daughter, Frances Leyburn.

'Did you say Leyburn?'

'Sure did. Anyway, there's an amendment to the will made two years after the original, leaving everything to Charles, because the other boy died. From the dates, I reckon he'd have been about twenty-one. I knew you'd ask me to look up Charles Miller's will so I've done it already. He left all his worldly goods to his wife May and her children, Elaine and Jack.'

'That's great.' It meant she'd skipped four generations. Didn't have to scour through all the birth registers for Eleanor's children, grand-children and their children and grandchildren.

She took a gamble the diary would be handed on down the female line where possible. May and then Elaine. Back to the marriage indexes, the more recent entries, with neatly typed records, groom and bride together. She found it after about an hour. Elaine's marriage, to an Andrew Wilding, in Stratford-Upon-Avon in the autumn of 1967. Bethany's parents. Perhaps.

Stratford. The photograph of a canal that Bethany had given to Adam.

What you dread is never as bad as you think it will be. And what you long for is never quite as good. But when a decision's made for you, there's a feeling of relief, no matter what.

She'd found her. Or almost.

Had to be sure.

The birth registers. Based on the assumption that Bethany was now aged around eighteen to twenty-one.

It occurred to Natasha, as she scrolled through all the Wilding baby girls born in Stratford around two decades previously, that if Bethany was not Bethany at all the final conclusive stretch of the search could prove an arduous one, and extortionately, perhaps prohibitively, expensive and time-consuming. She'd have to ask for reference checks to be done on all the certificates to find which of the female babies had parents called Elaine and Andrew. Wilding was not a particularly common name but there were a dozen or so in each register.

Something in her resisted just contacting

Andrew and Elaine Wilding and asking if by any chance they had a daughter who fitted Bethany's description.

She needn't have worried. The Wildings had had to wait over a decade for their daughter but she was there. In the index covering the September quarter of 1981, there was the entry for the birth of Wilding: Bethany, E.

She went outside to call directory inquiries and get some air. The road was deserted, except for a boy in an England shirt who was kicking a football at a brick wall in what would have been the playground of the old school. The sky was a sickly yellow. The street lamps had come on, glowing amber, and overhead blinked the lights of a jumbo jet.

Natasha dialled 192 and was told there was only one A. Wilding who lived in Stratford. She scribbled the number down on her notepad.

Everything was falling into place, as if, once she'd turned her attention to Eleanor, she'd passed some kind of test, cracked the code. Everything was more straightforward than it might have been. The Wildings could have moved years ago, or possessed a more common name. But no.

She started to dial the Wildings' number then stopped. She didn't want to talk to Bethany's parents on a mobile. She found two pound coins in her pocket and went back inside to the pay-phone. A woman was already using it. Natasha tried not to pace impatiently. Eventually, the woman hung up, flashing Natasha an apologetic smile as she left the cubicle.

Andrew Wilding answered. She listened to his

voice intently, trying to catch any nuances of sorrow or anxiety, but it was impossible to glean anything. She told him she was a genealogist, researching the Wilding name. 'I'd like to come and talk to you if that would be OK?' She made an effort to sound calm. As if she had all the time in the world.

Andrew Wilding seemed a little baffled by her call. He asked when she was thinking of coming and appeared surprised when she said the next day. He expressed concern at her having to make a special journey, wondered if he couldn't perhaps answer her questions over the phone?

'I'm afraid I'm tied up tomorrow but the day after would be fine,' he said. She told him she was planning a trip to Stratford anyway, so it was no bother.

Natasha jotted directions in her notepad, and hung up.

Bethany's father had sounded nice, normal. Yet she had been so upset when Adam mentioned him, and never talked about her family. Why? It would be good to know before she had to meet them.

She stared at her notes. Eleanor's grandson had died young, like Harry Leyburn. What was it Katherine had said about Bethany? *When people come in for wreaths for the graves she'd be almost in tears.*

On automatic pilot, almost against her will, Natasha found herself going back to the registers, sliding in the fiche for the 1980s death records. She scrolled through the Wildings. Slid in another file, searching again.

278

Then Elaine Wilding's name, Bethany's mother's name, was staring back at her.

She had died in summer 1985. Fifteen years ago, when Bethany would have been four years old.

Natasha rang Will.

'How you doing? Not great by the sound of it,'

'Listen, Will. Do me a favour can you? Check the local Stratford-upon-Avon rag for a coroner's report for Elaine Wilding, summer 1985.'

'The girl's mother, right?'

'Right.'

Natasha couldn't face another coffee, opted for tea instead, plenty of sugar.

'You've opened one large can of worms this time,' Will said when he rang back. 'Forget the coroner. There's a front page article. Elaine Wilding died while she was swimming, it says. Wouldn't it be easier to say she drowned?'

'Just read it will you?'

'OK, OK. No need to bite my head off. I quote: "A dreadful blow to a family still recovering from the tragedy of losing their eldest child, Charlotte, who also died suddenly just last year, a few days before her thirteenth birthday. Andrew Wilding, father of Charlotte and wife to the recently deceased, Elaine, is helping police with their enquiries."' Will paused. 'Which is a polite way of saying they think he did it, isn't it?'

Natasha couldn't find her voice.

'Explains a lot,' Will commented.

No it doesn't. Andrew Wilding's voice. Nice, normal.

'Haven't found any follow-ups as yet,' Will said. 'No details of conviction or acquittal or whatever. Not as dramatic as a speculative story no doubt, so it's probably tucked away on the back pages somewhere. I'll keep looking.'

Natasha called Adam, told him she needed to see him. He didn't ask what for, just said that he'd come up to Snowshill. She was about to give him directions, but he said he didn't need them.

This remark came back to her later, when she walked into the car park and saw the Celica parked two rows down from the Alpine, a figure with a baseball cap pulled low over his face, sitting in the driver's seat, cigarette smoke curling from the opened window.

Enough was enough. She marched towards it, was perhaps ten car-lengths away when the Celica pulled out at some speed. The tyres made an abrasive crunch on the gravel as it did a sharp turn and roared away through the exit gate. Natasha memorized the full registration number, went back to sit in her car and called Broadway Police Station. She asked to speak to PC Walker.

'I think I'm being followed. In fact I'm certain of it.' She told him what had happened, gave him the registration.

He told her he'd call her back after he'd checked the database.

She was almost at Toddington. 'I'm not supposed to tell you anything, data protection and all that. Unless you're in danger.'

'Is it likely you'd be followed and not be?'

She'd hoped very much he'd deny that but he didn't. 'Name of Jake Romilly mean anything to you?'

It came as no surprise at all.

Thirty-Eight

She cut cross-country and headed back into Oxford.

Her mobile rang with a voice message. 'Peter Deacon. *Oxford Times.* We're running a feature on a photographic exhibition at Exeter College. Have a few questions for you.' *I've got plenty of questions of my own thanks very much.*

She held her finger on the buzzer at the studio. No response. She felt like kicking the door down. She stood back in the street. The slatted blinds were down in the architects' office, but she could see figures moving about.

She rang the bell.

The door was opened by a plump, grey-haired woman. 'Can I help?'

'I wondered if I could have a word with Christine?'

The woman let Natasha into the vestibule.

Christine's careful professional smile dimmed when she saw Natasha. She was dressed more glamorously than before, as if she was planning on going out later. Short black skirt and shocking pink top, matching lipstick and dangly silver earrings. Natasha pictured her in a ring of fire.

'Know where I might find Jake?'

Christine shook her head, cagey now.

'You do know something?'

'I know who you are, what you're doing. I know

281

you got me into trouble. Jake had a real go at me for letting you in last time. I don't want to get involved, OK?'

She turned to go. Natasha grabbed her arm. 'Jake's been following me. I think he broke into my house. I'm pretty angry and I'm also quite scared. If you have any idea what's going on tell me, please.' She felt the girl hesitate, relaxed her grip. 'Look. I've not had lunch yet, do you get a break?'

They found a wine bar round the corner.

Christine said she didn't want a drink. Natasha ordered a bottle of house white and two glasses in any case.

Christine sat chewing the inside of her lip. 'All I know is what I overheard them saying.'

'Who?'

'Jake. And one of the others?'

'Adam?'

'I think so, yes. He was certainly there that afternoon. I saw Alex – you know, who also uses the studio – in the morning. I saw him leave.' Natasha tried to be patient. 'I went out with Jake for about three months. That night I was working late, waiting for him to come back so we could go clubbing. I saw him go down to the studio. It was pouring outside and I didn't want to ruin my hair so I used the back stairs, planned on banging on the door until they opened up. I heard Jake's voice. He was talking really loud, panicky, to whoever was down there. Adam, or Alex maybe, like I said.'

Natasha waited a second. 'What was he saying?'

282

Christine shifted on her stool, lowered her eyes, started gnawing her nails, nails that were already chewed back to the quick. She looked up. 'He said, "She was just lying there. Like she was dead." He said, "I swear I didn't do anything." He said that a couple of times. "I hardly touched her."' Natasha felt as if she'd been kicked in the stomach. 'Adam, or Alex, said "Christ." Then asked Jake if he'd felt for a pulse or whatever. Jake said he wasn't thinking straight. He thought she was still breathing but he couldn't be sure, and what happened if she stopped? He asked if they should go back but whoever it was said no way.'

'Go back where?'

'I don't know.'

'When was this?'

'Before Christmas. About ten days before.'

After the *Ophelia* shoot, then. Around the time Adam said Bethany had left. 'You think they were talking about Bethany?'

'Jake was seeing her when ... before ... me. Alex likes to stir it. Like I said, I saw him that morning. He said Bethany had left Adam. She'd come round to the studio to pick up some of her things. Jake had been there and said he'd buy her a coffee before she went. She said no but he followed her...' Her voice cracked. 'I met her at the studio once or twice. I didn't talk to her ever. But I could see why Jake liked her. She was perfect for the photographs they were doing. Sort of sad-looking.' She looked up imploringly. 'I didn't know what to do. He said she was breathing so I thought...'

'Have you told anyone else?'

'No. I...' Christine looked close to tears.

Natasha put her hand on the girl's arm, pushed the glass of wine nearer. 'It's OK.'

'I didn't want ... my parents would hate me ... mixing ... with people like Jake. I didn't want them to find out.' Christine started gnawing at her thumb now. Natasha couldn't help feeling a twinge of pity for her. 'It wasn't really that I liked being with Jake, but I liked being with myself when I was with him, know what I mean? The photographs he took of me. Not just a nine to five office girl whose best offer to the world is the fact that I can type at ninety words a minute and know how to operate Excel and Windows and PowerPoint. I thought how I'd invite everyone from the office to the exhibition, all my bosses. I couldn't wait to see their faces. It'd give them all something to think about next time they gave me their coffee orders. Going out with Jake was better than girls' nights out and office parties and all that stuff that everyone else does.'

Natasha paid and they went outside.

'What are you going to do?' Christine asked.

'I'm not sure.

'You should ask Adam,' Christine said. Natasha remembered with a jab of dread that she'd have the perfect opportunity. He was on his way to Snowshill. 'Ask him about The Ravens.'

Thirty-Nine

Ask him about The Ravens.

What was that supposed to mean?

As she drove into Snowshill, Arnold was making his way, as he did on the dot of seven every night, down past the green towards the pub. He raised his hand in greeting, in the way a police officer would stop traffic. Natasha waved back. Earlier she'd vaguely entertained the idea of wandering across to the inn for supper before Adam arrived. Now it felt as if she'd taken a wrong turning, into a nightmarish parallel universe where it was ludicrous to end the day with a simple pleasure like a drink with friends.

Ask him about The Ravens.

The Ravens. The initials TR on the photographs? Adam's words in the pub at Little Barrington. *I've always liked the idea of the Pre-Raphaelite Brotherhood. Secret societies.*

The Ravens was a good name for one. As good a name as any.

She was in the kitchen when she heard the clunk of the car door, didn't go through to let him in until there was a knock.

'Hello again.' He was wearing a black v-neck sweater and jeans. His hair looked freshly washed, still damp at the ends, the curls a little tighter, darker. He held out a bottle wrapped in tissue paper, like a peace offering. Natasha didn't want

285

to touch it.

'I thought we could go over to the pub.'

He thrust the bottle towards her. 'And I thought we could stay here.'

She didn't trust herself to say any more, extended her arm, indicating he go through to the living room.

She escaped into the kitchen, rested her hands palm down on the table. She could feel her pulse in her finger tips. She realized suddenly how unprepared she was for any of this. And what a ridiculously sheltered middle-class life she'd led, surrounded for the most part by straight, moral people, her only brush with criminals and murderers through yellowing coroners reports and lists of long-dead convicts.

She took a deep breath, straightened up, swept her hair away from her face, reached for the bottle Adam had brought. It was expensive French red wine. She found the corkscrew. When she went through to the other room he was kneeling on the floor, looking through the CD rack. 'Mind if I choose something?'

'Feel free.' Boris, who had been sprawled out in front of the fire, now rose stiffly to his feet and nosed her hand, then ambled back to the rug and flopped down again close to Adam. Clearly no judge of character at all.

Adam slipped a CD into the machine. Nick Cave. *Boatman Calls*. She wished he'd chosen something else. Something she didn't like so much. She'd never be able to listen to it again without thinking of him, or rather, thinking of this moment, how she was feeling. Angry.

286

Confused. Scared.

'Haven't you forgotten something?'

He stared down at her hands. She'd not brought any glasses.

He followed her to the kitchen. She could feel him behind her, blocking the doorway. 'Nice place you've got here.' She poured the wine. Some splashed on the table. It tasted bitter in her mouth, seemed to make her tongue and lips even drier.

'You're wishing you hadn't let me come? You're suspicious of me, aren't you?' She didn't reply. 'You're right to be.'

She pulled out a chair and sat down. Her senses were primed, buzzing, a pure still clarity in the centre of her brain. Adam sat down too. They were facing each other across the table.

'I did doubt you,' she said, her voice sounding ultra-calm. 'All along I've had this feeling that you might be keeping something from me. But I didn't tell you everything either. I found a note. Underneath the cover of the diary. It looked like Bethany's handwriting. I thought at first it was a suicide note. I wonder now if you put it there.'

He forced a laugh that wasn't a laugh at all. There was a bemused disbelief in it, as if he thought she was cracking some crass joke. Then he stared at her, looking stunned, so she started to wonder what she'd done. At the back of her mind though, she could hear his voice, giving himself the kind of stage directions he gave at photo shoots. *You've just discovered your lover might be dead, and that someone thinks you are involved. You're devastated, and angry, but part of you can't accept any of it's true.*

Winding himself up to act a part. Faking it.

'I should have told you before,' she said carefully. 'Only I had this crazy idea that it would be cruel. I wanted to find her for you first.'

'What did the note say?'

She rose, went through to the living room to fetch the diary from her desk. She handed the piece of paper to him. He seemed to take a long time, going over and over the words, or just staring at them.

'What made you think this was a suicide note?'

'Doesn't it look like that to you?'

'Not really.'

A surge of relief, mingled with acute embarrassment. Then doubt crept in again. He would say that, wouldn't he?

'She was always writing down things like this,' Adam said. 'Snippets of poetry, she'd read and liked, some of it her own.' He was convincing, you had to hand it to him. 'It means nothing to me.' He looked at the note again, shook his head slowly. '"At last you will be mine." I've been hers all along. If she wanted me.'

'Are you sure about that?'

Adam slumped back in the chair. The atmosphere in the room was like the air before a thunderstorm. You'd hear a pin drop. Cut it with a knife. All those clichés. 'You think I'm not to be trusted?'

'Would I be wrong?'

He snatched his wine, drained it. 'No. You probably wouldn't.'

Natasha replenished his glass.

'So tell me about The Ravens.' He didn't seem

288

particularly surprised or unnerved. 'Your secret society?'

He gulped more of the wine, wiped his mouth with the back of his hand. 'It was my idea. At the time I thought it was bloody clever. It comes from Edgar Allan Poe's poem, you know. 'The Raven'? "Nameless here for evermore … dreaming dreams no mortal ever dared to dream before"? We adopted the line as a kind of manifesto. It seemed to sum up what we were about. "Nameless", as in the secret society gave us and our work anonymity, like the Pre-Raphaelite Brotherhood, of course. "Dreaming dreams no mortal ever dared to dream". Which seemed to have just the right hint of darkness and danger, the mortal bit a nice nod to the afterworld, let us think of ourselves as vampires, or with fame and fortune before us, *im*mortals. And the daring dream element gave us plenty of scope for experimentation, indulging our darkest sexual fantasies.' He took another swig of wine. 'It all started in college. There were about half a dozen of us. We modelled ourselves on the Pre-Raphaelites, like I said. Took it all very seriously. Drew up a code of conduct and voted in members, initiation ceremonies with lots of wine. We got up to a few pranks, left a calling card with a silhouette of a raven on it, got drunk and stoned. Rumours got round, everyone wanted to know who we were. But we only told those we invited to take part and they were sworn to absolute secrecy. The idea was for each of us to approach the most beautiful girls and get them to pose, for all the members in turn. The girls we …

recruited took pleasure in it too. We shot them in the woods at night and ruins of abbeys and castles, naked on tombstones, noirish shots in railway stations. The pictures were great actually. Only, it went further than that.'

'The Ravens didn't disband after you left college?'

'For a while we lost touch, then about a year ago I ran into Jake and Alex. Who you've met I believe.' She was about to say something, but he carried on talking. 'We came up with this idea to launch the Pre-Raphaelite project as The Ravens. To create a little mystique, a publicity stunt. Only ... everything got out of hand.'

'Because of Bethany?'

He nodded. 'It was me she chose. Jake couldn't take that. He wanted her because he couldn't have her. There's always been a professional rivalry between us, healthy, you know, stimulating. But after Bethany it ... turned into something else.'

He didn't have to tell her any more. 'Jake was the one who brought her into the circle, not you?' Jake who, out of spite, never told Adam he knew where Bethany worked. 'You lied to me about how you and Bethany got together.'

'No. I *did* buy her a coffee, in a café, near the studio.'

'But that wasn't the first time you'd met?'

'I'd seen her with Jake, watched him photographing her.'

'And then you didn't want to follow the rules any more? Didn't want to share her?'

Adam shook his head. 'He wouldn't leave her alone, kept coming round to the flat, ringing her

290

up, following her...'

'You think that's why she went away?'

'No. She got pissed off with it all right, but ... in a way I think she was quite flattered as well. Got a kick out of it.'

'She saw herself as some kind of Janey Burden, and you two as Morris and Rossetti?'

But did it work both ways? Did she have to compete for Adam's love? It was Lizzie Siddal Bethany really identified with. Lizzie, who had wanted only Rossetti, who couldn't bear to share him, who killed herself when she thought he was with another woman.

Natasha phrased the next question very carefully. 'Where did Alex stand in all this?'

'Oh, on Jake's side, they've always been best mates.'

Natasha grabbed at that. It was Alex who Christine had overheard Jake talking to that night. Adam knew nothing about it.

He massaged his temples. 'Y'know, before Bethany, the longest relationship I've ever had lasted about a fortnight. I thought I wasn't cut out for monogamy. You said we can blame all our problems on past generations, people who died before we were born. I don't know about that, but I'd agree to a certain extent. That it goes at least one generation back. It's true what they say about your parents fucking you up. Mine were always rowing. I couldn't stand it. They tried to hide it from me at first, to wait until I'd gone to bed. All day I'd catch these looks between them, eyes like razors, a sort of hissing in their voices, and then later their shouting kept me awake for hours. They stayed together for my sake. People should never do that.' He broke off, looked up. 'The thing is, it's like I'm hooked on that first stage of being in love, when you'd do anything for each other, and everything is perfect. As soon as it starts to change, when you become a normal couple who go to the supermarket together, I start looking elsewhere. Every time I think, this will be different, I won't let things change. But it always does. Except with Bethany. She *was* different, I don't know what it was about her. She appreciated little things. I still loved her even when I knew she was lying to me. She told me she lived at Chatham Place. Jake had written it down in the studio contact book. I went there one day, to surprise her. And the old lady who lived there said the only lodger she had was a middle-aged man. I told Bethany what had happened and she just laughed at me. I was so angry I ripped the page out of the address book, tore it to shreds in front of her. She just watched me. But it didn't change how I felt about her.' He paused. 'You're a good listener. I bet people always end up pouring out their hearts to you.'

'Seems to happen that way.'

'I almost told you everything before, right at the beginning. But I couldn't. I knew you wouldn't agree to help me.'

'You'd have been wrong.'

People got away with all kinds of things under the guise of artistic decadence. But she could easily understand the appeal of what Adam and his friends had done, how you'd come up with an idea like that, to add some spice to life, then get swept along with the danger and drama and romance of it. Life crossing over into art again. She didn't know what to say. Next door the music had come to an end.

'I think I've found her father,' she said. 'I'm going to see him at eleven o'clock the day after tomorrow.'

Adam looked as if he didn't believe her, never honestly thought she'd manage to pull it off.

'I found out a little about her family, too,' Natasha said. 'Her mother died when Bethany was a child. Bethany had an older sister, Charlotte, who also died suddenly.'

'My God. I want to come with you.'

'Your exhibition opens in a couple of days.'

'There's nothing much left to do now.'

'Is Jake going to be there, for the opening?'

'I expect so.' She stored that information away for later. 'I thought about cancelling the whole thing. It was Bethany who persuaded me not to. And then when she'd gone ... I won't work with Jake again. This is it.'

'I have to ask you this.' Natasha paused. 'Do you think there's any chance he might have harmed her.'

'No.' He shook his head slowly. 'Why do you ask?'

'I...' How could she tell him about what Christine had told her? It would become clear tomorrow at the Wilding's house. If Bethany and Adam managed to make a go of it, it would be up to Bethany whether or not she ever told him what had happened between her and Jake. 'No reason,' Natasha finished.

'Once she'd gone, once I didn't have her either, Jake lost interest,' Adam said 'Out of sight, out of mind.'

Maybe Christine had made a mistake. Got the wrong end of the stick. 'You know her better than I do.' Just pray he knew Jake.

Adam picked up his car keys. It was late. She was in half a mind to tell him he could stay. But something prevented her.

She opened the door and a blast of cold night air took her breath away. He turned. 'I couldn't understand why you seemed almost more determined than I that we keep looking for her. I can't believe you kept all that to yourself. That you'd do that, for a stranger. It's sod's law, isn't it? I go through my life never finding anyone I could imagine loving for ever. And then I meet two at the same time.'

Forty

Next morning, while Natasha ran a bath, she printed out all her notes on Bethany's case.

As she read them, lying in the tub, she understood exactly why Bethany had asked if some families could be cursed. If you believed in such things, you'd easily be persuaded that her family carried that blight.

Eleanor's grandson who died when he was twenty-one. Harry and Harold Leyburn, in all likelihood distant cousins but blood relations none the less. Bethany's sister who never reached her thirteenth birthday. Bethany's mother, who didn't live to see her youngest child start school.

A good old-fashioned curse, or one of the more scientific varieties?

Later she called Will. 'Have you heard of Harry Leyburn, young athlete who died a few weeks ago, suspected heart attack?'

'Mmm.' Said in a tone that indicated he was bracing himself for the next question.

'Don't suppose you've any wild theories about any hereditary condition that might have killed him?'

Will had agreed to meet Natasha at the Genetics Research Centre, a modern glass and concrete building on the outskirts of Oxford. He'd warned that he could only spare half an hour or so before he had to get back to Cheltenham for a meeting with the scriveners.

They met in the spacious reception area, and took the lift up to the canteen where they filled chunky white china cups with tea from the dispenser.

'I've had a word with Professor Holmes,' Will said, as they sat down by a wall of glass. 'He's one of the world's leading specialists in hereditary heart conditions, specifically something called Hypertrophic Cardiomyopathy.' He handed over a sheaf of printed notes. 'It's pretty scary reading.'

Natasha flipped through the stapled papers. A series of diagrams of the heart, cross sections of muscle, elongated diamonds with dots in them in, the diamonds aligned horizontally, neatly on top of each other, then, in an adjacent diagram, all over the place, some vertical, some diagonal, crossing over. Myocardial Disarray it said underneath. On another page were ultrasound pictures, which looked to the untrained eye like the pictures Mary had proudly shown her of the baby in her womb; on another examples of family trees, medical ones, that mapped heredity, males and females represented as circles and squares, those unaffected showing as clear shapes, those that carried the condition, shaded in.

Natasha looked at Will. 'Okay. Give me the basics.'

He took the notes back. 'The condition was first recognized in the 50s. According to estimates, one in five hundred births could be affected. In the UK alone it's thought that ten thousand people have it. Mis-diagnosis is common. There's a severe lack of knowledge about the condition, so it often goes undetected, even during an autopsy. As such, it's guessed that up to seventy per cent are totally oblivious that they've got it, or are carriers. The condition is transmitted from one generation to the next without skipping. Dominant inheritance. Each child of an affected male or female has a fifty-fifty chance of inheriting. Want a rundown of symptoms?'

'Go on.'

Will read aloud. 'HCM is marked by a thickening of the heart in the absence of an apparent cause – because of a genetic abnormality. Sometimes causes a blockage that results in the heart overworking. Patients may have shortness of breath, exercise intolerance, chest pressure, pain, fainting, or no symptoms whatsoever.' Natasha watched Will's eyes as he read, flicking from side to side. 'HCM is cardiology's great masquerader. Sometimes it simulates coronary artery disease, sometimes it resembles valvular heart disease with heart murmurs. Sometimes the heart seems normal. The condition may be present at birth or in childhood, is occasionally the cause of a still-birth, but it's much more common for the heart to appear normal at this time. Hypertrophy more frequently develops in association with growth and is usually apparent by the late teens or early twenties.'

'What does it say about people who die suddenly?'

Will scanned a couple of pages. 'Ah, here we are. Adolescents and young adults with no prior symptoms can suffer sudden death without knowing they have the disease. HCM is the most common cause of sudden cardiac death in young athletes and people under thirty years of age. It is suspected that ventricular fibrillation, a chaotic heart rhythm, is the cause of death.'

'What about cures?'

Will shook his head. 'Nothing to reverse the condition. Pacemakers and drugs can be used to control heart rhythm if the problem is detected early enough.' He turned the page. 'Conclusion: Developments are likely to come from the early detection of persons carrying the gene and treating them to prevent the development of hypertrophy. It is hoped in the future that gene therapy will help to bring about curative intervention.' He stopped reading, put the papers down, sipped his tea. 'Like any hereditary disease, they're using family histories to learn more about it, and to quantify the risk to particular individuals. Using extended family trees to actually find and warn those who are at risk. This girl you're researching: what makes you think she's affected?'

'I think she was related to the Leyburns.'

'And her mother and sister both died. Maybe her old man wasn't guilty. I've not had time to do any more checks on the Stratford papers, I...'

'Doesn't matter.'

She went over the symptoms Will had listed in her head. 'Her boyfriend said that she fainted.'

Will gave a slight nod. 'If you're right, then she's fortunate that she's got you working for her. She'd be one of the lucky ones. Like I said, all too often someone drops dead and it just goes down as a freak heart attack. So the relatives carry on unawares. When you find her, you make sure she goes and gets checked out. ECG or angiogram might pick something up. There might even be a genetic screening test already developed for her family.'

Natasha stared at him. 'You mean there might be details of some of her family on files here? You couldn't–?'

Will silenced her. 'No. I definitely couldn't. Those patient records are highly confidential.'

'Of course.' Natasha looked down at her tea meekly. 'But...'

'But nothing.'

'OK, I get the message.' Natasha thought for a moment. 'What would it show up as in death certificates, before the condition was identified?'

'Sub-aortic stenosis. Heart attack. Heart failure. But then that covers a multitude of sins. It's what everyone dies of in the end.'

Natasha thought of Lizzie. 'How about the nineteenth century. General malaise, weakness, undiagnosable?'

Will pursed her lips. 'Possible, I suppose.'

And Lizzie's baby. HCM was a cause of stillbirth.

Natasha looked out of the window to the street below, a mother pushing a buggy, an old man making his way stiffly over the pedestrian crossing, leaning on a walking stick. 'What's the death rate for those affected?'

'Same as always,' Will said with a smile. 'One per person.'

'Thanks Will. I'll let you get on.'

They walked back towards the lift. Natasha spied the sheaf of notes tucked under Will's arm. 'Could I get a copy of those?'

'Yeah. We can stop off at the machine on the way down.' They got out at the third floor. 'Just be a tick,' Will said. As soon as his back was turned she flew in the opposite direction, frantically peering through doors for an empty office. She found one, the computer not in screensaver mode. Just pray whoever had been using it had just popped out for a cup of tea and she wouldn't need a password to access data.

She was in luck.

In the 'patient details' box she typed: Wilding.

No Results Found.

Leyburn.

No Results Found.

So much for luck. She pushed the chair back. Then remembered. The e-mail that had come in from the Genealogical Research Directory, from Sue Mellanby, who remembered being taken to the Marshall grave as a child.

She typed: Mellanby.

Four names popped up. Two from Cambridgeshire.

Genetic condition: HCM.

Natasha clicked on one of the names. Rachel Mellanby. Age 22. She scanned the screen. Whizzed the mouse to the box that said 'affected members'.

She hit enter and a medical family tree spidered across the screen, similar to the one in Will's notes, showing those who were dead, probably due to the condition, and those who were definitely free of it. She scrolled upwards. No recognizable names. Then along the right. John Miller was there, one of the names she came across at the Gloucester Records Office. So he was an ancestor of the Mellanbys. He was also Bethany's distant ancestor.

The old lady who'd spent her younger days researching her family tree, and who remembered hearing of a little girl called Bethany. Sue Mellanby was not on the tree but it was a rare enough surname, with a high proportion of the family coming from Cambridgeshire. They'd just not traced the link to her yet.

Faced with that fragmented family tree, with all its gaps and question marks, Natasha had an overwhelming sense of a race against time. To fill in those gaps, to find all the scattered members and warn them before it was too late. She saw for the first time what Will meant when he said that genetic research was bringing a new importance to genealogy.

One thing required no question mark next to it. The Mellanbys detailed here had HCM. And they were related to Bethany's family.

Natasha looked more closely at the names of those who'd died. In one generation, there were five teenagers.

The escape button.

She peered out into the corridor. All clear. She snuck out, sauntered back to the lift.

Will was waiting, looking impatient.

'Had to pop to the ladies,' Natasha smiled.

'You took your time about it.' Will handed over the copied notes. 'There you go.'

'Thanks. Don't worry about coming down with me. I can find my own way if you've got things to do.'

Will linked his arm through hers. 'Why is it that I find I'd feel happier if I knew I'd escorted you off the premises?'

Forty-One

The Alpine needed petrol. Natasha called in at a station on the way to Stratford. Copies of the local papers were on display on a newstand outside. The *Worcester Evening News. Cotswold*

Journal. Oxford Times. She'd completely forgotten about the call from the reporter who'd wanted to ask her about Adam's exhibition. She picked up a copy of the paper as she paid for the gas.

She drove to the small railway station at Stratford-Upon-Avon and parked outside. She was a few minutes early and the train from Oxford was delayed according to the arrivals board. She scanned the paper. Oxford United's latest victory on the front page. Photos of school children on a sponsored run, a story about a local computer games business that had just won an award. What was the reporter's name? Peter Deacon. She scanned for his byline, turned to the arts pages. MYSTERIOUS MODEL MISSING. A grainy black and white copy of Bethany as Ophelia. The caption underneath: *Do you know this girl?*

Controversy surrounds a photographic exhibition, due to open at Exeter College tomorrow, by a radical group of anonymous young artists who go by the name of The Ravens. The model, Bethany Marshall, the star of the showpieces, walked out several weeks ago after a row with her lover, who has hired Gloucestershire-based private detective, Natasha Blake, to find her. Intriguingly, it appears the girl left no clues as to her family or possible whereabouts. So far the search has proved unsuccessful.

Get your bloody facts right at least! Now she'd be getting calls from jealous husbands wanting her to tail their wives.

How had they got hold of this shit? Someone had fed it to them, been obliging enough to give them a copy of the photograph for God's sake. Was Jake Romilly unscrupulous enough, just to get his name in print, to settle scores?

Adam's train slid up to the platform, left again as a trickle of passengers appeared. Natasha watched all the usual little dramas of train stations, people saying goodbye running into each others arm's, embracing.

She noticed that Adam had made a touching effort to smarten up. Freshly shaven, a well-ironed white shirt beneath his black jacket.

He opened the passenger door, sat down beside her. She handed him the paper.

He didn't look at it. 'It wasn't me, OK? Angie offered to handle the PR for the show. She sent the paper a Jpeg of *Ophelia*. Some reporter rang to ask for Bethany's details. Angie happened to mention that...'

'Happened to mention? Are you absolutely sure about that? I mean, it's a great publicity stunt, isn't it? Look at these adjectives. In one fell swoop you're radical, controversial, mysterious.'

He snatched the paper, ripped it in two and screwed it into a ball, getting out and dumping it in a bin. 'Garbage,' he said when he came back. 'You're talking absolute rubbish. And what does it matter anyway? Bethany might see it...'

She might. 'And so might her family.'

'Lucky we're going to see them then.' He looked at her. 'Forget it, all right?'

They had forty-five minutes to kill. Natasha suggested they find somewhere for coffee. She took the Alpine round to the station car park and they walked down Greenhill Street, past the pinnacled clock tower, and turned right onto the High Street.

They found a café that overlooked the water and the Nine Arch Bridge. They sat at a table by the window, and in silence mostly, drank coffee, watching the brightly painted narrow boats in their moorings in the canal basin.

There was a sense of marking time, like sitting in the waiting room at a doctor's surgery, making polite conversation. The coffee was making Natasha feel hyper. The toast she'd eaten for breakfast sat in her stomach, her body too pumped with adrenaline to tackle digesting it.

Natasha noticed that Adam's hand, as he held his cup, was not quite steady.

He'd said he'd leave the talking to her, but she didn't have a clue what she was going to say to Bethany's father. She was trusting the right words would come when she needed them. What she was really hoping was that Bethany had gone back to him after she'd left Adam, that she would be there at her childhood home, and that Natasha could tell her what she'd discovered, then exit from the proceedings, her role completed. But she just knew it wasn't going to be that simple.

Adam leant back in his chair, distractedly picked up one of the magazines he'd brought with him on the train, a style title aimed at teenagers, with arty photographs of moody musicians, reviews of films and advertisements for the kinds of clothes Natasha used to buy from Kensington Market when she lived in London.

He dropped it onto the table, said he was going to the bathroom. She understood his inability to sit still.

It was just after ten-thirty and the café was emptier now. At the next table a young couple lingered over their drinks, in no hurry, sharing a single serving of chocolate cake.

The girl glanced at Natasha as Adam paid their bill. For a moment Natasha saw herself and Adam as others would. Another pair of lovers, spending a long weekend away.

Perhaps in just a few minutes they'd find Adam's real love. An ordinary twenty-year-old girl, listening to CDs or chatting to her friends on the telephone, painting her nails in her bedroom.

Or perhaps not.

Forty-Two

Number 19 Elsinor Road was a large detached mock Tudor house, with a wide gravel drive and double garage on a new housing estate on the western periphery of Stratford. The paintwork was pristine white, and net curtains hung at the downstairs windows. An Audi estate with a brand new registration plate was parked at an angle outside the red front door whose brass knocker looked as if it was polished daily.

Natasha formed an instant picture of Bethany's childhood home as similar to her own. But familiarity, in this instance, only made her more anxious. She imagined how Ann and Steven would react to someone like herself coming to see them with someone like Adam to discuss their family history, even before she got started on what she'd found out from Will. Ann would resent the invasion of privacy, strangers nosing around in her family without her permission. Steven would be deeply suspicious of Adam, doubting his sincerity, automatically believing him in the wrong, despite the evidence of his daughter's lies.

'Meeting the parents is always supposed to be a bit of an ordeal, but this takes the biscuit,' Adam muttered.

Natasha gave him what she hoped was an encouraging smile.

Bethany's father opened the door, tall and trim, in his late fifties. He was smartly dressed in dark grey flannel trousers and a navy sweater.

'Natasha Blake,' she said.

He shook with her. 'Andrew Wilding.'

Adam offered his hand. 'Adam Mason.'

A vague frown signified Andrew Wilding's puzzlement.

They were ushered through a blue carpeted hallway into a neat sitting room, with a pink, velour three-piece suite, beige carpets and creamy walls decorated with watercolours of windmills, castles and rivers. The easy chairs were drawn up around a fake fire that looked surprisingly genuine but gave out no heat. Andrew Wilding told them to make themselves comfortable.

'I thought it was only the aristocracy that had folk researching their ancestry for them.'

Natasha smiled awkwardly. She was about to explain when Wilding went off into the kitchen to put the kettle on for coffee.

'It must be great, living in Stratford,' Adam commented awkwardly, sitting slightly forward on his chair, when Wilding returned moments later. Natasha thought it was the type of conversation Adam would have begun with Bethany's father if she had been there to make the introductions.

'I'm so used to it I take it for granted. I was Manager of the Swan Theatre for seven years.'

Natasha tried to make the two images fit. A theatre manager, and this conservative middle-aged man who lived in this neat, conventional house. But people changed, sometimes beyond all recognition. Long haired youths with their own band, metamorphosing into slick solicitors or accountants; not to mention Goths into respectable genealogists, just. She tried to make two other images fit. This diffident, conservative man and a man who might have murdered his wife. She couldn't believe it. But what did murderers look like? Like everyone else. 'I met my wife, Elaine at the theatre,' Wilding was saying. 'She was a costume designer. He glanced at the watercolours, and a photograph which stood on a HiFi cabinet by the window. 'There's the kettle. Excuse me a moment.'

Adam went to pick up the photograph. Natasha could vaguely see it from where she sat. A young woman, her long pale hair tied up in a loose ponytail with a big black bow; a little girl, no more than two years old, sitting on her lap, laughing for the camera, wearing a frilly theatrical party dress with big sleeves.

Andrew Wilding came back into the room carrying a tray set with china cups and saucers and a plate of neatly arranged digestive biscuits. 'Is this your daughter?' Adam still clutched the picture in his hand.

The frown on Andrew Wilding brow deepened. 'Bethany, yes. She loved having her picture taken. That was a fair few years ago.'

'I know,' Adam said, a response to both facts. Natasha's eyes flew to Andrew Wilding's face.

'You've met Bethany?' he asked.

'Yes.'

Andrew Wilding handed over cups and offered biscuits. 'I take it that it's my wife's side of the family you're interested in?'

Natasha realized he thought Adam worked with her and had met Bethany as a result of genealogical research they were involved in together. She was aware of Adam's eyes on her, waiting for her to explain.

'It's not a straightforward family history I'm working on. Adam came to me because he'd met Bethany and he wanted my help to get in touch with her again. She left an old journal with him, which he presumed belonged to one of her ancestors.'

Natasha was surprised by how *un*surprised Andrew Wilding seemed by this news. 'The diary belonged to Bethany's mother, that much I can tell you. I don't think Elaine was fully certain of its history. My wife died when Bethany was just a toddler.' He turned to Adam. 'She didn't tell you

308

that, did she?'

Adam shook his head. 'No.'

'You're lucky she told you her name and gave you this address.'

'She didn't. Natasha traced her through the diary.'

Andrew Wilding gave a little cluck with his tongue, turned to her. 'Well, I never. How ingenious.' Then he looked back at Adam, the frown still there, as if it was permanently etched. 'Bethany took the diary with her everywhere. I can't understand her just leaving it behind. May I ask how you know her?'

'I'm a photographer. I ... took some pictures of her...'

'You're very good,' Andrew Wilding's face was transformed with a smile of recognition and understanding. 'She sent some of them to me. I've had the one of her in a long white dress framed. It's in the bedroom upstairs. Best one of her I've ever seen. But they're all remarkable. You have a real talent there.'

'Thank you. I'm glad you like them.'

'I asked her about you, naturally, but she was very evasive. Which instantly made me think there was something going on between the pair of you.'

'I love your daughter,' Adam said, matter-of-factly.

'I see.'

Adam dropped his voice to a whisper. 'Is she here?'

Andrew Wilding shook his head, more a nervous tick than a shake really. 'I'm afraid not.'

309

'But you know where she is?'

A hint of anxiety in his eyes. 'No. I'm afraid I don't.'

Natasha had been preparing herself for the absolute worst. For Andrew Wilding telling them that Bethany was dead. But now she didn't know whether to be relieved or even more concerned.

It seemed Wilding was prepared to say no more. Natasha noticed Adam's body tense with a frustration she felt too.

'Mr Wilding. May I ask why you said Adam would have been lucky if Bethany had given him this address?'

He stared into his tea.

'I really don't mean to pry,' Natasha continued. 'But it's just that we've come such a long way. I don't mean miles. We've traced her over half a dozen generations.'

Wilding pinched the bridge of his nose. 'I wouldn't know where to start.'

'Her mother?' Natasha suggested gently.

Andrew Wilding turned to Adam. 'Bethany would never have forgotten the diary. It was too special to her. She must have wanted you to have it. In which case you must be very special to her too. So I suppose you have a right to know.' He brought his hand to his mouth, coughed. 'My wife died when she was thirty-three, just after Bethany's fourth birthday. It was June. We'd taken a few days holiday. Our first since...' he broke off, his eyes glazed. 'Bethany had an older sister, Charlotte...' again he left the sentence hanging. 'Elaine and I had had a disagreement, something trivial. Things were difficult for us, after Charlotte. Anyway, Elaine just said she was going for a swim in the river. Bethany was on the bank, picking flowers. I remember that, because when I ran into the water, to … to get to Elaine … I looked back and Bethany was just standing there, in her little white sundress, a posy of buttercups and daisies in her hand.' Natasha heard the tremor in his voice, knew he'd forgotten who he was talking to, that he was talking to anyone at all. He'd gone back to that day in his mind. 'The police were involved of course. They took me to a cell, kept me there for days, months it seemed. Questions. So many questions. They went on and on until I thought I'd go mad. They dredged up everything about Charlotte, all over again. What else could I tell them? My daughter was playing tennis and we found her lying in the grass. My wife went swimming and I found her lying in the water. Suspicious circumstances. Oh, I could see why they were suspicious all right. To much for one family.' He took a deep breath. 'But eventually they had to let me go. Just like that. Never bothered me any more.' He was talking slowly now, almost as if he was in a trance. Natasha had the sense that he'd never poured out his feelings like this before, that now he'd started he couldn't stop. 'Sometimes I wish they'd locked me away – away from all those twitching curtains and wary glances. You can't blame them. When a death, two deaths in the same family are so sudden, so inexplicable. I refused to move house; too many good memories mixed up with the bad. And people round here forgot, eventually. But

311

Bethany ... she didn't forget. I always told her the truth, never kept anything from her. I'd catch her looking at me sometimes, as if she hated me. Or worse still, as if she was frightened of me. I still lie in bed at night and see it all through her eyes. Her mother, face down in the water and me standing over her, panicked, shouting, trying to pull her out, drag her back to the shore, as if I was fighting with her, as if I did it. Sometimes, I think I *am* to blame.' His voice trailed off, came back stronger. 'There was an autopsy of course. The verdict was heart failure. Same as Charlotte. And Elaine's brother, Jack, ten years before. Elaine didn't smoke, didn't drink much. Charlotte had been in the school gymnastic team. Their hearts should have lasted them until they were in their eighties.'

'I'm *so* sorry.' Natasha reached out, touched the back of his hand. 'Mr Wilding. I think I might know why Elaine and your daughter died.'

He looked at her, stupefied, shook his head as if to clear it. 'How can you...'

She glanced at Adam's tense face. 'You know Harry Leyburn?'

Wilding sighed. 'A little. I'm not entirely sure how we're related. Elaine's side. But we took an interest, as you do. Bethany and I followed his progress in the papers, went to see one of his races, hung around afterwards and said, 'Hello.' That's about it.'

'You know he died?'

A pause. 'Yes.'

'I think he had a hereditary heart condition. I think Elaine's branch of the family also inherited it.' She tried not to let the look on his face deflect her. 'There are precautions that can be taken to control the condition. The important thing is to detect it early enough.' She told him a little of what Will had told her, what she'd seen on the database.

His eyes clouded over and he looked away. She wanted him to say something, anything, didn't dare look at Adam again.

'Mr Wilding. I hope you don't think I've done the wrong thing in telling you this but...'

'Done the wrong thing?' He clasped her hand in both of his. 'Of course you haven't done the wrong thing. If what you say is correct, then it's the greatest relief. I can't tell you... It means Bethany and I... His voice cracked and he let go of her hand, fumbled in his pocket for a cotton handkerchief. He blew his nose, dabbed at his eyes. 'It's the most terrible thing, not knowing why, not being able to do *anything* ... I think what happened to her brother was always at the back of Elaine's mind. She was worried about having children. She once said to me, how you can never know what you're passing on to them... In Bethany's case it's fear she's left with. Fear and anger. She's terrified the same thing will happen to her. She's terrified that her father might be a murderer. Oh, she's never said a word but I see it in her eyes.' He reached for the handkerchief again.

'Has Bethany ever had any tests?' Adam's voice was croaky, as if he'd not spoken for weeks.

Andrew Wilding cleared his throat. 'She's always been a frail little thing, prone to getting

313

colds and chest complaints. A couple of times she's passed out, fainted, after she'd been doing aerobics, running for a bus. It happened once when she was small, when she had to give a blood sample for something or other. I didn't think much of it then. I don't like the sight of blood myself. And the more recent attacks I put down to stress over exams, not eating enough. But of course blackouts are a sign of a weak heart. Though Elaine and Charlotte never...' he let his head fall into his hands. Then he seemed to shake himself, dropped a sugar lump into his tea and stirred it slowly, the spoon chiming against the china. 'Bethany has had a couple of ECGs and angiograms but nothing has shown up.' He looked directly at Natasha. 'I encouraged her to find out about her ancestors. I hoped if she saw that they lived to an old age, it would put her mind at rest. That's what I thought, when you called, why I wasn't all that surprised really.'

'I did have a meeting with her,' Natasha said. 'But she never asked me to do any work.'

He nodded abruptly. 'Cold feet I expect. I hoped knowing more about her family might make her think less harshly of her mother,' Andrew Wilding explained. 'The worst thing is, Bethany resented Elaine for having left us, kept saying her mother was selfish.' He dropped another sugar lump into his tea, started to stir again, as though he'd forgotten he'd already done it. 'I kept trying to make her believe that being given the chance of a life, even if it turns out to be a short one, is better than never existing. I told her what you're supposed to tell people who've suffered bereavement. Better to have loved and lost than never to have loved at all. The trouble is, I'm not so sure that's true. I told her that I'd have married her mother knowing what I now know, that I wouldn't have had it any other way. But she never believed me. Sometimes, God forgive me, I didn't believe it either.

'I had to give up my job, get a sensible one, with sociable hours, running an office instead of a theatre. It felt as if my life had ended too, in a way. Except for Bethany. She was all I lived for. But that's a terrible burden for a child, for anyone. And children are so much more intuitive that we give them credit for. I tried to keep it from her, but she saw what a struggle we had, and she swore never to do the same to anyone, never to let anyone fall in love with her. She's stuck to the pledge with a firmness you can't help but admire.'

He turned to Adam. 'I'm telling you all this because ... well... it seems only fair. A boyfriend Bethany had in school wrote long letters to me for months after she'd gone off to London and not given him her address. I couldn't understand why she didn't put the poor fellow out of his misery, tell him she'd found someone else, or the truth even. I've had a string of them over the years. But she clams up on me whenever I try to talk to her about relationships, all that kind of thing. I'm not very good at it. It's not easy for a man to bring up a little girl alone.' He gave a tired smile. 'I even learned to cook and take an interest in clothes. But it's not the same, is it? I knew one day she'd really fall for someone and I worried about what would happen. Like I said, she never said much about you or mentioned you by name but I had a feeling there was someone special...'

Natasha bit the inside of her lip.

'Do you have any idea at all where I can find her?' Adam said.

Andrew shook his head. 'I want nothing more than to see her settled and happy, believe me. But I've not spoken to her in over a month. I know she's left the flat she was renting in Highgate. She's grown so distant since she left home. It's as if now she doesn't have to live with me she can't bear to have anything to do with me. We'd agreed that I was going to spend Christmas with my sister in Scotland, and Bethany wanted to stay in London. She said she might go travelling afterward. If she's fallen in love, that explains things. I dare say she's gone somewhere to sort herself out. She's taken off before now. I'll get a dutiful postcard or a reverse charge call from some far-flung corner of the world, or she'll turn up on the doorstep in the middle of the night, wanting a hot bath and a decent meal. It's just how she is.' He looked at Natasha. 'It'd be so easy to be over-protective, possessive. But I've always tried to let her live her own life, feel entirely free.'

Natasha felt Adam's eyes on her again. But she knew that they could ask no more just now. Couldn't tell this man, who had no way of contacting his daughter, that she might not have gone travelling at all, that she might never come home.

'When she does come back, I expect you'd like me to let you know?' Wilding said to Adam. 'I can't promise that she'll agree to see you, mind. She has her mother's stubbornness, that's for sure.'

Natasha realized then that she might never know the end of this. There was one crucial thing she had to follow up with Jake Romilly. But in the usual run of things she'd done her part, would collect her fee and never see Adam or Andrew Wilding again. If Bethany had simply gone travelling like Wilding said, there was no reason for Natasha to ever know if she came home, or if her father kept his promise and got in touch with Adam, and if Bethany agreed to see him. She could ask Adam to drop her a line maybe, but with what had passed between them, that didn't seem a good idea.

'Mr Wilding, I can tell you that some of Bethany's ancestors did reach old age. It'd be no trouble to order up copies of the certificates so you can show them to Bethany.'

'Could you? That would be tremendously kind.'

Someone who needed no convincing that knowing about the past could really affect the present. 'This may seem a strange request. Bethany's grandmother, the one who left her the diary, did she leave anything else?'

'Junk mostly. All in the loft. May died ten years ago now, but I've never got around to sorting it all out.'

'Would you mind very much if I had a quick look?'

Forty-Three

Andrew Wilding showed her upstairs, took a long pole from an airing cupboard to hook open a latch in the ceiling, and dragged down an aluminium stepladder. 'The light switch is on the floor, right hand side.' He stayed to make sure she'd found it. 'I'll leave you to it.'

'Thanks.'

The loft was a long boarded space beneath new, exposed rafters and wads of insulating rock wool. It looked as if the Wildings had considered converting it at some point, had got around to putting in a small skylight, cobweb encrusted now.

There was hardly any foot-room between piles of cardboard boxes, suitcases, plastic carrier bags and bin liners of clothes and blankets. Christmas decorations, two wooden trunks, a small painted chest of drawers. The top drawer was half open, displaying jewellery; heavy brooches and garnet necklaces. There was an old record player, a stack of LP's, shoe boxes of birthday cards, postcards, letters.

Remains of a life. Several lives.

In one corner was a stack of photograph albums. Natasha picked one up, cradled it in the crook of her arm and opened it. Black and white photographs secured with black corner mounts and white writing under each one, Brighton,

Falmouth. The pictures were of a blonde woman in a woollen twin set and slacks, with short, curled hair, holding a baby straddling a breakwater. Then a little girl with an ice cream cone and a broderie anglaise sun hat, perched on a donkey.

In the album beneath, the little girl was older, in another she was wearing a school uniform, white socks and a smart tie. In the bottom album she was a young woman. 'Elaine's 18th birthday' the caption said.

Kneeling on the floor, Natasha opened the first of the trunks. It was stuffed with clothes, evening dresses with sequins, a beautiful black stole, gold strappy shoes, a 1920s diamanté-studded tiara. She tried not to be distracted.

A box at the bottom was crammed with more postcards. Pictures of Loch Lomond, Tintagel. They were postmarked 1987, 1989, a later one from the Loire Valley. All addressed to Granny, signed Andrew and Bethany.

Natasha opened the other, larger, trunk.

It was packed tidily with children's toys and drawings, wooden building blocks, an ark with tiny pairs of lions and swans and flamingos, the paint chipped, a knitted rainbow scarf, with holes where stitches had been dropped, handmade dolls' dresses, neatly sewed, a recorder a tennis racket and pair of rusted ice skates, a cloth doll and one in a crinoline. Jigsaw puzzles of a water wheel, King Arthur and Guinevere.

Lizzie Siddal in Millais' *Ophelia*.

And beneath the toys, paintings. A toddler's daubs and pencil scribbles, dozens of them. They were all neatly dated on the back, 1950s. Elaine's then. Then the more sophisticated ones, touched by a maturing, individual eye. A treasure chest of memories. May had kept every single thing her daughter had ever painted, ever made or ever written.

Natasha closed the lid and, turned her attention to one of the bulging suitcases, where she discovered that May had kept all her daughter's clothes too.

Did all mothers do that? Ann certainly didn't. Selected items yes. But every single scrap?

It was almost as if, deep inside, May had somehow known what was going to happen, had known that she would not have her daughter for long, would suffer what every mother must dread most of all, to outlive her child. She had known that every tiny piece was precious and must be carefully stored away.

But there was nothing of Jeanette or Eleanor here.

Natasha threw the ladder back into the void, looked round for the pole to close the hatch. Then she noticed a door with an oblong ceramic sign on it, decorated with pink flowers. 'Bethany's Room'.

She opened it, and saw a single pine bed with a lilac and white quilt, and on the wall Pre-Raphaelite posters, slightly faded, of *Ophelia* and Arthur Hughes' *April Love*, with coordinating purple flowers. There were collections of shells, a row of pearly nail varnishes, framed swimming certificates and a photograph of Bethany in what looked like a school play, wearing an ermine cloak and a crown. It could have been Natasha's

320

bedroom at her parents' house.

Adam looked relieved to see her, as if conversation with Andrew Wilding had been stiff going.

'Find anything?' Andrew Wilding asked.

'I'm not really sure what I was looking for.'

'I just thought of something that might interest you, actually.' He went over to a bureau in the corner of the room and opened a little drawer. He handed her a heavy silver locket on a chain, engraved with flowers.

It was antique, Victorian.

Natasha slipped her nail into the tiny clasp to open it. No photographs inside. Just a lock of red-gold hair coiled into the right hand side, the strands tied together with a thin strip of black silk ribbon.

'Elaine said May told her it belonged to her great-great – I forget how many greats – grandmother. The diarist perhaps?'

Natasha tried to remember if Jeanette had ever mentioned the colour of her hair, didn't think so. She touched the coil very lightly, felt a sense of completeness, connecting to the past. A girl had sat in front of a mirror, in candlelight, brushing those curls until they shone, before she went to sleep. She had wound them into a bonnet on Sundays, plaited and decorated them to go to the opera, to meet Mr Brown. Then she had been ill, and someone close to her would have stroked those same tresses which splayed out on the pillow. She had died, and that same someone, the girl's sister perhaps, little Eleanor, had taken a pair of scissors and gently, with tears in her eyes, cut a few strands away from the girl's head, twisted them carefully around her own finger and slipped them into the necklace.

Reluctantly, Natasha handed the locket back. 'Thank you for letting me see it.'

'Thank *you*.'

Andrew Wilding kissed her as she said goodbye. He stood at the windows to see them off, a forlorn figure framed by lace curtains.

'I can't ever thank you enough,' Adam said when they were on their way back to Stratford. He sounded distant and formal, like a chief executive thanking a faceless junior member of staff about whom he'd received a glowing report.

Natasha kept her eyes fixed firmly on the road. 'I wish I could have found her properly for you.'

'You've done more than that. If what you said about the heart condition is true, you've probably saved her life.'

She swallowed hard. 'Listen, Adam, there's something…'

He didn't hear. 'What you said…' – he wiped the window with the back of his hand, pointlessly, since the dirt was on the outside – '…About taking chances at certain times of your life because of your ancestors.' Natasha didn't think he'd been listening to that conversation she'd had with Bethany outside the inn at Little Barrington. 'The note Bethany left … do you think it has anything to do with what happened to her mother? That Bethany might have wanted to…'

'No.'

They were at the station already. She felt

churned up inside. Hadn't said anything about Christine. Better that way. She'd do what had to be done on her own. There was nothing Adam could do to help anyway. She didn't need him interfering, trying to stop her, confronting Jake Romilly himself.

She stopped the car. A phrase came into her head. Have a nice life. 'I wish you all the luck in the world,' she said. Her mouth felt stiff, and she couldn't make it form a smile. 'I hope the exhibition goes well.'

The passenger door was open, Adam was leaning behind the seats to retrieve his magazines. Then he ducked back inside and kissed her on the lips, slipping his hand behind her head to hold her to him. She felt his tongue, just for a second. His fingers snagged in the tangle of her hair and she felt a sharp little pain against her skull as he pulled away. 'Good luck to you, too,' he said.

She heard what she thought must be his train, and then the sound trailed off into the distance, into the past already.

Forty-Four

Natasha switched her mobile on as she drove. There was a message from Mary. 'No news from this end. What have you been up to?'

Natasha called her back, gave her a summarised update.

323

'Poor kid.' Mary's voice had gone very quiet. At once Natasha regretted opening her mouth before her brain was engaged. A story about a mother who died and left her child is not the kind of thing Mary would want to hear right now. 'So that's that,' Mary concluded.

The job done, but not resolved. 'Not quite. I've promised to send her father some details of Bethany's ancestors.' Refusing to let go?

'I can get those for you.'

'Shouldn't you be resting?'

Mary groaned. 'You're as bad as James and my Mum. She keeps ringing me up to check I'm not doing anything.'

'It's nice she's worried about you.'

'About the baby more like. She's been waiting for me to produce a grandchild from the moment *I* was conceived. I can't count the number of times she's told me she's saved my Christening gown.'

It occurred to Natasha that Ann had never once dropped hints about weddings or grandchildren. Given her present circumstances, Natasha wasn't sure if she was glad about that or not. 'OK, if you're certain you're up to it, there is something you could do. All I need to know is what Bethany's ancestors died of. I need death certificates for Elaine Wilding's parents and grandparents at least.'

'Consider it done.'

'Order them on twenty-four hour delivery will you?'

'Course.'

Bethany liked travelling because it made the days seem longer, Adam had said. She refused to talk about the future. Didn't have time for dreams. She got a kick out of Jake Romilly's pursuit of her. Because she wanted to live life to the full, open herself up to as many experiences as possible. She used a false name so she'd be able to disappear when she wanted. Also because a different name let her become a different person, escape the curse of her family.

I have a bad heart.

She told Adam he mustn't rely on her always being around. When she sensed him falling in love with her she disappeared from his life because she was afraid she might be like her mother and her sister, like Harry Leyburn. Even more afraid, perhaps, that she was like her father, and what she wrongly thought him capable of.

She'd become fixated on Lizzie Siddal, a tragic heroine who'd killed herself.

Her Mother died when she was swimming, and Bethany wanted to pose as *Ophelia,* who drowned.

She'd started to see death not as a threat but as an answer, a way out.

Natasha drove to the studio. No sign of life, the architects' office closed for the weekend. She should have thought of a way to find out from Adam where Jake was staying. She'd have to ask Christine first thing Monday morning.

Home. Natasha put the key in the front door. It wouldn't turn. She twisted it the other way. It locked. So was unlocked before. She tried to tell herself that was all for the good. If Jake Romilly had come back it would save her the bother of having to go looking for him.

She pushed the door open. Boris didn't come bounding out to see her. The hallway felt warm. There was the pungent smell of smoke, the crackle of flames. She flew into the living room.

The only fire was one blazing in the hearth. Boris was stretched out contentedly in front of it, and Marcus was sitting in the armchair reading *The Pre-Raphaelite Dream*, as if he'd never been away.

Natasha felt tears start in her eyes.

He looked at her, closed the book. 'Sorry for making myself at home, but it was freezing out there.'

He stood and she went into his arms, stayed there as long as she could. She wiped the tears away, didn't care if he noticed. She couldn't begin to tell him how glad she was to see him.

Delicious cooking smells were wafting from the kitchen. 'Thought you might be hungry,' he said looking into her eyes. 'Nothing exciting I'm afraid. Just what I managed to rustle up from your rather bare cupboards.'

Which wasn't exactly true. It smelt like roast chicken and potatoes. Potatoes she had, but chicken definitely not. He must have bought it specially.

He suggested they went for a walk while they waited for the meal to cook. There were perhaps a couple of hours of daylight left if they were lucky.

They took the Alpine.

'Strange name, Fish Hill,' Marcus said as they stood, catching their breath after the climb. 'When there's not a lake or a river or the sea in sight.'

It was a strange *place*, strange and beautiful. And once, long ago, it must have been under the ocean. Natasha told him the name came from a fossil that had been found in a quarry close to the summit, abandoned now, nothing but a scar. She told him that the limestone beneath their feet was also encrusted with fossilised shells.

She glanced at him now, fed him a line, knowing he'd appreciate it. 'We're eight hundred feet above sea level so I suppose it's no wonder the fish...'

He laughed. '...were petrified.'

They fell silent, but she kept watching him out of the corner of her eye, wanting to know what he was thinking, but happy just to keep reassuring herself that he was there. Some of the items of clothes he was wearing she'd not seen before. Dark blue jeans, a chunky, chocolate pullover. A fawn suede jacket that had once hung in her wardrobe. She knew it would bend in the shape of his arms when he wasn't wearing it. He took a long breath of the crisp air, his hands lightly clasped behind his back and his deep, dark eyes, like a captain of a galleon, scanning the views that she felt she knew better than she knew herself.

Ancient fields and time-weathered dry stone walls that moulded into the landscape and looked as if they'd grown there. In the far distance, cut out against the darkening sky, the Malvern Hills and the Edge, with the road to Winchcombe running along it, rising from the valleys of the Severn and the Avon. Timeless, mysterious, steeped in pre-history. The Bronze Age barrows just a few miles south west of Snowshill, where they found the 3,000-year-old bones of a warrior; the massive earthworks of the Dobunni Celts at Bagendon; the fort on the top of Burhill; the vast earthwork at Belas Knap, like the back of a great whale. Close to where they stood now, the ancient roads, the White Way and Buckle Street, had once formed a crossroads high in the hills.

'When you stand here,' Marcus said. 'The past seems so close you could step back into it. Is that just an illusion, do you think?'

She knew which past he was referring to, couldn't bear to talk about that now.

'I worked it out,' she said. 'My grandmother just about remembered Queen Victoria's funeral. Her great-grandparents would have been born at the time of the French Revolution. Ninety generations and you're back to when Jesus was born. When you look at it like that, time shrinks, doesn't it?'

Marcus turned to her, running his fingers through his dark fringe, wrestling with the gusty wind to keep it out of his eyes. 'I've missed this.'

As they walked on he slipped his hand into hers.

This was where she'd taken him on the first weekend he'd come to Snowshill. The past and the present and the future sliding over each other like tectonic plates shifting in the earth.

Back then they'd brought a flask of coffee and had drunk it, passing the cup between them as they sat in the long grasses in the lee of a dry stone wall flowered with lichen. There was the plaintive sound of lapwings and the chatterings of starlings. Further down, two boys were flying multicoloured kites, one shaped like a bird of paradise and the other a spacecraft.

'Do you want to have children?' Marcus had said.

'What, here, right now?'

He'd smiled. 'If you like.' Then, 'Seriously?'

Despite the fact that it was only five days since she'd first met him, that it was only the second time they'd shared each other's company, it had seemed a perfectly natural question to ask.

'Yes,' she'd replied, her imagination taking flight, soaring high as the kites, to bucket and spade holidays and Christmas trees.

'I worry,' she'd said to him later. 'That if I have children I might...'

It was an accepted psychological fact. That the abused became abusers? Did the abandoned become abandoners?

'I'm sure you'll do everything you can to make sure you have the kind of relationship with your children that you've missed out on.' That was what *he* did. Drove all the fears and ghosts and dark spaces away. Let her sleep at night. 'If you had a little girl, what would you call her?'

'Catherine.'

He had looked at her as if she'd said something revelatory, tugged at a tuft of long grass by his foot and cast it onto the wind as if he was testing for direction. 'Why?'

'The name my mother used. It's a regal name, and strong. From Russia as well as England, which seems appropriate. Katherine of Aragon the most popular of Henry VIII's wives, and Catherine the Great, Russia's most famous empress.'

He turned to her now. 'Katie thinks you're great. I'm sorry I never got around to introducing you before.'

'It's me that should be saying sorry.'

'Consider it said.'

The trouble was, too many other words had also been said and hung in the air between them.

They drove back to the cottage and she went to serve up the roast while Marcus got the fire going again. Like old times.

When she took the roasting dish over to the table she saw that Marcus had taken her post and laid it in a neat pile. There was a package, in a slim padded envelope. She ignored it.

After they'd eaten they took the wine through to the living room where the fire was still blazing.

They sat on the rug in front of it.

'You want to know about my family?' he said. He took her hand, turned it over as if he was a fortune-teller about to read her palm, and then placed something in it, curling her fingers over it. It was a small object, cold and heavy. She opened her fingers and saw a miniature silhouette, a cameo of a shadowed face in profile, framed in a band of gold.

'A self-portrait of my grandmother. Catherine. Katie was named after her.'

You could tell she was beautiful, just from her profile, the aquiline slope of her small nose and the spiral curls of her hair, cut out against the whiteness.

'It tells you a surprising amount about her,' he said. 'Someone artistic who was interested in the past.'

Just like him.

'Also unconventional.' When he looked puzzled Natasha explained. 'She chose to specialize in a medium that was redundant. Two centuries ago silhouettes were the cheapest and easiest ways for people to capture a likeness of their loved ones. A poor man's oil painting if you like. Until photography took over.'

Later, lying in his arms, it struck her that if there was something ironic about her choice of profession – researching people's ancestors when she had no way of finding out about her own – there was also something poignant about the career Marcus had chosen. As a boy he was given a silhouette, a shadowy outline, onto which he had to project his own image, just as he constructed faces from ancient bones.

Sometimes, as he touched her, she wanted to ask him if he used his medical art training, his understanding of anatomy and muscles and skin, when he was making love. If that was the reason he knew how to make her feel as if she came alive beneath his fingers like the faces that he created from clay. But she'd never asked because she'd never wanted to interrupt, for him to stop what he was doing.

This time though, it wasn't the same. When he kissed her, his tongue finding hers, his fingers unpicking the buttons of her shirt, cupping her breasts in his hands, walking his fingers down her spine, it felt not like an awakening, but an exorcism, the end of something for him. He was clasping her to him at the same time as he was pushing her away. She couldn't help thinking he'd just come back to finish it properly. So he could draw a line, move on.

When they separated, she could feel his sweat drying cold on her skin. And what made her colder still was that, just for an instant, it was Adam's face she saw.

She woke at seven, turned over, automatically slipped her arm around him. Not tight enough.

He brought her coffee in bed like he'd always done. Except that he was already washed and dressed. He told her he was flying back to Canada at four o'clock. 'Take care of yourself,' he said.

She managed to say, 'You too.'

'Goodbye.' He made it sound so final that the lump in her throat stopped her answering.

From the bedroom window she watched him drive away. She wondered if he felt better now.

She went to rinse their cups under the tap, couldn't bear to wash the one he'd drunk from, set it to one side, and disconnected her brain.

Forty-Five

She carried the post through to her desk, peeled the adhesive tape off the padded envelope, and slid out the contents.

It was like pass the parcel. Another brown

envelope and white piece of paper, embossed with the emblem that distorted in front of her still-watery eyes. The logo said St Mary's Hospital, Norwich. The writing was sloped almost horizontal, practically illegible. A doctor's handwriting.

Dear Natasha.
Nigel Moore gave me your address. He said he'd tried to contact you but had no luck so I thought I might as well send this on anyway. I met Nigel very briefly years ago, through a friend of a friend, when we were both training at Edinburgh. He tracked me down because I'm a direct descendant of the surgeon John Marshall who I believe you are interested in. John Marshall's son, also John, was my great-grandfather. As they say, it's a small world, and the medical one is even smaller. As you can see, I've followed in my ancestor's footsteps, not only in name.

I do hope the enclosed is of interest. It's a letter to my great-grandfather from his sister. It's been in my family for years – I'd be thrilled if you could shed any light on its meaning, or should I say, on the identity of the mystery lady. The other scrap of paper has always been kept with the letter – something, or nothing?

Please return at some point – no hurry,
All the best,
John Marshall

P.S. I received an e-mail recently, from another lady, in Cambridge, who is also researching the family (and who I'm ashamed to say I haven't had the chance to get back to yet). Her name is Sue Mellanby and I'd be happy to give her your details if you think it'd be helpful.

No need. Natasha carefully tore open the smaller envelope.

The letter was two pages long, the writing instantly recognizable from Jeanette's diary, albeit not as neat, some of the strokes were quavery, as if the hand that had held the pen was weak, not quite steady.

15 November 1872
My dear brother,
I am afraid a grave responsibility must fall to you which it had been my hope to spare you. I shall give you the facts and trust to your wisdom and compassion to deal with them as you see fit when I am gone.

It concerns the child you were led to believe Papa took in, out of the goodness of his heart, our dear little Eleanor.

It has long puzzled me, how you men can call us the weaker sex when you are such helpless imbeciles before us. I am not alone in believing that one patient of Papa's cast her spell over many, not least her own husband, unintentional as it may have been.

No doubt she attributed Papa's attentiveness and care, his inordinate distress on failing to pinpoint the cause of her ailments and his despair when his remedies failed to revive her, to the natural conscientiousness of a dedicated physician. I assume Papa was a great comfort to the poor girl, for I understand her husband did not find her sickness easy to cope with, leaving Papa as her protector and confidante. The one on whom she depended to relieve her pain, both mental and physical. Indeed one must see Papa's attempts to cure her as a selfless occupation! For if she were made well, she would have no further need for his ministrations, and he would be no longer permitted his daily visits.

I like to think it was some strange enchantment that befell him on the night he attended her confinement. For so it seemed when he sent for me, and I arrived at her apartment to find him, his hair and face wild, a pathetic bundle in his arms, hidden in a blanket. In the previous weeks Papa had spoken about his fears for the infant, since it had stopped moving in the womb and on first sight I believed her surely dead, for she was quite blue and made no sound.

But, fearing for Father's state of mind, I did as I was bid when he urged me to hurry to our fireside, swaddle the infant in warm blankets until his return. Whereupon I witnessed what I can still only describe as a miracle, as I watched him rub the tiny limbs until the colour returned and finally she gave the faintest mewing sound, so much like a kitten. He believed that his understanding of the workings of the circulatory system could bring about what others would deem a miracle. He called on the power of God to heal and said he felt it flowing through his finger tips.

Believing that unfulfilled hope is more danger-ous than no hope, Papa had immediately told the baby's mother that she was born dead. He did not consider this a deception, since he'd discovered only the faintest of heart beats and believed it more than likely that the event would happen soon. He deemed it better for its mother never to have seen the child than to have to exhaust what little reserves of strength she herself had in tending and nursing her, only to watch her slip away after a matter of hours or days.

I have always believed that it was Papa's intention to attempt to restore the child to full health and return her to her mother, who, he trusted, would be so overcome with gratitude and delight that she would not question his actions.

I would like to say that I advised him against this course of action, and beseeched him to think again. But I did not. He seemed so sure, so steadfast. I assisted him in the care of the infant and grew very fond of her. Papa of course fell under a second enchantment. He could not help it, so alike was she, even from the first, to her mother. That same delicate face, sleepy eyes and wraith-like disposition. I feared that he would never be able to part with her, and admit the prospect was painful to me too.

And alas the parting was never to come. On the night of 11 February, when I was nursing the child by the fireside, Father was called out to attend her mother. He returned some hours later and took little Eleanor, for so we called her from the start, into his arms. He would not speak to me and there were tears in his eyes. I went to fetch him a glass of brandy and returned to find he'd left the room and taken the child with him. Fearing what I thought the worst, that Papa's actions had been discovered and he was reuniting the child with her rightful mother, I sat beside the fire, and waited, my own heart about to burst. It was then I noticed a scrap of paper at the edge of the fire, crumpled, as if it had been thrown there. I did not understand the meaning of the few words written upon it until I heard the news the next morning.

I suppose her poor husband in his grief never noticed it. Father's motives for taking it I cannot explain, for he does not know I ever saw it or have it still. I do not know if he feels guilt for her death, or if indeed he should. That surely rests with her husband if anyone. But with her melancholy disposition, perhaps no one could have made her happy, not least a demanding, sickly child. Papa had of course dealt before with those who had taken their own life, and I suspect he did not want that slur to sully the poor girl's reputation, for her to be denied a Christian burial. This last service to her memory, to pronounce her death an accident and destroy the evidence to the contrary, I am certain he saw as his atonement.

Of course I cannot tell little Eleanor of all this whilst Papa lives. Indeed I do not know if it is ever right to tell her, or how much she should be told. It is a decision in which, once again, death will intervene, will save me at least from having to make.

Your devoted sister, Jeanette

The coil of red hair in the locket. Bethany's great-great-great-grandmother. It might not be Jeanette Marshall's hair at all. It might be a

337

strand of the most famous red-gold hair in art history.

A tingle went down Natasha's spine. The shadow on the Little Barrington photos. When Bethany had been posing as Ophelia. As Lizzie Siddal. She cursed herself for not saving them now. She could so easily have smuggled them out of the studio under her coat.

Someone was knocking at the door, loud and persistent. The letter still clutched in her hand, Natasha went to answer.

James was standing there. 'Have you gone deaf?'

It took a few seconds for his grinning, exhausted, unshaven face to catapult her back to the present.

'Last night,' he said. 'Mary just got back from the Records Office when it started.'

She flung her arms around his neck. 'Congratulations.'

He was still grinning and she laughed. 'Well, come on, give me all the details.'

'He was born at eight o'clock, at home. Seven pounds and three ounces.'

'And Mary?'

'She's terrific.'

'When can I see them?'

'Now, if you like.'

Mary was sitting up in bed, a woollen cardigan draped around her shoulders, her hair pulled back into a ponytail. She looked pale and tired, and as if she wouldn't have it any other way.

The baby was cradled in her arms and the

curtains were closed, the bedside lamp casting a pink glow like dawn.

Natasha tiptoed over, peered at the little red, crumpled face held against Mary's nightshirt, the minute, perfect hand clenched in a fist. She reached out a finger and stroked the downy black hair on top of his head, then looked at Mary. 'He's beautiful,' she whispered, then bent over and gave her friend a peck on the cheek. The baby snuffled, stirred. Looked at her. 'Hello there, little fellow.'

This was what it was all about then. The next generation. As Natasha looked into those blue unfocused eyes she couldn't help thinking. Where do you come from?

It was enough to make you believe in reincarnation, or the separate existence of the soul, or in something. Hard to believe that this little being was created from genes, and cells dividing. At least here was one baby welcomed by both its parents, who was coming into the world with the odds stacked in its favour.

'What's his name?'

'Kieran.'

The baby gave a whimper and Mary slipped her little finger into the tiny mouth which instantly fell silent, started to suckle. Natasha sat down on a wicker nursing chair by the bed, watching them gazing into each other's eyes, trying not to feel left behind. There was a completeness and rightness about the two of them together, a mother nursing a child, a scene replicated throughout thousands of years, across all continents and races.

339

An experience which Lizzie Siddal had been denied.

The letter was still in her hand, the current Dr Marshall's note on top of it. His address and the title were printed in the top right hand corner of the letter. 'Consultant Paediatrician'. Atonement for the sins of the father? Or a great-grandfather to be precise.

The young John Marshall would never have been able to tell Eleanor her story. He had died not long after Jeanette, long before his father.

She re-folded the letters, opened the envelope to slide them back inside, and saw another piece of paper tucked down at the bottom. The scrap Jeanette had referred to in the letter.

It was fragile and small, with scrawled, looped handwriting. Natasha didn't recognize.

The words though, were familiar, and made Natasha's heart leap into her mouth.

Say no goodbye.
I am gone to a distant land
Where at last you will be mine.

Forty-Six

Natasha headed for the centre of town, avoiding Exeter College.

The exhibition opened today.

The Cornmarket would soon be thronged with January bargain-hunters but first thing in the morning there were just a few early birds with their bags. Natasha crossed Beaumont Road in time to see the doors of the Ashmolean Museum opening for the day. One other early visitor was walking up the wide stone steps between the Doric columns as Natasha hurried up behind him.

She could barely contain her excitement. It was the sort of find every historian dreamed of. The answer to a mystery that had lain buried for over a century.

At the information desk in the marbled entrance she was told that Lizzie Siddal's manuscripts and sketches were retained in the Print Room, that a request would need to be telephoned through if she wanted to view them. She watched the girl dial a number, explain what she wished to see, and then replace the receiver. 'If you'd just follow me.'

Natasha knew the museum well. She was led up the main stairs to the first floor, past the Egyptian section, the displays of ancient Greek vases, the artefacts from Dark Age Europe, then down a back staircase into a little corridor and lobby with oak doors. Her escort opened one and she was shown into a long, quiet room lined with shelves of boxes, old books and framed prints.

Lizzie was there ahead of her again, waiting, at the back of the room, staring down from her gilded window. It was the original of one of the portraits from the book of sketches, the picture that had also hung in the corner of the room in Blackfriars.

Natasha imagined Lizzie, lifting those large, sad

eyes now, watching the proceedings with interest.

Readers, wearing white cloth gloves, were writing with pencils in notebooks, poring over the contents of large boxes that were opened out on the long polished wooden table in the centre of the room. Manuscripts and sketches, watercolours and maps were propped up in front of them on wooden frames.

A girl climbed up a set of library steps and pulled down a box which she handed to Natasha, along with a pair of the white gloves.

Natasha went to sit at the table, and carefully lifted back the lid of the box.

There were several paintings and sketches on top.

It was so much more poignant, actually touching the drawings rather than seeing them displayed behind glass on a gallery wall. There was a rawness and immediacy about them, about viewing alone and at such a close quarters the rough sketches and jottings that Lizzie surely never intended for the public gaze.

More than with a polished canvas, you could imagine her hurrying to find her pad, making each mark on the paper, scribbling down some vision before it faded.

It was like looking inside Lizzie's mind.

Natasha studied one flimsy little sketch, then another, sliding the previous ones into the lid of the box: a pencil outline of the figure of a girl lying on the ground, a phantom raising from her body. Another of her standing in a boat, drawn with frenzied lines.

The poems were underneath the sketches. They

too were mounted and framed. The writing varied, reflecting with startling clarity Lizzie's erratic health, her varying mental states and the influence of laudanum. Two of the pages were pasted side by side, both pieces edged in black. Lizzie had written one of her poems on mourning paper.

I lie among the tall green grass
That bends above my head
And covers up my wasted face
And folds me in its bed
Tenderly and lovingly.
Like grass above the dead.

The writing was particularly scrawled, trailing off at an angle across the page. Natasha had the fragment of paper from Dr Marshall tucked safely in a small board envelope in the back of her notebook, but she didn't need to take it out for comparison. The truth was right in front of her.

Lizzie Siddal had taken her own life. She had left a note.

But one piece of the puzzle still didn't fit. Bethany, Lizzie's descendant Natasha now knew, had somehow written down the same words without having seen the original.

She was about to put everything back when she saw at the bottom of the box, beneath the poems, a larger, completed painting. She lifted it out. It was a watercolour entitled *Madonna and Child*. Only the child wasn't the baby Jesus, but a little girl, held up to a window outside which flowers bloomed. The child was reaching out her hand,

343

her small fingers extended to pluck a rose. It was a picture of innocence, yet there was something troubling about it. The Madonna's hands were under the little girl's arms, which were out-stretched to form the shape of a cross. But the most striking thing about the child was that she had the brightest red hair.

Natasha wondered when the picture had been painted, if Lizzie had been pregnant at the time. She gently lifted it up to read the picture's history.

Collection of WM Rothenstein
Exhibition at Leicester Square Galleries
June 1946, purchased by JN Bryson.
Bequeathed in 1977

There was no other date.

But also revealed beneath the frame was the place where the artist had signed her initials in the bottom right hand corner of the picture. EES.

Natasha stared, her mind returning to the weathered gravestone in Highgate. EES. Elizabeth Eleanor Siddal. Of course. All this time she'd been preoccupied with the naming of the Marshall children, the similarities between the names of Lizzie and Bethany. Yet Dr Marshall's choice of name for the baby who was raised as his youngest child was obvious and touching. Or another way of securing a piece of Lizzie for himself?

Eleanor *was* named after her mother, not after Ellen Marshall senior, the doctor's wife, nor Ellen Jeanette. Elizabeth *Eleanor* Siddal.

344

Forty-Seven

Natasha called Andrew Wilding. She asked him if, as well as calling Adam, he'd get in touch with her too when Bethany showed up.

'Of course.'

She gave him her phone number.

'I didn't realize how popular my daughter is,' he commented. 'Another fellow called by just after you and Adam left the other day, said he was a friend of Bethany's too.'

'Jake Romilly?'

'That's right.'

She tried to keep her voice normal, chatty. 'What was he after, then?'

'Just wanted to know if I'd heard from her lately. If I knew where she was. If she was all right. Funny, I asked him how he knew where I lived and he said Bethany told him. That must be a first.'

Bethany had told him nothing. He must have followed them. He'd got better at it. But then, she'd not been looking.

Andrew Wilding read back the phone number Natasha had just given him. 'Where's that then?'

'Snowshill. The Cotswolds.'

'A lovely part of the world. Elaine's mother lived in Kelmscott. You probably know it.'

'Very well.'

'Bethany loved it there. To tell the truth I've

345

never cared for it myself but I kept the house on after May died, for weekends and Christmases. For Bethany's sake.'

'Who lives there now?'

'Nobody. It's up for sale.'

Natasha was travelling into darkness. She'd set off in daylight, but the winter dusk descended swiftly as she drove.

She concentrated on the road, the red tail lights of the cars in front growing more prominent as evening approached, the cats' eyes starting to wink.

Patches of mist drifted across the nut-brown fields, twisting themselves around the naked trees, like smoke from sporadic forest fires. The signs for Kelsmcott loomed out of the greyness and she took a sharp left.

She slowed as she came to the outskirts of the village. She remembered Kelmscott from a summer visit as a student. A genteel, straggling little place, surrounded by water meadows, picturesque in a disorderly way.

She wound down the window to see better, a blast of cold air snatching her breath. In the dimness she could make out grand houses along one side of the main lane, interspersed with ramshackle farm buildings. On the opposite side of the road at the heart of the village, were areas of scrubby paddocks and meadowland, where sheep and cows would graze. They were partially flooded now, the sheets of water glittering with spangles of silver in the darkness.

Among the farm buildings were some fine

Queen Anne and Jacobean houses, typically Cotswold, with undulating stone roofs and gables. Natasha had presumed that it would be one of those that Bethany's grandmother had owned, but she wished she'd probed Andrew Wilding for more details. Still, she'd only have to ask one of the residents which of the houses were on the market and where May had lived. If she could find anyone, that was. It was eerily deserted.

She passed the church on her left, a small, unpretentious little building with a square tower and a small graveyard where, she remembered, William Morris was buried, as well as Jane and their daughters. The road curved to the left, past a quaint inn, The Plough. The lights were on. If she had no luck finding the house or anyone to ask, she'd come back.

The road ahead was flooded, after which it forked, with a sign to the Manor House and the Thames Path. It looked as if there'd be nothing else up that way so Natasha backtracked.

Beyond the village hall was a house, with an estate agent's board dug into the garden, the only one she'd seen. The house was detached, of medium size, with mullion windows and a stone porch over the front door. She drew up outside an iron gate that led to an overgrown front garden with a mossy brick pathway.

No lights showed at the windows and the curtains, if there were any, were all open. The place looked utterly abandoned.

When she opened the gate the rusted iron screeched on its hinges. In a little recess beside the front door was an antiquated bell pull. She

347

dragged on it and heard the responding peal, then silence. She tried once more. Still nothing. She noticed a nameplate screwed to the wall. Magdalene Lodge. She pushed open the heavy letterbox and crouched down to look through it, but could only vaguely make out a hall, with a wide staircase sweeping up from it.

She went back to the Alpine for the torch. Again she peered through the letterbox, shining the light around inside. In more detail now she could see the entrance and stairs, the threadbare carpet, flocked wallpaper discoloured with age or damp. She pushed against the door but it was firmly secured.

Angling the beam of light at her feet she walked round the side of the house. There was a stone gateway with an arched wooden door from which a large rusted padlock hung loose. The back garden was even more overgrown, large as a paddock, dotted with what looked like fruit trees.

By the back door was a crumbling patio with weeds between the stones. This door was also locked but a ground floor casement window to the right was open a couple of inches. She gave it a push and the window swung wide on its hinges, probably just about big enough for her to squeeze through.

She hesitated. She couldn't just climb in.

Who's going to stop me? She lifted a foot onto the ledge to lever herself up, gripping the inside of the frame with both hands and heaving. She twisted herself sideways so that her upper body was through the gap, then bent double, pulling her legs after her, and dropped down the other side.

She found a switch on the wall and flicked it. No light. She cast the beam of the torch around. She was in a large kitchen. There was a strong smell of damp. An old house smell. Not unpleasant. Aga. Belfast sink. Toaster on the dresser, utensils suspended from a game hook in the ceiling. Everything neat, disused. There was no sign of obvious habitation.

In the hall she tried another light just in case the bulb had blown in the kitchen, but that didn't work either. The electricity must be disconnected. Then she noticed that the ceramic of the sink was stained beneath the tap, as if it had suffered a persistent drip. It was dry now. She turned it. No water came.

The house was clearly, officially, uninhabited. It must be the house Andrew Wilding had talked of.

Her breath was coming fast, vaporising in front of her face, making her realise how cold it was. It felt several degrees lower in the house than it was outside. Surely no one could be living here.

Natasha turned back towards the window. There was a loud clatter at her feet. She flashed the beam of the torch round, creating wild shadows, and saw that she'd kicked over a tin waste bin, its few contents scattered on the floor. An empty plastic mineral water bottle, two chocolate bar wrappers and a banana skin. She looked at the skin for a moment. It was still yellow and soft, not blackened as it would have been if it had been there for even a couple of days.

She went out into the hall. There was another door directly opposite the kitchen. She pushed it open, flashed the torch around. A living room. It had a bulging lathe and plaster ceiling with cracks running adjacent to a thick black central beam. A door led off to another room, a little parlour or dining room, with a mahogany oval table, polished but covered with a film of dust. An old dolls' house stood on it, like a scene from an earthquake, with the front ripped away.

The stairs creaked and groaned alarmingly as Natasha trod on them, so that she expected someone to appear at the top at any moment. She was wrong to be here, an intruder, but anyone staying in a house with no electricity or water was also here illegitimately. It didn't make her feel a whole lot better.

The door at the top of the landing was open, showing, in the glare of torchlight, an empty room with white walls, a frayed rag-rug over bare boards. A single heavy curtain in the corner by the stairs revealed another flight, twisting and narrow, leading to what must be an attic. Across the landing was a further door which revealed a bathroom. There was one door left, firmly closed, with an iron handle. Natasha paused outside it, almost considering knocking. She seized the latch and pushed it down.

The figure lying on the iron bed was so slight it would have been easy to believe there was no one there at all. She lay on her back on top of a faded pink candlewick counterpane, with only a rough grey blanket over her. One arm was flung up over her head, the other resting on the cover. As the torchlight flashed across her face, casting her skin a deathly white, she didn't flinch, her closed eyelids registering not even a flicker.

Natasha stood looking down and whispered 'Hello.' When there was no response she raised her voice. Still Bethany didn't stir.

Gingerly, Natasha reached out, slid the cover back a little. Bethany was wearing a black top in some flimsy, slippery fabric, a black crocheted cardigan over it. Natasha forced herself to touch her hand. It was icy. She felt for a pulse, didn't find one.

She remembered the discarded banana skin, thrown into the bin surely just a matter of hours ago. Then Adam's face and the face of Andrew Wilding flashed across her mind.

Keeping the beam angled towards the floor now, Natasha inched closer to the bed. *I spend every day of my life with the dead but I've never actually seen a dead body.*

She remembered something you were supposed to try, grabbed a small mirror from the wall, held it in front of the girl's face. Then looked at it. She saw her own reflection, gaunt in the uplight from the torch. And a faint mist that had formed on the glass.

She dragged back the thin blanket. There were bruises around Bethany's neck and on her arms, faded to yellow-purple, not that recent.

Natasha knelt, lifted her own hair away from her ear, laid her head on Bethany's chest.

There was the slightest lift and fall.

Her mobile phone was in her pocket. Fortunately, there was a signal. Taking off her coat and heaping it on top of Bethany, Natasha dialled 999, asked for an ambulance, gave detailed directions, then went downstairs to unbolt the

351

front door.

Shivering, she watched the minutes pass on the carriage clock on the mantelpiece above the small iron fireplace. It was clockwork, which meant that recently, someone – Bethany? – had taken the trouble to wind it.

She called Andrew Wilding and told him to come to where she was sure Bethany would be taken, the John Radcliffe Hospital. Incredibly, he was almost breezy, not wanting to hear or believe any of it. After she'd hung up, Natasha had a sharp image of him, packing a clean pair of socks and his shaving kit, cancelling the milk, locking the front door behind him, driving towards Stow in his gleaming Audi. Even in his distress, making sure he remained within the speed limit at all times. Then reality slowly dawning on him, slamming his foot too hard onto the accelerator, the grief he'd taken such care to hide for his daughter's sake for twenty years finally exploding.

She'd made the call standing by the bedroom window, her back to the bed and its silent occupant, shifting the position of the phone until she had the strongest signal. The window gave a view of the tangled garden. It would have been beautiful once, when Bethany played there as a child.

Natasha sat on the edge of the bed, looked down at Bethany. She couldn't quite shake off the feeling that she'd acted according to some pre-ordained design, that discovering her this way was not entirely accidental. A shadowy chamber with a single iron bed, a perfect Pre-Raphaelite setting.

She wondered if Bethany had any sense that someone was there.

Film and TV doctors always gave instructions to talk to unconscious patients as if they were awake. Did it really do all that much good? Or was it just a device to increase dramatic effect, to give the characters the opportunity to voice their innermost thoughts? Natasha reached out and took Bethany's hand in both of hers. It felt small and light, like a child's hand. Natasha almost expected her own fingers to pass right through.

She looked so peaceful. Natasha shuddered and forced that word from her mind, such a clichéd way of describing death.

And death was near in the room; a sweet, sickly smell; a presence, hovering, waiting. The ghosts gathering to claim another. Lizzie, Eleanor, Bethany. Their identities had become so mixed up Natasha couldn't be sure of whose hand she held.

She'd heard a theory that those who came into contact with death early in life remained for ever close to it, as if a part of them had already passed over to the other side. She thought of Bethany as a child, crying because her mother had left her alone. She held the hand tighter.

As she chaffed it gently, it was possible to believe a little warmth gradually returned to the skin.

She thought of Gabriel Rossetti reaching into Lizzie's coffin, doing the same thing, convincing himself that the blood was still pumping through her veins.

I have a bad heart.

The bruises on her body. Yellow-violet: old bruises, made a week or so ago perhaps. Before Christmas.

The beam of the torch flickered, like a candle in a draft. It steadied but the light was weakened, the battery running low.

On the floor beside the bed was a box of matches and a half-used candle in a wooden pricket holder. Natasha prayed the torch would last. She didn't fancy waiting in eerie candlelight. If there were ghosts watching, there were plenty of places to hide.

'You have to wake up. You have to be all right,' she whispered.

Eventually, there was the sound of an ambulance siren in the distance, then the strange, silent flashing of the blue light when the siren was turned off as the vehicle entered the village.

A rap at the door was followed by the sound of it being pushed open. A man's voice shouted, 'Hello?'

'Up here.'

Shadows loomed in the stairwell before being diminished by the two bright torches of the white-uniformed paramedics, a man and a woman.

With almost casual efficiency and speed, they began assessing Bethany's condition, at the same time firing a host of practical questions in Natasha's direction. Are you a relative? Do you know how long has she been like this? Is she on any drugs? Has any allergies to drugs? Do you know if she has any previous medical conditions?

Natasha felt completely useless.

She said she'd called Andrew Wilding, gave them his number but told them he'd be already on his way. All she could do was stand back, out of the way, and watch as all kinds of monitors were produced from cases and bags and pockets. Bethany's shirt was unfastened, revealing tiny childlike breasts, a thin ribcage and bony shoulders. More yellowing bruises. The paramedics shared a glance. A stethoscope was placed against her chest, her eyelids were pulled up, the lights shone into her eyes. Wires and sticky pads were attached to her body, what looked like a large digital watch was strapped to her arm to read her blood pressure. 'One hundred over fifty', the woman paramedic said. Natasha knew that was low, didn't know if it was dangerously so.

They lifted her onto a stretcher. An oxygen mask was placed over her face, attached round her head with elastic bands.

'Is she going to be all right?'

The woman answered, with a brisk smile of sympathy that was genuine for all it was obviously practised. 'Hard to say at this stage, I'm afraid.'

The stretcher was carried swiftly down the steep stairs. The village was still deserted. If any of the invisible inhabitants had heard the ambulance siren none appeared to have paid it any attention. The blue lights were still revolving silently. A mortuary colour. The woman paramedic climbed into the back, Natasha followed, and the door swung after her.

355

The sirens were turned on again once they'd left Kelmscott and were speeding back towards Burford and the Farringdon Road.

'Whatever was she doing there?' the woman paramedic asked Natasha.

That was one question she could answer. Bethany had come here, to her grandmother's house, for some space; a little peace and quiet to think. About Adam and what she was going to do with the rest of her life, however long that might be.

Except Jake Romilly hadn't allowed her that.

Forty-Eight

In accident and Emergency, one of the nurses behind the reception desk took down again the little information Natasha could offer.

She was shown to where Bethany had been laid on a bed and wheeled into the corner of a long ward, the curtains pulled around her. A heart monitor had been wired up, a web of coloured cables, the oxygen mask still over her face, the tank beside the bed. A young, white-coated doctor was inserting a drip into her arm, gripping her thin wrist lightly between his fingers and thumb. Her hand dropped lifelessly and almost fell back onto the bed as the doctor released it to scribble on a chart.

'Do you know what's wrong with her?' Natasha asked.

'Pneumonia. Could be other complications.'

He gave Natasha a perfunctory smile as he left.

She found a staff nurse, told her she had to go out for a while but would be back soon.

It was the start of visiting hours and a taxi was dropping someone outside the main entrance. Natasha asked it to take her to Exeter College, to wait and bring her back.

She sprinted through the quadrant, up the stairs to the Morris Room. She could hear the hum of conversations from meters away. The gallery looked entirely different to how it was when Adam had given her an exclusive sneak preview. The publicity had obviously worked a treat. You could hardly see the photographs for the throngs of people who fell into two camps. Expensive coats and coiffured heads with champagne flutes, ponytails in leather and denim jackets drinking bottled lager with limes inserted in the neck. She asked a couple of people if they'd seen Adam Mason. They all had but couldn't see him now.

Then she noticed Jake Romilly at the back of the room talking to one of the denim jacket brigade, who was armed with a notebook. A reviewer. What a sensation it would be, if they knew the truth. Lizzie Siddal's granddaughter, with a few greats thrown in, posing in a replication of the picture for which Lizzie would always be best remembered.

Christine was draped on Jake's arm. So the relationship wasn't exactly over. Christine was staring at him adoringly, as if all her fears had been expertly diffused. At that moment Jake turned, scanned the room as if the interview was becoming tedious and he was looking for someone more interesting or important. He stared hard at Natasha. Christine saw her too and her face went from red to grey. Natasha knew then. Once Christine had started talking about what happened that night she hadn't been able to resist confronting Jake. Had confessed to him, no doubt, that she'd already told Natasha what she'd overheard.

Someone tapped Natasha's shoulder. 'Mr Mason's over there.'

He was behind the door, beneath *Ophelia*, talking to Angie.

His look was one of surprised pleasure. He came towards her, then stopped when he saw her face.

'I've found her. She's in hospital. I think she's going to be OK. There's a taxi waiting outside if you want to come.'

He gave a brusque nod, went back to Angie, said something quickly to her.

Natasha glanced at Jake Romilly feeding the reporter a last line. Jake would see Adam leave with her. Would grasp the urgency. Should she tell Adam to tell Angie not to say anything to Jake about where they'd gone? What did it matter now?

Natasha took Adam to where Bethany still lay behind green and white flowered drapes.

As she turned to leave them alone, Natasha saw him lean over the bed and place a kiss first on Bethany's lips and then on each of her eyelids. Just like the handsome prince. Except the kisses

358

didn't wake her.

Natasha went to wait on a blue, moulded plastic chair in the visitors lounge, drank a cup of sour, scalding machine coffee. It was noisy, the usual mishaps of a Friday evening in the city, bleeding noses and cuts, a young man reeking of alcohol with gashes on his forehead, and a mother cradling a toddler with a finger swathed in cotton wool.

How could anyone work in a hospital? Surrounded each and every day by so much tragedy and suffering and pain? They gave her the creeps more than any graveyard.

She looked up, saw Adam, stood and put her arms round him. After Marcus, his body felt almost delicate. 'I need a cigarette,' he said.

Outside, he leant against the wall by the automated doors, inhaled deeply.

'Thank God you found her.'

Andrew Wilding arrived half an hour later, and after he'd spoken to the consultant he came to find them in the waiting area, dragging over another chair. It was a cliché to say someone had aged overnight, but Andrew Wilding's face seemed more lined, and he looked thinner. Even his hair appeared greyer than Natasha remembered it being a few days ago. 'They say she's got pneumonia.' He shook his head. 'She was dehydrated, is still running a fever. She was never very strong and she's been in that freezing house with no proper food and drink. Doctor said she might have been drifting in and out of consciousness for days.' He turned to Natasha.

'Heaven only knows what she thought she was doing there. Did she want to kill herself?' He said it incredulously, as if the idea was impossible.

Natasha thought that just because Bethany hadn't thrown herself from a bridge, or taken an overdose, or slit her wrists, it didn't mean she'd not intended to die. There were two ways to end your life, actively and through negligence.

Jake Romilly had done the greatest damage clearly.

'If you'd not found her...' Andrew Wilding let his words trail off.

A few hours later, and Bethany would have died on the opening night of Adam's show.

Andrew went back to Bethany's bedside and Adam leaned forwards, hung his head in his hands.

Natasha was suddenly afraid for him. She stood up.

He caught her fingers. 'Don't go.'

'I was going to fetch us another coffee.'

She slipped outside, called James, explained where she was and asked him to give Boris a walk. When she went back up, the ward was strangely peaceful, the lighting had been muted, the night shift preparing to start.

Adam had moved to the otherwise empty patients' lounge and was slouched in one of the low chairs, his feet crossed at the ankles on top of a coffee table. The television was on quietly, showing a western film. The picture was almost invisible through the electric snow but Natasha could tell he wasn't really watching. His elbow was resting on one of the chair arms, his head in his hand. She thought he might be asleep but his eyes were open, unfocused.

She touched his arm, sat down next to him.

He heaved himself up in the chair.

She handed over the coffee and a cheese roll.

'Thanks.' He took a bite. 'This place makes you feel ill even if you're not.'

'I know.'

'I found something out the other day,' she said quietly. 'Lizzie Siddal's baby didn't die. Rossetti's doctor, Dr Marshall, took her and called her Eleanor.' She looked at him. 'Bethany is Eleanor's descendant.'

'Are you sure?'

'There's a letter from Marshall's daughter, Jeanette, the diarist, explaining it all.'

'I don't believe it.' He stared up at the ceiling. Then shook his head in amazement. 'Actually,' he said. 'You know. I *can* believe it.'

She was about to tell him about Lizzie's note, but stopped herself. She felt somehow that Bethany should be the first to know about that.

'Will you tell her?' Adam said.

'If you want me to. It doesn't seem the right place somehow.'

'Surrounded by doctors? Andrew says she'll be quite at home, interested in all the things they're doing to her. I'm sure if it were me, ignorance would be bliss.'

'Her Marshall heritage coming through,' Natasha said. 'Even if it's not in her blood.'

'The nurture not the nature bit.'

'There's a genetic screening test that can be done, to see if she's at risk.'

'You were right all along,' Adam said quietly. 'About the past being important. We carry it with us, don't we? In every cell of our body. All that stuff you told Bethany. About, what was it? Ancestor Syndrome. I thought it was pretty cranky but it's true. You *can* inherit fate, not necessarily in a supernatural kind of way, but scientific, through your genes.'

'Yes.'

Adam uncrossed his feet, took them off the coffee table. 'I know what it is about her that's different now. She doesn't take anything for granted. All her life she's been living each day as if it might be her last.'

'Maybe not all her life. Someone once said to me, that you only really fear death when you find someone you can't bear to leave behind.'

Adam looked at her. 'I'm scared.'

She understood what he meant. While Bethany was lost it had been easier in a sense. Rossetti had yearned for a lover to idolise in heaven. Adam wanted to keep Bethany as a similar ideal, not allow the chance for their relationship to alter or go stale.

But that was no reason to give up.

She went to look in on Bethany, to say goodbye to Andrew. He had his daughter's limp hand between both of his. When Natasha asked how she was doing he said, 'She's comfortable.'

She looked anything but, lying on her back, propped up slightly in the unnatural posture of the ill. But the mask had been removed from her face and a delicate rosy hue had turned to her cheeks. Now that she was warm, with concentrated oxygen in her lungs and pumped full of antibiotics, her breathing was more regular. The starched white sheets, the hard bed, were a stark reminder of the picture Adam had taken of her as the Sleeping Beauty, as if the picture had been a premonition. *Who actually slept in that position?*

Andrew smiled at Natasha. 'It takes me back to when she was a little girl, and I used to look in on her at night. She used to lie just like this then, never on her side like everyone else. She hated to hear the sound of her heart beating.'

In case it stopped.

Natasha rested her hand for a moment on his shoulder. 'Can I get you anything?'

'No, thanks. I'm fine.' He turned to her. 'It would be nice if you came back when she wakes. I'm sure she'd love to see you again. The doctor said she should respond to the drugs within twenty-four hours or so.'

Bethany would be back in the land of the living, then. But Natasha didn't feel ready to meet her there just yet.

Forty-Nine

By the time Natasha had found a minicab to take her back to Kelmscott to fetch the car, the sky was the colour of pearl, a cold sun illuminating the drifting mist. The temporary lakes that were the submerged fields of the Thames flood plain were strange and beautiful, with tussocks of grass and trees growing out of the bright sheets of water.

Kelmscott was still deserted except for a chestnut horse and rider in the distance, where the fields met the sky.

The signs to Kelmscott Manor led through the heart of the village and out the other side on a track towards the Thames. Natasha paid off the minicab, got out and walked. As she rounded a bend she could see, over the high hedge and wall, the tapering north towers and gables of the Elizabethan house, the lichen-covered stones of the roof. She had looked round it once, had loved the ebonised furniture, the tapestries and caskets that dotted the wide windowsills. An 'out of the world' kind of house, as William Morris had described it before he agreed to lease it, sharing the rent with Rossetti as they also shared the same woman. Like all the best chivalric tales, they were rivals for mastery of the manor and for one woman's love.

She carried on along the potholed track, following the sign for the Thames path. It was slippery with mud. Cold water seeped through the leather of her boots. There was a stile and gate for bicycles, beyond which a footpath over grassland led down to the narrow band of river.

She vaulted over the stile and headed towards the bank, her ankles twisting on the uneven ground, squishing in the part-frozen mud.

The Thames. Flowing under the ancient crossing point of the Folly Bridge at Oxford, where Adam first asked her to help find Bethany. The river a shadow then of the mighty waterway it became at Blackfriars, where Lizzie died and where Bethany said she had lived. And now here, higher up, closer to the source.

A silver thread, linking everything together. Or a dark cord. Into which the Celts cast the bodies of the dead, and human sacrifices, littering the bed with skulls.

Elaine just said she was going for a swim in the river. I've never really cared for the place.

It was here that Bethany had seen her mother die. You'd think she'd never want to return. Or maybe she felt close to her mother here.

Natasha remembered she'd left the back window of the house open, the front door unlocked.

In the light, the house looked homely and friendly, though the stone roof was sagging badly. Natasha imagined the buyers the house might attract. Young couples who couldn't afford a place that was all done up, who were prepared to spend weekends and evenings doing the renovations and decorating themselves, turning it into a home where they could bring up a family. It was a beautiful house, the kind she and Marcus had talked of moving to.

Some developer would probably snap it up and ruin it completely.

She opened the front door, bolted it from the inside, turned the heavy key. Then she went back to the kitchen, heaved herself out through the window, the way she'd first come in, and pulled the casement shut behind her.

When she went round to the front again, Jake Romilly was leaning against the Alpine. She looked for the Celica, couldn't see it anywhere. He must have taken the trouble to hide it. She carried on walking up the garden path, one step at a time, shut the gate carefully behind her. She took her keys out of her pocket and went towards the car, towards him, trying to look as unfazed as possible.

'I've been waiting for you.' He thrust his hands in the pockets of his great coat. 'How is she?'

She remembered the pattern of bruises on Bethany's skin, levelled her eyes at him. 'How do you think?'

'I rang the hospital. They say she'll recover.'

'Your concern is very touching. How did you know I'd be here?'

'Hospital put me on to her father. I asked to talk to you and he most obligingly told me you'd gone to collect your car.' She could see the bulge of his fists in his pockets, clenched, or he was concealing a weapon. 'How about we go for a walk?' he said.

She glanced round at the empty dawn-lit lanes, houses with curtains still drawn, icy puddles. Adam and Andrew Wilding knew she was here, but beyond that...

'For some reason, I'm not really in the mood.'

He sniggered. 'In that case, I'll be seeing you around.' He spun back. 'You don't happen to know what time visiting hours are at the Radcliffe, do you? I must drop in and pay my respects.'

He was never going to leave Bethany alone.

'Wait.' The determination in her voice halted him. *Let him go. No. Put an end to it right now.* Her

366

reckless streak won through. 'I wanted to ask you. How do you plan to shut up your friend, Alex?'

He looked round, snorted. 'He's not exactly lived his life on the right side of the law. Believe me, I know enough about him to be sure he'd never breathe a word.'

'With friends like that...'

Slowly, he retraced his steps. 'I hardly touched her.'

His face was just a few inches from Natasha's but she stood her ground. 'Hardly?'

'I didn't do anything.'

'Except harass her for weeks. Then follow her here. Scare the hell out of her. Forced yourself on her until she passed out?'

'If she goes to the police they'll not listen to one word.' His voice had a rasp in it. Gloating. 'We were lovers for three months. I'll tell them she told me to meet her here. It'll all come out, The Ravens, everything. Alex and Christine will vouch that Bethany was more than happy to be involved. On every level. When they see the photographs she let me take of her in private, it'll discredit everything she says.'

She stared him out. *Finish it now and be damned.* 'Photographs can be useful in other ways. Being around you guys gave me an idea or two. The bruises on Bethany's chest for instance. I thought they were worth preserving for posterity.' He backed off a little. Removed one hand from his pocket, held it down at his side, concealing something. Sunlight on metal. A set of keys. On the same ring, a Swiss army knife. Idly, he flicked the sharp little blade out, retracted it again. Out. In. *Don't look. Keep talking,* Natasha told herself. 'A secret society is one thing. But breaking and entering is quite another, wouldn't you agree? Going through my papers. Stalking, of course. Crimes where you know exactly where you are. And they know where you were, that's for sure. They've got fingerprints, from the desk. At first I thought you were on my tail because you still wanted her, wanted me to lead you to her. But that's not quite the whole story is it? You were shit scared when she passed out and you ran for it. Because you thought whatever it was you *weren't* doing to her might have been enough to finish her off.' She wasn't going to tell him that Bethany was prone to blackouts. Let him live with that. 'She'd told you as much about her family as she'd told Adam, zero, which put you in a bit of a fix, didn't it? No way to find out if she was missing, all right, or wanting your hide. It took me a moment, I must admit, to work out why you didn't just come back here. But you'd seen the For Sale sign, presumed there'd be estate agents and prospective buyers wandering in and out, nosing through the windows. You've obviously never had a house to sell, or you'd know, it all goes frustratingly quiet around Christmas. Or was it just that you thought Bethany's family would be arriving for the holidays? Is that what she told you? Just as well you were offered an alternative, Adam asking me to find her. You had to make damned sure you got to her parents first, or as soon as possible, to see what you were guilty of. When you found out

368

that piece was coming out in the paper saying she was missing, you got desperate, broke in to my house to see what you could find. How am I doing?'

After a moment, he slipped the knife back in his pocket, strode back to his car.

Natasha sank back against the garden wall, and breathed.

As she indicated right out of Kelmscott, she caught a final glint of the river.

The law would take its own course. But it wasn't there to protect those who chose to test the boundaries of normal behaviour. Children who played with adult toys, played with fire. Jake Romilly was probably right. If Bethany reported what he had done to her it might not even make it to court. There were no photographs of bruises, the police had found no fingerprints around the desk but Natasha's own. But so long as Jake Romilly thought there were, so long as he was worried enough to keep out of the picture, Bethany should be safe from him.

Fifty

They were walking, Bethany, Adam and Natasha, up through the deer park on Broadway Hill.

It was deserted, except for the grazing Cotswold sheep and the red deer themselves, like allegorical creatures, standing still as statues, or

369

skitting elusively between the shrubs. In the distance, shaggy highland cattle foraged in the rough grass.

The gatekeeper was a lad from Snowshill, and he had let Natasha drive James's Land Rover right up to the top of the park, for Bethany's sake. It had coped easily with the rugged terrain, which was why they'd taken it, rather than Adam's Lancia or the Alpine, to the hospital to collect her. Three people could sit fairly comfortably along the front seat. Adam had been at the far passenger side, Bethany in the middle, between him and Natasha, all the way from Oxford.

Bethany was wrapped up in black woollen gloves, a thick red scarf, and Natasha's black coat, which was so long on her it trailed to the ground. She was too thin, but the fresh air had brought colour to her cheeks, light to her eyes.

She was scheduled to go back for tests at the cardiology department in a fortnight's time.

It had been Natasha's idea to come here, and it was the perfect day to visit the Tower. The sky for once was bright blue, and the sun shone between occasional fluffy white cumuli. There was a strong breeze but it wasn't a cold one, and beneath the trees were the first scatters of snowdrops.

Ahead of them was the tower itself, a George flag flying high above its Saxon-style battlements. It was like a castle from a gigantic chess set, a stark presence, its stone darker than any found locally, a beacon that had been lit to warn of the approach of the Spanish Armada, and the end of the Second World War.

'What is it?' Bethany asked.

'Nothing particularly,' Natasha smiled. 'A folly. It was designed in the eighteenth century for the Earl of Coventry.'

'No wonder Morris and Rossetti wanted to spend their holidays here,' Adam said.

They entered the base of the tower, paid for their tickets, and Adam briefly studied the exhibition which explained the history.

Then, taking it slowly, they began to climb the narrow, curved stairway that wound upwards like a corkscrew, with a rope banister attached to the wall. Natasha led the way, followed by Bethany, who reached back her hand to hold Adam's as they ascended.

'Are you all right?' Natasha asked, turning her head.

'Perfectly.'

'It's worth it when you reach the top, I promise.'

The bracing air buffeted them as they stood overlooking the turrets, the flag right above them, cracking like a whip, fields and valleys and rolling hills undulating all around. You could see Edge Hill, seventeen miles away, and in the opposite direction, the Black Mountain and Wales.

'You're supposed to be able to see thirteen different counties,' Natasha said, not looking for them but for something in Bethany's face, as the girl compared the landmarks on the horizon to those on the 360 degree map that ringed the circumference of the tower.

In the photographs, Natasha had believed she glimpsed a similarity to Lizzie, even before she'd known the truth. But now, in the flesh, there was little sign of it, not even with her fragility making her eyes seem enormous and her head too heavy for her long, slender neck. In her chestnut hair there was no replication of Lizzie's fabled red tresses.

Adam took Natasha aside. 'That note in the journal. She says it was just something she'd jotted down, some lines that kept going round in her head. She thought they might be from a song or something. She says it meant nothing really.'

Lines that kept going round in her head.

A secret that had been passed on, hidden, like a coded message, in the lines Lizzie Siddal had scribbled on a piece of paper before she died, lines that had been handed down through the generations, like all the best stories and legends, in songs or poems or the words mothers whispered and sang to their children.

Say no goodbye
I am gone to the unknown land
Where at last you will be mine.

Inciting Bethany to do as Lizzie had done, or warning her not to?

Bethany was ticking the counties off on her fingers. 'Staffordshire, Shropshire, Dyfed, Hereford, Gwent.'

Natasha said, 'You thought Jeanette Marshall was one of your ancestors?'

'My grandmother told me she was.'

'It's not Jeanette you're related to.'

Bethany stopped counting, turned to Natasha,

who took Jeanette's letter out of her pocket and handed it over.

When she'd finished reading Bethany looked up. 'You mean Lizzie?'

'She's your great-great-great grandmother, yes.'

Her eyes flew to Adam, then back to Natasha, as if she'd made her wishes come true. She brushed a lock of hair away from her face 'I was sure there was something,' she said quietly. 'It was like I knew her, as well as I know myself.' She curled her small hand into a ball, held it in the centre of her chest. 'As if she was here with me, all the time.'

'She is.'

Adam slid his arm around Bethany's waist. She did the same to him, still holding the letter in her hand. She leant into him, smiled, shook her head in disbelief. 'I'm going to wake up tomorrow and think this is all a dream.' Then she turned to Natasha again. 'It's through my mother's side?'

'That's right.'

'Granny said she felt she was destined to buy her house in Kelmscott when she saw it was for sale because she had the diary, that was all. She wasn't particularly interested in Lizzie, in any of it really. And Dad told me he wanted me to be called Elizabeth, but my mother wouldn't have it, said she didn't like the name. She wasn't interested in her either.'

'You were different,' Natasha said softly. 'There was a connection. Lizzie was a mother who'd lost her baby daughter, and you were a little girl without a mother.'

As soon as Natasha said it and saw Bethany's

373

face, she wished she hadn't.

'Lizzie's baby was blue when she was born,' Bethany said. 'There was something wrong with her heart.'

'We can't know that now,' Adam cut in.

'Eleanor lived until she was sixty,' Natasha said. 'I've got a copy of her death certificate to prove it. And your grandmother was twenty years older than that. Your great-grandmother and grandfather all made fifty. Not bad going in those days. They all had the same genes as you. Even Lizzie might have lived a long life if ... it had been happier.'

'Natasha's right,' Adam said. 'If Rossetti hadn't messed around with other women, if they'd been able to bring up a family...'

'Things have a way of coming full circle,' Natasha said. 'So far your lives are not so very different.' She smiled at Adam, meeting his eyes. 'You fell in love with an artist, modelled for him. What happens next is up to you.'

She handed her the little note, Lizzie's words. 'Those lines can stop going round in your head now.' She let Bethany read it. 'Dr Marshall, Jeanette's father, found it on the night Lizzie died. Proof it was Lizzie's own choice to end her life.' Natasha looked at Adam. 'Secrets can be like a curse. But Lizzie and Eleanor's story isn't a secret any more.'

Adam moved closer to her and they stood together, staring out.

In her mind Natasha travelled to another hill. Fish Hill. When Marcus had asked her if it was possible to step back into the past. She should have told him yes. She should have said the past is always with us, is part of who we are. But he'd asked the question, hadn't he? That was the thing. He wanted it to be possible. He was willing to give it a try.

'That's Warwickshire over there.' Bethany pointed. 'I wonder where dad's house is.' Then she turned to Natasha. 'Your village is near here, isn't it?'

'Just half a mile up the road,' Natasha said, puzzled. 'Didn't you try to come and see me there, on New Year's Eve?'

Bethany frowned, shook her head. 'No, I was still in Kelmscott. Too ill.'

'It must have been someone else,' Natasha said.

A girl in a grey dress with long pale hair. A ghost?

The sun passed behind a cloud. Natasha saw Bethany shiver.

They watched a lark wheeling in the sky, riding the currents.

Bethany suddenly stepped towards the edge of the wall, as if to launch herself into flight. Natasha saw Adam's fingers clench tighter, pull back. She'd wanted to do the same.

Bethany was gripping the ledge, leaning right over to peer down. She was only watching a family below, tiny as dolls. A man and woman and two little girls.

With her eyes cast down then, her features in shadow, there was the most fleeting glimpse. Then she stepped back, looked up, and the ghost fled from her face.

Bethany turned her head, backlit by the sky.

The sun drifted free, struck golden rays across the hills to the tower. It picked out the natural highlights in her hair, made it shine as red as fire.

Epilogue

A week after the opening of The Ravens' exhibition, Bethany contacted the *Oxford Times* to offer herself for interview. What she told them caused a commotion. The following day the paper ran a double page spread of Adam's photographs. The story was picked up by the national press and television news programmes. Queues to see the exhibition stretched down Turl Street. There was talk of a nationwide tour for some of the works, kicking off at the prestigious Photographers' Gallery in London.

There was only one photograph everyone wanted to see. The photograph of Lizzie Siddal's great-great-great-granddaughter in a reproduction of the image which had made Lizzie immortal. It would give Bethany a degree of fame and immortality too. Everyone wanted to know about the photographer who had found her.

So, Natasha thought, Jake Romilly lost in the end, in the way he most hated to lose.

Afterword

The characters in this story are a mixture of real and fictitious. The real ones are Lizzie Siddal and Gabriel Rossetti of course, as well as some of the Marshalls. John Marshall was Rossetti's physician, his practice was in Savile Row and he did have a wife called Ellen, and a daughter called Jeanette who left behind a series of journals. John Marshall regularly attended to Lizzie Siddal during her long illnesses.

Lizzie and Gabriel's story is true in every part except for details concerning their baby daughter, who was stillborn. The exhumation in Highgate and Rossetti's request to be buried in Birchington, as well as him calling Marshall back to his apartment because he believed Lizzie was still alive two days after she had been pronounced dead are all true. *Beata Beatrix* was painted as a memorial to Lizzie.

There were rumours that Lizzie left behind a suicide note but this has never come to light.

I have taken a further artistic liberty regarding Chatham Place. This was the apartment where Lizzie lived with Rossetti and died, but sadly it was demolished to make way for the roundabout at Blackfriars.

The 1861 census returns for the district of Westminster St James are indeed lost.

Acknowledgements

Numerous books on both the Pre-Raphaelites and genealogy were invaluable in writing this novel. In particular Jan Marsh's *The Legend of Elizabeth Siddal* (Quartet Books, 1989) and *Dante Gabriel Rossetti Painter and Poet* (Weidenfeld and Nicolson, 1999) were crucial. All the details of Lizzie and Rossetti's lives, and in particular the descriptions of the Highgate exhumation, are taken from these books. (I take full responsibility for any errors in reworking.) Without Jan Marsh's extensive research and inspiring depiction of the people around which this novel hinges, it could never have been written.

Ancestor Syndrome: Transgenerational Psychotherapy and the Hidden Links in the Family Tree (Routledge, 1998) by Anne Ancelin Schutzenberger also inspired this novel.

Details of Julia Margaret Cameron's work comes from *Julia Margaret Cameron's Women* by Sylvia Wolf (Art Institute of Chicago, 1998).

Jeanette Marshall's diaries and the lives of her family are quoted and recounted in *The Precariously Privileged: A Professional Family In Victorian London* by Zuzanna Shonfield (Oxford University Press, 1987).

It was Marion Edwards who conducted the first research into Lizzie's history using PRO records.

I used numerous genealogical reference works, primarily, *Never Been Here Before* (PRO Publications, 1998) by Stella Colwell, the *Oxford Companion to Local and Family History* (Oxford University Press, 1996) and the *Good Web Guide to Genealogy* by Caroline Peacock (The Good Web Guide Limited, 2000).

The main sources for Cotswold and Snowshill history were *The Cotswolds* by Rod Talbot and Robin Whiteman (Weidenfeld and Nicolson, 1986) *Snowshill: Portrait of a Village* by Caroline Mason (Thornhill Press, 1987) and Susan Hill's *Spirit of The Cotswolds* (Michael Joseph, 1988).

Other books that were useful include *The Primal Wound: Understanding the Adopted Child* by Nancy Newton Verrier (Gateway Press Inc, 1999); *Making Faces: Using Forensic and Archaeological Evidence* by John Prag and Richard Neave (British Museum Press, 1997); *Highgate Cemetery: Victorian Valhalla* by John Gay and Felix Baxter (John Murray Publishers Ltd, 1984); *The Victorian Celebration of Death* by James Stevens Curl (Sutton Publishing Ltd, 2000) and *Love Beyond Death: The Anatomy of Myth in the Arts* by Rudolph Binion (New York University Press, 1993).

Thanks to William George Hunt, T.D., B.A., F.C.A., Windsor Herald at the College of Arms and to Kathy Wilshaw, who, just like Natasha, is a professional genealogist who lives in the Cotswolds.

Without the fascinating input of Professor Andrew Wilkie, Professor of Genetics, University of Oxford who offered information on Hypertrophic Cardiomyopathy and gave me a crash course on genetics, this novel would have probably been much easier to write but nowhere near as satisfying. For additional information on HCM, thanks to Dr Richard Winsley of the cardiology research unit at Exeter University. (Again, any errors regarding genetic or medical details of HCM are mine.) For advice on police procedure, my thanks to Detective Sergeant Rebecca Mountain. For rare insight into the workings and world of the Sunbeam Alpine, I am indebted to Geoff Woolf of the Sunbeam Alpine Owners Club!

For unfailing inspiration and encouragement and for giving me the necessary prod that brought the idea of Natasha to life, my thanks to Jane Wood at Orion. Thanks also to Rachel Leyshon, Sophie Wills, Laura Morris, Carole Blake and Julian Friedmann.

Fiona Mountain
December 2001

The publishers hope that this book has given you enjoyable reading. Large Print Books are especially designed to be as easy to see and hold as possible. If you wish a complete list of our books please ask at your local library or write directly to:

Magna Large Print Books
Magna House, Long Preston,
Skipton, North Yorkshire.
BD23 4ND

This Large Print Book for the partially sighted, who cannot read normal print, is published under the auspices of

THE ULVERSCROFT FOUNDATION